I0594197

LOVE AND
THE LAWMAN

ALEXA
ASTON

OLIVER
HEBER
BOOKS

All rights reserved.

No part of this publication may be sold, copied, distributed,
reproduced or transmitted in any form or by any means, mechanical or
digital, including photocopying and recording or by any information
storage and retrieval system without the prior written permission of
both the publisher, Oliver Heber Books and the author, Alexa Aston,
except in the case of brief quotations embodied in critical articles and
reviews.

PUBLISHER'S NOTE: This is a work of fiction. Names, characters,
places, and incidents either are the product of the author's
imagination or are used fictitiously. Any resemblance to actual persons,
living or dead, business establishments, events, or locales is entirely
coincidental.

COPYRIGHT © Alexa Aston

Published by Oliver-Heber Books

0 9 8 7 6 5 4 3 2 1

 Created with Vellum

CHAPTER 1

LOUISIANA—1870

Nora Cantrelle flinched as she entered the sick room. It had happened again. She'd go to hell for this.

She probably deserved to.

Yet to an unfamiliar eye, everything was the same as always. The bedroom was dark, save for the flickering candle she held in one hand. How many times had she wanted to fling open the windows and let the strong sunlight pour in? Or see gingham curtains sway in a gentle breeze that brought a whisper of honeysuckle and magnolia into the room?

Paul never wanted the windows open. He said light hurt his eyes. He insisted on heavy, damask drapes that looked as cheerful as a dour nun doing penance for an imagined wrong. So the room remained dim and the air stale and musty, a sickroom for a man who had chosen long ago to give up on living.

She glanced to the corner. The faint outline of Paul's prosthesis, propped against the wall, served as a reminder of the failures that blanketed the room.

Moving across the hardwood floor on tiptoe, she kept her gaze on Paul. He lay motionless in the canopied bed, propped against several pillows, the coverlet tucked snugly around him. His eyes were closed. A half-smile played about his lips, the first she had seen since before the War of Northern Aggression began. She bent and traced it with her fingertip, pushing back the deep longing that raged within her soul.

Nora picked up the empty bottle of laudanum and stared at it. The painkiller had been within easy reach. On a table next to his bed. Her husband was now dead.

Just as she'd wished.

Another death on her hands.

She pictured this room twenty years earlier. Not much had changed. Nora had been a child of six with a bedridden mother who wasn't afraid to use her waspish tongue, especially on her timid husband and only child.

Nora dreaded her daily visits to this room, and that day had been like all the rest. Her mother, who insisted that her daughter call her *Genevieve*, made everyone's life hard with her constant complaints and sarcasm. She berated and scolded her daughter incessantly, which filled Nora with despair. Genevieve didn't care that spring had just arrived and the birds were bursting with song, ready to usher in a new season, full of hope.

Nora had looked at her mother, a wilting beauty who faded more with each passing year. She finally broke down and prayed for Genevieve's death. Jesus really listened to prayer, just as all the sisters at St. Joseph said that Jesus did. He heard her plea.

Her mother died less than two hours later.

Of course, Dr. Ford said it was her heart. Always weak, it grew weaker during her pregnancy and Nora's subsequent birth. Genevieve remained an invalid ever since, growing more feeble and frail as the years passed. Heart failure was the official notation on her death certificate.

But Nora knew differently. It was because she had prayed for her mother to die.

She was so badly shaken that she didn't pray for a

2

long time after that, afraid if she did, her prayers would come to pass. She tried to think only pure thoughts, which didn't last long. Caroline Porter stuck Nora's braid in an inkwell and she wished the younger girl would fall down in the mud and dirty the golden locks she was so proud of. The bully of St. Joseph's School did trip Caroline on her way home from school that day. Nora panicked that Caroline would die, too.

But nothing bad happened to either child. Gradually, Nora relaxed, although she really never prayed again. She might desire something, but she never prayed to get it. A wish or hope was different from communing with God.

Until last night.

Only God knew she had been at her rope's end. Paul's bitterness drove her to exhaustion. She'd tried every way she knew to get him out of that bed and to force him to start living life again. She wanted her best friend back. She wanted him to be a real father to Robby.

Yet her husband's rage had gone on and on. He came home from the war angry and stayed angry. At his wife. At the son born in his absence. At his parents' deaths and the ruin of their family plantation. Paul's fury extended to the South losing the war and the Union taking one of his brothers to an early grave.

Yet the root of his rage was the fact he'd returned to Monroe minus his right arm and leg.

"Look at me, Nora! Just look at me!" he demanded for the thousandth time.

Her eyes swept over the bony frame that wasted away. Five years in that bed. Just like her mother.

"I'm looking, Paul."

"But do you see me?"

Tears glistened in her eyes "I do. I see a man too proud to start over, grieving for a life that no longer exists. I'm tired of it, Paul. Of you and—"

"You're tired? How do you think I feel, lying in this bed, day after day, year after year?" His voice grew peevish. "I can't get a moment's rest anymore, not with those boarders lurking about, making all sorts of noise. You know I don't sleep well. Now that complete strangers have the run of the house, I find it near impossible to catch any rest at all."

Nora sighed. "You know we need the extra income our boarders provide. The paper's not doing well, and it hasn't in ages. Papa said—"

Paul exploded. "I don't care what Albert said or what he thinks or what he feels. I resent that you bow to his every wish. If only we could live on our own. Then I know things would be better."

She snorted. "Live on what? We live on Papa's charity as it is. You take offense because he's generous to us? I don't see your brother helping us."

"Richard has come down in the world. He would help if he could."

Nora shook her head. "We've all come down to reality. The war saw to that."

Talk of the war brought a steely glint to his eyes. "You don't have to remind me, Nora. I'm the one who came home half a man."

Anger flashed within her. "You're not half a man. You've got a great mind. You survived the horror for a purpose. Do you honestly think I care for you any less simply because..." She choked on her words.

He sneered at her. "My darling wife. You are a fool."

"No. The only fool in this room is the one who refuses to get out of bed and live again." She shook her head. "You've become my mother."

Paul glared at her. "Just give me my glass and go. I want to be alone and enjoy the solitude before those boarders create another ruckus."

Nora automatically reached for the water glass as he'd demanded, as she'd done every time for five long years.

And suddenly it became too much. Paul running her ragged

*ever since he'd come home, refusing to do even the small tasks he
was capable of performing. Robby had been sick all day and
most of the night. Nora found herself physically and emotion-
ally drained. If the war had been a long nightmare, then the
aftermath was Hell itself.*

*His voice interrupted her thoughts. "Nora. I said to get the
glass."*

*She turned to leave and before she could stop it, the prayer
echoed in her head. She'd held it at bay for five years but like
Pandora's box, the evil of it broke free at that moment and the
words spilled out.*

*She met her husband's eyes. In a controlled whisper, void of
emotion, she said, "You're no good to me. To Robby. To anyone. I
wish you were dead."*

*She walked to the door and turned the handle. She hesi-
tated a minute, staring at the brass knob as if it held all the answers to her problems. Finally, she opened the door and closed it
gently behind her. Her footsteps echoed as she moved thoughtfully down the corridor.*

And now Nora took a deep breath and made a decision. She would hide the fact that Paul had taken his
life. She slipped the laudanum bottle inside her
pocket. She must avoid scandal and protect Paul's
good name or it would reflect on Robby. She already
would burn in Hell anyway. What was one lie on top of
two deaths?

She was thankful she'd closed the door. Neither
boarder they'd taken in during the past year had left for
work yet, as it was still early. Privacy had been hard to
come by with strangers living among them but this was
a private matter now. Nora wondered just how much of
their fight last night had been heard. She hoped Dr.
Ford wouldn't press too hard.

She fussed with the covers a moment. Paul looked
peaceful in death, incredibly young, and close to what
Robby looked like now. The boy was the spitting image
of his father at that age. Nora swallowed painfully. She

wondered how things might have been different if war hadn't torn the nation apart.

She bent and stroked her husband's cheek in a loving gesture, as she had done when she was sixteen, full of desire for him and hope for their future. Though the ardor had died long ago, she had continued to fulfill her responsibilities to Paul. She would do so now.

Nora slipped from the room of death and closed the door gently. Her hand gripped the bottle inside her skirt's pocket. She wouldn't even tell Albert. Her father had enough to worry about as it was.

❧❧❧

SILVER BLUFF—COLORADO TERRITORY

JACK DUNCAN WAS BORED. HE READJUSTED HIS HARD hat and stared at the wall before him, looking for the magical black vein that would indicate silver. He ran his hands over the rough edges, lost in thought.

An emptiness sat deep within him, growing stronger over the last year. He didn't want to mine silver. Sure, he'd set out to make his fortune in Colorado when he'd first arrived. Things were different now. The tedium overwhelmed him. He didn't know what he wanted out of life anymore.

He wasn't afraid of hard work and had seen his share. This was different, though. He made the decision to turn in his notice to Old Man Stevenson when his shift ended today. He didn't have a clue what he'd do next. At least he had some money saved.

Jack chuckled. Who'd have thought a man of thirty years wouldn't know what to do when he grew up?

"What's so funny, Duncan?"

He turned and saw Bran Stevenson making his way toward him. Behind the young man was the endless tunnel that branched off in many directions, held up by supports every few feet.

"Ready to get your hands dirty, boy?"

Bran grinned. "Pa says if I'm to run the mine one day, I've got to learn every aspect of it."

Jack nodded. "He's right. It's not just accounting and payrolls and shipments and contracts. You have to understand the back-breaking work that goes into mining."

The two men worked their way along the wall. Jack pointed out various subtleties to his younger companion. They passed one shaft entrance that had been capped off the week before because the foreman deemed it unsafe.

He explained, "Cave-ins are common in mining, Bran. It's a risk every man down here understands."

"But the pay is good."

Jack grimaced. "I suppose so."

Tell that to Bill Tompkins.

Two weeks earlier, Tompkins had been buried alive in a cave-in. Fortunately, he left no family behind. Mining was, for the most part, a lonely business.

They worked together in companionable silence until the shift ended.

"Thanks for your pointers, Duncan."

He looked at the youthful face before him—eager, hard-working, exuberant. Just like a thousand other seventeen-year-old boys. He liked the boss' son. Bran Stevenson was a good kid.

Just like Buddy and Sam. The thought of his younger brothers washed a wave of sorrow over him.

"Let's head in, kid."

They made their way slowly through the narrow tunnel, the air stale as it poured through their nostrils. Jack always treasured the first gulp of clean air when he exited the mine.

Then it happened. A sudden shift in the earth. A

startled cry. The world went topsy-turvy. He found himself on his back, the air knocked from him. Around him were muffled voices, a few moans, and then silence.

"Bran?"

He thought of the boy first, on the cusp of manhood, bright and eager to conquer the world. *Where the hell was he?* Jack sat up and tried to get his bearings, swinging his lamp around in all directions.

He couldn't see much of anything. Thick dust permeated the air. As he inhaled it, he coughed violently. Pulling a handkerchief from his pocket, he placed it over his nose and mouth as protection against the sooty grime. He slowed his breathing and closed his eyes, waiting for the dust to settle.

After a full minute, he opened them, gradually readjusting to the dim light. That was when he spotted part of a man. The wall support had collapsed around him. He crawled over and found the mine owner's son half-buried in the debris. One of the heavy beams lay across his lower legs, pinning him to the ground.

"Bran?"

The boy was barely conscious. Sweat gleamed from his face, one that had yet to mature fully, with round cheeks and a soft mouth now racked with pain.

"Oh, God..." Bran croaked.

Another rumble began. Jack felt panic crackle in the air. Heard voices calling, "Hurry!" Two workers crawled past them on their bellies, elbows scooting them along.

"Better step on it, Duncan," one called.

"Help me free Stevenson!"

Both men looked at him as if he were crazy. Without a word, they continued on their way.

"Go, Jack," whispered Bran. "You'll never get me out from this rubble." A sob caught in the boy's throat.

"No."

He hadn't been there for Buddy or Sam. Maybe he

could make a difference this time. "We're in this to-gether, son."

The boy smiled feebly. "Thanks."

He worked quickly with his pick, loosening the packed earth around Bran. He ignored the sounds around him. The straining wood. Bran's labored breath-ing. The low rumbles in the bowels of the shaft. He had to get this kid out before a cave-in occurred.

He pushed away the last of the dirt and pieces of wood. With great effort, he lifted the girder aside. He sucked in a hard breath. Bran's legs were crushed. He doubted the boy would ever walk again.

If he lived.

Jack flashed a confident smile. "Let's get out of here." He hoisted Bran upon his back and then half-crouching, half-dragging him, made his way to the top.

When he caught sight of daylight, it was the sweetest moment he could remember since he'd seen Lee's troops retreating from Gettysburg on a hot July day. A crowd had gathered around the entrance to the shaft. Raucous cheers erupted as he clawed his way to safety.

Men lifted Bran from him. Jack collapsed on the ground, too tired to move. Someone rolled him over and brought a bottle of whiskey to his mouth. He drank from it deeply. The liquor burned a hot trail down his parched throat to his belly.

Jack sat up and pushed the bottle away. He wiped his mouth with the back of a dusty, torn sleeve and stood. He brushed the grime from his jeans amidst pats on his back. So many voices spoke at once. He had trouble following any of them so he ignored them all.

He took three steps away from the noisy crowd be-fore his legs turned to rubber. He collapsed to the hard ground. He'd wait until he got his wind back. After all, the air was sweet and plentiful. He decided he was in no hurry. He inhaled slowly, enjoying the pull of clean air through his lungs.

"Mr. Duncan?"

Jack turned and focused on the shadowed figure in front of him, its face hidden by the surrounding sunlight. The words, though, rang loud and clear.

"You saved my son, man. Name whatever you want. It's yours."

CHAPTER 2

"S he always did have her head in the clouds. Why, Lord o' mercy, she acts as if nothing has happened. Just sitting there like she's made of stone."

Another harsh whisper joined the first. "Not a single tear shed for that dear husband of hers. Paul Cantrelle was the sweetest of those Cantrelle boys. Tip his hat to me and say, '*Isn't it a fine day, Mrs. Winston?*'"

A tongue clucked softly. "He will be missed by the fine folks of Monroe."

Nora bit her tongue hard and forced herself to remain calm. As if the fine folks of Monroe had visited Paul even once since the war ended. Had another widow held her tears, she would be called brave and stoic. Monroe's rumormongers labeled Nora Cantrelle hard and unfeeling.

"Mommy."

Robby tugged on her hand. She smiled down at her young son. She had wondered how she would manage to get through the funeral mass and graveside burial, but one look at him made even this tragedy fade.

"You're squeezing too hard, Mama."

Nora relaxed her hold on Robby's hand. His gaze returned to the black coffin before them, his blue eyes large, as if he didn't believe the events that had unfolded.

The two old women began sniping again, their murmurings soft but clear to Nora's ears.

"Why any Southern woman worth her salt would want to do a man's job is beyond me. It just isn't . . . feminine."

Her companion sniffed noisily for show and blew into her embroidered handkerchief. "None of the town's daughters behave in such a flighty manner. Genevieve Le Fall would be mortified to see her only child now."

"You know Nora was asked to leave St. Joseph when she was only seven? Imagine that. A child of seven."

A soft titter. "The nuns couldn't handle her. Or so I heard."

Nora wanted to scream. Of course she'd wanted to leave that stifling parochial school and go to the newspaper each day with her father. Albert was a far better teacher and not nearly as limiting as the somber nuns. The sisters took her as far as they could in her formal education, but Nora hungered for much more.

Who cared what these old biddies said? They'd had their noses out of joint ever since she'd married Paul. Her marriage gave them fodder for their ever-cranking gossip mill.

Yet the strong backlash after her wedding surprised her. Paul had been her greatest friend and champion from the time they were in diapers. Coming together as man and wife had been something they assumed at a young age.

Monroe looked at it quite differently. Albert Le Fall might be well-educated and enjoy a certain standing within the community, but Nora soon learned it unthinkable that a newspaper owner's daughter might attempt to transition into the highest echelons of Monroe society. Society's doors remained closed to her, despite the Cantrelle family's considerable influence. She refused to burden her new husband with such petty dealings when he was off fighting in a bloody war. She continued to hold her head high and ignore the town's pointed stares while she wrote to Paul of inconsequential things.

Father Deschard's monotone ceased. Nora realized the service had ended. She looked to her father, his abundant white hair hidden by the tall black hat perched upon his head. He gave her shoulder a gentle pat, which caused the first tears of the day to spring to her eyes. She loved him so much and was thankful he'd stood by her all these years.

The crowd began to depart, soon to descend upon the house bearing platters of fried chicken, sweet corn-bread, peach pies, and cucumber salad, as they reminisced about Paul and the days when the South ruled.

Nora dreaded an afternoon filled with such talk. Since the war had ended, she was eager for this New South all the politicians spoke of. She did her best to contribute to it by teaching two days a week at the local school for the children of freed slaves, working with students on their basic reading and writing skills. Even that was looked upon as suspect.

A man she knew only by sight made his way toward her. He was a prime example of how the white community of Monroe, now in genteel poverty, looked upon her. Only two days ago, he actually spit upon her as she exited the freedman school. Horrified, she kept the incident to herself. It would do no good to get her father —or Ben—stirred up.

"A shame 'bout your daddy." The man focused on Robby as he added, "I am sorry for your loss." He turned briefly to Nora, his eyes hard as he inclined his head.

She watched him and a hundred more like him leave the cemetery. She was slowly strangling here. She longed for freedom. Freedom from the South, which had crumbled long ago and refused to truly rebuild. Freedom to pursue a career as a writer, something that would never occur as long as she stayed in Louisiana, where women only strained their brains to consider if they'd gotten too much sun or how many beaux they should invite to their daddy's barbecue.

At least she and Robby were free from Paul's tirades. Still, she felt at loose ends. She visualized herself swathed in black, standing on a precipice that looked down into a canyon as far as her eye could see. Part of her wanted to leap off into the unknown. But where would it take her?

"Mama?"

Nora looked into her only child's face, upset by the dark smudges under his eyes.

"What, baby?"

He frowned at her. "I'm not a baby, Mama."

She giggled. "Your lip is hanging down farther than Old Man Simpson's hound dog's." She delighted in his sudden smile. "You'll always be my baby, hon. Even when I'm in my eighties and you have grandchildren of your own, I'll tell people, *There goes my baby boy*."

Robby crinkled his nose in disgust. "You're silly." His face relaxed and then he grew serious. "Why were those old ladies talking all through Daddy's funeral? It just bugged the dickens outta me, Mama. It wasn't polite."

Nora sighed. "I know, sweetie. It bothered me, too. They are old, though, and they were friends of your daddy's parents. Sometimes, we have to forgive older people for their faults."

"Well, Jess would've slapped 'em up side the head or popped 'em with her cup towel." He paused, a mischievous grin painting his face. "I wish she would've, too."

"Oh, you!" Nora exclaimed, ruffling his blond hair

affectionately. "Go on home with Ben now. I'm going to tell Daddy goodbye and then I'll be along soon."

Nora bent on one knee in front of the casket and stared at it. She scooped up a handful of dirt in her gloved hand.

"Goodbye, Paul. I hope you find peace."

She stood and scattered the soil across the gravesite.

"Nora?"

She turned and saw her brother-in-law, Richard Cantrelle, making his way toward her. He was Paul's opposite in every way. Where Paul had been tall and fair, Richard was stout and dark. Paul's eyes had reflected the blue sky, while Richard's were as dark as sin.

"Hello, Richard." She gave him a brief, social smile, the best she could manage since he was her least favorite person.

"We must talk."

She frowned. "Here? Now?"

"Yes." He took her elbow and pulled her aside to the shade of an old magnolia, its yellow and rose petals just beginning to bloom on this early spring day. Nora inhaled their sweet scent as she shook off his hand.

"What is it, Richard? Please get to the point."

"Always one for polite conversation, Nora." He studied her briefly, as if he'd noticed something for the first time. "What I've got to say is about Robby."

Nora waited.

"Well, aren't you interested?" Richard demanded.

"Go on." She fought the impulse to rip off a glove and bite her thumbnail, a lifelong bad habit that would betray her nervousness.

Richard took a deep breath. "I think Robby should come to live at Blair Oaks. You, too, of course," he quickly added. "It will be his one day."

"What's left of it."

He ignored her cutting remark. "You know my wife is in ill health. My girls will marry and leave one day. I would like Blair Oaks to remain in the family, with family to run it. I think it would be to your advantage—Robby's, too—to have us live together as a family."

"As a family?" Nora could hardly believe his words. "No, Richard, we don't want anything from the Cantrelles. Your parents never approved of me. They never asked Robby and me to live with them while Paul was gone. You yourself turned your back on the three of us, refusing to visit your brother for years."

"I couldn't bear to see him in . . . that condition."

"And you think that helped him? He became bitter and old before his time, thanks to people like you." Nora waved a hand around the graveyard. "The turnout today was exactly what would have been expected for a Cantrelle, yet where were all these people when Paul needed them? He fought for their way of life. Their dreams."

Her hard laugh was bitter. "No, they all stayed away, and Paul retreated further into himself until he had nowhere else to go."

She straightened her shoulders and looked her brother-in-law squarely in the eyes. "Thank you for your kind offer, Richard, but I choose to decline. Good day." She strode away briskly, hoping she'd done the right thing.

Once she walked the few blocks home, her temper cooled considerably, helped by a tall glass of Jess' sweet tea. She was thankful for that. It would take every bit of Southern graciousness she could muster to be attentive to the guests roaming about her father's home. It hurt to swallow her pride and cater to these people.

She did it, though. For Paul. Nora knew what was expected of her. His reputation was on the line, even now. This would be her last sacrifice for him.

Nora was pleasant to every caller the remainder of the afternoon, nodding occasionally when the conversation called for it, though her thoughts were far away.

She refused to be caught up in reminiscences of the past. She'd spent far too many hours at Paul's bedside to be trapped the same way today. She promised herself from now on she'd only look to the future.

Nora was weary by the time she closed the door on the last of the sympathy callers. She pulled the pins from her hair and let it fall to her waist.

Jess entered the room. "I put Master Robby to bed, Miss Nora. He was tuckered out."

She put her arms around Jess, finding comfort in the embrace. The only woman she'd ever thought of as her mother barely came to her shoulder.

"Let's clean up, Jess. It's been a long day."

"Ben and I can take care of that, Miss Nora. Your papa wants to see you in his study."

Nora laughed. "So, that's where he disappeared to. I know I haven't seen him for the better part of two hours."

Jess shrugged. "You know Mister Albert. He'd always rather be with books and his writing than with people any day. He gets downright bored with all that gossiping and recipe trading."

She raised her brows. "And I don't?"

Jess smiled. "I just taught you better manners, child. Not that you listened to what folks had to say today."

"Oh, dear. Could you really tell?"

"I could, Miss Nora. I doubt no one else except Ben could, though. We know you too well." She gave Nora a playful swat. "Go see what Mister Albert wants."

Nora put her hand on her hips. "I'm too old for you to go swatting me, Jess," she said with mock humor.

Jess beamed. "Don't you try me, Miss Nora. I'll take a cup towel to you if I have to."

She laughed, fondly remembering the times she'd been in trouble, Jess chasing her around the house, popping her dish towel as fast as her wrist could snap it.

Nora always remained out of Jess' reach, thanks to her longer legs.

"Not the cup towel," Ben moaned.

The two women turned and saw Ben put a hand to his forehead. "What am I going to do with you two? I turn my back for two minutes and you're ready to act like—"

"Like the sensible, mature women we are," Nora finished. "Why don't you and Jess go to bed, Ben? It's been a long day. We can clean up tomorrow."

Ben's face lit with a wicked grin. "You don't have to tell me twice." He took his wife's hand. "C'mon, now, Jess. You heard Miss Nora. She's ordering us to bed."

He gave her a quick kiss on the lips. Jess giggled like a schoolgirl.

"Goodnight, Miss Nora," they both called as they exited the room.

"Goodnight," she said softly, the ache in her heart throbbing as they passed through the doors. Even after all these years, they were so much in love. Nora wondered what love—real love—was all about.

She thought she loved Paul and was deliriously happy when they became engaged on her sixteenth birthday. Papa begged them to wait until she was eighteen to marry and they agreed, aware that her father still wanted her as his little girl for a while longer.

That was fine with Nora. She could wait because her feelings for Paul were so strong. He was a true Southern gentleman. When the town as a whole gossiped viciously about her every move, it was Paul who treated her with courtesy. He respected her for her mind and all she wanted to accomplish as a writer.

Then war broke out, just weeks after their engagement had been announced. Nothing had been the same since. Paul surprised everyone by volunteering to serve in the new Confederate army. Though tall and strong, Nora worried about him. His nature was so sweet, so

18

gentle and passive. She couldn't imagine Paul charging the enemy on a battlefield of smoke, bleeding men in his sight, when he couldn't even stomach the thought of the chicken slaughtered for dinner.

He came home a different man, returning to Monroe for a brief leave just weeks after Gettysburg. They hadn't seen each other in over two years but Paul expressed his eagerness to marry her the moment he arrived home, despite the protests from his family.

He had changed, though. She couldn't quite put her finger on the difference. Nora believed she married a stranger as they stood before Father Deschard and proclaimed their vows as family and a few friends witnessed the nuptial mass. Yet they had loved one another since childhood. Nora believed love would conquer whatever barrier had come between them.

Or so she'd thought.

Their wedding night turned into an abysmal failure. Intellectually, she was prepared for what would happen. Jess explained all the physical aspects to her, even down to the pain she would feel the first time she made love.

Nothing prepared her, though, for the lack of emotion she would experience. Their first coupling was terribly disappointing. They were both virgins and had a hard time coming together. Nora believed their awkwardness was due to nerves and their lack of experience, even Paul's physical exhaustion after months of campaigning with few rations and little sleep.

The second time confirmed they had made a mistake. No passion sparked between them. They kissed a few times before he returned to battle and she remembered those kisses as sweet yet unsatisfying. She supposed things would be different once they were free to act as man and wife in the privacy of their own home, where they would give each other their hearts.

Nora wrongly assumed her marriage would be like Jess and Ben's. She'd witnessed their wedded bliss growing up, a day-to-day love affair that deepened each year. She ran across them countless times in fervent kisses or quick embraces when they thought they were alone for a moment. The looks passing between them spoke more than any declarations of love from the lips of others.

Heat rose in her cheeks even now when she remembered the one time she accidentally walked in on them as they made love. They'd been oblivious to her, engrossed in their touches. Nora had quietly closed the door, but she longed for the time when she, too, would experience that kind of magic with her own beloved.

Yet Paul's kisses left her empty, as if she kissed a brother. The fire, the desire, all that she'd expected, never came. They had been friends so long that romance played no role in their marriage. Nora remained disappointed, afraid her mistake would never be remedied.

Paul left to rejoin Lee after two days, the longest two days in her life. She couldn't wait to see him go and experienced tremendous guilt when he rode off. She worried that he would die on the battlefield, that she'd never see him again, that she would never be able to make things right between them.

She brushed aside a tear and tamped down the jealousy that rushed through her. She should be thankful that Ben and Jess were still in love after more than twenty-five years together. They remained childless, while Nora gave thanks every day for Robby. He was the light of her life. Nothing would cause her to regret his existence.

She took a deep breath and exhaled slowly, gaining control of her emotions as she wondered what her father wanted. Probably something about the editorial she'd written. His mind remained fixated on his newspaper.

Nora knocked lightly on the door to the study and heard him call for her to enter.

He was seated behind his oak desk, a pipe in his hand. His eyes brightened as she took a seat in front of him. They'd sat this way a thousand times, discussing stories to run, ideas for editorials, and ways to make the paper turn a higher profit. The study was her favorite room in the house. Her happiest moments had been spent here with her father.

"Nora, we must talk."

He packed the pipe with a special blend of tobacco, his only concession to luxury in an otherwise Spartan life. Nora watched each gesture, compact and swift, until the pipe was lit. The sweet smell of tobacco slowly filled the room as he settled back in his chair.

"Would you care to leave Monroe?"

His blunt question startled her. "Tell me what this is about."

He closed his eyes and, for a moment, Nora could see how age had suddenly caught up to him. At this moment, he looked every one of his sixty years. She'd always thought him ageless yet, in the space of seconds, he looked like an old man. It wasn't his white hair. It had turned white almost overnight when Genevieve died. Still, his bushy brows had remained coal-black, and they were his most expressive feature.

He finally opened his eyes, mischief dancing in them.

"Papa, you've been up to something. What's going on?"

"You know how I feel about the South, Nora. I love it like an errant child. I have often disagreed with its politics, but I have lived here all my life. I would continue to do so if I thought it feasible."

"And it isn't?"

He shook his head. "No, it isn't. Business declined during the war and never picked back up. Money's hard to come by and will be for some time. People share newspapers instead of buying one of their own. They get their news off the streets and after church."

He stood and began to pace the room. "I see no future in this New South. It's nothing but talk. It's the same Old South with carpetbaggers taking advantage of everyone—white and black alike—until they milk us dry. Then these damned Yankees'll go home and where will we be?"

Her heart quickened. Nora had no idea what her father planned but it was obvious he'd given it great thought. "What do you propose?"

"I think we should pack up and move out West."

Her jaw dropped. No words came out.

He chuckled. "You're speechless, child. Perhaps I'll make this my lead story tomorrow."

Nora regained her composure. "You've threatened to make my actions your lead a hundred times, Papa. Go on." Her excitement grew by the minute.

"I have been thinking about this for some time, but it was impossible as long as Paul was in poor health. Colorado is fast-growing and full of opportunities. It's certain to become a state in the next few years. And where there are enough people to petition for statehood—"

"—there are enough people ready to buy a newspaper and read about it," she finished. "Papa, are you certain you want to go?"

He smiled. "Only if you do. Actually, Ben and Jess must want to go, too. I'd rather take them before you, anyway. They are much more helpful to me," he said playfully.

She jumped to her feet and threw herself into her father's arms. "You think Ben could write all those editorials for you?"

He took a moment to think about it before he answered. "No, he's not quite ready yet. I suppose I'll need to take you after all."

Nora danced around the room. "Colorado! I don't know much about it, but it sounds like heaven."

"I have acquired quite a few articles the last three years, Daughter. I'll let you read through them. Then if you think we should go, we shall."

Nora smiled at her father. "I'll read the information you've collected, Papa, but I can give you my answer now. If Ben and Jess agree, let's leave by the end of the week."

CHAPTER 3

"**M**orning, Sheriff."

Jack nodded a greeting as he made his way down Silver Bluff's main street. He glanced at the star pinned to his black vest. Although he'd been sheriff six months, he still wasn't used to seeing it there.

It surprised everyone—and maybe himself most of all—when he'd asked Old Man Stevenson to name him the town's lawman immediately after Jack's rescue of Bran. Silver Bluff didn't have anything remotely resembling a peace officer.

It came to him on the spot that the town needed one.

Silver Bluff boomed overnight when one of the richest strikes in Colorado became public knowledge. He was one of many intrigued by the find, who poured into the place, which didn't even have a name attached to it in those early days.

He took care of himself, which is more than he could say for some of the men who arrived looking for instant wealth. A rowdy element settled in for a short span. Ill-prepared for roughing it, a good number of newcomers found themselves cheated and beaten. Once no new discoveries were found, the worst of the riffraff moved on for greener pastures.

Jack had liked this place, though. After five years of wandering, he was ready to call Silver Bluff home. The air was sweet. The lake nearby danced with fish. The surrounding mountains took his breath away. He'd witnessed so much carnage during the war. He still dreamed of it most nights. If he planted roots here, at least he'd be assured of waking up to beauty, no matter what his nightmares held.

He joined the bulk of workers who remained and went to work for Stevenson's mining company. For the most part, his fellow laborers proved hard-working men —reliable, steady, and law-abiding. Only Saturday nights at the local saloon got boisterous.

Now, a general store stood on the main thoroughfare, and they'd completed the Methodist church a month ago. Silver Bluff had the makings of a real town. Jack aimed to see it stay on the straight and narrow. Burke Stevenson had cottoned to the idea of a sheriff and signed him to a one-year contract, renewable if he remained in good standing.

He wondered if that was the case now.

Pulling his hat lower, he strode down the street, a muddy bog due to recent rains. It was something he wanted to discuss with the new boss, William Kessler. Kessler had bought the Stevenson Mining Company and other interests Burke held in the town and beyond, as well as the two-story house half a mile outside town.

The old man had sold out, something Jack never anticipated, given Stevenson's interest in the mining process but one that was understandable. Stevenson took young Bran down to Denver for treatment immediately after his accident. After months of therapy, the prognosis for walking was just this side of hopeless. Burke Stevenson decided to pull up stakes and head back East in search of the best medical care available for his only child. Jack couldn't blame him.

He wondered what the new owner would be like. The transactions occurred in Denver and William Kessler had only arrived in town late last night. He hoped it was a good sign that Kessler summoned him so soon.

He continued down the small thoroughfare, almost empty at mid-morning. The bulk of Silver Bluff's working force toiled at the mine. Only a few scattered souls had business at this hour. The ones he passed gave their sheriff a polite nod of recognition.

Kessler's house loomed ahead, surrounded by a white picket fence and lush grass made green by the spring storms. He walked through the hinged gate and up a short flight of steps, pausing to lift his hat and run his fingers through his unruly hair before he knocked.

A slight Chinese man answered. Jack recognized him as Stevenson's butler. Probably smart leaving him in Colorado Territory. Although the small Chinese community here faced the same prejudice any Asians did in the West, he could only speculate about the look on the faces of Eastern callers if Chin Lee had answered their knocks.

"Chin Lee."

The man bowed low. "Greetings, Mr. Jack Sheriff."

He stifled a smile at the address. Chin had never quite gotten the hang of exactly what to call Jack when he visited the Stevenson homestead. He supposed this title was as good as any.

"Here to see Mr. Kessler, Chin."

The butler bobbed his head up and down. "Yes, Mr. Jack Sheriff. Mr. Kessler ready to see you." He motioned. "Come. This way."

Chin led him up the staircase, where they turned left. Apparently, Kessler would maintain the same office Burke Stevenson had used. All the furniture remained in place from the previous owner. He figured the mine owner sold the house and all its contents intact.

The Chinaman knocked on the study's door and popped in his head. "Mr. Jack Sheriff, Mr. Kessler. Can he come in?"

Jack stared over Chin's head and located Kessler. He was seated behind a large oak desk covered with papers, a frown on his florid features. He noted the graying hair and broad shoulders and placed his new employer in his early to mid-forties.

Without raising his eyes, the man spoke. "Come in, Sheriff. I'll be with you in a moment." He began to scribble furiously on the page in front of him in short, quick strokes.

Jack stepped into the room but did not take a seat. His mama had raised him with manners. He would sit if invited—not before. He gazed about the room, noting a few new filing cabinets that had not previously been present. Otherwise, the room remained unchanged. He wondered what Kessler had done before moving to Silver Bluff. Thick Persian carpets covered the floor and silenced his steps as he walked nonchalantly around the room.

He studied his new employer from the corners of his eyes as he did so. The man was handsome in a fleshy way. He'd probably done physical labor at one time, but his body spoke of how it had lost its edge over time. New money always seemed to turn a body soft.

Kessler rose and stepped away from the desk, offering his hand. His dark blue suit was well cut and brought out watery-blue eyes that were slightly bloodshot, even at this early morning hour. Jack had seen eyes such as these before. No wonder the name rang a bell when he'd heard it first mentioned.

"Pleased to meet you, Sheriff Duncan." Kessler favored him with a tight smile, one that did not quite reach his wintery eyes.

"Call me Jack."

Kessler eyed him speculatively before he nodded. He did not return the favor of being addressed so informally. Jack immediately sized up William Kessler as a smart man, one who would hold his temper well—and one who would play all the angles. He was sure in that moment that his new boss was somehow related to Ken Kessler.

"Glad you could come on such short notice." The new mine owner perched on the edge of his desk and lifted a box lid, withdrawing a cigar. He lit it and slowly inhaled.

He did not offer one to his guest.

"Tell me about yourself and Silver Bluff, Jack." Kessler stood and leisurely walked to the large window. The entire town could be viewed from this perch.

Before he answered, another man entered quietly. He had the same watery blue eyes, though his skin held none of the ruddiness Kessler's did. His hair was a medium brown, probably Kessler's color before the gray set in. He looked to be in his mid-thirties. He crossed to Jack.

"Sheriff Duncan, I presume?" He flashed a smile that displayed even, white teeth.

Jack's stomach roiled, but he thrust out his hand and managed a strong grip.

"I'm Ken Kessler. William's brother."

The man in front of him was one that was quick to anger and quicker to use his fists. He'd often wondered how Kessler rose to the rank of major. His face usually betrayed his thoughts. Right now, he looked at Jack as if meeting him for the first time. Had the war really been that long ago?

"Good to have you in Silver Bluff, Mr. Kessler." Jack broke the contact between them, ready to coat his hand in strong lye soap where Kessler had touched it.

"Ah, Ken. The name's Ken."

He looked at him steadily. "Then call me Jack." He waited for any sign of recognition. None came. At that moment, he was grateful his own face was made of stone. His mother had often teased him about it.

"Lord Almighty, Jack. If I didn't know you loved my mincemeat pie so, I'd be in tears right about now. You'd never know it from looking at that face of yours."

He turned back to the older Kessler in total control. He'd shown little emotion as a child. Since the war, he showed even less. If Ken Kessler was too stupid to recall him, he wasn't going to announce their previous connection.

"You wanted to know about me, sir?" He paused as Kessler nodded, his gaze cutting from his brother and back to Jack as he puffed away on his cigar, its sweet aroma floating through the air.

"I'm a great shot and a hard worker. I was a farmer in western Virginia before the war. Afterward, I moved West like so many others. Tried mining on my own. No huge successes there." He shrugged. "Was a bounty hunter for over three years. I can track with the best of them."

Kessler turned his back as Jack spoke, staring out the window again. He wondered if his new boss was even listening to him. For a long time, neither man spoke. Finally, the elder Kessler broke the silence.

"Why did you leave that profession?" He moved to face Jack once again.

"Bounty hunting pays well, but it's a transient life. I took to Silver Bluff. The opportunity to be sheriff presented itself at the right time."

Kessler returned to his seat behind the massive desk. "Your contract runs another six months."

It was a statement. Not a question. He wondered what Kessler was up to. Already he'd formed a strong impression of his employer. He knew it was colored by his former association with Ken Kessler, but Jack was a good judge of character, nonetheless.

He didn't like either Kessler.

The few minutes they'd spent together put him on edge. Leopards didn't change their spots and that included Ken Kessler. The man was a proven cheat, liar, and probable murderer. If Ken worked for his brother, Jack knew neither could be trusted. His instincts had never let him down before. His guard was up and would stay that way.

"Unless I'm derelict in my duties, I aim to fulfill the life of the contract. If I'm negligent, it's within your rights to terminate it."

He stared hard at Kessler, almost daring him to do so now. He'd thought the new mine owner simply wanted to meet with him as a courtesy. Get some background on the town. Now he sensed an ulterior motive as the room crackled with tension. It was as if Kessler were sounding him out, wanting to see if his sheriff could be controlled.

Jack decided to go with his gut and lay his cards on the table. If he'd read the look in Kessler's eyes right, he'd be gone regardless of what he said.

"I'm no puppet on a string, Mr. Kessler. I like my job, but I would never lower my standards. I'd rather be fired up front and move on than wallow in corruption."

The older man laughed harshly. His brother chimed in, sounded like a hyena. "No sense to do that, Sheriff. I'm determined to see Silver Bluff grow in the right direction." He frowned thoughtfully. "Tell me about the town. What it's like." He pointed to his brother. "Neither Ken nor I have ever lived in a place quite so small."

It surprised Jack that his comments went unanswered, ignored or simply dismissed by William Kessler. He would ponder that later. For now, he turned his focus back to the brothers.

"Started out as a mining camp, close to four years

ago. Mr. Stevenson bought up some of the land and set a half-dozen men in place, looking for silver strikes. The camp grew larger as a few claims of silver were made. No new loads discovered so most moved on to fresh sites.

"Then Stevenson's men found a mother vein. He set up a large-scale operation, wanting to establish a permanent company. He wasn't interested in migratory workers. The bank and general store soon followed."

"And I hear talk of a school?"

"A few of the men are married and brought their families, though a rough element still exists. I'm working on smoothing it out. Even though there's only a handful of school-age children, Mr. Stevenson was a planner. He'd rather have the school in place, if only with a few students, and let it grow naturally. It'll be finished next month. Methodist church was just built. I heard tell the Baptists might be next. About eight or ten families of homesteaders have arrived, too, with farms on the outskirts of town."

"A real little community."

Jack didn't like Kessler's sarcastic tone but continued. "We've also built a jail. It can house four prisoners. I work out of an office there."

Kessler steepled his fingers and nodded. "Good. I want this town run as tight as a drum, Jack. Silver Bluff may be in for big things. Tell our sheriff about this, Ken."

Ken Kessler sat up straighter in his chair. "I just got back from Denver. Word there is all about statehood. Most of the politicians predict statehood within five to six years. Enough people will have moved in by then to write a state constitution and apply for admission to the United States. The railroad's key, you know."

Jack nodded. "Denver's grown by leaps and bounds in the five years I've been here."

Ken's perfect smile flashed again. "That very railroad may run a connecting branch through Silver Bluff in the next few years. If it did, we'd be on the map. A real boomtown. Who knows how big it could get?"

William Kessler interrupted. "That's why I want a town with the lid on it. I need a man who'll keep things on the straight and narrow. I do not want trouble. Ever. Think you can handle that, Sheriff?"

Before he could answer, Chin Lee burst through the door. "Mr. Jack Sheriff! Come quick! Mr. Lowell got drunk again. He's gonna shoot his stinking mule, he says."

Jack placed the worn hat on his head. "If you'll excuse me, Mr. Kessler. Ken. Casey Lowell gets liquored up about once a month and threatens to shoot Gertrude, his mule, every time. I need to throw him in the jail and let him sleep it off."

As he took his leave, he caught a knowing glance between the Kessler brothers.

CHAPTER 4

J ack gritted his teeth as the ladies of Silver Bluff filed out of the bank, all four total, not a backward glance among them. How four scrawny women could give one man so much grief was beyond understanding. He stared after the last departing skirt as it whirled out the door. Jed Ragland, the appointed escort for the ladies, uttered a soft expletive and hurried after them.

He raised his eyes and met the timid glance of Mortimer Witherspoon, the town's banker and its sole employee. The slight man raised his bony shoulders and eyebrows in a show of camaraderie and gave Jack a half-hearted smile before returning his attention to the stack of ledgers in front of him.

Jack gave an inward sigh and raked his fingers through his hair. It was Witherspoon's own wife, Millicent, who'd made the most demands today. Between her and Jane Simmons, he'd been ready to rip off his badge and walk out for good.

Only a handful of women could want so much so fast. He explained to them it was too soon for families to be in Silver Bluff anyway. The town still had a wild streak to it. Wasn't the death of Rita Jean last week proof enough? Of course, as sheriff, he couldn't very well bring up a painted lady's murder to a polite gathering of females—even if he heard them gossiping about it when he arrived at their little get-together.

The fact that he'd even had to stop at the bank angered him. He'd left his meeting with Kessler to straighten out Casey Lowell. The fool always threatened to shoot his damn mule—whether he was drunk or sober—but Lowell only tried to make good on his threats when he had a little whiskey in him. Jack couldn't blame him. Everyone in town knew Gertrude had a mean streak a mile wide. How Casey put up with the animal surprised him.

Still, he had every intention to march back to Kessler's until Mr. Witherspoon stopped him and told him *the ladies* needed a brief word with him.

That brief word turned into ninety minutes of complaints about everything wrong in Silver Bluff to date. The unspoken words left hanging in the air were that the women felt it was all their sheriff's fault.

Dealing with unreasonable women and greenhorns was his least favorite part of the job. Neither should be here in the first place. Colorado Territory as a whole was too rough. At least with greenhorns, someone could play a joke on them. That always made for a good tale when the miners gathered in the saloon. The greenhorns either learned to tough it out or tucked their tails and left fast.

Women were another matter. Life was a heck of a lot easier before women arrived in Silver Bluff. The few present only came this spring, after things thawed. Here it was July now and they'd already cornered him for three of these so-called *meetings*. He pictured each of them calling on the Almighty Himself at the first snowstorm next season to complain how the snow might ruin the hems of their garments and would He please see that something's done about this?

Jack smiled at that thought as he gazed out the bank's window from his seat.

NORA LISTENED TO THE DEEP RUMBLINGS OF THE stagecoach, thankful they had made so much of their journey by rail. Although far from comfortable, the train was a most acceptable way to travel, compared to being tossed about like rag dolls inside this stagecoach.

She licked her dry lips, only to find the taste of dust upon her tongue. Dust lingered everywhere. In her hair. The folds of her clothes. Inside her boots. She figured it probably sneaked into the deep recesses of her ear canal, too, as well as behind her eye sockets. She dreamed of a wet cloth placed upon her eyes and a soothing cup of tea to settle her queasy stomach.

Would this leg of their journey never end?

Even with her eyes closed, she sensed the people crammed inside the stage. The man next to her had to be over two hundred and fifty pounds. She didn't know what annoyed her more—the fact that he took up more of her seat than she did or that he reeked of alcohol. Both things gave her reason enough to hand Robby over to Jess, who sat directly opposite her.

Thank goodness her boy caught some sleep. The stage had left before daylight this morning, and it was already mid-afternoon now. Nora wished she could escape from the noisy snores of her fellow passengers but found sleep impossible with all the jostling. The baby that cried so lustily from the beginning of the trip also prevented her from catching any shut-eye.

She longed to stand and stretch. Her bottom was numb. She imagined the thousands of tiny pinpricks that would dance across it once she stood. Maybe she was better off keeping her seat.

The coach began to slow. Nora's eyes popped open

to survey the landscape outside the window. Spectacular mountains in the distance showed tall peaks with a visible ribbon of snow adorning their caps. Everything here was green and vibrant. The colors were richer, the land so different from Louisiana.

Her father said the higher altitude created her nausea. Coming from flat, humid land, Nora had never experienced anything as this thin mountain air. She couldn't wait to gulp deep breaths of it once the stage halted at their destination.

The moment it came to a stop, she became the first to exit. Her legs wobbled as she touched the ground. She reached out a hand to steady herself, locking on to a large wheel of the carriage. She took a moment to compose herself and then inhaled slowly, deeply, enjoying the lack of dust as she looked at her new home. The queasy feeling in her stomach began to pass.

Nora gazed out over miles of endless green that met a sky the color of a blue jay. It took her breath away.

"Mama! Mama!" Robby scrambled down and latched on to her skirts. "It's beautiful, Mama."

She ruffled her son's hair. "Indeed it is, Robby boy. Do you think you'll like Colorado Territory?"

He nodded enthusiastically. "Grampy says we'll even get snow when it's winter." His eyes grew large at the thought before his attention wandered to the passengers disembarking. He ran the few steps to Ben, who assisted Jess and Albert from the coach.

She watched Jess take in the scenery. A smile played around the corners of Jess' mouth. She met Nora's eyes and nodded in approval. Nora crossed to her and took the servant's hands in hers.

"We've done a good thing, Miss Nora. This is a real good place. I can feel it in my bones."

The men approached them, and they stepped farther away from the stagecoach as more passengers spilled from its doorway.

Ben shook his head. "Don't know how they cram so many folks into one of them. At least we didn't ride on top."

Albert responded, "It's called profit, Ben. The more that fit inside, the more money they can make. The West is a place of opportunity."

They all laughed at his words of simple wisdom.

"Nora, I will see to getting us a couple of rooms at the local hotel. Why don't you check at the general store and see about our building needs? I want someone to start immediately on our new office. I don't want to leave the printing equipment in storage in Denver for too long."

"I'll get the luggage," Ben added.

Jess sighed. "I suppose that leaves me to watch Master Robby. Why do I get stuck with the hardest job?"

Robby grinned. "You have the best job, Jess. You're just pretending." He took her hand. "C'mon, let's go exploring." He eagerly pulled her along.

Nora glanced down the thoroughfare. The stagecoach had stopped at the very edge of town. To the left, she saw a small building with a hand-painted sign proclaiming it a bank. On her right, a general store stood thirty yards away. It looked new, with a large sign hanging above it, proclaiming its name in bold, black letters. Nora removed the duster the driver had offered each passenger, glad to be rid of its weight. The others traveling with her had all chosen to go without one.

She didn't know if they were foolish and dusty now, but she was hot and sweaty.

The mid-summer temperatures had climbed as they made their way from Denver. Nora patted at her hair, checking to see if her pins had held up. She found a few stray wisps and decided not to worry about them. She smoothed her skirts and checked the reticule draped across her wrist. She wished she had time to wash the travel stains away, but she was eager for information.

She moved from the middle of the street, a little surprised that no wooden walkways greeted her. She could only imagine what Silver Bluff looked like after a heavy downpour. As it was, the street was a mess from an earlier shower that morning.

Nora carefully picked her way down it, the words of an editorial already forming in her head. Without realizing it, she began mumbling them under her breath.

◆◆◆

JACK ROSE AND STRETCHED WHEN HE HEARD THE rumblings of the stage coming into town. If possible, he tried to greet those on it, whether they stayed on or were passing through. He tucked his worn hat onto his head and moved to the window. He would assess the travelers as they disembarked and make his presence known to those who looked questionable.

The vehicle barely came to a halt when the door flung open. A body emerged, encased in one of the shapeless dusters offered by the stage drivers. Although they did a decent job of keeping the dust off passengers, most refused to wear them in warmer weather. Apparently one passenger did take advantage of it.

It was a woman. He could tell that only by the trim black hat perched upon her head. Her eagerness in leaving the compartment meant, as usual, the company packed their paying customers in so tightly, many had trouble breathing. He noticed her face drained of color as she descended the steps unsteadily. She latched on to the wheel for support. He imagined white knuckles under her gloves.

Suddenly, a small boy appeared at her side. The woman managed a smile for him. As others poured from the confined space, Jack realized the pair must be mother and child. That meant more women, which meant more grumblings. He felt his temper rise again. Especially with a child in tow, this would be a woman who wanted a school and church meetings. and no saloon, to boot.

Didn't anyone realize he had more important things to deal with? He wanted the drunken miners off the streets. He needed to find a way to keep Billy Baker from beating the pulp out of his wife twice a week. And what about all the addicts over at the saloon? Those painted ladies overdosed quicker than a man could drink up his week's pay on a Saturday night.

He had way too much to handle before he could think about civic issues like town socials and potluck suppers at the church and ladies getting their fancy slippers muddy. His gut told him this would be a woman interested in those things.

She turned and surveyed her surroundings. He watched her assess the place as she shrugged out of the cumbersome duster. The minute he saw her raise her skirts and pick her way carefully around the few mud puddles in the street, his temper boiled over.

As Nora approached the general store, a sudden movement caught her eye. She turned to find a man striding across the street, aimed straight for her. She stopped dead in her tracks and then took a step back. He halted directly in front of her and swept off his hat, a scowl on his bronzed face.

Though taller than most women, she craned her neck to look up at the menacing stranger, who stood at least two inches over six feet. His brown eyes had an interesting ring of amber around them. Untamed, rich brown hair made him seem less threatening than at first glance.

She knew despite his dangerous looks, he must have had a mother who'd drilled manners into his head. The hat in his hand testified to that.

Nora decided to speak before he did, hoping to defuse the anger she saw on his face.

"Good day, sir," she said with confidence, although her voice trembled slightly. She clasped her hands tightly together to prevent them from shaking and continued. "I find it quite decent of you to take off your hat when meeting a lady. I wasn't sure what to expect coming out West, but I can see I worried for nothing. I'm sure good manners abound in Silver Bluff."

For a moment, the man was speechless. Nora noticed a scar that ran along his right temple, into his hairline. The hair that had grown back there was almost white. She'd never seen anything like it before.

Not wanting to stare, she introduced herself. "I'm Nora Cantrelle, newly arrived from Monroe, Louisiana. And you would be—"

"I don't allow unescorted women in Silver Bluff, miss. Any woman with a brain in her head could figure that out." His eyes bored into hers, causing Nora to take a step back.

"There's no need to be so harsh, sir. I—"

It shocked her when he reached out and took her elbow in hand.

"I'll excuse you this once since you're new in town. But unaccompanied women do not stroll the streets of Silver Bluff alone. That's the rule."

Her anger began to rise, as much from his words as the harsh tone he'd taken with her. "Why is that?"

He looked across the way at the bank and then down the street, which bothered her even more than his words had. A gentleman should look at the person he was having a conversation with. Just who did this man think he was?

"Because it's not safe yet."

She laughed and glanced around. "Not safe? There can't be more than four blocks of town. I went by myself all over Monroe and managed quite well, thank you.

At any rate, if the sheriff here did his job, it *would* be safe."

"I'm the sheriff."

Nora felt her cheeks turn crimson. She was also aware of his hand still on her elbow, an incredible heat pouring from it. She pulled her arm away as ladylike as she could manage.

The lawman still looked away from her, his mouth set in a hard line, his eyes unreadable. Were wild bandits about to ride into town and rob the newly-opened bank? Or worse . . . even wilder Indians on a vicious rampage?

She swallowed and tried to keep her tone light. "I'm sorry—I didn't know I'd chosen to move to such a rowdy place, Sheriff."

That finally got his attention. He glared down at her. "It's not rowdy, miss. I aim to keep it that way."

She started to speak, but he pushed ahead. "This was a mining camp until recently. The rough element has moved on for the most part, but I can't be every place at once. We're starting to grow, and growing pains can be tough. There's still trouble lurking around a few corners. A woman is just asking for trouble if she goes out alone."

She understood his words, but his arrogant attitude bothered her. "I assure you, Sheriff, that I will take Ben with me whenever I venture out from now on. He's been with me since birth. Now, if you'll excuse me, I have business at the general store."

He stepped aside and she passed, only to turn and call out over her shoulder, "And it's *Mrs*. Cantrelle, Sheriff."

His face remained impassive. Nora tried to still her heart and keep her steps steady as she moved away and entered the general store. She paused in the entrance and composed herself. If she hadn't thought he was still watching her, she'd rip off her glove and chew on her thumbnail for comfort.

In all her years, she'd never been addressed in such an uncivil tone. His uncouth greeting relegated her to the position of a second-class citizen. She found herself trembling more than on her worst encounter with the uppity ladies of Monroe.

"Welcome. You must be new in town."

Nora located the voice, which came from behind a wooden pickle barrel. She walked in that direction and saw a pair of feet sticking out. Slowly the feet pulled in and the body appeared from behind the barrel, rising to its full height.

"Seymour Simmons." Impish blue eyes were enlarged by gold spectacles. "Anybody I know always calls out a greeting when they come in. That's how I knew you were a stranger."

"I see." She already liked Seymour Simmons. He looked to be in his late fifties and had a friendly face. He also was skinny as a rail. She decided to invite him to supper once they established a home. A few of Jess' meals from heaven would fill out Mr. Simmons nicely.

"Just sorry my wife's not here to greet you but she should be back in a minute. She ran upstairs to sew on a button that came off. You can't run off until you've met."

"I'm Nora Cantrelle, Mr. Simmons, and I would like to meet Mrs. Simmons very much." She looked around at all the wares on display. "It seems you're well stocked."

"Yes, ma'am. Been open close to three months. Get deliveries every week from the stage, being only seventy miles north of Denver. We're actually closer to Cheyenne, though. Did you hear it's been named the new capital of Wyoming Territory? And the Colorado River's nearby, less than a day's journey on horseback."

He pulled the apron he wore over his head and

tossed it onto the counter. "What brings you to Silver Bluff?"

Simmons indicate a chair next to the pickle barrel and she sat.

"My father plans to start up a newspaper in Silver Bluff, Mr. Simmons. He published one back in Monroe. Since the mill started up in Oakville this spring, he'll have a ready supply of paper."

"Well, if that don't beat all." Simmons shook his head. "Getting a real paper." He mopped his brow with a large handkerchief. "'Course you'll need a place to build on. Does he have his own printing equipment?"

"Yes. We've managed to store it in Denver for the time being but are anxious to get started. That's why I came to you."

She smiled at Simmons conspiratorially. "I knew the proprietor of the local store would know exactly whom I should consult. What would your recommendation be, Mr. Simmons?"

Simmons puffed up with pride. "Got a couple of fellows that might do, ma'am, but I'd go with Harve Nelson. Does good work. Is a pleasant fellow, even if he's on the quiet side. Did you see the church yet?"

Nora shook her head. "We've only just arrived. I came straight off the stage to your store while Papa tries to secure us rooms at the hotel."

"Well, Harve's your man. Did a nice job on the church. Built the saloon, too." Simmons pinkened slightly. "Not that you'll need to see the inside."

She chose to skim over talk about the saloon. "Might Mr. Nelson be able to build a house at the same time? We'll need that, as well as a building to produce the paper."

"Harve could handle both for you. Hope you've brung plenty of money, though."

Before she could ask Simmons about his remark, a short, rather plump woman entered the store, coming through a curtain located behind the counter. She was fussily dressed in heavy brocade from her hanging chins to her heavy ankles. Nora wondered how she could take the summer heat in such material. She strode immediately down the aisle to where they sat.

"Who is this young lady, Seymour?"

Simmons rose and kissed the rude woman on the cheek. "This here's Miss Nora Cantrelle, honeybunch. Her daddy's gonna start up a newspaper here."

Mrs. Simmons clucked her tongue. "Bad for our business, Seymour. People come here to gossip and get the latest news as much as to buy goods." She extended her hand. "Still, it's a pleasure having a new lady in town. Aren't many of them here, Miss Cantrelle."

Nora rose and coolly offered her own hand. "It's Mrs. Cantrelle, ma'am."

"Oh?" The overweight woman looked her up and down, thoroughly taking in every detail. Though Nora never bothered much with her appearance, she knew others often judged her on it. Her faded gown was out of fashion. Money had been tight for years now, and she refused to spend any on updating her wardrobe when there were so many other needs. Instead, she and Jess had made her clothes over many times.

Now, though, she realized with her old clothes wrinkled and stained from travel, she must have made quite a poor first impression on Mrs. Simmons. The woman seemed the direct opposite of her friendly husband. Yet Nora suspected that Mrs. Simmons was a power in the town, simply because of her husband's position. She didn't want to get off on the wrong foot with her.

Much as she had wanted Silver Bluff to be different from Monroe, she realized it wasn't. The Mrs. Simmonses of the world seemed to abound. Though Nora dreamed of having the freedom to speak as she chose in her new life, she knew the newspaper was of utmost importance. She would do whatever it took, even curbing her tongue, to make it a success.

Placing a subservient smile on her face, she told the couple, "My husband was wounded in the war. He recently passed on. My family and I hope to build a new life here in Silver Bluff and not dwell on the past."

Mrs. Simmons nodded sagely. "Delighted to have you."

Her words might be kind, but Nora sensed an undercurrent that said otherwise.

"Once we get you settled in, dear, I'm sure you'll want to join our Tuesday quilting circle and our Bible study on Thursdays." She patted her graying hair. "There are so few quality ladies in town. I know you'll want to make all our acquaintances."

Nora dug her nails into her palms, painful despite the gloves she wore. This woman could drive a person to drink. She didn't want to alienate a pillar of the community on her first hour in town, though.

"I really am going to be quite busy, Mrs. Simmons. I'm afraid I'll have to turn down your kind offer for now." She pasted on her most ingratiating smile. "You see, I help my father in his work. I'm also raising my son. Both of these endeavors leave me little leisure time for now."

She flinched at the look that passed across the older woman's face. She had known her announcement wouldn't be well received, no matter how diplomatically she phrased it, but she was unprepared for the sudden change in appearance. Mrs. Simmons became an avenging angel, looking down upon Nora in her multitude of sins. Except Mrs. Simmons was very short. This angry angel had to look up at the wicked sinner.

"I see," she said briskly.

The door opened again, and Nora was glad for the break in conversation. A tall woman entered, her hair a flaming red, her clothes immaculate. She carried herself

45

so well that the nuns would have held her up as a perfect example of good posture.

She wished she might have been introduced to this woman first. Without even speaking, she already made a far better impression.

The woman nodded politely. A touch of sadness in her green eyes took Nora aback. It was as if she carried the weight of the world. Nora smiled warmly and almost spoke, but the woman moved to the far side of the store to the bolts of materials. Mr. Simmons excused himself to go wait on her.

"The Calico Queen graces us again with her presence."

Nora didn't understand the remark Mrs. Simmons made but she definitely understood its derogatory tone. Without thinking, she blurted out, "But she's not wearing calico."

The taller woman must have heard her remark. She lifted her gaze to Nora and smiled then went back to her shopping.

"Stay away from the likes of her, Mrs. Cantrelle, or your papa won't have a prayer of getting his newspaper off the ground."

"I don't understand what you're saying, Mrs. Simmons," she protested. "You said there were so few women in town. It seems a shame you would quarrel with one."

The proprietor's wife snorted. "I said there were few *ladies* in town. That, my dear, is no lady."

She studied the woman but couldn't discern why she wasn't a lady. Her hair was elegantly coifed, her clothing beautifully tailored. She did wear a few cosmetics on her face, something that brightened both her cheeks and lips, but other women back in Monroe did the same.

She turned to find Mrs. Simmons' eyes boring into her.

"You really don't know, do you, dear?" A malevolent smile crossed her plump features, and her chins wagged as she spoke. "That, Mrs. Cantrelle, is a soiled dove."

Nora looked blankly at the storeowner's wife, who cackled in response. "Take it from Jane Simmons. That woman entertains men above stairs at the local saloon."

Her eyes widened. She had heard talk of men paying for women's favors. Thoughts of her few couplings with Paul sprang to mind. She couldn't imagine a woman who chose to make a living that way.

"You say there are more?" Her natural curiosity needed to be satisfied.

"Oh, heavens, yes. When Mr. Stevenson set up the mining company, he also provided a saloon. Liquor, music and . . . those women." She clucked her tongue. "Men will be men, he said. They have certain needs that must be met. Mr. Stevenson provided this service for his employees."

"And it's legal?"

Jane Simmons shrugged. "I suppose so. Sheriff's never shut it down." Her eyes narrowed. "Just stay a good distance from them, Mrs. Cantrelle. You've got your reputation to maintain."

It distressed Nora that any woman resorted to that lifestyle to survive. She'd known of women in Monroe trapped in awful circumstances both during and after the war. Some married men they didn't love, while others hired themselves out, doing laundry or cleaning for the few affluent families still left.

The women at the saloon could have similar stories. Although the war had been over for five years, it was taking most of the country much longer than expected to get back on its feet. Until Silver Bluff grew, this was probably the only kind of available work for a woman.

As Mrs. Simmons turned away, Nora caught the eye of the redhead again and smiled broadly at her. Ideas formulated in her head. She was a born crusader. It would take time and thought, but she knew this dark cloud would have a silver lining in the long run.

Walking across the store, she thrust out her gloved hand. "I'm Nora Cantrelle. My family just arrived today."

The statuesque redhead gave her a radiant smile. "I'm pleased to make your acquaintance. My name is Marguerite Le Beau."

She heard Jane Simmons gasp. A quick glance showed her the woman had gone as white as a sheet.

"Miss Nora?"

She was roused from her thoughts by Ben's voice. He hurried toward her. The look on his face let her know something was wrong. Ben was the calmest of men, with a gentle, easy demeanor. He looked almost in a panic now.

"Mister Albert's gonna be in high trouble, Miss Nora. You better come quickly."

48

CHAPTER 5

Jack slammed the door to the jailhouse. Usually, he left it open when he was here. He enjoyed the breeze that passed through and could keep an eye out at the same time. Now, he simply needed time by himself to cool off. He tossed his hat onto the large desk and plopped into the chair behind it. He ran both hands through his hair, frustrated that that woman —*Mrs. Cantrelle*—had gotten under his skin.

He reached into the lower right-hand drawer and pulled out a piece of wood, one of several. He whipped out the knife from his boot and leaned back into the chair more as he planted booted feet atop his desk. Whittling always calmed him, and he definitely needed to cool his heels a spell.

The woman was Southern. The one thing he couldn't tolerate was a damned Southerner. His parents had been hard-working people, farmers in the mountains of western Virginia. They'd had no slaves. No desire to own them, either. They'd raised their sons with the idea that a man who couldn't do his own labor with his own hands was no respectable man. He'd lived by that creed—and he'd die by it, too.

Just like his little brothers. Buddy lost at Chancellorsville and Sam at Shiloh. It had been almost more than his parents could bear, hearing their two youngest died a lonesome death on a bloody battlefield. Not a day went by that Jack didn't regret their passing. He wished he could have protected them.

Their deaths gave him more cause to fight Mr. Lincoln's War with a vengeance. It instilled in him a deep hatred for all the rich, spoiled slaveowners. No better example could be seen than in his brief encounter with Mrs. Cantrelle. He saw the tired-looking Black woman who'd been ordered to mind the Cantrelle child while his mother marched around Silver Bluff causing havoc.

The woman had been downright haughty. Who was she to judge how he ran his town? She stuck her nose so high in the air, he wouldn't have been surprised to see a bird fly by and clip it off. Telling him that Ben, who'd been with her since birth, would accompany her from now on had gotten his goat. Didn't this woman realize slaves were now free? Someone better wake up both her and this Ben to the idea that Grant's boys had changed their world.

Thoughts of Grant and the war made Jack think of Felicity. Raw emotions washed over him anew. He ached at the unresolved issues between them. The pain of her betrayal and the loss of his parents swept through him. He deeply regretted the rift with his older brother, Joseph, but that gulf was too wide now to breach.

He'd promised himself again that he would forget them all. But it was taking a hell of a lot longer than he'd anticipated. Joseph scoffed at his dreams of wealth. That was all water under the bridge now. Jack hadn't made his mark as the newest millionaire in the West but he liked what he did for a living. Sure, some of it was mundane, but a lot more was worthwhile. It gave him purpose, and that's what he would focus on now.

He turned the wood in his hands, oblivious to the shape beginning to form. His thoughts went back to what Kessler was up to. After he'd convinced Casey Lowell not to shoot his mule, Jack had been on his way to Kessler's to finish their interrupted talk.

Unfortunately, he'd been waylaid by Mortimer Witherspoon's worst half and her brigade of do-gooders. Then he'd run into the Southern prima donna. She'd gotten under his skin, so he'd chosen to come back here and compose himself before seeing Kessler again.

The door squeaked on its hinges as Ned Sooner came in. He was a gawky lad of fourteen, but he reminded Jack of Buddy in a way. He smiled at the boy, ready to quiet the panic he saw on the boy's face.

"Sheriff, you better get to the hotel right away. Seems like Sonny's having a big problem. If one of 'em don't kill him, the other one will."

"What's up, Ned?"

"If'n I took the time to tell you, Sheriff, there might be no more Sonny. Come on!"

Jack shook his head. Ned had a tendency to exaggerate. He brought himself to his feet and decided to stroll over to the hotel, just in case.

❦

NORA MARCHED INTO THE SILVER BLUFF HOTEL, BEN hot on her heels. She'd managed to get the gist of the situation in the minute it took to go from store to hotel and she was ready to raise Cain.

As she approached the front desk, she saw Papa's bushy brows had taken on a life of their own as he berated the hotel clerk. His blue eyes raged in anger. He caught sight of her and hurried over. She took his arm and murmured in his ear.

"Papa, I want you to settle down. You're redder than a ripe tomato. Go look for Robby and Jess. I'll handle this."

Albert opened his mouth to speak but changed his mind. "Ben'll stay with you."

Nora nodded. "Of course. Now, go on." She brushed her lips quickly against his cheek and turned him in the direction of the door before she planted a smile on her face and headed towards the front desk.

The man seated there was in his early twenties, with hair already thinning. He rose to greet her.

"I can't thank you enough, ma'am, for soothing him. He was mighty riled up. He your pa?"

"Yes, Mister..."

"Smith. Sonny Smith. I been clerking for Mr. Hall six years, first in Denver and now here."

"Well, Mr. Smith, it seems a situation has developed involving my father. Can you explain to me what happened?"

Smith pulled nervously at his collar. "He wanted to rent a few rooms for you, but I can only rent two."

"Is it a space problem, Mr. Smith? Surely the Silver Bluff Hotel isn't full at this point?" Her smile remained in place, but she narrowed her eyes to show she meant business.

"Not exactly, ma'am. We just... we just don't rent to coloreds." He took a handkerchief from his pocket and mopped his brow.

"Why is that, Mr. Smith?"

"It's been Mr. Hall's policy since we opened." He swallowed hard. "This is the first time it's come up, though."

"Perhaps I should have a word with Mr. Hall? I'm sure we could straighten this matter out in no time."

"Can't do it. Zebulon Hall's done gone down to Denver yesterday. His son's marrying a real society lady, and he and Mrs. Hall won't be back for a week. If I know Mrs. Hall, she won't come back until next spring. She hates it here. Too small for her taste."

Nora was silent a moment as she studied the clerk.

"Then I suppose you'll have to make a decision on your own, sir." She fiddled with her reticule as she began to hum softly.

"I can't accommodate your entire party, ma'am. Mr. Hall'd have my hide."

"Have your hide?" Nora laughed softly. "Oh, I don't think so, Mr. Smith. I'm sure he'd be quite angry at all the business you cost him."

"Come again?"

She smoothed her skirt and then met the clerk's eyes. "Not only would we be paying for three rooms for an indefinite period, but we are ready to establish a newspaper here in Silver Bluff. That will attract people, Mr. Smith, lots of them. It always does. Many of them will need a place to stay and I would assume Mr. Hall's hotel would be their choice."

Nora shrugged. "Of course, if we find Silver Bluff not to our liking, I'm sure we'll just move on. Colorado Territory is a big place. I know we'll find the right town to start our paper. Pity, though. I would hate for you to lose such an opportunity." Her words hung in the air.

She could tell the man regarded her words carefully.

Ben hovered near the doorway, clearly uncomfortable with the entire situation. She gave him a reassuring smile.

Sonny Smith exhaled noisily. "Seems like you've got yourselves some rooms." He turned the register around to face her. "If you'll just sign in, ma'am. You'll be upstairs, turn left, the last three rooms on the left."

Nora took the pen he offered and scrawled their names, doing her best to suppress a triumphant smile.

"Thank you, Mr. Smith. I look forward to seeing you each day," she said sweetly, and she meant it. She wanted Silver Bluff to be a good home for her family. She'd always regarded Ben and Jess as part of that family. No one could tell her that skin color made a difference. If she had to convince each individual in Silver

Bluff of that, she would. Sonny Smith was merely a beginning.

She also planned to do something about those poor women who made a living on their backs, servicing the men of this town. She couldn't believe the sheriff allowed it to go on though she guessed he was their leading customer.

Nora walked to the door, ready to retrieve their luggage and get unpacked. She had so much to do. Ben opened the door for her, and she sailed through it.

She ran smack into Silver Bluff's sheriff.

❦

WILLIAM KESSLER TOOK THE CHINA CUP FROM THE tray the butler brought. He couldn't remember the man's name. Several servants came along with the house. Stevenson had been quite specific on that point. He was to keep each of them on a minimum of six months before the mine owner would agree to a bill of sale regarding the house. For now, Kessler merely rented the residence for a reduced fee.

He brought the steaming drink to his lips and sipped it slowly. He enjoyed a strong cup of coffee almost as much as he did sex. He'd always had real coffee, even during the war years. Some things he considered sacred. It had involved quite a bit of finagling, but then, didn't everything worthwhile during the war?

Kessler watched as Ken dumped three lumps of sugar and a good swig of milk into his cup and stirred the mix together. Finally, the servant left them alone. He never spoke in front of hired help. Too many spies. Too many secrets. They knew enough as it was, being always underfoot. That's why he limited his conversations in their presence.

"What do you think of our town's sheriff, little brother?"

Ken swallowed a sip of coffee and set the cup down, a thoughtful look on his face. "Don't think he'll cooperate, William. Not with anything." He paused. "I do think he'll keep things running smoothly for the time being."

Ken shifted in his seat. "He's dangerous—and not just in his looks. I'm sure that alone has kept trouble in Silver Bluff to a minimum. One look at our noble sheriff's size and chiseled features would tend to make even the most crooked con bypass him by a mile. He may be useful for a while. Do you agree?"

Kessler closed his eyes for a long moment. When he opened them, he said, "He may be valuable." His eyes burned brightly as he gazed at his brother. "But sooner or later, I'll need you to get rid of him."

His brother smiled. "It will be my pleasure. As always."

CHAPTER 6

The Cantrelle woman hit his solid wall of hard muscle. Jack caught her under her elbows as she bounced off him and steadied her.

"In a hurry, Miz Cantrelle?" He ran a slow eye over her, hoping to rattle her a bit. She didn't take the bait.

"Actually, I'm fine, Sheriff. Thank you for your concern."

"I heard there might be a little trouble here."

She laughed, patting her hair in an utterly feminine gesture. "Not at all. Just arranging rooms for our stay until we can have a house built. A Mr. Harve Nelson has been recommended to do the work. Do you know him?"

He nodded. "Nelson's a fair man and a good builder. He's a little busy, though."

"I plan to do what I can to sweet-talk him into not only starting a house for us but constructing our business, as well."

Jack imagined her batting those long lashes at Nelson and cajoling him in honeyed tones. She interrupted the sharp remark about to roll off his tongue.

"Sheriff, I'd like you to meet Ben Weaver." She gestured for him to come closer. "Ben, this is our new town's sheriff. He wants to be sure you're with me at all times if I step out on his streets. He's afraid something might happen to me unless I have you by my side."

Ben's dark face broke into a lopsided grin as he offered his hand. "Howdy-do, Sheriff. Pleasure to be in your town." He pumped Jack's hand rapidly as he spoke. "Don't worry about Miss Nora, though. She's been taking care of herself nigh on twenty-odd years. If anything, you'd best be warning people here about her."

"Ben!"

Jack watched as the Southerner swatted at the tall man in mock anger. As she admonished her companion playfully, his surprise grew. Before he could fully comprehend things, an excited voice called out.

"Mama! Mama!"

The Cantrelle boy rushed up, a huge smile painted from ear to ear, a mangy mutt cradled in his thin arms. The short, dark woman he'd seen earlier followed the boy, skirts swishing in her haste. As she stepped up behind the boy, she rested her hands on his shoulders. Bright eyes danced in her honey-brown face.

"You've gotta ask your mama nicely, Robby," she whispered in the boy's ear. "She has the final word at what goes on in our house and we ain't even got a house yet." The servant smoothed the boy's hair affectionately, her smile warm. "Take your time. Say it just like we practiced."

She pushed him forward a little bit with a swift pat on the rump. He looked over his shoulder and she nodded encouragingly.

"Mama. You know how I never had a pet 'cause we had to keep things quiet for Papa 'cause he couldn't be disturbed? And Papa said a dog would eat us outta house and home and we didn't have no money to spare?"

Jack watched Nora Cantrelle nod, a trace of a smile forming on her full lips.

"Well, Jess said nobody's gonna worry about barking

dogs now and this little fellow doesn't have much of a bark anyway and Jess says things'll be better for us now out west and can I please, please, please keep him? Please, Mama?"

Jack thought keeping the sickly-looking hound would be a poor decision on anyone's part. If a dog couldn't hunt, what good was it? He glanced at the boy's mother, her cheeks now flushed a soft pink. She ruffled her son's golden hair.

"You can keep him, honey. We'll just have to check with Mr. Smith in our hotel to see if the pup can stay in the barn."

The boy looked stricken. "Mama, he's gotta stay with us. He's a skinny little critter. He might get lonesome if he can't see me."

In agreement, the dog licked Robby's face and stared morosely at Nora.

Jack shook his head. This dog was going to be more cosseted than a spoiled child.

"We'll need to see about food and water for him then. Why don't we walk over to the general store and ask Mr. Simmons about it? I'm sure he'll fix us up."

The boy's scrunched up face relaxed into a terrific smile. He hugged his mother's skirts tightly, mashing the dog between them. "Thank you, Mama. He'll be good. I promise."

Jack looked up to see an older man making his way across the street to them. "Is this our newest family member, Robby?" He bent low to scratch the dog's ears.

The boy nodded. "He ain't got a name yet, Grampy."

"Then let's give him one. How about Odysseus? Just like the feller in the story we've been reading. We could call him Ody for short."

The boy tried out the name. "Hey, Ody. Hey, boy."

The dog perked up his ears and barked, a soft,

pitiful sound. He gave Robby another quick lick and nuzzled close.

The gentleman patted the dog again and then stood. He held out his hand to Jack.

"Albert Le Fall, sir. New to Colorado Territory."

He clasped the wiry man's hand, surprised at the firmness of his grip. "Jack Duncan. Sheriff. Welcome to Silver Bluff." He paused a moment and then added, "What brings you to town?"

"Starting up a newspaper, Sheriff. Had one back in Monroe. Plan to do it all over again here in Silver Bluff." He frowned. "Just found out, though, that Mr. Stevenson left town. Sold his silver mine and his other interests in the area."

His daughter interrupted, the concern evident in her voice. "Will that change things for us, Papa?"

"I'm not sure, honey. I have a signed contract with the paper mill in Oakdale. I'd think the contract would be good, even if the ownership has changed. I want to go see this Kessler fellow now and be sure we're all on the same page. He bought out Stevenson."

Jack spoke up. "I'm on my way over to Kessler's now. I have some business myself with him. Wouldn't mind company on the walk over."

"Then it's agreed." A worried look creased his brow. "Nora, did you secure rooms for all of us?"

"Yes, Papa. Mr. Smith was most accommodating. In fact, Ben can take our bags up to the last three rooms on the left any time."

Mr. Le Fall blew out a long breath. "I'm glad that's settled. The sheriff and I will go and see Mr. Kessler then."

"Jess and Robby and I will head over to the store and see what we need to do for Ody." Nora touched her father's shoulder briefly. "Take care, Papa."

Le Fall grunted in return.

Jack set out, the old man falling into step with him.

As the pair started down the main street, he tossed a glance over his shoulder. The pup's tail wagged happily as he followed Robby Cantrelle toward the general store.

❧❧

Marguerite Le Beau entered Kessler's library, her brows faintly arched. The advance word he'd heard about the woman didn't do her justice. Though close to forty, she looked a good five years younger. Her skin was as smooth as porcelain, with only faint lines around the corners of each eye. Vivid green eyes glowed brightly, matched in their splendor by the bright red flames of her upswept curls. He couldn't wait to run his hands through that fire.

"Good afternoon, Miss Le Beau. Won't you have a seat?" He indicated a settee in dark green on his left.

"Thank you, Mr. Kessler." Instead, she perched on the edge of a Queen Anne chair nearby. His blood raced at the thought of how fun the chase would be.

"I came as soon as I received your summons." Her voice was deep, almost mannish but one look at her bustline would dispel any doubts. He was surprised by her dress. It was very proper and of the current fashion.

"It was only a message, Miss Le Beau." His eyes traced her form slowly, savoring the curves.

"I suppose you wish to discuss the contract?"

He drew his attention from the curve of her hip and met her gaze. "Yes. The paperwork left by Stevenson was a bit... unusual."

One corner of her mouth turned up slightly. "Somewhat out of the ordinary. Mr. Stevenson was more than generous with me."

"He left you in charge of the daily operations at the saloon?"

"Yes, and I'm to receive a quarter of the girls' take. Before expenses."

"That's in addition to a salary, Miss Le Beau?"

The statuesque beauty nodded. "I'm very good at what I do, Mr. Kessler."

"The expenses are rather large."

"Not unreasonable for what Mr. Stevenson had in mind. He was aware that Silver Bluff would grow quickly. He knew women of integrity who settled the town would rather things be kept discreet. That's the reason for the rather luxurious upstairs parlor. It's very private. He also wanted each girl's room furnished in good taste, and monthly exams by a doctor. Mr. Stevenson was a thorough man." She dabbed a handkerchief against her brow.

"I can understand his reasons." Kessler moved from where he stood to sit near his visitor. "May I call you Marguerite?"

She gave him an enigmatic smile. "If you choose."

He took her hand in his. "I know you had an arrangement with Mr. Stevenson. I would be most enthused if that arrangement would continue. With me." He gave her hand a slight squeeze.

Marguerite removed her hand from his. "Thank you for the kind offer but I can't accept it."

Her words took Kessler aback. Rarely did someone refuse him. He might be past forty, but he still had a full head of thick hair, graying slightly. His last kept woman had called it distinguished. He knew he cut a fine figure —and he had money. If things went according to plan, he'd have even more wealth, as well as be a true power when the territory became a state.

"Maybe you didn't quite understand me, Marguerite—"

"I understood you. I'm not interested."

"Not... interested?" he sputtered.

"Correct. I'm only interested in the business end of

things. I've spent many a night on my back. I have no intention of doing so again. Burke understood that, and he's given me a way to provide for myself. The only sleeping I'll do will be with my pillow, I assure you."

Kessler held his temper. "If you change your mind..."

The green eyes sparkled. "You never know." She pursed her lips. "But I doubt it."

He stood in dismissal. "Thank you for coming by."

She offered him her hand. "The pleasure was all mine, Mr. Kessler." She turned and sashayed across the room and through the door.

Marguerite paused at the top of the stairs. Her heart pounded violently in her chest. She had heard Kessler was a tough man. She congratulated herself on maintaining her calm façade, when the entire time she'd been shaking like a delicate leaf on a blustery day.

She passed Chin Lee on her way down and nodded. "I'll show myself out," she told him. She reached the bottom of the wide staircase and readjusted her hat before opening the heavy door.

As she stepped out onto the porch, she saw two men coming up the path.

"Good afternoon, Sheriff," she called.

He tipped his hat. "Hello, Marguerite." He motioned to his companion. "This here's Albert Le Fall, new in town as of today. He aims to start up a newspaper this fall."

She turned her attention to the man Jack introduced. He had a kind face, a man whose eyes didn't run up and down in a quick appraisal of her generous assets. He was tall, with dark, bushy brows and hair that had long ago turned white. She placed him in his late fifties. Still, he had one of the most interesting faces she'd ever seen, and she had seen her fill in her line of work.

Marguerite was surprised at the gentle rush of warmth that filled her. He reminded her of the sweet,

Southern gentlemen back home, the ones full of genteel respect for all women. It had been many years since she'd encountered a man with that nature.

"It's so pleasant to meet you, sir." She offered him her gloved hand. He took it and raised it to his lips. A thrill rushed through her. "Why, a newspaper's just what we need in Silver Bluff."

"I thank you kindly for saying so, Mrs.—"

"It's Miss Le Beau, Mr. Le Fall. Judging from your name, I'd say we are from the same neck of the woods."

"Born and bred in New Orleans. Apprenticed with a printer near Jackson Square at an early age. Struck out on my own and traveled the whole state before I settled in Monroe. I print newspapers, flyers, handbills, programs. You name it, I've printed it."

"I'm from Louisiana myself, Mr. Le Fall."

She glanced to Jack. His face remained blank, but she could see the impact of her news in his eyes. She wondered if it would make a difference between them.

"You didn't know that, Jack." She leaned over and said, "Our sheriff isn't too fond of Southerners, Mr. Le Fall. Seems he fought against them in the War Between the States. I don't think he's forgiven us yet." She winked conspiratorially. "I lost my accent long ago. Seemed to do better without one."

She opened her pastel parasol. "Good meeting you, Mr. Le Fall."

Marguerite took her leave, but as she walked down the pathway, she heard Jack say, "Damned women. Never know what they're about."

CHAPTER 7

"Papa, I have no interest going to a *Methodist* church."

"Lower your chin a notch, Daughter, and try to be a little more humble. It's the Lord's Day—not yours."

Nora flushed at her father's words. He sounded as bad as the sisters from the convent back home. She placed both hands on her waist, fists balled tightly, tension flowing through her body. Actually, she had no plans to attend any church. Having been raised as a Catholic from the cradle, she had gradually drifted away from mass as she'd grown older. The Latin seemed remote and cold, signifying nothing personal to her.

She did remember with fondness attending church with Ben and Jess a few times on a special occasion. She always begged to go if a revival was being held. The cadence of the traveling preacher's speech and the rich spirituals sung with fervor caused her to be spellbound.

She shocked Sister Ruth Helen and Sister Margaret Mary when she'd taught the other children *In Dat Great Gettin' Up Mornin'*. Though the sisters preached tolerance and understanding, they explained to Nora that most Southerners wouldn't think highly of children who sang so freely of slaves escaping from their masters.

Nora had not defied them at school after that. She couldn't bear to see the hurt look on Sister Margaret Mary's face. She did continue to sing spirituals, albeit quietly, on her way home from school. She even sang them to Robby when she rocked him to sleep when he was a baby.

She'd raised her son with stories from the Bible, mostly those Ben had shared with her when she'd climbed upon his knee. She remembered how vividly he brought them to life. It delighted her that all these years later, Robby would clamor for the same tales of Daniel in the lion's den or David slaying the mighty giant, Goliath.

Nora thought it important to give Robby these tales to hold on to. Many lessons could be learned from the Bible, even if she no longer went to mass. She also taught Robby to live by the Golden Rule. She wanted to pass along the right kind of morals to her only son, not a litany of rote prayers that held little meaning, spiritual or otherwise.

The Golden Rule became her mantra over the years. Nora saw too much unkindness and injustice in this world. If more people chose to live by such simple words of truth, no war between North and South would have occurred.

She watched Papa fasten his tie. As usual, it was a lopsided mess. She crossed the room.

"Allow me." She undid the knot and began again, soon smoothing it flat against his crisp white shirt.

"My thanks," he murmured with a warm smile. "We should discuss the issue at hand." His stern look kept her from speaking. She docilely sank onto the nearby bed.

"I am a man who believes in good, Nora. You know that. I may not have always worshiped the Lord in one of His designated houses, but I have tried to respect Him and live my life according to His lessons."

He sat beside her and took her hand. "We have moved to a small town, Daughter. It will grow quickly, even more quickly than we could imagine, but I think we'll find its small-town mentality will stay for many years.

"We will go to church each Sunday, as a family, and continue to practice our good deeds during the week. If we didn't go to church, it would be a strike against us." His gaze bored into her. "That could affect the sale of newspapers if we're judged the wrong way."

Squeezing her hand, he added, "It'll be good for Robby. Children need the regularity in their lives that church brings. Although," and his eyes perked up with mischief, "he'll not get nearly as much thinking done, seeing as how the Methodists refuse to conduct their services in Latin. Always said that Latin droning on and on in the background was conducive to thinking."

"Oh, Papa." Nora hugged him tightly, knowing she had the best father in the world.

The door swung open. Robby bounded in, his dark slacks and slicked-back hair a sure sign of Jess' handiwork.

"Mama, these britches are getting short."

"Again?" She looked at the pants Jess had made only a month before they'd left for Colorado Territory. They fell a good inch too short. The hole in one knee didn't help. "I declare you to be the champion grower for boys born in 1864." She gave him a swift kiss and stood.

"Ready?" she asked her father.

"You know what going to church means, Nora? I'll get to hear you sing on a regular basis."

She smiled. She loved to sing. Her father told her she sang her words before she ever spoke them. Not much singing had gone on for many years. She'd all but given it up while she worked alongside Jess in the house. Paul complained that the pitch of her voice gave him a headache.

On her way home from the paper, if no one else was in sight, she'd sing a light, happy tune. Papa told her she always hummed when she wrote. He'd caught her at it several times, but Nora never realized it until after the fact. It might be fun to sing again.

She linked one arm through her father's, and the other through her son's, and went out to meet Ben and Jess.

"We're running real late, Mister Albert. Jess says we better get a move on it."

Jess poked Ben in the ribs. "I ain't saying we're late. We're pressed for time." Her lips fastened in a prim line.

"We do need to hurry, Ben. I'm sorry if my reluctance has caused us to be tardy."

It took them less than five minutes to leave the hotel and make their way to the new Methodist church. The outside was a bright white, testifying to its recent raising. Mr. Simmons informed her it opened for services four weeks ago.

Ben held the door and they all filed in quietly to the strains of *Come, Thou Almighty King*. The building had a high ceiling and several rows of pews, most of them filled toward the front of the church. Nora pointed to her right and slid in the last row so as not to disturb anyone. A Chinese couple with a boy about Robby's age were the pew's only occupants. She smiled at them and picked up a hymnal. She glanced to see what page to turn to and opened it, holding it low so Robby could follow along her.

"It smells new, Mama."

Nora nodded. Before her eyes returned to the page, she saw Sheriff Duncan enter from a side door near the front. He was dressed in his usual black pants and long-sleeved white shirt, partly hidden by a black vest. He slipped off his hat and moved his eyes across the crowd. The white patch of hair that ran along his right temple stood out. She wondered what it would be like to be a recipient of one of his smiles.

Startled, her eyes grew wide at the thought. She dropped them back to the hymnal and located the verse before she joined in the last strains.

❧❧

JACK SKIMMED THE CHURCH'S INHABITANTS. He wasn't a religious man but knew appearances were important. He attended services every now and then. Just enough to please the local populace. He'd enjoyed two conversations with Reverend Seabury and appreciated the fact that the man kept his sermons short and to the point. He had rarely known any man of the cloth to be brief, but John Seabury proved to be an interesting exception.

It didn't hurt, either, that Mrs. Seabury was a terrific cook. A man on his own enjoyed a home-cooked meal now and then, and the minister's wife had promised him one after church today. The least he could do was let his face be seen at morning services. He caught Mrs. Seabury's eyes and nodded.

His eyes flicked from pew to pew until they rested on the last one. In previous weeks, there had been a gap in the seating. The good people of Silver Bluff all clustered near the front of the church. Then a space of several empty rows occurred before the final pew. It remained open every service, except for Chin Lee and his family sitting in the far corner. No one in the town was ready to sit with Chinese just yet.

It surprised him that Chin came to church. He didn't think of the Chinese as being Christian. Jack wasn't sure whom they worshipped, but he was certain it wasn't a Jewish carpenter from Galilee.

Today, Chin's accustomed pew was full. He would've expected Ben and Jess to be there. They both seemed good people to him and even in the newly emancipated society, they would quietly assume their place would be at the back of any public building.

What he didn't expect to see was Nora Cantrelle, her arm around her son, like she belonged there. His eyes moved on and then came back to rest on her. She wore a straw bonnet trimmed in pale yellow ribbons. Her dress was of the same shade as the ribbons, perhaps a bit faded but very feminine, all the same.

The hymn drew to a close. He watched her replace the book and then turn to Chin Lee and hold out her gloved hand, right as rain. Chin took it, a funny look on his face as she pumped away.

Then she leaned over and did the same to Mrs. Lee. He couldn't hear her whispers from where he stood but she indicated Robby and then pointed at the Lee boy, all the while a smile on her face. Robby Cantrelle got up and moved next to little Tien Lee, happy as a jaybird.

Jack took a seat. He tried hard to listen to Reverend Seabury's interpretation of the Sermon on the Mount, but he couldn't get that Southern flower off his mind.

She was pretty. He'd give her that. Masses of honey-blonde hair piled up, with a few tendrils escaping from under her hat. Green eyes like a cat. Creamy skin. Some nice curves, although she was a little on the thin side, but then, who wasn't after the war?

Still, she was easy on the eye.

Jack struggled in his mind. He couldn't let her get to him. Not her emerald eyes ringed with long, dark lashes or her mouth that pouted as sweet as a blooming rose. He'd sworn off women long ago. Other than the occasional poke upstairs in the saloon, he had no reason to look at this woman.

Or think about her so much.

The offertory hymn was *For the Beauty of the Earth*. He had always liked music. He couldn't read it. He couldn't sing a lick. But he liked to feel it wash over him. Something about music calmed him. It drew him to this church the past two weeks.

Then he heard it. A voice above the rest. It had a purity to it, a freshness, like dew on the morning grass before anyone's trodden on it.

FOR THE WONDER OF EACH HOUR
    Of the day and of the night,
    Hill and vale and tree and flower,
    Sun and moon and stars of light:
    Lord of all, to Thee we raise
    This our hymn of grateful praise.

HE TURNED TO LOCATE THE SWEET SOPRANO THAT lilted above the mostly off-key crowd. He realized he wasn't the only one searching for the source. Every eye of the congregation came to rest on Nora Cantrelle. She was oblivious to the stares, lost in the words of praise.

The song ended. Jack joined everyone in turning quickly back to the front. It was as if the magic spell that hung in the air would break if the songstress became aware of the attention focused on her.

Jack couldn't wait for the closing song. He wasn't disappointed when the strains of *Come, Ye Thankful People* began. Mrs. Seabury had pounded this song out at two previous Sunday services. He was beginning to remember the words without having to look at his hymnal.

Once again, Nora Cantrelle's voice transported him to another place. She brought a sweetness to the melody that didn't exist before. Jack stared at her. The Southern woman had her arm around Jess, whose own arm encircled her employer's waist as they sang joyfully to the Lord.

It startled him. They looked like mother and daughter. He was mystified.

In that moment, he decided he needed to know what made Nora Cantrelle tick, even as he fought against this compulsion.

He was reluctant even to talk to a woman nowadays. Where was this driving force coming from?

"Just a few announcements, my good brethren." Seabury's English accent cut through Jack's thoughts. He turned to the minister.

"The Quilting Club would like to have it known they'll be meeting at my house this Tuesday from nine until noon. Mrs. Seabury has promised to make scones again."

A buzz swept through the church. He saw several women nod their approval and he hid a smile.

"We also are ready to instigate our monthly potluck suppers next month. These are to be held the third Saturday of each month. It will give us a nice chance to welcome those moving into Silver Bluff, as well as partake in fellowship with those already residing here."

The preacher beamed a smile to the back of his church. "I would especially like to thank our newest residents for their attendance today. I've quite forgotten your names already. Not good for a minister, but that's why I married Mrs. Seabury." He grinned sheepishly. "That—and her scones."

Mrs. Seabury's voice carried to the rafters. "That's Mr. Le Fall. His daughter, Mrs. Cantrelle, and her boy, Robby," she pointed out. "Next to them are Ben and Jess but I don't have a last name on you yet, dearies. We'll chat afterwards." She waved her fingers at them.

"Then I say God bless you all until we meet again," Reverend Seabury pronounced in his rich tones.

The congregation began filing toward the back of the church. Nora noticed the favorable nods sent her way and melted with the nice welcome she experienced.

She turned to speak to the Lees again, but they had already left the pew. She saw them slip out of the church, only the little boy raising a hand in farewell. They seemed rather shy. Maybe she could have Mrs. Lee over for a good chat while the boys played. She was so happy to see at least one child Robby's age. Papa had assured her more would follow as the town grew.

They stepped out into the strong light of the July day. Nora loved the fresh scent in the air. It contained none of the mugginess of Louisiana, which threatened to drag a person down into a bog.

"Mrs. Cantrelle?"

She turned and slipped her hand into Reverend Seabury's. He was a good two inches shorter than she. At his side, Mrs. Seabury was the same height as her husband, but she probably outweighed him by fifty pounds.

"A pleasure to have you in our fine town, Mrs. Cantrelle, you and your father." He shook Papa's hand.

"Delightful sermon, Reverend," Albert replied. "And an even more delightful accent."

Seabury cleared his throat. "Mrs. Seabury and I are English born and bred. Anne is a descendant of Mr. John Wesley, the founder of Methodism." He beamed at his wife. "Thanks to your Great Awakening, the Methodist Church has flourished here in America. I am only too happy to be spreading the love of Christ to Colorado Territory."

"We are happy to make your acquaintance, Reverend, and will worship with you and yours on a regular basis." Papa patted the preacher on his shoulder.

"Mrs. Cantrelle, will you join our Quilting Club?"

Nora gritted her teeth but managed a sweet smile. "I would love to come and quilt with you, Mrs. Seabury."

Jess laughed and shook her head. "Miz Seabury, you

might want to think twice before you go asking Miss Nora to come to your house and quilt."

Nora blushed as Mrs. Seabury turned her puzzled expression upon Jess. Jess smiled politely. "Jessymyn Weaver, ma'am, and this here's my better half, Ben."

Mrs. Seabury greeted them both. "Why wouldn't I welcome Mrs. Cantrelle, Mrs. Weaver?"

Jess' dark eyes shone with mischief. "I'll have to say Miss Nora's a true beginner. Has been for nigh on twenty years now." She looked at her mistress. "Don't worry none, Miss Nora. I bet you'll get off to a real fine start on quilting. This time."

Mrs. Seabury said kindly, "Even beginners are welcome, my dear. And you, too, Mrs. Weaver."

"Why, thank you, ma'am. I do believe I'll come." Jess put her arm through Ben's and moved away. Even though her back was to them, Nora could see the quick, bobbing movements indicating Jess was trying to keep in her laughter.

She turned to Mrs. Seabury. "We would be delighted to come quilt with you." She pushed her reluctance deep within her. Surely, it wouldn't be as bad as in the past.

CHAPTER 8

Nora tied the grosgrain bow under her chin, her fingers shaking. The bow came out lopsided. She sighed and untied the mess. It was her third attempt at trying to look presentable for the ladies who would be at Mrs. Seabury's this morning.

Frustrated, she pulled the bonnet from her head and placed it on the pine bureau. She adjusted one of her pins which had come loose, trying to calm the swirling butterflies in her stomach.

"It's not Munro," she whispered to the image reflected in the mirror.

Nora had gone a-quilting before. The end results were disastrous. She still remembered Betty Munro's tomfoolery.

"Oh, Nora, do be a dear and come work on the Dresden Plate," Betty cooed in a syrupy tone.

Nora stood frozen to the spot. She had no idea what a Dresden Plate was. She'd barely mastered the one stitch Jess had drilled her on for the last ten years. She so wanted to make a good impression among the ladies present today.

Paul's mother was a member of this circle and an expert quilter. Nora knew the woman would expect no less from her son's wife. Not that they were married yet, but she expected Paul would propose soon. Her sixteenth birthday was right around the corner. Even if Papa thought her too young to marry, she could get engaged, couldn't she?

All eyes focused on her as she walked unsteadily around the frame. A few muffled giggles made her mouth go dry. What on earth was a Dresden Plate?

"Over here, Nora."

Thank goodness for Penelope Lowman. They weren't exactly friends, but Nora knew Penelope had it in for Betty ever since Betty stole her beau the year before. Betty, being Betty, had tossed the boy aside after a month, but Penelope had never forgotten—nor forgiven the incident.

She walked with a little more confidence toward Penelope, a shaky smile on her face.

"There's no Dresden Plate, Nora. Betty's just teasing you." *Penelope tossed a glance at her rival.* "This here's a Log Cabin, honey," *she said.* "You won't find any plates on it."

She wanted to wring Betty Munro's neck. The girl had taken a sudden liking to Paul at the Sweetheart Dance six weeks ago, batting her thick lashes and begging him to retrieve punch for her, when she knew good and well he'd come with Nora. To top it off, Betty was a terrific quilter who did everything well.

She smiled sweetly at Betty, who'd slipped over to sit next to Mrs. Cantrelle. The two women were engaged in conversation, but Betty threw Nora a triumphant look.

Nora was miserable.

"You ready yet?"

Jess' voice startled her from her reverie, placing Nora's bonnet on her head.

"I'll fix you up nice, Miss Nora." *She hummed as she adjusted it to her satisfaction.* "You're gonna be the prettiest girl there."

"What does that matter, Jess? I can't quilt. I'm not going to fit in."

Jess shook her head. "Don't go talking that way, baby girl. We all gonna like Silver Bluff and they gonna like us. Don't worry too much, Miss Nora. You know a little bit about sewing. Just sit by me. I'll get you through this."

Jess picked up her sewing bag, the material faded with age and use. They locked the room and made their way down the long, carpeted hallway to the staircase that led to the hotel's lobby. They stepped out into the bright morning sunshine. A slight breeze caressed her face. Immediately, she felt better.

"If you wind up the creek without your paddle, honey, then I'll push you to the kitchen. You are the queen when it comes to cooking. When we get us a house built, we'll have to invite all of Silver Bluff over to sample your cherry tarts. They are the best I've ever had, and Jess Weaver doesn't lie about things like that."

Nora beamed at the compliment. "You are a sweetheart, and you are the one who taught me to cook. I may shine at desserts, but you do everything well, Jess."

They approached the Seaburys' house, a white clapboard with dark brown trim. A white picket fence surrounded the small parcel of land. An abundance of flowers bloomed around the porch and walkway.

"Mr. Albert is counting on us to make a fine impression today on these ladies. We're gonna talk up this newspaper now, hear?"

She pursed her lips to hide a smile. Jess had always been proud to be part of a newspaper family. Her reverence for the written word first interested Nora in reading, then writing. Her father had taught the three of them—Nora, Jess, and Ben—to read and write after his wife's death.

That was when he had given both Weavers their freedom, well before the war began. Nora grew up with the two former slaves as members of her extended family. Only later did she understand her father's remarkable actions. These thoughts gave her a warm feeling, which helped calm her jittery nerves.

"I see that smile, Miss Nora."

She arched her brows. What smile?"

They were almost at the open door. "Remember to hide your knots and rock the needle, honey. And stick with the ladderback stitch."

Nora smothered a laugh. That was the only stitch she knew. "Yes, ma'am."

"Mrs. Cantrelle, Mrs. Weaver! How are you?"

Mrs. Seabury appeared at the door and ushered them in from the morning light.

"I am so happy you could come." She put her arm through each of theirs and led them around the large frame standing in the center of the room. "You must meet Mrs. Malone. Her husband is our local doctor. They've come to us from Kansas."

At the mention of her name, a woman in her late forties turned. She was small and trim, with a thick bun of hair turned white gathered at the nape of her neck.

"Iris Malone. So nice to meet you both." She pressed each of their hands warmly. Her friendly greeting touched Nora as so different from the ladies of Monroe. She stole a quick glance at Jess. Their eyes met and they smiled their approval. Even though they were weeks away from putting out their first paper, Nora knew they'd made the right decision in coming to Colorado Territory.

"And have you met Mrs. Simmons?"

The storekeeper's wife had been caught off-guard, plopping a warm scone into her mouth. She turned, eyes wide, unable to say anything.

Nora offered the plump woman her hand and pumped it enthusiastically, glad she wouldn't be able to answer. "Oh, yes. I met Mrs. Simmons at the general store the day I arrived," she said sweetly. "Mr. Simmons was most friendly and helpful."

She was unhappy at the look that Mrs. Simmons gave Jess. She had worried about Jess being accepted as an equal in Silver Bluff. She hoped more people would respond as Mrs. Malone had. Nora would take one of Jess over a dozen of Mrs. Simmons.

As Mrs. Simmons tried to choke down the scone, a shadow crossed the doorway.

"Mrs. Nelson, do come in." Mrs. Seabury went to greet the newest guest, and motioned Nora and Jess over.

"Mrs. Nelson's husband designed and built our church here in Silver Bluff."

"He'll be putting up a newspaper office before long," chimed in Mrs. Nelson. She held out her hand. "Glad to meet you, Mrs. Cantrelle. Mr. Nelson says you have quite a good head on your shoulders. He's very impressed at the layout you sketched for him." She smiled mischievously, eyes twinkling behind gold frames. "You've challenged him, dear. He's been working hard on the final plans to show your papa today."

"I've heard nothing but compliments about him, ma'am," Nora replied. "And the church is lovely." She motioned to her right. "Have you met my friend, Jessymyn Weaver?"

She introduced the two women. Jess asked, "Did your husband build the quilt frame we're dancing around? It's mighty fine workmanship, that frame."

Mrs. Nelson glowed. "He did indeed. Built it right here in this room. If the Seaburys ever want it moved, they'll have to take down the walls!"

All the women laughed. Mrs. Seabury explained, "The reverend knows quilting brings women of a community together. We never had little ones so this is the ideal place to gather. I'm able to leave the quilting frame up all the time. And when we've no quilt, the frame stands easily against the far wall there. That leaves us plenty of room for meetings and receptions."

She smiled at Nora and Jess. "We are so glad to have you here today, ladies. Now, we'll have six hands to work on this quilt. We'll be finished in no time." Mrs. Seabury sighed. "I guess we should get started."

"I'll get the scones," called out Mrs. Malone quickly.

"I'll pour the lemonade," answered Mrs. Nelson.

Relief flooded Nora when she realized getting started meant eating and not quilting. She was far better at nibbling and conversing. As far as she was concerned, the quilting could wait while she got to know her neighbors.

Mrs. Malone shared with them, "One simply can't quilt on an empty stomach. We'll be much more productive if we eat some of Mrs. Seabury's scones before we start."

She soon realized it was the chitchat as much as the scones that brought the women together. The talk quickly turned to events in the town, the rapid growth of Colorado Territory, and what every gathering of women means—talk of their children.

Nora did notice Mrs. Simmons avoided speaking directly to either her or Jess. The woman had a cold manner the others easily ignored. Maybe the storeowner's wife wasn't the power she would like to be.

"We got a letter from Sally yesterday," gushed Mrs. Malone. "I have three sons and two daughters scattered all over the country, and I still hear from each of them once a month," she bragged. Pushing her glasses up the bridge of her nose, she added, "Our first effort together was a star pattern for my daughter, Lucy. Her baby's due at the end of September. If I must say so, we did an excellent job."

Mrs. Seabury interrupted. "We've been piecing a red and white Irish Chain for my niece in Pennsylvania since that. This morning I had the reverend set up the frame because we're ready to quilt again." Her smile grew wide at the thought. "Emmy'll be married in the new year. My sister tells us the boy is as good as gold, a hard worker and steady churchgoer."

She paused a moment. "Minnie says it was love at first sight for those two. Says the boy can't take his eyes from Emmy and she's the same way. They already have such a deep, abiding love. Just the same as the reverend and me." Mrs. Seabury's eyes misted over as she spoke.

Nora's mind flashed on Paul and the dismal experience their marriage had been. She drifted in and out of the conversation for a few minutes, her thoughts bouncing between the past and the future that lay before her.

"... so my Tamara is often too busy even to write on a regular basis," Mrs. Simmons said stiffly. "Of course, she is a busy hostess for her husband, and a wonderful mother."

An awkward moment of silence followed her remarks before Mrs. Seabury announced, "Well, ladies, I say we better get started if we're going to make any headway on this wedding quilt."

The women all rose quickly, leaving their plates and half-empty glasses of lemonade on the side table. With an easy companionship, they all settled into their accustomed places. Mrs. Seabury made a spot for Jess, who reached into her bag for her favorite quilting needle, anticipation evident in her eyes.

"I think I'll just clear up these dishes if you don't mind, Mrs. Seabury." Nora began picking up plates to return to the kitchen nearby.

"You don't have to do that, Mrs. Cantrelle," Mrs. Malone protested.

"Honestly, ma'am, I won't be able to lay a stitch unless this mess is cleaned up."

"Nonsense, my dear," declared Mrs. Seabury. "You are my guest. I won't hear of it."

Iris Malone chuckled. "What she won't hear of, Mrs. Cantrelle, is anyone in her kitchen. Mrs. Seabury is quite fussy about such matters." Her eyes twinkled as she glanced mischievously at their hostess. "Must be something about the English."

Anne Seabury shook her head. "You've got me there, Iris. I am quite particular." She gestured to Nora. "Come take a seat, dear. We've got lots of work to do."

Nora reluctantly pulled up a chair next to the minister's wife. She took her time getting out her quilting needle.

Mrs. Seabury leaned over and whispered, "I know you are a novice, Mrs. Cantrelle. Don't worry. You are among friends."

She shook her head. "I've so enjoyed the conversation today, ma'am. I just wish I could enjoy this part. Sewing is not my forte, I'm afraid."

She cautiously threaded her needle. That had always been a tricky part. She looked up to see if anyone noticed the trouble she had with this simple task. Mrs. Simmons locked eyes with her and shook her head in disapproval before she returned to her work, her frown creasing her wide brow.

Nora glanced around the group. She didn't know what moved faster—their fingers or their tongues as they gossiped away. No one else paid a bit of attention to her. She began to relax and almost by magic, the needle seemed to thread itself.

"I do declare you can always find an occasion deserving a new quilt," said Mrs. Malone. "I've lived by the rule that it's never too soon to start one."

"Jess sold many of the quilts she made over the years during the war," Nora offered as she began a few tentative stitches.

"Did you now?" said Mrs. Simmons coolly. Nora didn't like the woman's tone.

"We would have starved if not for Jess," she told them. "She's the best quilter I've ever seen."

"What are your favorite patterns, Mrs. Weaver?"

asked Mrs. Simmons. "I find I'm partial to the Gentleman's Fan. The curves are always such a challenge."

Jess nodded. "A good choice, ma'am. I like Milady's Fan a touch better, though, or maybe Nine Patch or Beggar's Block." Her fingers worked with steady rhythm as she spoke. All the women's eyes were drawn to her stitches.

"Have you ever tried Drunkard's Path, Mrs. Simmons?" Jess asked.

Nora knew the tone sounded innocent, but she was well aware of how complex the patterns Jess mentioned were. She had worried about the racial problems Jess might experience today. Nora now realized that through a demonstration of her sewing talents, Jess had upped the ante. She could sew circles around Mrs. Simmons. Color made no difference. It was talent that counted.

"Why, I do believe you get a good ten stitches to the inch, Mrs. Weaver," Mrs. Seabury exclaimed in fascination as she watched Jess work.

"Ten some days." Jess shrugged. "I try for twelve."

"That's impossible!" exclaimed Mrs. Simmons, her face going beet red.

"Oh, no, dear, I've seen it done before," assured Mrs. Malone. "But it's a master quilter that does it—and I think we are in the presence of one."

An appreciable silence followed her words as the others admired Jess' work.

Mrs. Simmons broke the spell. Her scowl darkened her full face. "I suppose we should get back to work."

The quilters pulled their eyes away from Jess' stitches and went back to their needles and talk.

Nora started and stopped several times over the next few minutes, concentrating carefully with each up and down motion of her needle. She found it hard to believe women did this for relaxation. She stopped when her fingers began to cramp and watched the circle of women, happily chatting as their fingers moved, almost unaware of their motions.

She looked at her own work. She'd tried to catch more than one stitch, as Jess had taught her, but she'd had little success. The thread before her was unevenly spaced. Her frustration at her lack of skill grew with each stitch.

Nora sensed Mrs. Simmons watching her as the hour passed. She refused to give the woman the satisfaction of intimidating her into stopping.

"Is that a ladderback stitch you have going, Mrs. Cantrelle? I wasn't quite sure."

She gritted her teeth at Jane Simmons' remark. "Yes, ma'am," she replied evenly, not taking the bait.

It was hard pushing the needle through the thick flour sacks the women had used as backing. The material was first used during the war when better quality cloth was scarce. Nora wondered why on earth they still used them. It made a tedious task even more difficult. Her neck hurt from bending over, as well as her back. She longed to be in the kitchen or scribbling a story on a tablet or even ironing. Anything was more exciting than quilting.

"Ouch!"

Nora jumped. The needle that pierced her skin pulled away. A spurt of blood shot across the white surface of the quilt.

"Oh!" She yanked her handkerchief from her pocket and tried to blot the stain, angry that her mind had wandered and caused such a mishap.

"You've ruined it!" cried Mrs. Simmons. She jumped up and tore Nora away from the quilt. "Who do you think you're fooling, Mrs. Cantrelle?" She looked down at Nora's messy work, fast being eaten away by the spreading stain.

"You aren't a quilter at all. You don't even sew well. Anyone watching you thread your needle would see

83

that, quicker than eggs frying in hot grease. You're clumsy and foolish and have remarkably bad—"

"Good morning, ladies."

A deep, drawling voice pulled everyone's attention away from Nora to the shadow hovering in the door.

"An open door is an invitation to one of your scones, Mrs. Seabury. If you object, I'll just have to confiscate them all as evidence."

Nora's face flamed with humiliation. Not only had she made a fool of herself in front of the few women in Silver Bluff, but the sheriff was also party to her embarrassment. Things couldn't get much worse.

"Come in, Sheriff. I do believe I heard the scones call out your name a while ago. I'm surprised it took you so long to hear them." Mrs. Seabury fluttered around, quickly serving up a plate.

Jack hesitated for a moment. Entering a room full of women was worse than being thrown into the lion's den with Daniel. For all their sweet smiles, their claws could be much sharper. He avoided this group as much as possible. Still, he remembered Mrs. Seabury would be serving scones.

A sliver of doubt tugged at him. It wasn't just the thought of fresh-baked scones that brought him here. Against his better judgment he'd come, curious to see if Nora Cantrelle would be here. He hadn't wanted to seek her out, but after what he'd just heard, he felt obligated to rescue her all the same.

He stepped across the threshold and accepted the plate Mrs. Seabury offered him. "I'm afraid I'll have to take these to go, ma'am. I've got to get back." He couldn't think of a reason why. He hoped no one would be curious enough to ask as he slid the two scones off the plate.

Jack met Nora's eyes. "If Mrs. Cantrelle wouldn't mind accompanying me, I can escort her over to Harve's office. Your papa and Harve were looking over some plans and could sure use your input on a few things. I've never seen two grown men at such a loss."

Jess had already wrapped a handkerchief around Nora's finger as he spoke. "Go ahead, Miss Nora. This here spot'll come out in a flash. I knows just what to do." Jess glared at Mrs. Simmons, daring her to challenge her words.

"Yes, of course, Mrs. Cantrelle. You mustn't keep the men waiting," added Mrs. Nelson. "I told you how much Mr. Nelson respects your ideas. He was having a few problems about some corner nook you'd requested."

"If you're sure..."

He watched her look from face to face. Thank goodness it was only the Simmons woman who wore a hateful expression. If Nora Cantrelle decided to stay, she'd soon learn that people would rather shake a stick at Seymour's wife than give her the time of day.

"Shall we?"

Jack offered her his arm. It was the polite thing to do. Nora slid her hand through the crook of his elbow.

He was surprised at the sudden rush of heat at the contact. A light, sweet, jasmine scent floated from her and went straight to his head.

He forced one foot forward. Thankfully, the other one followed. They stepped out into the warm summer day and down the path. Jack opened the gate and closed it behind them. Once more, he offered her his arm.

Glancing down at her bandaged finger, he said, "Looks like you were wounded in action, Mrs. Cantrelle."

CHAPTER 9

S he held up her wrapped finger for his inspection. A few drops of blood spotted the white linen handkerchief. She studied it a moment, a frown creasing her brow. Then she broke into a deep, hearty laugh.

This woman kept surprising him.

"I have tried many times to get out of quilting. Or sewing. Or needlework." She sighed. "The thought of stabbing myself with my needle and bleeding over a strange quilt hadn't occurred to me before." She smiled mischievously. "I suppose I won't be asked back again. Most of them were so nice, though."

Jack snorted. "I suppose you would be omitting Mrs. Simmons from that group?"

Nora looked up innocently. "Mrs. Simmons? Now, which one was she?" she mused.

It was his turn to laugh. "I do believe she's the one giving you the hard time, Mrs. Cantrelle. I'm sure you remember her."

She laughed again, a rich sound that made his fingers tingle. He had a sudden longing to stroke the long, white throat that protected such a musical rumble. The strange thing was, this random thought didn't even sur-

86

prise him. He realized instinctively he'd wanted to touch her from the minute they'd first clashed in front of the general store.

That was why he'd been drawn to the Seaburys' place. It wasn't the promise of fresh, hot scones that led him this way. No, it was the hope of seeing Nora Cantrelle. He'd thought he was through with women. With feelings. Felicity had seen to that. She'd proclaimed her eternal love before the war, only to go behind his back and marry his older brother.

That one act hardened him against all women. He swore he'd never become involved with one again. Sure, he was a man, and occasionally he moseyed over to the saloon and visited a whore there. His physical needs were met in a very pleasant and thorough way, with none of the commitment that most females demanded before they gave their favors.

Lately, it hadn't been enough. He'd spent the years since the war ended wandering. Searching. Keeping to himself. As his town grew about him and he saw other men with homes and families, it dawned on him with sudden clarity that he wanted what most men want—a woman to come home to every night and share what went on during his day. Kids to crawl into his lap after a home-cooked meal.

And a woman to hold in the still of the night. A time when secrets were whispered with tender affection and love was made, sweet and slow. As a small child, he would awaken in the loft he shared with his brothers, sometimes in the dead of night, only to hear the quiet, loving laughter of his parents below. It gave him a warm feeling, knowing how they loved one another. He wanted that with his own wife.

Felicity had ruined that dream. Part of him—and his dreams for the future—died with the news that she'd married Joseph.

Jack wasn't sure Nora Cantrelle was the woman he'd been longing for, but he couldn't deny the feelings this Southerner brought to the surface. He hadn't even put a name to what ailed him as he'd shut himself off from human emotion for so long. He wasn't sure if he was ready to jump in again just yet.

He took her arm once more and started a slow stroll. "I'll admit that it sounded like you needed rescuing, Mrs. Cantrelle. I heard Mrs. Simmons dressing you down."

Jack felt her stiffen. "I wouldn't worry about her too much, ma'am. She's mostly tolerated around here. Seymour Simmons is universally liked. Go figure how such a kind man got himself hitched to a shrew."

He added, "The only lady in town who is her friend is our local banker's wife." Jack shook his head. "Now, that woman is one to watch out for." He turned to Nora and stopped a moment. "Don't ever try to match wits nor words with Millicent Witherspoon. She's like a viper, that one. Best give her a wide berth."

"What's she done that's so terrible, Sheriff?"

Jack hesitated, seeing the inquisitive light dance in her eyes. "No use in dredging up old gossip, ma'am. Just suffice it to say you'd make better use of your time spending it with Mrs. Seabury or Mrs. Nelson."

"I wonder why Mrs. Witherspoon wasn't at the quilting circle today. Seems like that would be a missed opportunity on her part, with a new woman come to town to inspect."

"She's got a dilly of a head cold. Heard about it from Mortimer. He told me she awakened with it yesterday and was miserable. Still must be troubling her today."

Nora was thoughtful. "Since you rescued me from Mrs. Simmons, I suppose I don't need to stop by and see Mr. Nelson and my father, do I?"

"I can walk you over anyway. It's on my way. Harve

Nelson told me just the other day how helpful you've been in designing the plans."

"My father and I ran a newspaper back in Louisiana. It's all I know. I grew up with ink smudges on my fingers and a pencil behind my ear, ready to jot down any story idea that came along. I'm more at home with the noise of a running press than I am with a needle in my hand."

He smiled. "Your mama let you run wild?"

At the mention of her mother, her mouth tightened. The earlier frown returned.

"My mother passed away when I was six, Sheriff. I don't remember much about her."

"I'm sorry to hear that, ma'am." He paused a moment and then took a new route, trying to prolong their stroll. "You have plans for your new home?"

She visibly relaxed and began happily chatting about the house Nelson would soon begin to build for them. Jack listened to her quietly, nodding here and there, making a suggestion or two along the way. He was pleased that she responded well to his ideas and wasn't the type of woman to pass a good idea by simply because it wasn't her own.

He became aware that they'd stopped walking and had been standing together in the street for a while, amused that he couldn't begin to guess how long.

They were interrupted by distant shouts. Jack looked up to see two boys running in the distance.

"I see your boy has made a friend," he observed.

Nora shaded her eyes and spotted the boys. "Yes. Tien Lee showed up yesterday morning at the hotel. I don't know how long he'd been sitting outside our door before I opened it. He wanted to play with Robby. They had a wonderful time."

She smiled. "I saw them eyeing each other at church so it didn't surprise me. I'm so glad Robby has someone his age to pal around with."

Surprisingly, she didn't seem upset about the fact that Tien Lee was Chinese. He wondered if she was aware of the town's prejudice against the few Chinese that lived in Silver Bluff. It might cause her and her son trouble down the road.

"Tien Lee's papa works up at Mr. Kessler's place. Name's Chin Lee. He's a good man. His wife, Sung Moon, cooks and cleans."

Nora brightened. "Oh, I'd love to learn to cook some Chinese dishes. Maybe Mrs. Lee will teach me. I could show her how to do Creole—"

"Mama! Mama!"

Robby interrupted her. Tien Lee came flying behind him. Both boys bent, hands on their knees, trying to catch their breath after their long run.

"What's all the excitement about, Robby?"

He raised large eyes and blurted out, "Ody got sprayed."

Tien Lee added, "Skunks are no good. Ody went up to smell him. The skunk shook his back side and turned. He sprayed everywhere." The small boy shook his head, looking more like a somber judge as he pronounced the skunk in the wrong.

"Oh, dear," Nora said. "We must see if Mr. Simmons carries any fresh produce. We'll need tomatoes, lots of them, to negate the smell."

Jack spoke up. "I have something that should help. Got it from an old mountain man I helped out a while back." He looked at the boys. "Let's get a rope to tie your pooch with and take him back to my place. I have the feeling he might need a little persuading right about now."

"Oh, Sheriff, you don't have to—"

"No problem at all. Let's go find the dog."

They walked to the general store to get a length of rope. He quickly explained what it was needed for.

Mr. Simmons laughed. "Poor pup. He's learned a tough lesson. Take the rope, Sheriff. No charge."

"Are you sure, Mr. Simmons?" asked Nora. She didn't want him to be in trouble with his wife.

"Of course, Mrs. Cantrelle. You just gotta promise to tell me what happens. I'll get more mileage from this story than most. People will flock in to hear all about the skunked-up dog. They'll buy a thing or two while they're here, I'd suspect." He winked. "I should be paying you to take the rope."

"Thank you, sir. I'll be sure to give you a proper report at the end of our adventure."

As they left, the sheriff asked the boys where Ody was last seen. Once they'd described the place, he named it immediately.

"You boys must be talking about Rocky Steeps, near the old fishing hole." Tien Lee's head bobbed up and down in confirmation.

He turned to Nora. "Mrs. Cantrelle, it might be a bit difficult for you to follow along, seeing as to how it's a narrow ravine clogged with briars. We can drop you off at my place. You can wait for us there. It's on the way."

Nora hesitated, feeling uncomfortable at the thought of being left alone where Jack Duncan lived. It didn't seem proper somehow. She was still aware of how she wanted a fresh start in Silver Bluff. It wouldn't do to jeopardize her reputation the first week here.

He sensed her dilemma. "It's not a problem. We'll need to clean the dog there anyway. The hotel wouldn't look kindly on you if you brought him back there."

She quickly agreed, wanting no more run-ins with the management. She still worried about how she'd secured a room for Jess and Ben under duress. The hotel's owner was scheduled to return soon. She didn't want any added trouble.

They walked to the outskirts of town and then half a mile beyond. Nora spotted a cabin made from pine that faced north. It was a large structure, two-storied, with a wraparound porch that ran the length of its front and beyond. In her mind it called out for a family to occupy such a huge homestead. She wondered if Jack Duncan was ever lonely in such a big house. Or if he was courting someone right now that would help him fill it to the rafters with children. She blushed at such a thought.

"That's my place."

Nora heard the pride in his voice. Sheriff Duncan seemed so remote before today, showing little emotion. Now he was rescuing not only her but also Ody. She wondered at the sudden shift. Was it really a difference in him—or her perception of him?

"Stay here a minute, boys." He escorted her to the front porch, gesturing toward an oak rocker. "You're welcome to sit a spell or if the breeze is too much, feel free to step inside. Your choice, ma'am."

He tipped his hat and ambled down the steps. He turned back to her. "Shouldn't take more than fifteen minutes, I'll wager. He's close by and I've handled this before."

Nora admired his broad shoulders and slim hips as he led the boys down the road. It startled her as she realized that she was looking at Sheriff Duncan the way a woman looked at a man. She collapsed into the rocker, her legs no longer sturdy enough to keep her standing.

When was the last time she'd experienced that little rush? The one where just looking at a man did funny things to your insides? She thought back to the times she'd sat on her own front porch, waiting for Paul to come courting.

She remembered the feeling of anticipation as she sat. The jumping of her heart as he turned the corner and approached their gate. Her palms would go damp and her mouth dry as he unlatched and then pushed through the gate, his eyes twinkling as he spotted her. When he walked toward her, a spring in his step, her heart pounded with sweet joy.

It had been a long time since she'd been that happy girl.

She'd thought she would be overcome with joy at her wedding, all those giddy feelings magnified a thousand-fold. Instead, she helped hold Paul up during the ceremony since he was so weak from the fight at Gettysburg. He'd seemed a stranger that day and had continued to be one that night. The things he'd asked her to do repulsed her. And they'd hurt. Neither of them had been good at any of it, all awkward limbs and sweating bodies. Her dreams of sweet kisses and tender pillow talk quickly flew the coop, replaced by a hollow actuality.

When Paul left after his brief sojourn, Nora was secretly pleased to see him go. She hadn't experienced a moment of happiness with him after that. She'd simply done her duty as a wife when he came home a broken man and nursed him until his death. When he returned, she hadn't asked if he was capable of the physical act of making love. She hadn't wanted to know. Thankfully, he'd never spoken of it either. The only sparkle in her life had been the time spent with Robby.

Until now.

The deep longings suddenly triggered by the town's very attractive sheriff frightened her. She didn't want to be involved with Jack Duncan. Not in that way. Look where it had gotten her with Paul. Her head in the clouds, full of anticipation, until harsh reality set in.

Nora shook her head. No, love and giddiness and happily-ever-after only existed in the minds of schoolgirls too young and inexperienced to know any better. She was a mature widow with a son to raise and a newspaper to get off the ground. Jack Duncan would only be a distraction and a disappointment. She would concentrate on other things.

Besides, Jack Duncan seemed dangerous. He was all male. In a way Paul never had been.

And her growing attraction to him scared the hell out of her.

CHAPTER 10

Nora fled into the house. She felt exposed on the wide porch. These feelings, overwhelming and new, had her face so flushed that she was sure if any passerby saw her, they would know exactly what she had on her mind.

As she leaned against the solid door she'd just slammed, she admitted to herself what her heart had already discovered. She was wildly attracted to Jack Duncan, a man she barely knew. A man who'd been harsh and quick with her. A man about whom she knew nothing at all. Yet she'd give her right arm to have his mouth on hers.

She didn't know what shocked her more—the fact that she wanted to kiss a man, or the fact that Jack Duncan was the particular man she was interested in kissing.

Nora thought back to stumbling across Ben and Jess on more than one occasion when she was a child, spying on them as they spooned in the kitchen or behind the woodpile. They seemed to take great pleasure in it, with all kinds of little noises and smacks.

She had practiced kissing after that. Of course, she didn't want to embarrass herself in front of any little Monroe boys, so she'd rehearsed with her own dolls.

She would lift them tenderly and tell them how much she loved them, stroke their hair and then pucker her lips and press them to her doll. She would think of things such as strawberries dipped in chocolate or fresh peach pie, and the appropriate sighs would follow.

She thought she became adept at the business of kissing, but she wanted to try it out to be sure. Unfortunately, Sister Mary Joseph caught her and Tommy Lee Smith in the cloakroom, thanks to their giggles.

The nun sternly warned of the tortures before them if they insisted on corrupting their bodies with lewd behavior.

After that, Nora couldn't find any more takers willing to experiment and chance going straight to Hell. Grudgingly, she had pursued other interests. She hadn't given kissing much thought until Paul Cantrelle wanted to. That's when she was fourteen.

Paul had been a friend to her for most of her life. At first it was hard to think of him in a romantic way, but gradually things changed. Their kisses had been sweet, short and always closed-mouthed. They had stayed that way for a long time, forbidden kisses in stolen moments when no one was looking. They had given her a thrill. She wasn't sure if it was because they happened on the sly or if the kisses themselves excited her.

It wasn't until they went to their marriage bed that Paul tried any other kind of kiss. These weren't romantic at all but slobbery and messy. Nora had very little response, much less felt any great passion, as their lips and then tongues touched. It started the first of many doubts about her marriage.

Now, she suddenly yearned to kiss a man who was practically a stranger—and not a prim, chaste kiss at that. She wanted him to give her a deep, passionate kiss. One that would stir her soul and make her blood boil.

Nora shuddered and licked her lips nervously. How

could she ever look at Jack Duncan again without betraying her thoughts? At least she had what her father called a good poker face. She'd been hurt more times than she could count by the good ladies of Monroe, her mother-in-law chief among them, but they never knew how they cut her to the quick. Maybe in another life she had been a stage actress in London.

Her eyes adjusted to them dim light in the house. She'd never been one to be without light. Surely the sheriff wouldn't mind if she opened up a few of the shades.

She did so and pale sunshine peeked into the room. Nora found herself in awe. Jack Duncan must earn a hefty salary as Silver Bluff's sheriff. The room was full of some of the best quality furniture she'd ever seen.

She touched the table next to her. It was as smooth as glass, with fine lines in its legs. She even knelt and ran her hand along one, observing the detail carved into it. Nora stood and went around the room from piece to piece, noting the subtle mix of different woods.

Curiosity got the better of her. She wandered into a small kitchen off the main room. A table and four chairs stood at one end. Nora pulled up a chair and sat. She spread her palms wide and stroked the tabletop. The set was a work of beauty. She wondered from how far away the sheriff had it shipped. San Francisco? Back East?

Ben would love to see the sheriff's place. He was always dabbling in wood. She was sure he would pick up some terrific ideas if he were allowed to examine the workmanship of the furniture here.

A sudden noise startled her. It was the front door thrown open. The pungent scent of skunk caused her to crease her nose and grimace.

"Mrs. Cantrelle?" Jack Duncan's voice called to her.

Nora scooted the chair back and quickly replaced it. She walked to the doorway. "I was sitting a spell at your kitchen table, Sheriff. I hope you don't mind." As she walked toward him, the foul smell grew stronger.

"Not at all, ma'am." He looked a bit sheepish as he stood in the doorway. "I don't want to come in just yet. I might smell up the place."

"Then I'll come out with you."

He stood back to allow her to exit the house and then closed the door behind her.

She spotted Robby and Tien Lee immediately. Ody was nowhere in sight.

"Did you have any trouble finding Ody, Sheriff?" She looked around as she spoke.

Both boys erupted in giggles. They pointed to some bushes next to the house. A long piece of rope disappeared into them.

Jack sighed. "Not again." He bent and picked up a blanket lying on the ground and then walked over and knelt next to a clump of bushes.

"Ody boy, we've been through this before. No sense in acting like your feelings are still hurt. We're here to help you, you mangy mutt."

As Jack moved into the clump of bushes, Nora heard the pitiful whine.

"Jack had a dickens of a time getting Ody, Mama." Robby beamed from ear to ear. "He finally had to give him a bear hug just to get the rope around him." Robby leaned closer to whisper, "Jack says Ody's mighty embarrassed and his pride's hurt, is all."

"Either Mr. Duncan or Sheriff Duncan, Robby," Nora chastised.

"No, Mama. He said Tien and I can call him Jack."

The lawman emerged from the bushes, a wiggling Ody swept up in his arms. He quickly tied the rope's end to a tree in the yard, which still gave Ody a little room to run about as he barked. Nora backed away as the dog leaned toward her, straining against the rope, eager for a swift pat.

"You smell awful, Ody," she proclaimed.

The dog immediately crouched, his belly flat on the ground, his head resting on outstretched paws.

"Now, Ody, she didn't mean it." Jack strode back to them, a rusted bucket swinging from one hand. He knelt beside the dog and stroked him slowly. "She knows it's not your fault."

Jack surprised himself talking to a dog this way. He'd never had much regard for animals. It had been his younger brothers who'd treated their hunting dogs as well as their human friends. And yet when he'd seen the sad look on the dog's face, something spoke to him. He somehow knew that Ody was humiliated by what had happened to him. Hell, *he* would've acted the same if a skunk sprayed him.

In that moment, Jack bonded with the mutt. It was something else that felt good. Maybe he'd look into getting himself a dog.

"Boys. Come here."

The two children rushed over. "I've got a few more buckets in the shed out back. Fill all of them at the well. Bring the soap, too, and the scrub brush next to it."

They hurried off at a gallop, laughing as they went.

He turned to Nora. "You can sit up on the porch, Mrs. Cantrelle. This is going to be some nasty business."

"Nonsense, Sheriff. I helped clean Ody up in the first place. He was a sight when Robby brought him home."

"A Southern lady like you dirtying your hands?" He regretted the words the moment they popped from his mouth, but she didn't seem to take offense.

"I've done a lot more than get my hands dirty." She left it at that, and he didn't pry.

"What needs to be done first?" she asked.

He took the lid off the rusted bucket. "Got this

from a tracker. He must've been eighty years old. It's vinegar-based. I can smell some in it. Other than that, it's a mysterious concoction that he said would do all kinds of interesting things." Jack dipped his hand into the can. "Never had cause to use it before now."

Nora leaned closer, got a whiff of the contents, and took a quick step back. He liked the way she crinkled her nose. Even above the stink in the can, he'd once again caught the scent of jasmine as she drew near. He wanted to pull her close and bury his hands in that thick, honey-blonde hair of hers.

The return of the boys pushed those thoughts from his mind.

"Where do we put the buckets?"

"Just set 'em down, Tien. Fill any others you can find."

The boys hustled back. "And don't forget that soap!" he called out.

He turned to see Nora Cantrelle rolling up the sleeves of her blouse.

"Do you want me to hold him or spread the goop?"

"I think I better hold him. At least at first."

Jack knelt beside the dog and wrapped his arms around him, effectively pinning him in his grasp. "Just dip your hands into the bucket and spread a coat of the stuff on him. Not too close to his eyes, though."

Nora didn't hesitate as she reached in and scooped out the concoction. She rubbed it along the dog. He whined at first, but she kept cooing to him softly, telling him it was for his own good. Jack had an image flash in which she moved her hands across him, echoing the same sweet words.

He swore softly under his breath.

"I caught that, Sheriff." Her gaze captured his. He saw her fight to keep from smiling and then she laughed aloud. He joined in.

It took forever to sufficiently cover the dog's coat

with the mysterious mixture, working it deeply into his fur. Ody's cooperation would have been nice, but they weren't getting it today. It took an even longer time to rinse and soap the mutt several times. Eventually, they wound up with a wet, clean dog.

"Why don't you boys let him off his leash now?" Jack suggested. "He's probably ready for a good romp and even a roll in the dirt."

Robby undid the knot that released Ody from the restraining tree. The dog took off, both boys chasing after him.

"He was pretty patient. More so than I would've been under the same circumstances," Nora said. "I can't imagine he'll try to befriend another skunk anytime soon."

"Let's get ourselves cleaned up." He laughed, looking at their bedraggled state. After repeated washings, they probably wore as much of the soap as Ody had. Thankfully, most of the smell was now gone. Still, he couldn't wait to rinse himself.

They both picked up the buckets scattered across the yard. Jack led her around to the back of his house.

"I'll take these and put them in the shed. Why don't you draw some water from the well?"

He took the cans from her. Still aware of her. Still wanting her. He walked toward the shed and dumped his armload on the ground then stacked the buckets along the wall. He spied an old work shirt hanging from a hook, frayed but still decent enough. He popped the buttons on the shirt he wore, which wouldn't even make a good rag after today, and quickly stripped it off. He slipped into the replacement and quickly buttoned it and closed the shed door behind him.

As Jack came out, he paused a moment. Nora was next to the well, her back to him, her hair gleaming in the sunlight. It had escaped from its pins at some point during the dog's bath and now spilled down her back in soft waves, slightly damp.

She was unaware he approached as she dipped her hands into a bucket and then poured the water over her forearms. She reached for a bar of soap in a stand next to the well, but his hand covered it first.

"Here. I got you into this, Mrs. Cantrelle. Let me help you clean up."

"Then please call me Nora. I've never stood much on formality."

"Nora then. And I'm Jack."

He rinsed his own hands in the bucket of water she had brought up and then poured it out and raised a clean one. He took the bar of soap and dipped it into the bucket to moisten it first and then worked it into a nice lather.

Nora watched him as he took hold of her hand and worked the lather around her fingers. His fingers were long and slender, but she sensed great strength in them. He was nothing but gentle, though, as he cleansed each finger and her palm with his rough, callused hands.

Then he began to work his way up in slow, sensuous circles, first to her wrist and then up her forearm. Nora found she couldn't breathe. She was afraid to inhale. It was as if she were deep under water, holding her breath, with the surface nowhere in sight.

She would perish if he didn't stop. Or perhaps if he did.

He finally stopped and poured cool water over her soap-slickened skin. She managed a quick breath before he took her other hand and repeated the process.

This time, she began to relax as he stroked her fingers up and down. She became aware of the sweet scent of pipe tobacco mixed with horse and leather and soap. He continued as before, gradually moving from palm to wrist to forearm, the motion causing her heart to race faster and faster.

Couldn't he feel it in her pulse? She herself could see the erratic vibration causing her skin to jump. He had to feel that as he worked his way back down to her hand and rinsed it again. She felt a dampness between her thighs now, a pulsing, its rhythm steady and strong, unlike anything she'd experienced before. Nora thought she might go mad.

And then he kissed her.

LOVE ON THE RUNAWAY

CHAPTER 11

I t was sweet and tantalizingly slow, a kiss with a life all its own.

A brush of his lips to start, then his mouth fully encompassed hers, tender yet firm.

Jack's callused hand slid down Nora's wet arm and then back up again. It moved to the back of her neck, his palm warm and moist, pulling her close as his other arm encircled her waist. He could feel her heart racing as he brought her against him, her soft breasts crushed against his muscled frame.

His tongue painted a ring of fire around her mouth, and he heard her soft sigh. Encouraged, he gently urged her lips apart, easing his tongue into her mouth. Her sweetness overwhelmed him as the scent of jasmine wafted about them. He explored her thoroughly. Leisurely. She was stiff at first, as if she'd never kissed before, but she caught on quickly. As his tongue mated with hers, slowly at first and then more insistent, she became a full participant. The kiss turned fierce, possessing, all-consuming. She gripped his shoulders, her nails digging into flesh.

It was pure heaven.

Jack's grasp on Nora tightened. He couldn't bring her near enough. As he stroked her tongue, he reveled in her—her touch, her scent, her sweet abandon. He had never kissed a woman with such intensity or need.

And that's what made him stop.

He jerked away, breaking the contact without warning. Nora stumbled at the sudden release. Jack reached out and steadied her. Their eyes met, hers full of unanswered questions. He almost succumbed to temptation and kissed her again, but he controlled his actions for both of their sakes.

He tried to steady his uneven breathing. In a low voice, he apologized. "Forgive me, ma'am. I have no excuse for my actions."

Nora looked at him with a dazed expression. He noticed her own ragged breathing. She shook her head back and forth, her mouth slightly open but no sound came out. Her hair, pure gold in the sunlight, hung about her in waves. He had to fight to keep his hands from leaping into it, running through the silky mass.

What the hell just happened?

He better keep his hands busy, else they'd begin to roam over Nora Cantrelle again. He turned away and reached for the wooden bucket from the well and tossed it aside.

"I must beg forgiveness myself, Sheriff."

Jack couldn't avoid her gaze any longer. As he met her emerald gaze, her head bowed but not before he saw the dark irises glazed with passion.

"No, ma'am," he said humbly. "I take full responsibility for my actions."

She raised her head, a trace of a smile at the corner of her mouth. "Then I will take full responsibility for my reactions."

Her words took him aback. He'd have expected her to slap him or go into hysterics at his outrageous behavior, but she'd done neither. Whatever else the Southern beauty had, she possessed spunk.

"May I escort you home, Mrs. Cantrelle?" he asked

formally, not trusting himself to call her Nora as she'd asked.

She nodded. "I would appreciate it, Sheriff Duncan."

He offered her his arm. She hesitated briefly before she took it, but when she did, he saw the resolve in her face. Jack admired the courage it took for her to go on as before the kiss occurred. He knew, too, he'd better get her home quickly, before his own determination unraveled and he swept her up into his arms again.

They walked at an easy pace toward town, chatting about inconsequential things as if nothing earthshattering had happened between them.

"I couldn't help but notice your furniture, Sheriff," Nora told him after a quarter of a mile. "It's very handsome."

He nodded but gave no other response.

She pursued it further. "The wood is beautiful, of course, but it's the lines of each piece that hold the real beauty. Don't you agree?"

"Yes."

"We brought very few items with us from back home, which means we have an entire house to furnish in a few weeks." Nora paused. "Is it the work of one craftsman? I don't think we'd be able to afford much from him, but I would like to buy a piece or two."

"That could be arranged, I suppose."

Nora stopped dead in her tracks, a hand coming to rest on her waist. Color spotted her cheeks.

"You are an impossible man, Jack Duncan. First, you're mean as the dickens to me, then you rescue me from excruciating pain, you help clean Ody up, you kiss me senseless, and then you have the audacity to string me along as to who carved your furniture. I won't have it."

She stomped off, giving him an exceedingly nice view of swinging hips and rounded bottom.

"Ma'am?" he called out.

She turned to face him. "What?"

"What excruciating pain?"

She snorted. "Why, quilting, you fool."

He strode a few steps to reach her. "I made it."

Nora frowned. "You made what? You made me angry?"

"I made the furniture."

Her jaw fell. "You made it."

"Yes, ma'am."

"All of it."

"Yes, ma'am."

"Why . . . you're very talented, Sheriff."

"Thank you, ma'am."

They fell into step together again, a thoughtful look on her face.

"Would you make me a table?" she asked, her voice quiet. "A kitchen table, with chairs for us all?"

"Might take a while."

Nora's smile lit up her face. "That would be no problem. No problem at all."

They continued to walk again. They made it another ten feet before she stopped again.

"Would you invite Ben over to see your work? He's tinkered a bit with furniture over the years. I'd like him to see a real master's work."

Her words secretly pleased him. Jack hadn't heard praise in a long time, and he wasn't sure how to react. Carving furniture was a soothing way he passed his time once his day in Silver Bluff ended. It was a part of him and had been from childhood.

Instead, he shrugged. "Fine by me."

They continued in silence until they reached the hotel.

"I do thank you for your help, Sheriff. You went above the call of duty today."

"Just part of the rounds, Mrs. Cantrelle. Send Ben

over on Saturday morning. He can bring the boys with him."

"The boys?"

"I promised them I'd take them fishing at Slaughter Creek. That is, if it's okay by you."

"I won't mind at all." She paused. "Of course, my father will."

He was confused. "Come again?"

"My father's favorite thing in the world is fishing. Not writing. Not eating. Not sleeping. Fishing. He'll be heartbroken unless he's invited along."

He grinned. "I knew I liked that man. Well, tell them all to come by about seven-thirty. We'll pack a lunch and make a day of it."

"I will," she said softly. Nora turned quickly and glided up the steps of the hotel without a backward glance.

Jack walked down the street, numb, trying to shake off all that had happened in the last hour with Nora Cantrelle. He resorted to his customary routine, desperate to cling to something familiar. He wasn't ready to think just yet.

He stopped at the general store and gave Seymour Simmons a complete report of their dealings with Ody, knowing full well the man would also demand an account from Nora. He stopped by the bank and inquired about Mrs. Witherspoon's health and then wandered back to his office, thankful to be alone.

He collapsed in his chair and rubbed his hands over his eyes. He lifted the worn hat from his head and placed it on the desk in front of him. He couldn't avoid it any longer.

He could kick himself. He should at least pay someone to do it for him. His anger began to permeate through his pores. How could he be so stupid?

He yanked open his drawer and took out his whittling.

It felt good having something in his hands. But as Jack looked down at them, he noticed a slight tremble, which caused the anger to bubble over. Anger at Nora Cantrelle. More anger at himself.

Gripping the wood, he forced the shaking to still. Better to hold hard wood than a soft woman any day, he lied to himself. Women were nothing but trouble.

Then why did he kiss her?

How could he not?

The woman was a little on the thin side, but he'd enjoyed the feel of her breasts against his chest. The taste of her mouth. In a brief span of time, he'd kissed her with more emotion than he'd ever given in to, not with Felicity, much less any woman since.

And she was a damned Southerner.

Jack felt his fury begin to flow again, denying any passion was mixed in with it. He let his thoughts drift with each angry stroke of the knife until he yelped in pain. He looked down to see the piece of wood he'd started with worn down to a bare nub. He'd nicked himself but good. A few drops of blood dribbled onto his dark trousers.

Pulling a worn handkerchief from his pocket, he wrapped it around his grazed index finger, all the while thinking of Nora Cantrelle's similar injury. He kicked back his chair and threw the wood and his knife in the drawer and slammed it for good measure. He needed to get out, clear the wool that had gathered in his fuzzy brain.

A quick trip to the saloon would lift his spirits. Thoughts of a quick tumble in the sheets made him smile briefly. That would get the Southern vixen off his mind.

He adjusted his hat and stepped out into a fine Colorado summer day. He took a deep breath, and with long strides, made it to the saloon in less than a minute.

Jack squinted as he entered. The saloon was poorly

lit and as quiet as a dead mouse. A few stray customers sat at scattered tables in the late afternoon. Some of the girls ate an early dinner before they readied themselves for their night's work. Being a Tuesday, they probably wouldn't see much action.

He acknowledged their presence with a tip of his hat and slowly cruised toward the bar. He perched on a stool and propped one elbow on the counter.

Lola separated herself from the others and took the stool opposite him. "How're you doing, Sheriff?" she asked lazily, placing a slim hand on his taut thigh.

"Been better, Lo."

She smiled at him seductively. "Maybe I could make you feel better." The hand glided across his thigh in a gentle caress.

"Not now, honey. I'm working."

Lola laughed. "When has that ever stopped you?" When he made no reply, she added, "Then maybe when you get off, you'll come see me?"

"Maybe."

The girl gave his leg a squeeze and winked. She returned to her companions.

Jack was dead to her touch. He experienced absolutely nothing in that moment. He clenched his jaw, wishing to shake some sense into himself. Lola was the pick of all Marguerite's painted ladies. She'd pleasured him many times before. What was wrong with him?

"It has to be a woman."

The low, sensual voice caught his attention. He spun around on the barstool. Marguerite Le Beau stood behind him, lovely as always, in pale green satin that brought out the green of her eyes.

"You look pretty down, Sheriff."

"Just a little bored, that's all."

Marguerite eyed him expertly. "Not my diagnosis, dear heart. Is it Nora Cantrelle?"

He remained cool. "Whatever are you talking about, honey?"

The experienced madam chuckled. "Oh, Jack. I never thought I'd see it." She linked an arm through his and led him up a wide, carpeted staircase to the upstairs parlor, seating them on a camelback loveseat the color of butter.

She took his hand in hers. "You have that look, my friend."

Before he could deny it, she added knowingly, "And I saw you with Lola."

He lay his head back against the soft cushions of the sofa for a long moment.

"She's a looker, that Southern belle."

His head popped back up. "You've seen her?"

Marguerite smiled. "She came over and introduced herself. Right in the general store." She chuckled. "Almost gave the Simmons woman apoplexy. Jane Simmons was explaining to Mrs. Cantrelle exactly what I did for a living. In my earshot, I might add."

She smoothed the folds of her gown. "I would've thought our newcomer might run screaming from the store or gaze at me with ice in her eyes—but she marched straight to me and introduced herself, real ladylike and all." She tightened her hold on his hand. "I like her."

He grunted in reply.

She patted his hand dismissively. "We don't have to talk about it now, but you know I'm here if you need me."

"Nothing to talk about."

Marguerite touched a hand to his cheek. "Deny it all you want, Jack Duncan."

He refused to humor her any longer. Nothing, absolutely nothing, was going on between him and Nora Cantrelle. "Drop it, Marguerite." He stood, ready to leave.

"Then maybe you'll want to hear something I learned about our Mr. Kessler today. You better hold on to your hat, cowboy."

CHAPTER 12

"Where on earth have you been, Miss Nora? You look like some kind of swamp rat dragging in. I thought you were helping your daddy and Mr. Nelson."

Nora ran a hand wearily through her mussed hair. She realized that she'd left her bonnet back at Jack Duncan's place. Apparently her pins, as well, since her hair hung limply.

"I've been bathing a skunk-sprayed mongrel, Jess." She explained Ody's misadventure and how the sheriff volunteered to assist them clean up their pet.

Jess helped her out of her damp clothes and into a robe. She caught Jess studying her in the mirror as she belted the robe.

"You're wearing a sly smile, Jess. What are you up to?"

"Nothing, Miss Nora." The servant switched topics. "We met us some fine women today, didn't we? They were all nice, except for that Miz Simmons. She's a handful now, ain't she? And not half the quilter she brags on being, that's for sure."

"They were nice, weren't they? I enjoyed myself."

"And they don't mind that you don't quilt, Miss

Nora. They said to bring you back anyway and you could keep 'em company while they stitched." She leaned in. "I told Miz Seabury that your buttermilk pie would give her scones a run for the money. She's eager to have you make one and us eat it while we quilt."

Nora sighed. "If only I had my own kitchen. I wonder if Papa will have news about that."

At that moment, he swung the door open. "Hello. Hope you had a—" He stopped short, obviously worried about her bedraggled appearance.

"It's nothing, Papa. Ody tried to make friends with a local skunk and was sprayed for his troubles. I've been trying to get rid of the smell and clean him up."

"With Sheriff Duncan," Jess added. "He helped track Ody down. They took him out to the sheriff's place and scrubbed him good." Jess nodded sagely. Her father returned the nod.

"What?" Nora cried. "Is there something you're not telling me?"

"Maybe something you're not telling us, Miss Nora?" Jess prodded.

She felt the flush race up her neck. She reached for her brush on the bureau, tugging it through her hair as she watched in the mirror as her father and Jess exchanged another glance and the servant left.

Nora focused on her own image. The brush halted in midair. She brought a hand to her face. It was tender to her touch. The whisker burns she'd been oblivious to stood out like a sore thumb. No wonder they had looked at her with amusement.

"I have some good news."

Papa seated himself and went through his ritual of packing his pipe. She calmed as she observed this routine, familiar to her after so many years.

"Mr. Nelson says the house will be built in two weeks' time and the newspaper facilities in less than a month."

"That seems fast."

"He has a crew of three who're full-time workers. They're the ones that built the church. The wood's already cut and we staked both lots this afternoon." He frowned. "The house is a basic box, Nora. We're going for speed over beauty. It won't be quite what you're used to but then I suppose we can add on to it once we get on our feet."

"How many rooms to start?"

"We'll have a parlor and a kitchen and then three rooms beyond that. Ben and Jess will be together, and you'll need to share with Robby for a while. We'll use the last one as our home office and I'll have a cot put in for sleeping."

"That's more than I had expected, Papa, but a cot?"

Albert coughed, a deep, hacking noise that bothered her. She had harped on him for months to have it checked, but he refused to go to the doctor, saying they didn't have the money to bother with a tickle in his throat. Nora hoped once they came West that the air would be better for him and the cough would clear up. His recent shortness of breath was another cause of concern.

"You know how restless I am nowadays. A cot is more than adequate. I'm up more than down at night. It's a problem we older folks experience."

Nora wasn't so sure. When their finances had grown tight, her father insisted they sell his bedroom furniture. Made of carved oak, the set contained a large bed, headboard, armoire, and dresser. The carpetbagger that replied to their advertisement bought it for a song, but the money it brought in fed them for a few months. When it ran out, they gradually sold off a piece at a time, until she decided to take in boarders. Albert insisted the cot he slept on was comfortable, but she often wondered why he spent more time out of it than in it.

"They begin tomorrow at first light." He struck a match against his shoe and lit the pipe, puffing until the sweet smell of tobacco began to fill the room.

"Besides his regular crew, he's got a group of men from the mine that work swing shifts. In their down time, they'll put in a few hours for him. They're eager to pick up the extra cash and Nelson pays well. With so many of them, even working part-time, they can have both places done in no time."

"That's good news. It will be nice to cook our own food and sleep in our own beds."

"We need to think about furniture. We've got the presses and desks for the newspaper, but we'll need to make a trip down to Denver to buy some of the basics. Harve gave me the measurements to place an order for the windows while we're there."

Nora sat on the bed next to his chair. "I've already commissioned someone to do a kitchen table for us."

"Oh, have you now?"

"Sheriff Duncan carves furniture in his spare time. He's agreed to make us a set. You might put a bug in his ear when you go fishing."

Papa's face brightened with pure joy. "When?"

She smiled. "This Saturday morning. You're to take Ben and the boys. You can look at the work he's done in his own home to see if you approve."

"I'm sure I will, Daughter." A dreamy expression crossed his face. "I wonder what kind of fish they have in Colorado. Catfish? Bass?" He leaned back in the chair, a contented look on his face. "Fishing. Saturday, you said?"

"Yes."

"I wonder if I could bring what I catch to dinner."

Nora was puzzled. "What are you talking about, Papa?"

"Oh, didn't I tell you? Mr. Kessler asked us to dine

with him and his brother Saturday night. It'll be both for business and pleasure. We're to be there at seven."

"You and I?"

"That's right, dear. I don't know if any other guests will be present." He eyed her

speculatively. "Maybe our town sheriff?"

She stood and returned her brush to the bureau. Every time the man was mentioned, she flushed beet red.

An arm touched her shoulder. "It's good to get out and mingle again. Nothing wrong with that. It's time to let go. Don't mourn Paul anymore."

She stiffened. "Are you saying I should seek out the company of other men?"

Papa gave her shoulder a squeeze. "I'm sure they'll seek you out."

Nora swallowed hard. The thought of being in the company of men again hadn't really occurred to her before. She'd been so busy packing and traveling and thinking about ideas for the new paper. Yet Silver Bluff was filled with nothing but men.

And one of them was on her mind now.

"I think I'll go for a little stroll before dinner." He winked and eased out the door.

Nora sat on the bed and groaned. She balled her fists and slammed them against the mattress. She knew he was headed for his daily visit with Jack Duncan. The thought brought fresh embarrassment to her.

She'd certainly acted as unladylike as possible this afternoon. She'd actually responded to the sheriff's kiss.

And what a kiss it was. Nora had no idea that a kiss could be so intimate, so soul-baring. Or that it could go on for an eternity and yet seem only a moment long.

She was thankful that at least one of them came to his senses and stopped before things got out of hand. They had been in public, for goodness' sake. It had been reckless, crazy, stupid.

And the most satisfying thing that had ever happened to her.

⚜

THEY SAT ALONG THE BANK, A SOFT BREEZE BLOWING a gentle wind across the water. The sun was bright for nine in the morning, but it was July, almost August. Jack closed his eyes, basking in the warmth of the day and his good spirits.

He hadn't asked anyone to fish with him since the days when he used to take his brothers to the pond at the back of their property. That was before the war. They'd had good times together, joking and playful, before they quieted down to wait for the fish to bite. He could almost smell fish frying in a skillet on an open fire.

"I got one!"

Robby bounced to his feet, pulling on the pole, looking excitedly at the two men and then gleefully back at the water. Jack saw the familiar splashing and grinned.

He and Albert ambled to where Tien Lee danced alongside Robby, as caught up in the drama as if he had the fish on his own line.

"Be patient. You've got to reel him in nice and slow." He placed his hands on the pole atop the boy's hands. "Don't let him think he's in charge. You're the one calling the shots now. That's right."

With infinite patience, the two managed to bring the fish to shore.

"Whoo-eee!" Robby hooted. Tien Lee echoed his cry of triumph.

They placed the fish in a basket and closed the lid, hearing it slap and pop inside the encasement.

"I'll get a fish, too," Tien Lee declared.

He tugged on Tien Lee's long queue of hair, drawn into a tight ponytail. "I'm sure you will, Tien."

The older men helped settle the boys again and returned to their places some twenty yards in the distance. Jack regretted that Ben hadn't joined them. He'd been intent on studying Jack's tools and furniture. When Jack encouraged him to try his hand with the tools and produced a few blocks of wood for him to practice on, Ben opted to stay behind.

They sat on the grassy bank and picked up their poles again, once more lapsing into a comfortable silence. An hour passed. The two men finally began to speak quietly. Jack found himself telling Albert more than he'd shared with anyone since he'd left Virginia. He'd learned not to get too close to someone during the war because you never knew when that man might wind up with a bullet in his gut. He'd shared even less about himself since that time.

"You're a good listener, Albert. I've spilled my guts. Why don't you tell me about your newspaper?"

"It's all I've ever known. I apprenticed in New Orleans at an early age with a printer. Worked in his shop doing handbills, flyers, programs—whatever came our way. Eventually partnered with the man and then got interested in the newspaper business.

"Finally took off on my own and found myself starting a paper in Monroe. Business was good until the war. Money was hard to come by. People shared papers or got their news off the streets."

"And after the war?"

Albert snorted. "Politicians speak of the New South, but there's no future there. The carpetbaggers took advantage of most people's trust. The freed slaves had nowhere to go and no education. They're the ones who have had it the roughest."

He was curious about Ben and Jess. "Is that why

your servants came out West with you? They had nowhere else to go?"

Albert laughed. "Nora wouldn't have come without them. Ben and Jess are family to us. See, my folks never had slaves. We were simple people who accomplished things with our own hands. I freed Ben and Jess even before the war began. When my wife, Genevieve, passed on. They were part of her dowry.

"They helped me raise Nora. She was just a bitty thing. Jess has been more a mama to her than her own ever was. When we decided to head West, it was all or none."

The older man's revelations took Jack aback. Every preconceived notion he had about Southerners, and Nora Cantrelle in particular, was shattered. Yet looking back, he could see the warm affection between all of them.

"Why Silver Bluff?"

Albert bent a knee. A loud pop resounded. "Did a little research. Wanted to find a place that was on its way up. One that still didn't have a newspaper but would be ready to embrace one as it grew. And," he added, a twinkle in his eyes, "one with a lot of men."

"Why?"

"Because I'm dying."

Jack was startled at the blunt words. Albert seemed a bit frail, but who wasn't at that age? Yet upon more serious inspection, he caught a look in the older man's eyes. He'd seen that look of desperation during the war, among those wounded who knew they wouldn't make it. Albert had put up a good front until now, and Jack was humbled to see the older man let his guard down around him.

"My ticker's no good. That's what the doctor in Monroe told me. He also was worried about all the congestion in my lungs. Said mountain air would be a heck of a lot better than breathing what comes from those humid swamps." Albert shook his head. "Nora doesn't know any of this. I'd appreciate you keeping this under your hat. She's had a rough time. Her sweetheart went off to war and came home all shot to hell. War turned a kind-hearted young boy into a bitter cripple."

Albert stared hard at him. "I'll admit I indulged Nora growing up. She was a bit spoiled. Always had lively opinions on this and that. But she's had to shoulder a heavy burden for a long time, dealing with a husband missing his arm and a leg and no will to live. A little boy who's always into something. That's why I came West. For her to find a better life. And maybe for someone to help her shoulder her burdens."

He chuckled. "If I can get this newspaper off the ground, it won't matter to most people who runs it. Nora is as happy as a flea on a dog when she's writing and running a newspaper. Ben knows enough now to help her run it. They'll manage fine once I'm gone. Of course, I'd rather her be settled with a man to take care of her and Robby. There are plenty here. With the shortage of women, I suspect my daughter will have her fair share of gentlemen callers before long."

Jack knew Albert spoke the truth. Nora was a real beauty. Already he heard her name in town on almost every man's lips. Once Harve Nelson finished their house next week, he knew a line would form at the gate.

"Are you sure you shouldn't talk this over with her?"

"I will when the time comes. I've been better since we arrived here. Maybe mountain air does have some magic in it. I'm just a little tired, that's all."

Albert removed his hat and mopped his brow with a handkerchief. "Most men won't do for Nora. Knowing her, she won't even think to look at a man for quite a spell. But once she does, I want him to be good to her. And if I go before she's settled with someone, will you look after her, Jack? Make sure that whomever she marries is a good soul? She's been hurt so much, my girl. She's like a wounded bird."

He folded the handkerchief, tucked it into his pocket and replaced his hat. "You struck me as a man with good judgment from the moment we met. Could I have your word? Will you agree to watch out for Nora in case I can't?"

Jack cleared his throat. "You can count on me."

CHAPTER 13

J ack carefully fastened the only jewelry he owned, a cufflink, into his sleeve. Marguerite had advised him to invest in a decent pair. She'd convinced him that he would have opportunities to use them, and she'd been right. Burke Stevenson had invited him to dinner several times before he sold out and left Silver Bluff. Usually, the occasion witnessed an important visitor passing through. He wondered if that was the case with Kessler tonight.

Chin Lee had appeared on Jack's doorstep the day before, just as the sun began to dip along the horizon. He'd sat in a rocker on his porch, enjoying the canvas of colors as he worked on sketches for Nora Cantrelle's table and chairs. It surprised him at how anxious he was for her reaction.

The Chinaman scurried up to the gate and through it, his queue swinging from side to side in his haste. He waved an envelope in one hand.

"Greetings, Mr. Jack Sheriff. Tien says you're going fishing?"

"I'm taking him and his new friend up to Slaughter Creek tomorrow. Has he ever fished before?"

Chin shook his head sadly. "No, Mr. Jack Sheriff.

Tien has never fished. I'm a bad father. I have no time to teach him this."

Jack protested. "You're a great father, Chin. Just a busy man. I guess Kessler keeps you that way." He wasn't averse to doing a little fishing of his own.

"Yes, we're very busy. Mr. Kessler wants you to come to dinner. Tomorrow night. Seven sharp." He thrust the envelope into Jack's hands. "Very important you come. Some big man is coming to visit. You'll meet him then."

"Who?" Not a carriage pulled up nor a rider passed through that Jack didn't know about. Kessler's guest must've arrived in the dead of night and remained in the house at all times for him not to get wind of his visit.

The servant shrugged. "An important man, Mr. Jack Sheriff. We change his sheets—wash, dry, iron—every day. Yesterday, he made us do it two times. He's a particular man. Mr. Kessler says we must make him like it here."

Jack wondered why. It also bothered him that a stranger had taken up residence in Silver Bluff without his knowledge. Before he could ask Chin more, the little man rushed back down the path.

"I'll see you tomorrow, Mr. Jack Sheriff. You'll have a fancy dinner. Sung Moon is working very hard. I'm helping her. Goodbye."

He wished he had more time to pump Chin about this mysterious visitor. He'd followed up and asked Tien Lee a few questions that morning, but the boy was so captivated with the art of fishing, Jack let the matter drop.

He did wonder at the last-minute nature of the invitation. It was almost as if Kessler didn't want him to sniff out any information about his mystery guest. Still, this was the first time he'd been asked to dine at the big house since William Kessler had arrived. He'd keep his ears—and eyes—open.

Jack smoothed his shirtfront again and reached for his tie. It was thin and black. Marguerite had taught him how to tie this, as well. He hadn't much use for ties in the mountains of western Virginia. Dressing up for a special event merely involved pressing a clean shirt with a hot iron and slicking back his wavy hair with water. Whether wedding or funeral, everyone arrived looking pretty much the same—clean but humble, no fancy dress among them.

He picked up a comb and ran it through his hair, curious if any other guests would attend. It made him uncomfortable to think he'd be around the Kesslers all evening. He didn't think the pair was up to any good.

It didn't surprise him. He'd crossed paths with Ken Kessler briefly at the war's beginning. At twenty-one, Jack was ready to fight Mr. Lincoln's War and personally force every secessionist to his knees for daring to leave the Union. He didn't realize in his idealism that many of his Northern compatriots were shady characters, out to make a fast buck on the war and not caring about the politics.

Ken Kessler had been one of those men.

Kessler started as a captain and rose in rank to major. His older brother held the rank of colonel. After raids in the area, the two men took the confiscated Southern goods and shipped them home as personal property. Rumor had it they sold these goods on the black market to Northerners and Southerners alike, gaining a small fortune.

Ken also had a reputation for dealing dirty. Idle army gossip placed on him the disappearance of three, possibly four men, in his command. Officially, the men were listed as deserters. Local hearsay had them put down as murdered victims who tried to cross Ken Kessler.

Jack was a green kid who'd never left his home county before the war. When he reported for Union duty under Ken's command, the first soldier he'd encountered warned him to lie low, keep his mouth shut, and don't interfere with the Kesslers' operation. Jack had already seen too much too fast in his brief stay in the army, but the level of corruption he'd witnessed left a bad taste in his mouth for all officers, though he never even laid eyes on Colonel William Kessler.

He secured a transfer from their command as soon as possible, though it meant immediate battlefront duty. He later heard his replacement was killed in a skirmish by friendly fire. He wondered if the boy, whom he'd met briefly, tried to report the goings-on at the camp to a higher authority. Jack had issued the same warning he'd received but the peach-fuzzed kid had shrugged it off. He regretted hearing about the youngster's death, but by then it was just another burden placed upon him. War brought a heavy blanket of guilt to its survivors.

Earlier in the week, he'd made subtle inquiries about the Kesslers from the town's citizens. Though gossip usually didn't interest him, it had proved interesting. The Kesslers were buying all surrounding land in the area for a hundred-mile radius. He wasn't sure why, but he'd find out. Maybe Chin's "big man," who'd apparently slipped into town while he'd been fishing today, would hold the key.

Jack set the comb down, lifted his jacket from the back of a chair, and slipped into it. He took a passing glance in the mirror, satisfied with his appearance. The hat followed. He was ready to face the Kessler brothers once again.

NORA WATCHED WITH RELIEF AS MARGUERITE LE Beau walked through the drawing room door, wearing pale yellow satin, her upswept red hair worn high atop her head. They made eye contact and Marguerite flashed her a genuine smile. The older woman then joined the social circle and greeted William Kessler and his guest, a Mr. Thomas Morrison, visiting from San Francisco. She chatted with them easily for a few moments before she took Nora's arm in hers.

"I'm sure you gentlemen can keep yourselves occupied for a while." Marguerite batted her lashes with good effect. "Mrs. Cantrelle and I must catch up on things."

Kessler nodded curtly and turned his attention back to Morrison.

"It's so nice to see you again," Nora said with pleasure. She thought about what Mrs. Simmons had spoken of that day in the store. Nora's memories of what a couple did in private were those of awkward discomfort and sweating, tangled limbs. She couldn't imagine this elegant woman in such a circumstance, much less accepting payment for it from a stranger.

If it were true—and she still had her doubts—she wondered at how Marguerite must be ostracized by the few women of the town. She, too, had experienced that isolation by the finer society matrons of Monroe. Nora made up her mind that whatever local gossip held, she would make a friend of this woman.

They crossed the paneled room to where Albert stood next to the fire, leafing through a book Kessler had wanted him to see soon after they arrived.

"Have you met my father, Albert Le Fall? Papa, this is Mrs. Le Beau."

Marguerite smiled as Albert set aside the book. He took her hand and brushed a kiss across it in a courtly manner.

"I met Mr. Le Fall last week when you had barely arrived. You were coming to visit Mr. Kessler, I believe."

Papa's eyes sparkled. Nora hadn't seen him look so perky in many months.

"Mr. Le Fall? Please come settle this argument," William Kessler's commanding voice called out from across the large room.

"If you ladies will excuse me."

"Thank goodness you are here. I needed a woman to keep me company," Nora told her companion.

"Hmmm. Most women prefer the company of men, Mrs. Cantrelle."

"Please call me Nora. I hate to stand on formality."

"Then Nora it shall be. I am Marguerite." She flicked a piece of lint from her sleeve. "I was happy to see you, too. I had thought tonight would be a boring diversion, at best."

"Then why did you accept the invitation?"

"This is the first dinner party William Kessler has held since coming to town. I suppose I'm here to adorn the table. I think he's hoping I'll entertain his guest. After dinner."

Nora turned to the fire, her back now to the men across the room, the meaning of Marguerite's words clear.

Marguerite kept her composure, but Nora could see the twinkling in the older woman's eyes.

In a quiet tone, the redhead said, "Don't worry, Nora. Kessler has a lot to learn." She smiled like a cat who'd found the cream unattended. "What brought you and your papa here tonight?" Nora detected a hint of Southern drawl as Marguerite spoke.

"We were invited to talk about the newspaper we'll launch in a few weeks." She tilted her head slightly to flash a quick look at their host. Thankfully, he was deep in conversation with his guests.

Her gaze returned to Marguerite. "At least that was the impression I received. I was mistaken, however. I tried to enter the conversation several times in the few minutes since we've arrived, only to be ignored. I may be opinionated, but mine are educated opinions and not flights of fancy." She thrust her chin a notch higher. "I know quite a bit about running a newspaper."

"Kessler doesn't think any woman has the brains to have an opinion, honey. Much less run a business."

"Then I was sadly mistaken about Western men." Nora shook her head and confided in a low voice, "I was led to believe that Westerners were different. That they respected the work women have done here. Why, I was certain that I would be able to vote in my lifetime!"

Marguerite brushed Nora's cheek in an affectionate gesture. "I'll let you in on a well-kept secret, honey. Western men aren't any different from any other men—anywhere, anyhow, anytime. I should know."

She paused and leaned closer. "And Kessler's brother, Ken? Well, my advice to you is stay out of his way. He'll chase anything in a skirt."

Nora drew in a long breath. "Thank you for the warning. I haven't met the other Mr. Kessler yet." She took Marguerite's hand in hers and squeezed it. "I'm so glad you're here."

At that moment, she sensed another presence in the room. Turning, she spied Jack Duncan at the threshold, or rather whom she assumed was Jack Duncan. The last time she'd see the sheriff he'd been dripping wet, wearing both the gunk from the tin can and a layer of soap, with a liberal dash of skunk spray thrown in. The man who now stood across the room looked a perfect gentleman. He wore a stiffly starched white shirt with a plain but elegant black tailcoat and vest over it. His boots were polished until they gleamed like mirrors.

He swept off his hat and handed it to Chin Lee, then greeted his host with a handshake. He was newly shaven, and his thick, dark hair was swept back from his face. Nora bit her lip and looked away. She'd feared he would be invited tonight. Her feelings were so fragile now, she was scared she might shatter into tiny shards if their gazes met.

"Chin up, honey. Just act like you own the place."

"What?" She looked at Marguerite with surprise.

"Don't let Jack intimidate you. Deep down, he's a good man, but a restless soul. I know you've sparred a bit. Best thing you can do is hold your ground and don't give him the time of day." Marguerite smiled. "It'll drive him crazy."

Nora instantly decided to take her advice. Why should she be upset that Jack Duncan was here? It was Saturday night, and she was at a dinner party for the first time in ages. She was ready to enjoy herself, have some food and drink, and enjoy stimulating conversation. That is, if William Kessler would let her join in.

"May I ask to make your acquaintance, ma'am?"

Nora looked up to see a younger, more handsome version of her host standing next to her. Marguerite's warning echoed in her mind.

"You must be Mr. Kessler."

His lips twitched in amusement. "I most certainly am. I assume you're the fair Mrs. Cantrelle."

Nora blushed at the brazen compliment. "I am Nora Cantrelle."

"Your name has been bandied about everywhere I've gone this week, Mrs. Cantrelle." He lifted her hand to his lips and lingered over it a bit longer than was acceptable. His touch caused a chill to ripple down Nora's spine. "Now I see why."

"Good evening, ladies. Hope I'm not interrupting." Jack Duncan bowed formally to them.

The two women both murmured their greetings.

Marguerite said suddenly, "Please excuse me. I think Mr. Le Fall is motioning me over."

Nora tossed Marguerite a look that showed her displeasure.

"Don't worry, Mrs. Cantrelle. I'm sure we'll be able to amuse you."

She looked back at Ken Kessler. Marguerite was right. He was a smooth talker. She would trust him about as much as she would a water moccasin sliding around her bare feet. Kessler was easier on the eyes but seemed far more deadly.

"Would you care to sit?" Kessler took her elbow and led her over to the settee. She perched on its edge as he sat down next to her, a little too close for comfort.

"And how is Ody doing, Mrs. Cantrelle?" Jack Duncan followed them over and hovered close by.

Nora tilted her head back to stare up at him. "I'd say he's none the worse for his encounter with the skunk."

Jack shrugged. "He's a young pup, but it's a good lesson to learn. Is Robby exhausted after today's outing?"

"You wore him out. He talked a blue streak when he got home, but he ran out of steam about an hour ago. Jess helped him undress and then he fell into bed. I'm sure he'll be dead to the world until church tomorrow morning."

His eyes burned into hers. Despite her air of nonchalance, Nora felt the goose bumps rise on her arms. Fortunately, her gown featured sheer sleeves that hid them. Unfortunately, she felt a warm flush rise up her neck, which her rounded neckline did not disguise.

"I'd love to hear about where you came from, Mrs. Cantrelle." Ken Kessler

inched imperceptibly closer. "And why you came to Silver Bluff."

She realized that the sheriff had excluded Kessler from their conversation. He had done a good job. Nora had totally forgotten the man next to her elbow.

Good manners prevailed, despite her aversion to her host's brother. She focused her attention on her seat mate for the next few minutes as she described the plans they had for their newspaper venture in Silver Bluff. As she spoke, she became aware of both men's rapt attention. At first, she was uncomfortable, but then she decided to take Marguerite's advice and enjoy herself.

Both men laughed at a story she related and the one she told after it. Jack offered to get her a glass of Madeira. Ken helped plump the cushions behind her back. Jack asked if she would like a footstool. Ken complimented her dress. Jack praised her hairstyle.

The unspoken competition increased between the two men. Nora caught herself pursing her lips to keep from bubbling over with laughter. It seemed so unlike the rock-steady sheriff.

Then she saw William Kessler staring at her from across the room. His eyes glinted with something cold. She glanced away, troubled by what she'd seen, wondering just how deeply her father was involved with the man.

"Dinner served. Come, please. This way."

Chin Lee bobbed his graying head a few times and motioned the guests to follow. She rose, only to find each man offering her an arm.

"I dare not offend either of you, gentlemen. Would you both care to escort me into dinner?"

Neither looked pleased, but they each took an arm and led her to the dining room, paneled in deep mahogany. Nora had never been a part of the elite set but for a fraction of a moment, she felt every inch the Southern belle.

Dinner passed pleasantly. Conversation flowed between the men regarding the growth of the town, the likelihood of Colorado becoming a state in the next few years, and the growing cattle market for beef back East. Chin Lee and Sung Moon flitted in and out, serving several courses before they brought dessert. It was an apple pie with cream on top, one of the best Nora had tasted.

As Sung Moon passed, she lightly touched her arm. "I would be honored if you would share this recipe with me, Sung Moon. I have pined to make a pie ever since I left my kitchen in Monroe."

The servant nodded, a nervous smile on her delicate features, her eyes darting quickly from side to side. Nora looked straight at the source of her discomfort. William Kessler narrowed his eyes and glared at her, a twitch in his cheek indicating his suppressed anger. She realized her mistake in speaking with Sung Moon. A man like Kessler would disapprove of any mingling between his guests and servants. She hoped there would be no trouble afterwards for the Chinese couple.

Once dessert was finished, their host cleared his throat. "We'll excuse you ladies to have your coffee in the parlor. When we've finished our brandy and cigars, we'll join you."

The gentlemen rose as Nora and Marguerite stood and moved toward the door.

"Tell you what, William," Ken said, his voice silky smooth, "I think I'll keep the ladies company. Coffee sounds like it'll hit the spot tonight." He looked to Chin Lee. "Maybe with a dash of brandy in mine, Chin?"

Nora watched William Kessler's face darken. She half-expected him to growl a fierce "no" to his brother, but his response surprised her.

"By all means. See to the ladies."

The women moved down the hall, Nora conscious of Ken's hand on the small of her back.

Jack watched Nora go with regret. He'd like to break Ken Kessler's wrist, if that would keep his hands off her. The man had preened like a peacock all night, hovering around Nora as if he'd owned her.

Or wanted to court her.

The thought left a sour taste in his mouth, despite the smooth brandy he sipped. He would have liked to adjourn to the parlor, too, but he didn't know what he might miss if he did so. He should have, since William Kessler droned on about nothing for half an hour, only to be matched by Mr. Morrison's monologue on mining in northern California.

As Morrison spoke, Jack racked his brain. The visitor looked vaguely familiar, but he couldn't place him. He knew he hadn't done any bounty hunting for the man since he'd come West. He'd never seen Morrison in town before, so he doubted Morrison was connected to the mine, at least while Stevenson owned it.

What troubled Jack most was the undercurrent running through the two men's conversation. Something didn't add up about this Morrison and Jack aimed to find out. He'd hit up both Seaburys and the doctor and his wife after morning services tomorrow. Heck, he was curious enough even to stop by the general store on Monday and compliment Mrs. Simmons, if that's what it took. He wanted fast information and as much of it as possible about Thomas Morrison.

He also made a mental note to ask Marguerite if the Californian had stopped by for a night's entertainment at the saloon. The girls always seemed to inspire confidences from their customers.

Jack was ready to stretch his legs as Kessler finally drained the remainder of his brandy and stood. The men rejoined the others in the parlor. Albert Le Fall, silent during the business talk, instantly gravitated to Marguerite. He wondered what the crusty editor was up to with the local madam.

He looked over at Nora Cantrelle, her low voice sounding mystical and promising as she spoke to her companion. He was ready to break Ken Kessler in two.

"Mrs. Cantrelle?"

Jack's voice was as smooth as honey as he addressed her. "I know it's getting late, but you did promise you'd go over your instructions for the table and chairs with me. If I'm going to start them tomorrow, we'll need to discuss it tonight. Might I escort you home? We could talk on the way back to your hotel."

He watched Ken's mouth tighten. It twitched slightly. Jack could see how the man fought to control his temper.

"I was hoping I could accompany you home tonight, Mrs. Cantrelle."

Jack cleared his throat. "Sunday is my only day to work on carving the furniture Mrs. Cantrelle ordered. If I don't get started tomorrow, it'll be a week before I touch it." He looked at her steadily. "I know how soon you'll be in your new home and how eager you are for me to begin."

He caught the glimmer of amusement in her eyes.

"Yes, Sheriff, I am enthused about you starting as soon as possible. Let me take my leave with our host and thank him for his kind invitation."

She turned back to Ken. "It was nice making your acquaintance, Mr. Kessler."

He took her hand. "The pleasure was all mine, Mrs. Cantrelle."

Jack saw the warm caress in Ken's eyes as they roamed over Nora. He forced his fists to stay by his sides. No sense brawling in his host's home. He would look up Ken Kessler when the time was right and explain to him to stay away from Nora Cantrelle.

Jack accompanied Nora to thank William Kessler for the night's outing. He caught a wink from Marguerite.

Chin Lee led them into the foyer and handed Jack Nora's wrap.

"Good to see you, Miss Nora. And you, too, Mr. Jack Sheriff. Tien Lee is full of good thanks for your biting fish. We'll fry some up tomorrow morning. It will be a big feast."

He opened the door for them. "See you in church, Miss Nora. Bye-bye now."

Jack took Nora's arm to help her down the stairs. He tried to think how to begin a decent conversation for their walk back into town. He didn't have to worry long. She let out a low whistle, probably learned from that indulgent father of hers, and shook her head, her brows arched high.

"What in tarnation is this all about, Jack Duncan?"

CHAPTER 14

J ack looked at her innocently. Nora scrutinized him carefully, but he remained silent.

"Why were you in such a rush to get me out of there?"

He shrugged and began walking down the path. She followed him and passed through the gate he opened.

"I wanted to discuss furniture with you." He latched the gate behind them.

"Pish-posh!"

To her surprise, he opened his jacket and slid out a sheaf of folded papers, the same guileless look on his face. He offered them to her. Nora took them, hastily opening the bunch. She rested them on top of the fence to leaf through them, pausing a time or two as she studied the drawings on the page in the strong moonlight.

"These are incredible, Sheriff. You should consider moving to a larger city. You would have clients bickering left and right for your services if you took up crafting furniture."

He shrugged. "Silver Bluff suits me just fine." He peered at the papers. "Any design appeal to you?"

She laughed. "They all appeal to me." She thought a

moment. "I did like this last set, though." She separated one page from the rest and handed it to him.

"I thought you might." Wearing a satisfied look, he returned the sheet to her and reclaimed the remaining pages. He refolded and placed them inside his coat pocket.

"How did you know I would favor this design?"

Jack shrugged. "I have a good feel for matching a person with a plan. You," he said as he gazed at her steadily, "like something practical and comfortable but you also want it to be pretty. Not too feminine, because you know the men in your life would scoff at it. You want fluid lines and a large table surface." He grinned. "Close enough?"

Before she could reply, he took her elbow and began a slow stroll. Nora was immediately aware of the heat he radiated and the tingle glistening up and down her spine at the light touch of his fingers. This was the first time they'd been alone since Ody had tangled with the skunk.

Since he'd kissed her.

A flood of warmth sizzled through her at the memory, his mouth on hers—hot, hard. Nora was grateful for the cover of darkness. Passing clouds hid the moon for the moment but Jack seemed to know where to step. She forced herself to look up from her feet. She caught the pale glow of lights in the distance. Silver Bluff lay straight ahead.

She bit her lip to bring her back to a different reality, one in which she could calmly discuss business with her handsome escort. He had apologized for the unexpected kiss and probably gave it no more thought. She would curl up and die of embarrassment if her own thoughts became known to him as they walked along on a cool summer night.

Alone.

"Are you really going to start tomorrow?" She

winced as her voice came out a high-pitched squeal. "I mean . . . on my table and chairs."

"If that's what you'd like." His gait remained slow and relaxed.

"All right then." She fumbled for words. "How much of a down payment would be sufficient?"

"None needed. I know where to find you." He grinned. "Just don't plan on leaving town anytime soon."

"That's the last thought on my mind." She studied his profile a moment, its outline clear in the bright moonlight, thanks to the shifting clouds. "You still haven't answered my earlier question. And don't tell me it was all about furniture. Why did we leave William Kessler's so suddenly?"

He stopped and looked at her steadily. "Let's just say I knew of the Kesslers during the war. You don't want to know them any better than you have to."

She snorted. "That's going to be a little hard. William Kessler has become a small investor in our newspaper."

Nora heard him sharply inhale. Obviously, this was one fact the local sheriff had been unaware of.

"It's only twenty percent, what Papa agreed to with a Mr. Burke Stevenson when we first decided to come to Colorado Territory. It also includes a separate contract for supplying us with paper. A paper mill to the northwest is another venture that Mr. Kessler assumed when he arrived in town. You must be aware of that. Papa said both contracts are still legal and binding, despite the change in parties."

They walked in silence for a few minutes. Nora could tell Jack was thinking on what she'd said. She, too, had been concerned when they'd reached town and found the original correspondent gone. Still, she'd always trusted her father's business judgment. After Papa met with Kessler, he'd been comfortable enough to continue with the agreement. He told her Kessler was only looking for ways to diversify his income. He would not seek to play an active role in the newspaper, other than with monetary support.

That had satisfied her. Until now. It worried her to think their only remaining capital was tied up with someone of questionable scruples. What exactly did Jack Duncan know about the Kesslers from the war years? Her instincts sensed something that begged further investigation.

Yet Silver Bluff's sheriff was a man of few words. She didn't think he'd take kindly to being pumped about his past. She sensed reluctance on his part to discuss the Kesslers any further. Much as the thought brought distaste, she might have to stop by the general store and cozy up to Mrs. Simmons. The woman seemed to know everything that went on in town. At least Nora would be able to visit with Mr. Simmons at the same time. The man was a saint to put up with his wife's obnoxious behavior.

The scattered lights grew closer as they neared town. She found herself reluctant for the evening to end. The clouds had passed on and the night sky sparkled with scattered stars. A lone wolf howled in the distance.

She loved the fresh, clean smell of night in Colorado. As hard as it had been to leave behind the magnolia and oak trees of her youth, she knew she would pine away if she were swept from this new land. It surprised her after so short a time that this was home. She envied Robby a bit, knowing he would grow up in this paradise. Always think of it as home. Marry and raise his family here.

As they entered the outskirts of town, Nora wondered what Silver Bluff would look like by the time her son was her own age. Would it be part of the United States, with bustling crowds flowing along paved sidewalks, the latest fashions displayed in a corner window? Would there be a milliner's and a school and a feed store? New homes and several churches?

And where would Jack Duncan be? Would he still be sheriff, the white streak along his temple blended into a mane of white? Or would he be a man who went bald, complete with a paunch and bags under his eyes? Somehow, Nora doubted the wide shoulders would bend in a stoop. He would cut as fine a figure in twenty years as he did now.

They continued along the main street, noise from the saloon floating across the night air.

"Do you mind if we check in at the jail?"

She shook her head, trying to clear the flights of fancy from her head. She was certain she could—as soon as Jack Duncan's fingers left.

"I guess it's convenient to have your office across from the nearest watering hole."

He laughed. "That's by design. Most trouble starts at the saloon. Not much of a walk to bring any rowdies across the street and lock 'em up for the night."

"Does that happen often?"

"Just about every Saturday night. That's why I wanted to go this way. It's early yet but I didn't think it'd hurt to breeze by and make my presence known."

Actually, Jack was thinking of any way to prolong this evening. He hadn't pursued a woman in years, and now Nora Cantrelle was all he'd thought about this past week. What had this Southern belle done to him? He hadn't been himself since she'd arrived in town.

Anyone who vaguely knew him would think he'd been chomping on loco weed for breakfast. One minute he couldn't stand to be in her presence. Her smooth drawl would prickle his conscience, and he would remember his baby brothers and how they would never live to marry and have children, much less leave their marks on the world. The next minute he vacillated into a simpering fool, wishing Nora would favor him with one of her sweet smiles.

It was enough to drive a man to drink. Or worse.

It had been agony walking alone with her in the moonlight. Her very nearness caused his blood to pump loudly in his ears until he couldn't hear himself think. She smelled like water lilies tonight, sweet and fresh. He longed to nuzzle her throat and inhale her intoxicating scent up close.

They reached his office. Jack had every intention of asking her to wait at his desk in safety while he made a quick turn around the boisterous saloon. Then he would be free to escort her back to the hotel.

Instead, he caught sight of the swell of her bosom. The curve of her throat. Something in him broke. He threw open the door, grabbed Nora's wrist, and pulled her inside as he kicked the door behind them shut. Without any thought to the consequences, he pulled her into his arms. "There's not a woman in all Colorado that can hold a candle to you."

His mouth came down on hers. Hard. His arms tightened around her. He could feel her heart thumping wildly against his chest as he crushed her to him. She tried to speak but as her mouth opened, he slipped his tongue inside.

She tasted like honey, rich and sweet. He'd dreamed of her, night after night, but the reality of kissing her was earth-shattering. Desire coursed through him. He'd never wanted a woman more.

The heat grew between them, his kiss more demanding. He wanted to know her. All of her. As he drank from her sweetness, one hand clasped her nape, his thumb rubbing back and forth across the smooth skin. The other cupped her breast. She made a sound, stirring his desire as his fingers explored her breast, teasing the nipple as it became taut beneath his touch.

He broke the kiss, his lips moving to her jaw,

planting little kisses along it. Then they moved lower, brushing her throat, finding her pulse beating wildly. He licked that spot and she shuddered.

A gunshot shattered the quiet.

He immediately pushed her behind the desk and down to the ground, following her as he unholstered his gun. He cocked it and listened to the noise in the street.

"Stay here," he warned. "It's probably the usual Saturday night rabble-rousing but I want to be sure."

Laughter sounded, followed by the sound of shattering glass. Though his body remained tense, he broke into a smile. Muffled voices spoke and then more laughter filtered through the night.

He stood. "Sounds like Casey Lowell again. He's always threatening to shoot his mule. I need to take care of this. Will you be all right?"

She nodded and he helped her to the chair next to his desk. He strode quickly to the door and went outside.

Nora shivered. She brought a hand to her mouth and brushed her fingertips against her lips, lips that had only moments before been next to Jack Duncan's. He'd told her the Kesslers were dangerous—but what about him? Silver Bluff's sheriff was the most dangerous man she'd ever met. She'd been foolish enough to kiss him not once but twice.

Those kisses shook her to her core.

She was frightened. Jack Duncan stirred feelings in her that shouldn't surface. Not now, not ever. She was a respectable widow with a child to raise and a newspaper to launch. She had no business getting involved with a stranger, albeit a devastatingly handsome one. Gossip could kill her reputation and certainly harm the paper before it even got off the ground.

She wouldn't be alone with him again. That was the simple solution. She hadn't enjoyed marriage the first time around. She doubted a man like Jack Duncan would offer marriage anyway. Let him ply another woman with his kisses. She was not interested.

Loud groans came from the other side of the door. Nora could hear Jack's voice over the crowd.

"Show's over, folks. Get back to your business. Better yet, go on home."

He returned to his office with a man in a headlock, casually dragging him across the room as if this were an everyday occurrence. She didn't know whether she was shocked more by the sheriff's actions or the sour stench that now permeated the room. She hadn't realized another human could smell so foul from so far away.

The drunken man hiccupped loudly and caught sight of her.

"Evenin', pretty lady," he slurred through bloated lips.

Her eyes widened. She was grateful when Jack slipped a set of keys from his pocket and used them to open a cell door.

"Sleep it off, Lowell," he said cheerfully to the drunk who collapsed on the cot, rubbing his head.

"Damned mule. Almost bit my ear off."

Jack chuckled as he closed the barred door and locked it again. "I heard it was the other way around."

He crossed to Nora and casually asked, "Shall we go?"

She wondered how he could be so calm. Between the kiss and the gunshot, the blood still raced through her veins. She raised her chin a notch. "Yes. It's been a long night." She was glad she sounded composed.

He took her arm and walked her straight to the hotel.

"Nora—"

"Sheriff," she interrupted, "I appreciate the escort home. However, I feel we must come to an understanding."

He frowned at her as she took a cleansing breath and plunged ahead.

"I think you have received quite the wrong impression of me. You have now kissed me twice. Both times uninvited, I might add. I need to set the record straight. Although I realize you have become a friend of my father's, I do not look to you for any type of friendship. Especially in that respect. I am not interested in pursuing any kind of relationship with a man. I—"

"Miz Nora! Am I glad to see you."

They turned and saw Ben coming down the steps to the lobby.

"Master Robby's got a fever. He woke up all hot about an hour ago." The servant mopped his brow with a handkerchief. "Jess has been with him but you knows how a boy wants his mama."

"Excuse me, Sheriff." Nora avoided directly looking at him. "Thank you for accompanying me home." She turned to walk up the steps.

"I'll come with you."

Hadn't she made herself perfectly clear? Politely but firmly, she said, "Thank you. That won't be necessary." She lifted her skirts and took the first step up, but he was at her side, his hand cupping her elbow.

"I'd like to look in on the boy, if it's all right. If need be, I can fetch Doc Malone for you."

She studied his determined expression. There didn't seem to be any point in telling him she could always send Ben. Besides, Robby was crazy about this man. Maybe it would lift his spirits to see him a moment or two.

"If you wish."

They hurried to Robby's side. Jess sat next to him, a damp rag in her hand.

"Happened all of a sudden, Miss Nora. He started moaning in his sleep and thrashing around."

Nora bent and placed her open palm on her son's

forehead. It was scalding hot. A quick surge of panic flooded her. It did every time Robby fell ill.

She always worried that she would lose him. She tried to quell her alarm. After all, it was only a fever. Robby always took sick suddenly, but he was almost always over it by the next day. Surely, this time would be no different.

"Thank you for taking care of him, Jess. Why don't you and Ben try to get some rest now? I'll call if I need you." She hoped her voice sounded more confident than she felt. "I'll let you know if there's any change."

The servants slipped from the room. Jack pulled up a chair on the other side of the bed as she dipped a rag in a basin of cool water. She twisted the water from it and placed it on Robby's head. She took his hand in hers, refusing to believe anything would happen to her boy.

They sat for almost an hour before Robby began moving restlessly. She'd almost forgotten Jack was there. He found a second cloth, and they worked together bathing the boy's limbs in silence. Finally, after several hours of their ministrations, Robby seemed to settle back into a deeper, more peaceful sleep. Nora breathed a sigh of relief as she touched his brow.

"The fever's broken." She soothed Robby's eyebrows with her thumb and caressed his cheek. His even breathing comforted her.

Suddenly, the tears that had threatened to spill earlier streamed down her cheeks. She pushed back her chair and stood abruptly. Not wanting Jack to see them, she turned away.

Almost immediately, warm hands rested on her shoulders. "Go ahead and cry."

He pivoted her so she faced him and wrapped his arms about her. A sob escaped and she buried her face against his chest.

Nora didn't know how long they remained that way.

She heard Jack speaking, but the words all ran together. They were comforting, though, gentle and quiet.

She finally raised her face and wiped one cheek with the back of her hand. "I'm sorry. I seemed to have made a mess on your shirt."

He shrugged. "It'll dry." He looked into her eyes. "I know the boy means the world to you."

She swallowed hard. "I didn't realize I wore my heart on my sleeve, Sheriff."

"Jack," he said softly and slipped his hand around hers.

She wanted to object but she was so tired. Her weariness stemmed as much from lack of sleep as from the worry that invaded her when she saw Robby lying on the bed, so small and sick.

Jack ushered her to the other side of the bed and backed her against the mattress. "You need to get some rest now." The minute her knees made contact with it, she collapsed.

He gently guided her down to the inviting pillow. She could feel her boots' laces being loosened and then lifted from her feet. A quilt was placed across her. She wanted to protest at his ministrations. They were so personal. Had he not heard a word she said earlier? Nora fought to keep her eyes open, but they refused to do so.

Her last conscious thought was of a soft kiss pressed against her brow.

CHAPTER 15

Nora awoke and immediately reached for Robby, eager to see if the fever had returned. The place next to her was empty, yet still warm to her touch. She sat up in a panic, worried that he'd fallen ill again. Where could he be?

She bolted to the door, only to hear her son's laughter coming through the thin walls. She sighed in relief and walked down the corridor to the next room.

Robby sat upon Ben's knee, his arm around Ben's neck, a smile on his face.

"Mama!"

Robby caught sight of her and slid from his friend's lap. He hugged her waist tightly.

"I was real sick, Mama. I ain't never been so hot."

"I've never been so hot," Nora automatically corrected. "Yes, you were a sick boy. What I'm wondering is why you're out of bed."

He looked at her, appealing. "But I'm all better now, Mama. Jack said so."

Jack.

She remembered his touch as she drifted off to sleep.

"Jack said he'll take me and Tien fishing again real soon. He said we were naturals, Mama, and next time

we could take what we caught back to his place and fry
'em up and have a feast. Do you think—"

"I think that you need to be in bed, young man."

"Ah, that's for babies."

"Bed is for babies and sick little boys."

"But I ain't—"

Nora used her best Sister Mary Joseph look. She had
been the recipient of it more times than she wished to
remember, but it came in handy when she needed
Robby to do something he balked at.

"All right," he mumbled. "But I'm not a baby."

"You are my baby until you die, Robby Cantrelle.
That's how all mothers feel about their children."

"I bet Jack's mama doesn't think he's a baby." He
plodded to the door and dutifully opened it to return to
his bed.

Nora tried to sweeten the pot a little. "I'll read to
you if you like."

Robby's eyes lit up and he scurried back to their
room. She told Ben, "I think we'll skip church today.
He's still weak despite all his bravado. Later, I might try
to order him a bath."

"That'll make him feel mighty fine, Miss Nora. You
go ahead now."

She did her best to casually ask, "When did Sheriff
Duncan leave?"

"Not ten minutes ago, I'd reckon. He brought
Master Robby over when he woke up so you could get a
little more shut-eye." Ben smiled. "He a fine fellow, that
sheriff."

Nora swallowed hard, confused by her sudden rush
of emotions. She nodded and returned to her room.
Robby had already propped up the pillows and had
three books scattered across the bed.

"You can pick, Mama. I like all of these best."

She chose one at random and began to read, but her
mind kept wandering. Did Jack still have a mother?

What did she make of her grown son? Where was she now?

"Mama, you keep messing up," Robby complained. He took the book. "I'll read it to you."

She settled against the pillows, her arm around her son, concentrating as best she could on the adventures of Hans Brinker.

⊙⊰⊙

JACK ROTATED HIS NECK AS HE WALKED TO THE JAIL, rubbing at the soreness in it. It was early yet, and he enjoyed the quiet of the summer morning. The only noise was his boots scuffing in the dirt as he made his way down the deserted street.

He opened the door only to have the silence ruined by Casey Lowell's snoring. Jack slammed the door, hoping to disrupt the drunk's sleep, but the wheezing went on undisturbed.

He pulled a ring of keys from his pocket and unlocked the cell door, swinging it wide. Lowell was on his back, his mouth opened and showing the few teeth that remained.

His booted foot nudged the drunk. "Wake up, Lowell."

The man yawned broadly and peered at him with one eye. "Is that damned mule dead?"

He shook his head. "Nope. I think you'd better sell it. Less trouble that way."

Lowell sat up and groaned. His hands went to his temples and rubbed tenderly. His stomach growled and his hands traveled downward to rub it, too.

"Need some grub."

"Be sure you get some. Stay off the sauce," Jack warned. "If you don't, someone'll get hurt."

Lowell shuffled by him. He smelled the sour stench of too much whiskey and months-old sweat.

"And take a bath," he called. "Might improve your disposition."

The old drunk stopped. "My disposition's just fine, Sheriff. It's Gertrude's that needs workin' on."

He shuffled out. Jack wondered if that was his true gait or if the old codger stayed drunk all the time.

He picked up the blanket that lay on the cot. It would have to be laundered. Old Casey's odor clung to it. He tossed it over by the door before locking the cell door again.

Jack consulted his pocket watch and decided to shave here, rather than make the trek home. Sometimes he stayed overnight if the situation called for it. He always kept a clean shirt and a razor handy. He went out back to fetch some water for his shave. Better cold water than a dry shave, although he would've preferred the water warmed.

The war had taught him how to focus on a task, blocking out all else. He used that skill to his advantage now. It wouldn't do to appear in public with nicks covering his face from carelessness. He would only think about the blade and removing the whiskers that already dotted his cheeks.

He would not think about Nora Cantrelle.

Jack finished shaving and tossed the water out back. He changed into the clean shirt, adding the old one to Casey's blanket. It was almost time to take his laundry over to Quon Lee Son anyway. The man pressed and starched Jack's shirts to perfection.

"Better than a wife could," he declared aloud to the empty room.

He left to walk over to the church but passed it by. He didn't really want to go in. After passing three times, the pull of the music lured him inside. He stood at the back, arms crossed, as the hymn drew to a close. Reverend Seabury winked at him. He felt guilty for being in church. You weren't supposed to come to

God's house with lust in your heart—and his heart was full of lust for a Southerner, if that didn't beat all.

He recalled watching Nora as she slept. Her chest rising and falling in a soothing rhythm. Her face was that of an angel, all soft and pretty, full of sweet innocence. It took every ounce of control not to reach out and stroke her cheek. She and Robby were a tender picture together. It brought longing for a family to the surface again.

Jack slipped from the church. He'd get a quick fix for his longings at the saloon. Lola would be just the thing. As he hurried down the empty street, though, he realized it was Sunday morning. The girls would all be fast asleep after a busy Saturday night. And he was in no mood for Marguerite's probing, should she be awake.

He decided to head home. Before long, he was frying up eggs and bacon, which brought brief satisfaction. He tried to read for a while but he couldn't concentrate on the words and returned the book to its place on the shelf.

He couldn't understand his restlessness. What had Nora done to him? He could count the times he'd spent with her on one hand yet those few incidents seemed some of the most important encounters he'd experienced. He liked Albert and he was already crazy about Robby.

What did it mean?

Jack was afraid he already knew the answer to his question. He wasn't certain if he was ready to think about it, much less act upon it. And what about her declaration when they'd reached the hotel last night? That his kisses had been unwelcome. Well, maybe he hadn't asked but she sure hadn't stopped him. He knew she'd taken as much pleasure in them as he had. Why would she go from enjoying them one minute to telling him to mind her own business the next?

Women.

He could stew over this for hours and had no intention of wasting such a pretty day on gloomy thoughts. Given a million years by the Good Lord, he might never figure Nora Cantrelle out.

Instead, he went to his shed. He would start on her kitchen set. Might as well be productive. He'd always been able to comfort himself with a plank or two.

Jack threw out a tarp to work on and chose the block of wood he wanted. Based on what she'd said last night, he would use the last design she'd looked over. He lined up his tools, perched on his stool and began.

He lost himself in the pleasure of the wood. Its smell. Its color and shape. The feel of it in his hands. Wood meant magic to him. He forgot all his problems when touching it. Carving had helped him survive his many losses. His brothers' and parents' deaths. Felicity's betrayal. His innocence given up during the war. Wood soothed his soul.

Right now, it was all he wanted to touch.

CHAPTER 16

Nora stood in the center of the room, the smell of new wood and fresh paint invading her nose. Home. The sweetest smell imaginable. Life in a hotel room had gotten old fast.

Her eyes swept over the walls with pride. Harve Nelson beat his promised deadline. With his original crew and overtime from several helpful miners, the house was now complete. She and Papa had spent two days in Denver choosing a few pieces of furniture that would arrive tomorrow. Eventually, they would add more as they could afford it.

Harve's crew had also finished the newspaper office. On the same trip to Denver, they arranged for the presses held in storage to be delivered during the next two days. Ben was waiting for them round-the-clock, eager to begin work. He would do the heavy set-up while Albert fine-tuned things. Nora had given Jess a free hand in setting up the household because her own time would be devoted to working on the first edition. She had people to interview and stories to write. Their goal was to begin a print run two weeks from today. Fortunately, subscriptions to the new venture had sold like hotcakes.

"I love it, Nora." Marguerite walked through the doorway, her admiration obvious. Albert trailed her, much like a puppy eagerly dogging his master's steps.

"It did turn out nicely." She looked at her father and hid a smile. Marguerite had been a constant companion to them both these last few weeks. She was easy to talk to and had made all kinds of suggestions for story ideas, having lived in the area several years. She knew something about everything going on in Silver Bluff and the surrounding areas.

Nora wondered if their first lead story might be a wedding announcement and wondered how the town would view its new editor taking the local madam in holy matrimony. Actually, she didn't think it would raise much fuss. Besides Mrs. Simmons, Nora found most very accepting. She had learned from Marguerite that many former soiled doves took husbands and were received in polite society with no problems, further distinguishing her new home from Monroe.

She'd also discovered the scant women in Silver Bluff had a soft spot for Marguerite. She'd taken tea with Mrs. Seabury and Mrs. Malone a few days earlier and mentioned that her father and Marguerite were keeping company.

"Mrs. Le Beau has such a kind heart," Iris Malone told her. "A cave-in occurred several months after we arrived in town. One miner was seriously injured. Mrs. Le Beau saw to his medical expenses and even allowed him to stay above the saloon while he was on the mend."

"Of course, he could never go back to mining," Anne Seabury piped in. "He became the barkeep."

Mrs. Malone had striven to finish her story. "He recently married and moved to Denver. I hear he's working in a dry goods store and has become a church deacon."

"It's not the first time she's helped those in need," Mrs. Seabury pointed out. "She's been very discreet, but I could confide several other instances of her kindness." The reverend's wife smiled at Nora. "Your father may be just the man she's needed."

She had to agree—especially as Marguerite brought a spring into Albert's step that had been sorely lacking. He seemed more energetic these days. Between his happiness and this new house, Nora knew their move West would bring a contentment that had been missing. They only had to launch the newspaper and hope for its success.

"Good morning to you, Miss Nora Cantrelle."

Chin Lee and Sung Moon stood in the open doorway, both beaming.

"Come in." Nora shook Chin's hand, as was their custom, but she gave Sung Moon an affectionate hug. She had come to know the Lees well. Tien was always underfoot, and she had come to think of him—and the Lees—as extended family.

"I brought this for you." Sung Moon thrust a basket with a handle at her. She removed the red-checkered napkin from the top and took a whiff.

"That smells heavenly."

"It's chicken dumplings. Mr. Kessler says I make them better than his granny." She smiled shyly.

"Then stay and we'll eat them together."

"No, no," Chin protested. "We must go to the general store and stock up. Mr. Kessler needs many things. We can visit more later when you're ready for company."

"Thank you for the dumplings," Albert said. "I've missed home cooking the most. We will have you over for a meal as soon as we get settled."

The couple nodded and turned to go, but Jack Duncan blocked their way.

"Morning, folks. See you've got a full crew." He

looked around the room, his eyes avoiding Nora. "Got your table and chairs done. Thought they'd come in handy."

She shivered despite the heat of the day. Since that night when he'd kissed her at the jail, Jack had acted as if she carried the plague. He was cordial but kept his distance and made sure they were never alone together. She had asked him to leave her be. He had been respectful enough to do so.

Why did that bother her so much?

Had she imagined the feelings that passed between them? When she thought back to that night, it all seemed hazy now.

She was better off without him. An exciting time lay ahead, between launching the newspaper and preparing lessons for Robby and Tien. She'd promised the Lees that she would see to both boys' education until the town hired a teacher. The school would soon be completed. As things stood, she had no time for a fickle sheriff.

No matter how good-looking he was.

As she watched him from the corners of her eyes, Nora wondered if she'd made a mistake. She remembered the feel of his mouth on hers. The quickening of her heart. His hands pushing through her hair. A part of her ached, wishing she could take back the words she'd spoken.

The Lees took their leave. Tien and Robby went with them. Marguerite and Albert excused themselves to return to unpacking Albert's books in his study. Nora found herself in awkward silence with Jack Duncan, who seemed fascinated by the floorboards that ran alongside his boots.

"I suppose you can bring the table and chairs in now." She took pride in how even and neutral her voice sounded.

"All right."

Jack retreated to a wagon parked in front of their house. She sucked in her breath as she saw Ken Kessler making his way up the path. He'd been underfoot since the night they'd had dinner at his brother's house. It seemed every time she looked up, Ken Kessler was there, stopping by to say hello or asking how the building was going. He'd wanted to know what kind of stories they expected to run in the first edition and how often they would publish.

Nora imagined at least half of the instances were contrived. She had successfully put off his more-than-friendly overtures so far, but his invitations had become more persistent. The last thing she needed was some slick rich boy courting her. She'd rather have drunk Casey Lowell as her beau. Or better yet, his mule.

Kessler entered carrying a large crate in his hands, which he set on the ground. Jack Duncan followed him in, a chair in his hands. He placed the chair down and put one foot on the tarp covering it, idly studying the situation.

"Brought you a housewarming gift, Mrs. Cantrelle. Mrs. Simmons helped me choose the items."

Ken flashed a brilliant smile, which she realized would melt most women's hearts. It left her cold—and any gift Mrs. Simmons had a hand in left her suspicious.

"If you've got a crowbar handy, I'll uncrate it."

"What is it?"

"Kitchen items. Mrs. Simmons figured you needed a few things."

Nora shifted uneasily from one foot to the other. "It's very kind of you, Mr. Kessler, but I'm afraid it's simply far too much to accept."

"No, ma'am, I insist. Just look upon this gift to your family as from both William and me." His eyes narrowed. "You wouldn't want to offend my brother. He's a powerful man and a good ally to have. Surely it wouldn't be worth spoiling our friendship over an iron skillet or two?"

She hesitated. "If you put it that way..."

"I know it'll all be put to good use." He cocked his head to one side. "I've heard Mrs. Malone and Mrs. Seabury mention what a fine cook you are. Perhaps you could repay me by fixing me a meal . . . or something?"

Nora immediately picked up on his suggestive tone. What had her attention, though, was the fire she glimpsed in Jack Duncan's eyes. She wasn't imagining that. The man oozed hostility

All directed at Ken Kessler.

Maybe those kisses had meant more than he let on. Just maybe, she'd found a way to show him that she'd changed her mind. Nora decided to see what would happen if Jack were pushed a little. She decided to flirt openly with her would-be suitor.

"I do love to cook, Mr. Kessler. I find it very . . . relaxing." She looked up at him through her thick lashes and saw the interest in his eyes. "Perhaps you could come for dinner one night next week."

Kessler grinned wolfishly. "You can count on it, Mrs. Cantrelle."

She giggled. "Oh, please, call me Nora. I've heard that the West doesn't stand on formality. We're all such close neighbors here in Silver Bluff."

"Yes, indeed." He looked at her hungrily. For a moment, the unveiled desire Nora saw frightened her. She'd never played the coquette in her life. Too late, she realized what a bad idea this had been.

Then she looked at Jack and saw trouble. His face was a blank mask except for the raw anger in his eyes. He looked ready to take someone apart. She didn't know who his first victim would be—her or Ken Kessler. But she was certain now that Jack Duncan was anything but neutral toward her. She knew she was far from impartial toward him. Probably more than was good for her.

In ignorance, Kessler chose that moment to leave. "I've got business to attend to, Nora." He took her hand in his. She prayed he didn't feel its slight tremble. "I look forward to that dinner." He touched his lips briefly to her knuckles before he released her hand. "Goodbye."

Jack averted his face and turned to retrieve another chair from the wagon. He swore to control his temper and get every piece in the house before he strangled Nora Cantrelle.

"Good day, Sheriff," Kessler said as he sauntered by him, a smug smile on his face. For a moment, Jack had thoughts of throwing out a foot. Seeing this preening cock sprawled on the ground would be a nice start. He did, however, like being sheriff of Silver Bluff, and kept both feet close to his body.

He brought in the rest of his work, one piece at a time, unwrapping each from the tarp that lay protectively around it to prevent any scratches on the short trip over. He didn't speak to Nora in the process.

As he climbed from the wagon with the last chair, he still hadn't decided if he would throttle the little minx or stare at her until she turned into a pillar of salt.

Then it hit him as hard as a mud landslide. Nora had acted entirely out of character.

She had been deliberately flirting with Kessler.

Jack smiled.

Nora Cantrelle wanted *him*. Not Kessler. Him. Else she wouldn't have behaved so outrageously.

He'd avoided thinking about Nora for an entire week and had ignored all the longings she stirred within him. He'd tried to play the gentleman and respect her wishes. He didn't know what had changed her mind. And didn't really care at this point. All he knew was the woman had let him know she was interested. He wasn't about to disappoint her.

He stepped through the door with the last chair in hand and watched as she laid her palm flat on the table's surface and reverently stroked the wood.

He saw a look in her eyes, an appreciation for both his own talent and the end result that he'd never seen before, and probably wouldn't again in his lifetime.

"You put a lot of yourself into this, Jack. Thank you."

A warm feeling washed over him.

Nora pulled out a chair and ran her hand along its back before she sat in it. She closed her eyes, a wisp of a smile playing about her mouth. She looked right in that chair. In fact, everything about her seemed right.

He realized it didn't matter where she came from or what had happened to either of them before this moment. The past was the past. His future was with this woman.

Might as well make a start.

Nora was just opening her eyes when Jack placed his hands around her waist and pulled her from the chair. She gasped as he swung her around and placed her next to the wall. He planted both hands flat on each side of her, hemming her in.

"You will never lift a finger to feed Ken Kessler. If I can help it, you'll never be in the same room as Mr. Kessler. You will not bat your eyelashes at him or give him coquettish smiles.

"And you will definitely not..." His voice faded away. He could only look at her. A shining light appeared in those emerald eyes, one that radiated passion and heat. It was even better than the look she'd given his furniture.

"Yes, Sheriff?" She deliberately fluttered her lashes.

Jack grinned lazily. "You will definitely not go for

more than a day at a time without being thoroughly kissed."

Her eyes widened. "By whom?"

"Who do you think?"

His mouth came down on hers and he felt her smile.

CHAPTER 17

Jack thought their mouths were a perfect fit. An electricity ran through him as he touched her. It had been nothing like that with Felicity. This woman was all heat, bringing a liquid warmth that raced through his veins until he was on fire.

He placed his hands next to her face, marveling at her smooth complexion. Then before he knew it, his fingers pushed into her honeyed hair as he'd imagined a hundred times, only this was far better. As her pins fell to the floor, he ran his hands through the spun silk. Her hair fell in soft waves to her waist. His hands followed there and back up.

He deepened the kiss, pressing his body against hers, crushing her breasts against his chest, his hands still buried in her hair. If he spent eternity like this, it wouldn't be long enough.

He finally broke the kiss, his breathing harsh and heavy. Jack rested his forehead against hers, his eyes closed. If he was drained after one kiss, what would making love to this woman be like?

"We need to talk." He looked over his shoulder. The only furniture was what he'd brought in earlier. He also didn't know if or when Marguerite and Albert might walk in. He decided they needed more privacy.

Taking Nora's hand, he led her outside. Harve had built a wraparound porch and it was here Jack helped her sit down, along the steps that led up the porch itself.

He kept her hand in his, their fingers laced together. As he gazed at her, her eyes glimmered with unspent passion. Her mouth trembled. Her hair was still mussed.

She was the most beautiful creature he'd ever laid eyes on.

"We don't know each other well," he began. "Maybe that's best. We've both got a past that probably needs to stay there." He sighed. "At least we'll have a fresh start together."

"What does that . . .mean?"

He noticed how her voice quavered. How the pulse point in her throat fluttered. How those brilliant green eyes now narrowed, and a slight furrow creased her brow.

Jack squeezed her hand. "It means marriage, love. Spending the rest of our lives together, discovering just who we are together. Learning all about each other and accepting what's to come in our hearts."

Nora pulled away from him and stood. She began pacing the length of the porch, mumbling to herself, her arms wrapped protectively about her. He let her think it through as she walked back and forth. Finally, she halted in front of him.

"This is too much, too fast, Jack Duncan." She pushed her hair from her face. "I've got a newspaper to start up, Robby to care for. Papa depends upon me to—"

"You want time?" He leaped to his feet and cupped her elbows, holding her still a moment. "You have it. You want to be courted? I'll do it. But," he said, swallowing the catch in his voice, "I won't be made a fool of." Even now, he couldn't escape the ghost of Felicity's betrayal.

Nora lay a hand against his chest. "You're nobody's fool, Jack," she said softly.

"I like how you say my name." He leaned down and gently pressed his lips against hers.

She broke the kiss. "You promise that we'll spend time getting to know one another?"

He nodded. "I figure by Christmas we ought to know each other well enough."

How he could hold out from loving her until Christmas would be a miracle, but he'd worry about that later.

"I want us to be a family by then. I promise you, Nora, that I will love Robby as my own. Hopefully, we can even make a few more."

Her instant look of panic surprised him. He wrapped his arms around her, pulling her head against his shoulder. He felt hot tears through his shirt.

What the hell was going on? Whatever it was, he would help her get over it. Maybe she'd had a hard time carrying Robby to term. He'd ask Albert later, though how he was going to bring up that particular subject to Nora's father would be interesting, to say the least.

She lifted her head and turned to him. "You don't mind if . . . that . . . I've been married before?"

"No," he said quietly. "That was your past. The future is what we make it." He stroked her hair reassuringly.

She gave him a crooked smile, her eyes brimming with unshed tears. "Robby will be pleased. He already talks about you constantly. Jack this, Jack that."

"Was he close to his daddy?"

He felt her stiffen. "No," she said after a moment. "Why?"

Jack shrugged. "I was wondering if he would ever want to call me Daddy."

She cried out and grabbed on to him tightly. A fresh flood of tears fell down her porcelain cheeks.

"Oh, honey." He wiped them away, only to have them replaced by a river of new ones. Finally, he brought her head back to his shoulder. "It's all right," he muttered soothingly, stroking her hair.

He let her cry out whatever needed to be released. She reached up and wiped her eyes with the back of her hand. "I'm sorry. I'm a mess."

He lifted her chin. "You're beautiful to me."

She gave him a smile that would light up the darkest night. "No one but Papa has ever said that."

"Then all your admirers were blind or fools. Or both." It made him all the more curious to speak with Albert. "Tell you what. Why don't you go wash your face? I need to get back to town. We'll talk more later."

She nodded. He gave her a swift kiss and escorted her into the house. Jess stood there, her mouth agape.

"Why, Sheriff, you outdid yourself! The furniture's beautiful. I can't wait to sit and break cornbread at this table."

"I enjoyed making it, Jess."

He watched her glance up at Nora and then do a double-take. Jess started to speak but then went to Nora and put an arm about her waist.

"It's a big day for us, Miss Nora. And we have so much left to do."

"Is everything packed at the hotel?"

Jess nodded. "Mr. Nelson told me he'd put our things on one of his wagons and have someone bring it all over."

Marguerite and Albert walked in, both looking a little dusty but with an air of joy about them. They admired the new table and chairs. Jack caught a questioning glance from Marguerite, and he nodded at her. She broke into a huge smile.

She walked to Nora and linked their arms. "Let's see what else needs to be done."

Jack offered to open up what Kessler had brought. All three women peered over his shoulder and admired all the goodies the crate contained, except for the dull orange cup towels.

Marguerite lifted one up for closer inspection. "I declare these are the most godawful color I've ever seen." She tossed it back into the crate.

Jess picked it up and shook her head. "I don't want to know what Mr. Kessler paid for this. 'Cause whatever it was..." She shook her head, not even finishing the sentence.

Nora spoke up, a wry smile on her face. "When Jess was busy the other day, I went to choose material for new curtains in the house. I remarked to Mrs. Simmons how much I disliked orange. 'Give me anything but orange,' I declared." She shrugged.

He gritted his teeth. "That woman is the biggest meddler I've ever seen. Do you want me to take them back? Seymour'll give you a store credit."

"No," Nora said. "I won't give her the satisfaction of knowing she offended me." She brightened. "I'll take them to Ben. His hands always get filthy when he's setting type. A few days of removing ink from his hands and we won't even know these towels' original color."

Jack looked at her. "If you're sure." She nodded.

"We've got us a mess of work to do," Jess declared.

"Then we need to get started," Marguerite agreed. "Although after going through all those books with Albert, I need to wash my hands."

"If you ladies are going to deal with household affairs, I think I will accompany our fine sheriff back into town. I want to see if any deliveries have been made at the office."

Jack clapped Albert on the back. This was better

167

than he could have orchestrated. "Let's go, Albert. We've got a lot to talk about."

Nora flashed him a panicked look. He grinned at her. She blushed a bright red and spun on her heels, heading for the kitchen without a backward glance.

The two men walked to the wagon and climbed in. Jack took the reins and started off.

"You seem a bit out of breath, Albert."

The editor waved a hand at him. "Need to take a little break. That Marguerite'll wear a man out."

Jack chuckled. "Exactly what's going on between the two of you?"

Albert raised his brows. "Going on? Does it look like something's going on?"

He laughed. "It certainly does."

"Well, there's a little bit going on," Albert admitted, his eyes sparkling. "There's a whole lot more I'd like to see happen," he declared.

"Are you going to make an honest woman of her?"

Albert nodded. "I am. She may not know it yet, but she'll be Marguerite Le Fall before the year's out." He paused. "Haven't said a word to Nora yet."

Jack frowned. "Do you think she'll object?"

"Nora? Oh, good heavens, no. It's just a lot for her to adjust to, is all."

He grinned. "Well, Nora might be talking to you about something."

Albert looked expectantly at him. "Such as?"

He concentrated on the road ahead. "She and I have come to an understanding."

"About?"

"That we'll be spending a lot of time getting to know one another. That by Christmas, she and Robby will be moving in with me."

"Are you going to make an honest woman of her?"

Jack smiled as Albert echoed his question. "Yes, sir. I hope she'll make an honest man out of me."

Albert offered his hand. "I admire you. You're taking on one stubborn woman, but she has a good heart. You won't regret it."

They pulled up outside the jail. Jack planned to take the wagon home later. "Care to come in a minute?"

Albert agreed. Jack hitched the horse to the rail. Almost every day since the old man had arrived in town, the two of them talked, usually over a glass of whiskey he kept in his bottom drawer. This time was no different.

Albert opened the drawer and removed the bottle while Jack retrieved two shot glasses. Albert poured the amber liquor into each.

"What's on your mind, Jack?"

"Nora's first husband."

Albert picked up the bottle again. He added enough so that each glass was now at the brim. Jack looked at him questioningly.

"We'll need it." Albert picked up his glass carefully and took a sip. "Is this just natural curiosity? Or is there more to it?"

"More." Jack lifted his own drink and took a small swallow. The liquid burned going down. He wasn't much of a drinker, but if the whiskey would help Albert share confidences, he'd drink the entire bottle with him.

Albert leaned back in his chair. "Where do I begin?" He settled himself and took another sip.

"Paul Cantrelle was the second son of the richest planter in the area. His people went way back. Paul was about two years older than Nora, but from the time they were children, they were as thick as thieves."

He laughed. "Not that the Cantrelles were pleased about that. We Le Falls were not quite of their social circle, so to speak." Albert toyed with the glass in his hand. "I think Paul was attracted to her spirit. Nora always was eager to learn and try new things. Didn't mind being in trouble with the nuns at school. Would stand up to anyone bullying someone weaker. Yes, my Nora was quite a spitfire. Still is," he chuckled.

"They married without his family's approval?"

"Pretty much. They became engaged on Nora's sixteenth birthday. I insisted they wait two years. I thought things might change. And they did. War broke out weeks later. The South was full of idiotic young men ready to ride out and conquer the world. Most everyone around Monroe thought we'd whup them Yankees in a matter of weeks."

Albert paused. "Sorry, Jack."

He nodded. Many of the men in their surrounding area had felt the same. He'd actually lived in Virginia when the war broke out, but his pocket of mountain folk had always taken issue with the cause of slavery. Things grew so heated that his entire part of the state broke off and entered the Union as West Virginia. He understood the mentality of those eager to fight the war.

Albert took a sip of his drink. "Paul insisted on going off to experience the glories of war. Didn't have to, mind you, being a planter's son, but he'd always been second in his daddy's eyes. Maybe he thought if he came back a hero, his old man would respect him."

"Did they get married after the war?"

"No. During it. They exchanged letters. Nora was as ready as ever to marry, stars in her eyes. Until Paul came home on a brief leave. It was right after Gettysburg."

A chill ran up Jack's spine. He'd been at Gettysburg. He wondered if his path had crossed Paul Cantrelle's during those three godforsaken days.

"Paul came home a changed man. Distant. Quieter than before. Hardened. I suppose that's what war does to a man's soul."

Albert poured more whiskey into their glasses.

"I begged Nora to wait, but she said she owed it to

him. She was worried he wouldn't return. He'd always been a sweet kid, with a gentle nature. Paul convinced her he'd only survived because he wanted to come back to her. He needed her as the reason to keep fighting.

"She was terribly frightened, Jack. She didn't want to go through with the marriage. The boy she'd always known had come back a stranger, but Nora felt honorbound to wed him. Two days later, he returned to the front."

"Did they find any happiness?" he asked softly.

Albert shook his head. "None. She admitted to me after he'd been gone several months that she had wanted him to leave. She was racked with guilt because of it. Said she'd made a terrible mistake. That it was like kissing a brother. She was despondent. Said they'd never have what Ben and Jess had."

He frowned. "Meaning?"

"That was always Nora's gauge, you see. Those two have been deeply in love since I've known them, and that's been over twenty-five years. Nora's mother died when she was little. Genevieve and I wouldn't have been good role models for her anyway. But Ben and Jess were how Nora knew what love was all about. And she didn't have that with Paul."

"I assume she was pregnant when he left?"

Albert nodded. "It was a hard labor, but Robby was all she lived for, then and now. You see, the Cantrelles didn't welcome Nora after the marriage. In fact, they kept doors closed to her that should've been opened once she married into the family. Gossip abounded about how she wanted to be a man, simply because she wrote for my newspaper."

Jack seethed at the words, hating that Nora had suffered at the hands of her in-laws.

"She worked for me. Cared for Robby. Volunteered to nurse the wounded that returned. She kept her mouth shut, though. Never wrote Paul to tell him how shabbily she was treated at home. Didn't want to worry him."

"Did things change when he returned?"

Albert stood up and walked to the window and looked out. "Paul came home minus a leg and arm and without any love in his heart for his wife—much less the child he'd never seen. He was bitter before his time.

"Nora encouraged Paul, but he'd already given up on living. His parents died in the last weeks of the war. His brother, Richard, only visited him once before his death. Didn't offer any financial support either, and Blair Oaks was in much better shape than we were. Paul slept around the clock. When he wasn't sleeping, he was feeling sorry for himself. Ran my girl to the bone. I never saw him touch her again. No love, no affection—only sorrow and misery and complaints all the day long."

A deep ache filled Jack. "How did he die?"

"Finally killed himself. Drank a bottle of laudanum. Nora hid that, but I found out. Never told her, though. Whole town turned out for Paul's funeral. Not one of them had offered an ounce of support during those five years he lived after the war. Not one."

Albert sat heavily in the chair again. He was ashen. The retelling of this story had drained him of his strength. Jack wondered if he should summon the doctor.

"She's suffered, Jack. My girl has love in her heart, but she won't know how to give it to you. I'm surprised you got her to make any kind of commitment at all."

Jack smiled sheepishly. "I'm afraid I blindsided her. She was a little skittish, though, when I mentioned children."

He could see why now. Probably both had been virgins when they consummated their marriage vows. Nora had, in effect, married a total stranger. He doubted Paul had been gentle with her. Then he'd come home a cripple, both in body and mind, and had ignored his wife and child.

Jack was amazed that Nora's spirit endured. His admiration for her grew tenfold. His gut told him deep inside her lay a passionate woman who needed to be roused. He longed to help her discover herself in this way. He would quiet her fears about what physical love meant. They would learn together the beauty of the bonds of love between them.

Albert placed his glass on the desktop. "I better head over to see Ben before I'm too drunk to walk."

He saw that Albert's color had improved but he was still short of breath. "Should you let Doc Malone check you over first?"

"No. I'll be on my way." He stared at Jack a long time. "I'm glad it'll be you taking care of my little girl." He offered his hand to Jack.

"So am I."

CHAPTER 18

William Kessler was aggravated. He had better things to do than try to sweet-talk obstinate homesteaders. That was Ken's job, one in which he'd been fairly successful.

Until Nora Cantrelle came along.

His brother was infatuated with the attractive widow. Kessler could understand why. Just one look at her and he'd been ready to cart the woman off to his bed. Her pure beauty made her seem untouched somehow.

His opinion changed the minute she opened her sweet mouth. While her voice was pleasant, she proved to be opinionated and overeducated. He tolerated neither in his women. Pity, too. A war widow would have made fine window dressing on his arm during the governor's race down the line.

Ken, however, chased her like a dog in heat. He doubted she would know what to do with a rutting fool like his brother. She seemed passionate about her writing, but he didn't see her as particularly sensual. Ken, for all his gentlemanly airs, was base in his desires. He didn't see a long-term relationship for them and had told Ken so. He advised his brother to see his needs met at the saloon because there wouldn't be any lasting happiness with the Cantrelle woman.

That only made a determined Ken dig in his heels. William would give Ken credit for that. He would woo Nora Cantrelle as long as it took, before he took her and used her up. It had always been the same story. William got Ken out of far too many scrapes of the same nature. Why the boy couldn't use his energy on whores was beyond him.

He reined in his horse as he hit the top of the rise and looked out over Seth Appleton's property. It was a nice piece of land. One he had to have. If the railroad came through this way, he would make a killing. That is, *if* he could buy up all the land on its supposed northern route. He prayed to God Tom Morrison's information was correct. Morrison owed him a huge debt. For them both to cash in on a new Denver-to-Casper line would go a long way in fulfilling the obligations of the past.

So far, his venture had been successful. He'd authorized Ken to cut the current homesteaders good deals but not enough to cause suspicion. Most jumped at the generous offer, not caring whom it came from, much less why it had been tendered. He'd recognized this wanderlust among many of the people who came West after the war. They claimed they wanted to put down roots, but they also took off for parts unknown at the drop of a hat. It was odd but it had been very effective for him.

Except for a few holdouts like Appleton. His family came out in '62 when Congress passed the original Homestead Act. Appleton wouldn't budge. Ken had spoken to the farmer on three separate occasions to no avail. That's when he'd decided to step in. Appleton was a leader in the small but growing community. He might convince other homesteaders to stay on. Kessler would see him gone—lock, stock, and barrel.

He cantered down the slope and caught sight of Appleton. He was coming from the barn, a toolbox in his hand. He rode over to the farmer.

"Good day, Mr. Appleton." He tipped his hat for good measure. Wouldn't hurt the farmer to think he actually respected him and the work he did. "I'm William Kessler."

Wariness filled Seth Appleton's eyes. "You the one who took over Stevenson's silver mine?"

"I am." Kessler dismounted and fell into step with Appleton. "I would appreciate a few minutes of your time."

Appleton's eyes narrowed. "Is this about selling out? If it is, I ain't doing it. Your brother done been here nigh on three times now." The man's jaw set, and Kessler could tell he'd already decided to refuse any offer that came his way.

"I'd like to offer you a good price, a more than fair price, for your land."

Appleton shook his head. "My wife's partial to these mountains. Silver Bluff's our home. When all the miners came and went, we stayed and worked this land." He pulled a handkerchief from his pocket and wiped the sweat from his brow. "Done a damned fine job of it, too."

"You're saying that whatever the price is, you won't reconsider?" He stared at Appleton and saw no hesitation in the man's eyes.

"No, sir."

"As a man who works the land knows, things can change pretty fast, Mr. Appleton. You might want to think about that before you turn down my offer. I hope to hear from you by the end of the day."

He watched the farmer's eyes narrow, knowing his message had been received. Whether or not Appleton would act soon enough to suit him was another matter.

Kessler remounted his horse and rode off, kicking up dust as he went. If he hadn't received word of this hick changing his mind by nightfall, drastic measures would be necessary. He smiled. Ken would enjoy that. His brother had no qualms about using force of any kind. He'd proven it time and time again during the war. Hopefully, the Appletons would be the lesson given in order to convince any others of the need to sell.

Whistling, Kessler continued into town and through to the other side. He needed to check with his foreman at the mine. Now was just as good a time as any.

⚜

"JACK, IT WAS A DAMNED THREAT! I KNOW A THREAT when I hear one."

"Calm down, Seth. Take it slowly. From the beginning."

"He wants my land, Jack. He's been buying up property left and right since he arrived." Seth Appleton shook a finger. "He's up to no good, that one and his brother."

"What did he offer you?"

"He done sent his brother out three times, each time sweetening the pot a little more. Hell, I didn't even give him a chance to make an offer this go-around. The answer was gonna be no."

Jack studied Seth. The man had always been level-headed, someone the few farmers that had settled around Silver Bluff could trust. Appleton was a good judge of character. Jack knew from his own investigations that William Kessler had bought quite a bit of land since his arrival.

"How many others haven't sold out yet?"

Seth scratched his head. "Well, lemme see. There's Paxton to the north of me. Leavenworth to the north-west. Don't know about Middleton. Haven't seen the ornery sumbitch in a month of Sundays."

The door opened and Nora walked in. His heart

skipped a beat, just like a schoolboy with a crush on his teacher. She was wearing mint, which only made her eyes even greener. He wished Seth Appleton was a blind man at the moment, because Jack would steal a quick kiss.

"I'm sorry. I'm interrupting."

Seth shook his head. "No, ma'am. You're just the person that needs to know about this."

"I don't think—"

"Let Mr. Appleton finish, Sheriff," Nora said calmly. She turned to Seth. "You were saying?"

"It's that damned Kessler, ma'am, excuse me for saying so. Maybe you and your daddy can do a story about him."

Jack saw intrigue light her face. He'd like to squelch it, but he knew if she talked to enough people, sooner or later she would hear. He just didn't want her charging off blindly, prying into things and getting into all kinds of trouble. Maybe it was better if she found out about it now.

And maybe cows really could jump over the moon.

"Kessler's bought up land since he took over the mine. Not land around the mine, mind you. Land surrounding the town. Especially up to the north, toward Wyoming Territory."

Jack kept quiet that a wider range of property was involved, much of which lay south of Silver Bluff.

Nora had already taken a small tablet from her reticule and was scribbling on it. She looked at Seth. "How much land, Mr. Appleton?"

"I'd say eight, maybe ten homesteads. Offered a pretty price, if you know what I mean. More than the land is worth. Me? I don't aim to go no place. Annie's fond of it here. Why should we be run off our own land?"

Her eyes widened. "Did he threaten you in any way?"

Appleton sighed. "Not in so many words, ma'am. But it was there all the same as we talked." He looked at Jack. "I want something done."

"Not a thing that can be done, Seth. Man's offered you money and you've turned him down. There's been no verbal threat. He's brought no harm to you or your property."

"What if he does?"

"Then we'll do something. I'll check on you every day. You, too, keep your eyes peeled. Don't go anywhere without your shotgun. I'll ride out and visit with your neighbors, see if they've been pressured to sell."

"I'd like to interview you in more depth, Mr. Appleton. If it leads to a story, you might make our first edition of the *Silver Bluff Gazette*."

The homesteader pumped her hand. "Annie'll be tickled pink. Say—does that mean I can get a free copy?"

Nora smiled. "You had already paid your subscription, but I think we could start that up after this first edition."

Appleton beamed. "I gotta go tell Seymour, Mrs. Cantrelle." He opened the door. "Let me place my order and then we can talk a spell."

"When you finish there, please head over to the newspaper's office. We'll conduct the interview there."

The door closed. Jack pulled Nora to him and kissed her soundly. He hoped by doing so it would erase all thoughts of investigating William Kessler.

He'd told her before that he didn't want her to know the Kesslers any better. Now that Seth had whetted her appetite, he doubted his warning would suffice. He needed to do some exploring on his own. If there was something dirty to be found, he wanted to beat Nora to the punch.

"My, Sheriff, what if someone came in?"

He grinned. "Got that all figured out. No one can

see us here behind the door since the window is over there. And if anyone approaches the door, I'll hear his boots when they hit the planks. That gives us a good two, three seconds to pull apart and act like we're almost strangers."

He kissed her again, a more lingering one. Its sweetness left a longing inside of him.

"I want you, Nora," he said huskily.

She tensed slightly. He cupped her face and visibly saw her trying to relax. He knew she waged some inner war with the pleasures her body was experiencing versus what she had known before.

"I can't wait until Christmas, darlin'." He kissed her slowly, his hands stroking her back up and down. He felt any resistance slowly melt. She slipped her arms around his neck and he pulled her close. She smelled like wildflowers today. He smiled.

"When can we get married?"

Nora looked surprised. "I thought you were going to give me some time, Jack. You said we were going to get to know one another."

He slowly massaged her shoulders and the nape of her neck. "I know all I need to know. You're smart. A good mother." He paused, a wicked grin crossing his face. "And a great kisser."

"Jack!"

He kissed her again, glad to see she responded so readily to his touch. "When's the date?"

"Can you give me . . . a month? Just let me get two issues of the paper out. And let me talk to Papa."

"I can do that." He rubbed his thumb along her lower lip. "I think he may already have a good idea."

Nora pulled away. "In that case, why don't you come for dinner tonight? Jess is frying chicken and I made an apple pie this morning."

"That's all you had to say."

They heard heavy footsteps outside the door and sprang apart as the door opened. It was Seth again.

"Got my order placed, Mrs. Cantrelle. Would you like to walk over and get to business now?"

She glanced at Jack. "We'll see you later then, Sheriff?"

"You bet."

As they left, he glanced at his pocket watch. He had enough time to ride out and visit Paxton and maybe Leavenworth. He picked his hat up from the desk and left.

CHAPTER 19

Nora dipped her biscuit in the cream gravy. Jess' gravy was always a little touch of heaven on earth. She glanced at Jack, who was in an animated discussion with Robby. She ate the last bite and took a deep breath, full and relaxed and very content.

Albert and Marguerite were also talking rapidly, each finishing sentences for the other. There was a glow about Marguerite, one that added to her beauty and charm. Her father also looked different. Nora still worried about his shortness of breath, but he did seem to have more energy these days and the persistent cough no longer lingered.

She decided to share what her research today had revealed. "I think we found our lead story today."

The table grew quiet. Everyone present sat up with anticipation.

"I hope it's not about Casey and his mule," Marguerite joked.

"No, it focuses on William Kessler. He's buying up chunks of land around Silver Bluff and beyond." She related what she'd learned from Seth Appleton that afternoon.

"I also stopped by Mrs. Seabury's. She knows most

everyone in the area, thanks to her husband's work as a minister."

Albert leaned forward. "Did she have anything interesting to add?"

"Four other families have left since Kessler arrived in town. She said it had surprised her, with all the work they'd put into their places. She was certain that two of them had sold out to Kessler. Both had shared with Reverend Seabury that they'd received a more than generous price for their land."

"But she didn't know about the other two?" Albert asked.

"She knew they'd left the area, but she didn't know if Kessler bought their property or not. One was a family that kept to itself. The other was an older couple that decided to go back to Missouri to live with their daughter."

"I wonder how we can find out."

"I already did," she said. "The transfers were a matter of public record. Each of the four families deeded their land to William Kessler in transactions at our local bank. All four properties were to the south and southeast of town."

Albert cleared his throat. "Where does Seth Appleton live?"

"Just to the north of Silver Bluff. Seth believes there's a real danger present. He's not an easily intimidated man, either."

Jack spoke up. "I visited with two of the men who have claims near Appleton's. Ken Kessler's approached Neal Leavenworth. He's thinking it over. He left me with the impression that he'll stick by Seth and go along with whatever he decides."

"Who else did you see?" Albert Le Fall began the ritual of lighting his pipe as he spoke.

"Walt Paxton. No one's made him an offer yet. He's

greedy, though, and fairly lazy. I think he'll take the money and run, truth be told."

"What can you do, Mr. Jack?" Ben's voice was quiet, but he carried the thought that was in all their minds.

Jack raked a hand through his hair. "Not much from a legal standpoint. No harm's been done. All Kessler has done is buy land surrounding his town and pay a fair price for it. He has that right. Everything's been done above board. All parties have been in agreement. I can't go arresting Kessler on some gut feeling Seth's had, especially when no one else has complained."

His voice dropped a notch. "But I can be sure that I watch both Kesslers very carefully."

Jack turned to Nora. "That's where it'll stay for now, Nora. You can write your story about Kessler's land purchases if you want, but it's my job to watch for trouble. Don't go stirring any up."

She bit her lip, holding back a flood of accusations. Did Jack know something he wasn't saying? Was he covering up something Kessler was involved in and that's why he hadn't given much credence to Seth's fears? Did her fiancé actually expect her to sit on what might be a major story?

Jess spoke, cutting the thick tension in the room.

"Let me bring out that pie. Miss Nora makes the lightest crust." She winked at Jack. "You just wait and see."

Nora busied herself with cutting the pie and passing plates around. Appreciative sighs became audible as first bites were consumed. She began to calm inside. She would ask Jack about what he knew as soon as they were alone.

Albert cleared his throat. "I know Nora's been working on a few articles, but I have an idea for another one."

She paused, her fork in midair. "What, Papa?"

Albert puffed on his pipe thoughtfully. "Well, it's

not really hard news, but it's big news, all the same." He reached over and took Marguerite's hand.

"I know this may seem sudden, but we know our minds. Marguerite has promised to be my wife."

Chairs scraped across the floor as those present rose for hugs and congratulatory handshakes.

Jess beamed. "You sly old fox, Mr. Albert. You're plucking the prettiest hen from the coop."

Marguerite gazed adoringly at Albert. "I think I'm the lucky one." She looked at everyone. "It may have crossed your minds and I want to reassure you. I will give up all claims on the business I run. I would never hurt or embarrass this family."

Nora touched her shoulder. "You will always be an asset to this family, Marguerite."

"Amen!" Ben echoed. "You're a lady through and through. I'd want you in my family any day."

"I think Lola is savvy enough to manage the saloon." Marguerite chuckled. "It will give Mrs. Simmons more to complain about. She and Lola have had a few run-ins."

Laughter followed her words. The storekeeper's wife would never be a popular person in the Le Fall household.

Marguerite turned to Nora and Jess. "I hope you'll both continue with the housekeeping. I know nothing about that." She laid a hand on her fiancé's arm. "I think taking care of Albert will be a full-time job as it is."

Jack interrupted. "You'll have plenty of room to do that, Marguerite." He glanced at Nora and took her hand. "We'll be getting married next month." Then he turned to Robby. "That is, if Robby here gives me permission to marry his mother."

Robby grew round-eyed. "You're asking *me* if Mama can marry you?"

"I most certainly am. You see, Robby, I wouldn't just

be marrying your mama. In a way, I'd be marrying you, too. We'd be a family. We'd live together. If the two of you will have me, I promise I will do my best to make you both happy. So, what do you say?"

Her son turned to her, his eyes bright. "Mama?"

"Say yes," she urged.

Robby swung back to Jack. "Yes, sir. You can marry Mama. And me!"

Congratulations were enthusiastically given, as Jack picked up Robby and swung him through the air. Nora delighted in her son's squeals of pleasure, which had been rare before they arrived in Colorado.

"That means you're gonna be my new daddy?" the boy asked.

"Yes," Jack answered as he set Robby on the ground. "You'll always be my Number One. Why, you'll have to be the one that helps me run the place and keep your brothers and sisters in line." He ruffled Robby's hair. "I'll depend a lot on you."

"We've got to think about your wedding dress, Miss Nora." Jess exclaimed. "And what kind of food to serve after the wedding."

Ben laughed. "That's all you women think of." The light that shone in his eyes told Nora exactly what Ben thought of his wife.

Nora knew Jack Duncan was a good man and he would make for a wonderful father. After all, he had included Robby in their marriage announcement, a gesture that touched her—and told her exactly the kind of man he was. She doubted there were many men who would have taken into account the small boy's feelings about the matter. Jack had not only involved Robby in the proposal, but let the young boy know in no uncertain terms that he was loved and would be a treasured member of their family.

She wondered about her own fragile feelings toward Jack. She'd been afraid to examine them too closely. She only knew when she was with him, she didn't want to be anywhere else. His presence dominated a room and even her thoughts when she was alone. His kisses excited her and frightened her, too. He was so much man.

She wondered if she were woman enough for him.

৩৫৯

NORA AWAKENED EARLY. SHE EASED FROM THE BED, tucked the covers around Robby, and slipped on her dressing gown. Tiptoeing from the room, she went to the kitchen to make coffee.

Morning was her favorite time. She loved to rise while the house was quiet and take private time to think. Sometimes, she came up with ideas for stories; other times she simply let her mind drift where it may.

She'd decided to go with the Kessler story. She intended to investigate more fully exactly what Kessler had purchased since arriving in Colorado Territory, be it land or business interests. She was curious, too, about Thomas Morrison. He'd been present at Kessler's dinner party. Albert said the man spoke knowledgeably about his mining interests. She wondered if Morrison might be involved with anything else regarding Kessler.

Why would Kessler want vast amounts of land? He wasn't a rancher. He had city boy written all over him, with his expensive suits and manicured nails. Could he be planning on expanding his mining operation? Had gold or silver been discovered in the hills where he was purchasing land? Were the homesteaders being cheated out of an unknown windfall?

Nora thought the discovery of precious metals in the area was a definite possibility. But what else?

She doubted Kessler would become involved in cattle. Maybe lumber? He had bought the paper mill they would use to produce paper for the *Silver Bluff Gazette*. Did he want to add to those enterprises? She couldn't be sure. Anything at this point was pure speculation. She knew from experience that it would take research and hours of interviews to get to the bottom of this mystery. If she were a gambler, she'd lay odds on it being silver. That would explain Kessler's hurry to rush the settlers off the land before news of the discovery leaked.

The water began bubbling. She stopped her wool-gathering to see to the coffee. As she poured herself a cup, Albert shuffled in. She automatically handed the cup to him and got herself another one.

Nora knew better than to speak. Her father might be the sweetest man in the world, but that was only after he got a good amount of coffee in him. They sat in silence until he'd downed two cups.

He grinned. "What do you think about getting a new step-mama?"

She placed a hand over his. "I think it's wonderful, Papa, though I can't imagine casting Marguerite in the role of my wicked stepmother."

"Not that she couldn't play it to the hilt."

Nora laughed. "I'm sure Marguerite would do the part justice on stage. However, in real life, I think she's a pussycat." She grew serious. "It's about time you found some companionship. Mama's been gone a long time."

Albert snorted. "Haven't needed a woman before now. My little girl kept me happy." His eyes shone at her. "With you gone, it'll be nice to have Marguerite around."

"Do you like him, Papa?"

She'd never asked whether or not he thought well of Jack. She assumed he did, seeing that they spent time with each other daily.

He placed a hand on hers and gave it a squeeze. "He's a Yankee—but he's a damned fine one, Daughter. I will be proud to have him as my son-in-law."

Tears sprang to her eyes. Although he'd been fond of Paul, Papa had never given her such a strong affirmation as he did now regarding Jack.

"I hope we'll be happy," she said wistfully.

"Do you love him?"

The question startled her. She hadn't really thought about love and Jack together. Everything was still so new between them. She did know that his kisses took her breath away. That he drew every eye in the room whenever he walked in. She knew if she never saw him again, she would wither as quickly as a hothouse blossom taken from its protective nest. She knew deep down in her soul that he excited her and frustrated her and could drive her wild all with one look.

Was that love?

Would they be like Ben and Jess in the years to come, a smile lighting one's face when the other entered a room? Did she really even want love? She thought she'd married for love the first time around. Look at what a disaster that had been.

No, this time, she would marry for stability. Robby needed a father and he'd taken to Jack easily. Jack had a solid job in a growing town. He would be a good provider. If love grew between them, it would be icing on the cake.

"I don't know," she answered. "He's a good man, Papa. I know Robby and I can depend on him. That's why I'm marrying him."

Albert laughed. "Well, at least you're honest. Just give the fellow a chance. I think that you'll build a good life together."

"I hope so. I know he'll be good for Robby."

"Jack will be good for you, too."

She drained the last bit of brew from her mug and set it on the table.

"I'll fetch more water for your shave, Papa. You're

looking a bit scraggly. We can't have Marguerite seeing you this way."

He shrugged and took another sip of his drink.

Nora caught the smile he hid in his cup. She quietly opened the door and walked the few paces to the well they shared with the Malones, grateful it was so conveniently located.

She tightened the sash of her dressing gown. The chill in the morning air was brisk. She loved the clean smell of it, as well as the view of the mountains in the distance.

As she brought up the bucket from the well, she heard a noise nearby. She turned and saw a figure covered in black soot from head to toe marching straight at her. The pail slipped from her hands as the stranger blurted out, "I'll kill the sumbitch! He's burned us out!"

CHAPTER 20

Nora immediately recognized the voice. She doubted she would've known the man without hearing it. The grime covering him had turned his skin as black as night. His clothes were torn. He was missing one shoe.

It was Seth Appleton.

"I told Jack what that dad-blasted fool was up to. He didn't believe me." Seth's eyes blazed hot.

"What's happened, Seth? Where's your family?"

The farmer looked startled. "Why, I guess . . . I . . ." His voice trailed off. "I took out like a bat from hell. They're still back home."

Albert stepped onto the porch and hurried over. "My God, Seth. What happened?"

"Kessler done burned me out. That's what happened." He spat on the ground in disgust. "I lost my barn and all my animals. My crop. We was gonna be harvesting soon."

"And your family? Are they all right?"

Appleton's mouth set in a hard line. "We got out in time. I sleep like the dead, but my Annie heard a loud banging." He snorted. "Was enough of a warning to wake us and time enough to get out before the house went flaming."

Nora swallowed hard. "You lost everything?"

"Yes, ma'am." The hatred that glittered in Seth Appleton's eyes was frightening. "Even slit my dog's throat. Guess so's he wouldn't bark and wake us up."

Nausea filled her. How could Kessler—if that's who was responsible—stoop so low? Thank God the Appleton family was alive.

"Did you see Kessler do it? Hear his voice? Do you have any proof, Seth?" Albert's words hung on the gentle, early morning breeze.

Seth glared at Albert. "Hell, no. Them Kesslers are sly ones. If'n I'd seen either one of 'em, I'd have shot first and asked questions later. Sheriff better put them bastards in jail quick, else I will shoot 'em full a holes. They gotta pay for what they done."

Albert flashed a look at Nora as he asked, "You haven't been to see Jack yet?"

"No, I was fixing to," Seth mumbled. "I was on my way to try and kill both of them Kesslers, then I saw Miss Nora at the well." He scratched his chin. "I figured mebbe that's not such a good idea."

She shuddered. Thank the stars they were the first house on the north end of town and that she stepped outside when she did. If not, Jack might be on his way now to arrest Seth Appleton for a double murder.

"Why don't you and I go and bring your family back here, Seth? Papa will go find Jack. He'll take care of everything."

The farmer nodded woodenly. He seemed drained of all energy and on the verge of collapse.

"Papa will get you some coffee. I'll throw on some clothes and we'll go see to your family."

Albert led a trembling Seth inside the house as if he were a small child. Nora slipped down the hall and hurriedly dressed.

IT WAS WORSE THAN SHE COULD HAVE IMAGINED. THE thick, acrid smell permeated the air, even as the blackened ground glowed warmly with faint embers. As they drew close in the buckboard, courtesy of Doctor Malone, Nora swallowed the bile that rose.

"Such a waste," the doctor said.

She was glad he'd come. Since they had neither cart nor horse, she had gone to borrow the Malones' wagon, knowing Seth's property was several miles away. He'd actually run the whole way into town. Now that his initial excitement had died, the homesteader looked twice his age and shook like sugarcane swaying in the breeze.

"Let's find your family, Seth," she said gently, as they climbed from the wagon.

"Mrs. Appleton?" Nora's voice rang clear in the unnatural silence. Not a bird sang in the stillness. The only sounds were pops and crackles in scattered parts where the fire was slowing dying.

"Over here," a voice answered weakly.

If she hadn't recognized the sound of defeat in the woman's voice, she certainly saw it as they approached. Annie Appleton's eyes were dull and lifeless in a face of ash gray. She bore no resemblance to the woman Nora saw in church, her slightly off-key voice singing the loud praises of the Lord.

"Oh, Seth." Annie collapsed into her husband's arms. Three children, dressed in their nightclothes, huddled around their parents. The group clung tightly to one other. She averted her eyes to give them a moment of privacy.

"Did Seth give you any idea who might've done this?"

Nora's eyes met the kind physician's. "Yes."

Malone studied her a moment. "But you think it best if I hear it from him?"

She nodded. "Thank you for coming with us."

"Not a problem. I want to take a look at everyone

once they've had a spell together. Make sure they're all right."

She and the doctor stood quietly for a few minutes, waiting for the Appletons' reunion to conclude.

Seth eventually waved them over. "Check 'em out, Doc. Don't think anything's wrong, other than a broken heart."

Seth pulled Nora aside while Malone began talking to the Appleton family.

"I ain't never seen my Annie like this before. She don't want no trouble. Says if Kessler would do this, he'd do a lot worse if we made this fight public. I've got to get her out of this godforsaken place."

Her stomach twisted into knots. "Are you telling me you won't press charges, Seth?"

The farmer shook his head. "First, I'm gonna bury my dog. Then I'm gonna get cleaned up real nice and go tell William Kessler I've had a change of heart. The money will be enough to put some clothes on our backs and buy supplies enough to head up to Wyoming. Or maybe Montana." He sighed. "Or I hear tell California's nice. Maybe we'll go there instead."

Nora wanted to scream at the injustice, but she realized Seth was only being practical, protecting his family the best he knew how.

JACK CLENCHED HIS JAW TIGHTLY AND GRIPPED HIS reins. The closer he came to Seth Appleton's place, the madder he got.

He blamed himself. He'd heard rumors back during the war of what Ken Kessler was capable of. He'd learned that war made most men just a little bit crazy. Jack figured that the past was the past and hoped the Kesslers would've changed by now. Sure, he wasn't happy they'd come to his town, but neither had given him any reason to suspect such treachery. Until now.

His gut told him they were involved up to their eyeballs. He also knew he wouldn't find a shred of proof that they'd torched Seth's place. He regretted he hadn't taken Seth's concerns more seriously. Though he'd made a pass by the Appletons' place after the farmer voiced his worries, Jack really hadn't thought it would go this far—much less this fast.

To top it off, he'd been fishing when it probably happened. He suffered bouts of insomnia from time to time, a little gift from the war. Since he'd come to Silver Bluff and become sheriff, he'd put a stop to all that tossing and turning by slipping out to fish. The lake was why he'd built nearby. The best fishing happened between three and five in the morning, and he usually got a good breakfast out of it.

His guilt ran heavy, though. Thank God the family got out with no serious injuries. Arson and destruction of property were bad enough. Murder was unthinkable. He had seen such a waste of lives during his years in the army. He'd hoped never to witness that again.

And now, both Kesslers were in town—his town— and he could smell their touch.

Albert told him poor Seth was crazy with rage and ready to kill both Kesslers. Jack knew he'd better ride out and calm down the homesteader, as well as see the damage for himself.

He came down the slope, immediately spying the others. At least Nora had convinced Seth to return home and check on his family instead of charging hell-bent into Kessler's place.

He dismounted, surveying the ruins about him. The crops. The house and barn. All gone. Nothing left but rubble. An icy hand ran along his neck.

"Seth. Annie. You all right?" He looked around at

the three stair steps, not remembering any of the children's names at the moment. Annie was drawn and pale.

What haunted him most were Seth's hollow eyes. Jack recognized the emptiness that lay within them, because it had lived with him. Thank God Nora finally came into his life and rid him of its existence. She'd taken her own sweet time getting here, but he already needed her more than he would ever let on.

He offered Seth his hand. "I'm sorry about what happened here. Everything was fine when I rode by last night. When did the fire break out?"

Seth hesitated a moment before he took Jack's hand, but he pumped it with true feeling.

"Annie heard something what woke her. Don't know what time it was."

Nora spoke up. "Seth arrived at our house a little before six, if that helps any."

Jack nodded. "Why don't we work on finding you all some clothes and—"

"—and then we'll leave town." Seth waved his hand. "Don't try and stop me, Jack. You owe me that much after not taking Kessler's threat seriously."

Appleton walked back to his family and spoke to them in quiet tones.

Nora turned to Jack. "They're frightened. They want out. If Kessler is behind this, they want to be as far from his reach as possible."

He looked at the family, huddled together in the only clothes they owned. Annie Appleton cried quietly. "They'll take Kessler's offer?"

"That's what Seth plans to do."

He looked across the burned land, a sick churning in his gut. This was only the beginning and he hadn't a clue what to do to stop what came next.

THEY BROUGHT THE APPLETONS BACK TO ALBERT'S house. Jess fussed over the children, making a mound of flapjacks they gobbled down as fast as she could flip them. None of the adults had an appetite.

One of Jess' dresses fit Annie. The two boys, only ten months apart, both fit into pants Robby had recently outgrown. His shirts were a little big for them, but sleeves were easy to roll up and grow into.

Mrs. Malone came over to see if she could help, and she brought back a blue and white calico dress she'd finished the day before.

"It was for my granddaughter," she confided to Nora. "I love making clothes for a little girl. It's a good thing I missed the post yesterday else it'd be on its way East."

Nora called over to the littlest Appleton. "Sally, would you like to try on your new dress?"

The girl clung to her mother's leg, her face buried deep in the folds of the skirt. She brought the dress to Annie instead.

"She's been through a lot. No wonder she's a bit shy." Nora stroked the girl's head and was rewarded with a shy smile.

"I thank you for your kindness. As soon as Seth can see . . . that man, we won't impose on you any longer."

"There's no rush, Annie. You can stay as long as you wish."

Annie's sad eyes brimmed with unshed tears. "Thank you but we'd like to head out as soon as we can."

Nora wondered how Seth's encounter with William Kessler would go. Jack had taken the farmer back to his place to bathe and provide him with a change of clothes.

She moved close to Albert and said quietly, "I think we should go to the paper, Papa. We've got a story to write."

He looked at her with weary eyes. "And much to discuss, Daughter."

⚜

WILLIAM KESSLER DISMOUNTED AND TOSSED HIS reins to a young kid. He stepped into his foreman's office. Fortunately, Sam Spivens was out.

He sank into the chair behind the desk and sighed. A confrontation with Jack Duncan was inevitable. The sheriff would be investigating the fire at that country bumpkin's place. He smiled, glad he'd had the foresight to send Ken to Denver early this morning. He didn't need his little brother's hot temper misfiring when Sheriff Duncan came calling with a dozen questions.

He took out paper from the desk drawer and doodled a quick map onto it. Scribbled "Xs" indicated the land he'd bought long before his arrival in town. Most of them were far apart. He doubted anyone would make the connections until much further down the road. By that time, he would own everything between here and the Wyoming border, and a good bit of what lay south between Silver Bluff and Denver.

With satisfaction, he folded the slip of paper and tucked it into his suit pocket. When the railroad came this way, he would become a very wealthy man. Not that the war hadn't already made him one. He'd seen to that.

As a Union colonel, he made sure once his troops were stationed in the South, the raiding parties had taken not only food for his soldiers and usable supplies, but anything that hadn't been nailed down. Consequently, goods shipped north as personal property included such Southern treasures as heirloom jewels, Persian carpets, and fine art and wines. Southern gentlemen knew how to live in luxury.

Those quality items sold on the black market during

the war at sky-high prices. He now lived off those profits. His countless acquisitions had bankrolled him as he bought into several businesses at war's end. The money would also see him through the governor's race here in Colorado. He knew it was only a matter of time until enough settlers moved into the territory and petitioned the United States to take their rightful place on the red, white, and blue.

And why stop at governor? He was still a relatively young man. The graying temples only gave him a distinguished air. The Senate? Perhaps a run at the presidency? He would be a war veteran who was also a self-made man. The public couldn't resist his kind. If they let a butcher like Grant run the country, then anything was possible.

As long as Jack Duncan didn't interfere.

Stevenson had sung the man's praises loud and long. Insisted Kessler keep Duncan on as sheriff. Well, his mama hadn't raised no fools. William Kessler knew enough to keep a man like Jack Duncan close by. He wanted to be able to watch his every move.

For the most part, the sheriff had a sweet deal. Duncan kept Silver Bluff running like clockwork. He had the respect of the miners and even let them blow off a little steam on Saturday nights. If things got a bit wild, he stepped in and handled the situation with ease. Duncan made sure the bank paid a fair price for the gold brought in to be measured. He kept an eye out for the whores at the saloon. All in all, Duncan had done an excellent job of taking care of Silver Bluff, which gave Kessler more time to devote to his own business interests.

The incident with Appleton bothered him, though. To this point, to a man, they'd all been willing to sell. He hadn't had to instruct Ken to get rough with anyone. Some had needed a little time and some needed the pot sweetened more than others, but until Appleton balked, trouble had been avoided.

He hoped Duncan would see no connection could be made between him and this local yokel and simply go about his business.

After escorting Seth Appleton and his brood out of town, of course.

Kessler stood, his stomach grumbling in protest. He had skipped breakfast. That Sung Moon was too fine a cook. He already felt a tightness in his pants from the weight he'd put on since arriving in Silver Bluff. Hustling Ken out of the house gave him a reason not to eat this morning. He regretted it now.

He decided to walk down to the mine. He needed to check with Spivens on a few things. As he opened the door, the previously muffled noises now hit him full blast. Cold sweat instantly broke out on his forehead.

"Damned war," he muttered under his breath. He'd only been involved in two engagements, both brief, but they still haunted his dreams and even his waking hours. Whenever a sudden noise occurred, the cold washed over him anew. He doubted it would ever leave him, no matter how many years passed.

He headed straight for the mine and found Spivens. He barked out his instructions, Spivens all the while nodding like a China doll on a spring.

Satisfied, he decided to head home and have a little breakfast after all. Maybe even an early lunch, as he consulted his pocket watch.

"Jack! Hey, Jack!"

"Good to see you, Sheriff."

Kessler looked up immediately and snapped the watch cover closed. Jack Duncan strode towards him like the Devil himself, oblivious to the greetings called out.

"He's a hero, Jack Duncan," he heard one man say.

Kessler was aware the sheriff had saved Bran Stevenson's life in a nasty cave-in. That fact soured the good mood that the thought of Sung Moon's cooking had brought. He steeled himself for their conversation, barely noticing that Seth Appleton accompanied Duncan.

"Good morning, Sheriff. Appleton," he said pleasantly. "What brings you to the mine?"

"I've been out at Mr. Appleton's place. Thought it'd be the neighborly thing to do to accompany him here." Duncan placed a hand on the homesteader's shoulder briefly.

Kessler began walking away from the noise of the drills and shouts of his crew. He didn't want their conversation shouted aloud and easily overheard. The two men fell into step beside him.

"What can I do for you, Mr. Appleton? I thought we'd concluded our business yesterday. At least that's what my brother told me. That you weren't interested in selling at any price."

"We didn't have any business yesterday. We do today." Appleton's jaw was set, his mouth a tight line.

"What business might that be, sir?"

"I aim to sell. Is your offer still good?

Kessler shrugged nonchalantly. "I could put an offer on the table." He named a figure that was just the right side of fair. He couldn't afford to be overly generous. He didn't want Jack Duncan to sniff around more than he had already.

"I think Leavenworth could easily match that amount, Seth," the sheriff said good-naturedly. "He'd probably dance a jig to be able to have the adjacent property for that price. Why don't you let him know what Mr. Kessler is willing to part with and see if Leavenworth might match it—or raise it a bit?"

Kessler wanted to kick his fair-minded sheriff in the teeth. He planted a stiff smile on his face and said, "No need for that, Appleton." He quoted the farmer double his offer and watched as the fool's eyes widened.

"You have a deal," the homesteader said shakily.

He hoped he did. What did the poor bastard have to go back to? A few smoking pieces of wood and a burned crop? He'd be insane to turn down the kind of money offered.

"We can finalize things at the bank," he said agreeably. "Today, if you like. I have business there around two this afternoon. Shall we say a quarter to three? My other transactions should be completed by then."

"I want it in gold," Appleton said stubbornly.

"Whatever you'll accept." He turned to Jack. "A minute of your time, Sheriff?"

Quietly, Jack told Seth, "Go on back to Albert's. Better yet, head over to the general store. I bet you want to get started on what you need to buy before you leave town. I'll meet up with you there."

Appleton nodded his head wearily and shuffled off. Kessler almost could feel sorry for him. He regarded the man in front of him for a moment before he said, "Didn't know you and Seth Appleton were friends."

"What happened to the Appletons was wrong."

He paused, trying to hide his amusement. "Something happened to them, you say? Is that why Appleton changed his mind about selling?"

Duncan quickly grabbed a fistful of his shirt and brought him close. Kessler felt his face go beet red. He prayed to God they were out of his workers' sight.

"You know what happened. Don't lie to me. I aim to find who burned him out. Fair warning's now issued."

The lawman relaxed his hold. Kessler coughed and gasped for a breath of air as the other man studied him.

"You think I'd be involved in something sordid? You don't know me at all, Sheriff. Not at all. Why, I'm an upstanding member of this community."

The lawman walked away. Kessler felt the old, familiar rage build inside. Who did this small-town hick think he was?

He called out, "Do you remember who you work for, Sheriff?"

Duncan stopped and looked over his shoulder. "You might pay my salary, but I work for the citizens of Silver Bluff." He strolled away without a backward glance.

Jack Duncan would have to go.

CHAPTER 21

"We're in a fine pickle."

Albert plopped into his chair at the newspaper, his breathing choppy. Nora wondered if it resulted from the quick walk from home to the office or the mess they were now in.

"It's a huge problem, Papa. I agree."

Ben snorted. "We're way past the problem stage, Miss Nora."

"Ben's right," Albert chimed in. "What will we do?"

She waved a hand impatiently. "Just hold your horses, you two. Yes, we have a problem. It's not one that we have to deal with just yet."

"Come again?"

She smiled at the puzzled look on Ben's face. "We've got a story to write now. A sad one, but a story that needs to be reported all the same. News sells. And bad news sells twice as fast. We need to let the town know about the arson at the Appletons' place. You always taught me to write objectively, Papa. We'll go strictly on the facts and hit every 'W' we can."

"The who, the what, the when, the where—I can see all of those, Daughter. It's the *why* that's giving me fits."

"Correct." Nora seated herself at the companion

desk across from her father's. "Not every news story can tell that the first time around. We may *think* we know why. That for some reason William Kessler wanted Seth Appleton's piece of property badly enough to scare him into selling in the worst way. It's not a fact that we can prove. Yet."

"We're gonna be impartial." Ben grinned at his use of such a fancy word.

"Exactly. That's good journalism. In the meantime, we dig. As deeply as we have to. But we'll either prove or disprove a link between the fire and the Kesslers."

Albert removed his pipe from his pocket and stroked it in his hands. "What if we find that one or both Kesslers are involved in this offense? Do we run with it?"

She slammed a fist on the desktop. "I don't know!" Tears of anger burned in the back of her eyes. "What would we risk if we eventually write that story, Papa? Kessler only has a twenty percent interest in the paper. We have the control."

"But that twenty percent is important, Nora. It's not something to be taken lightly."

"And setting fire to a man's home and property isn't a matter to trifle with either."

"Calm yourself, Daughter. I'm not disagreeing with you. I'm just thinking of all the angles. What if Kessler withdrew his support, including the paper mill contract? What if he demanded his original investment back? What if he claimed the story was a pack of lies that slandered him and he sued us for every dime we have?"

"Are we puppets or journalists?" She began pacing. The new floorboards creaked as she walked a steady path across them.

"Seems to me we're fretting over things way too much," Ben quietly added. "Miss Nora should just write the story first. Mr. Kessler can't be angry with her reporting the news. Especially if he ain't involved, he can't be mad."

She placed her hand on Ben's shoulder. "You're right, Ben. We do the job at hand."

"Write it up, Nora," Papa said. "Both stories. Arson at Appleton's place will be our lead story on the front page. A smaller story, not so prominently placed, can report on Mr. William Kessler investing in property around his new home of Silver Bluff. Keep it understated. Report the bare-bones facts.

"In the meantime, I'll start the detective work. I'm heading over to the bank now. With no lawyer in town yet, Witherspoon must house all documents, such as deeds."

"Unless they were filed in Denver. It may take a trip there, especially if the sales were far enough away."

"True. But it's a start. I'll push Mortimer as hard as I can." Papa mopped his brow with his handkerchief. "Once I leave the bank, I think I'll go home and rest a spell. You do what needs to be done here. I'll trust you both to see it done properly."

He shuffled out the door. Nora immediately exchanged looks with Ben.

"Mr. Albert's moving slow."

"I know."

Worry blanketed her momentarily. She knew, though, that the best way to lighten her father's burden was to get the *Silver Bluff Gazette* off and running to a good start. They definitely had the stories to do so.

An hour later, Nora chewed on her pencil thoughtfully before the final phrase came to her. She got her thought on paper and rested the pencil on the desk. Stretching her arms high above her head, she cracked her knuckles for good measure.

She always felt complete when she finished a story. The one about the Appletons' losses was hard to write, seeing she knew the people involved and had witnessed their pain firsthand. She read over both it and the brief story concerning Kessler's real estate transactions a final time and then pushed the sheets across the desk.

"Let's start setting the type for this, Ben. It'll be our lead story."

"Headline?"

"You decide. You're better at coming up with headlines anyway. Papa says you should've headed for New York long ago. Do you know there are actually men who make a living at nothing but writing headlines?"

He looked at her as if she'd lost her mind. "You're joshing me, Miss Nora." He took her copy and read over it slowly, nodding to himself a time or two. "I'll get started on this. You gonna go check on Mr. Albert?"

"Yes. I hope he found out something at the bank."

"Don't get your hopes up too soon, Miss Nora. That Mr. Kessler, if he's involved, is a sly one. It'll take time. Be patient."

The door opened, startling them both. Chin Lee hurried in, closing it behind him. He bowed to both of them and then offered Nora his hand to shake.

"Greetings, Miss Nora, Mr. Ben. Are you in good health?"

"Yes, Chin, we're well. What brings you to the paper?"

Chin looked sorrowfully at them. "I heard what happened to Mr. Seth and his family. Tien Lee told us. He said Mr. Seth said bad things about Mr. Kessler."

"We don't know yet how the fire started, Chin. Jack will find out. Don't you worry."

Chin beamed. "Mr. Jack Sheriff is a good man. He'll find the bad man who did this terrible thing."

She noticed that Chin seemed to hesitate. "Is there something you came by to tell us?"

The servant frowned. "Mr. Kessler is a very private man. Very quiet. But maybe if I hear something, I'll tell you?"

Nora beamed at him. "Chin, I could just kiss you." She watched him blush.

"Miss Nora should save her kisses for Mr. Jack Sheriff. He's . . . how do you say?"

"He's sweet on her?" Ben added helpfully.

Chin grinned. "Right."

She chuckled. "I'm saving all my kisses for Jack. We're going to be married soon."

The Chinaman's mouth formed a perfect "O". He ran to her and pumped her hand repeatedly until she laughed.

"I'm so happy for you. He's a good man, that Mr. Jack Sheriff. You will be very happy together."

Then it hit her. She'd actually told someone other than family that she was getting married—and she'd liked saying it.

She shook Chin's hand again, her happiness spilling over, a grin on her face.

She was actually marrying Jack Duncan.

She rather liked the sound of that. Jack Duncan. Mrs. Jack Duncan. Nora Duncan. Would he make Robby a Duncan, too? She hoped so.

"I'll tell Sung Moon. She will be happy for you." Chin waved goodbye and left.

"Well, Ben, I guess the cat's out of the bag."

"That cat didn't need to be in a bag. Cats like to run around so everyone can see them." Ben beamed. "Before you go home, Jess told me to remind you to stop at the store and look at material for your wedding gown."

"I'm glad you reminded me. I hope she's already been there and chosen it. Jess has a better eye than I do."

"Go on, then. See to that and Mr. Albert. I have plenty to do." He began whistling as he set to work.

Nora went down the street and pushed open the door to the general store. Seymour Simmons had several stacks of goods on the counter. He leaned around one to greet her.

"Good afternoon, Mrs. Cantrelle. Just getting the last of the things ready for the Appletons. Kind of you to take them in. Fine family. We'll miss Seth."

"Well, I won't miss that Annie Appleton," came a voice from the back stockroom. A moment later, Jane Simmons leaned around the corner, her mouth twisted. "She can't sing a lick, that woman. I might actually enjoy the Lord's music this Sunday without her warbling bothering me."

Nora wished she was a man at that moment. She'd never understood a man's urge to fight until now. If she was a man and if she was close enough, she would've hauled back and punched the lights out of Mrs. Simmons.

Instead, she sweetly said, "I so enjoy when people raise their voices in praise of the Lord. I'll miss Annie Appleton dreadfully."

She caught Seymour Simmons stifling a grin.

"At least they're making good money out of the mess," Mrs. Simmons added. "Seth says they may go north or west."

"You, too, will make a nice profit, Mrs. Simmons," she pointed out. "It's fortunate that you'll be able to supply them so well."

She wandered over to the bolts of material on the opposite side of the store. "Has Jess been in today, Mrs. Simmons?"

The storekeeper's wife waddled in her direction, a sour look on her face. "Can't say I remember her coming in. You seen that woman, Seymour?"

He took out a handkerchief and wiped his brow. "No, ain't seen Jess for nigh on two days now. Do you need to pick something up for her?"

Nora fingered the material before her. "No. She was going to look at material for me. If we can find what we

ALEXA ASTON

want here, she'll decide how much will be needed. If not . . ." Her voice trailed off and she moved to another grouping of fabrics.

Mrs. Simmons followed her along. "Are you looking for something special?"

"Mmm-hmm." Nora continued to play with the different bolts of cloth. She came across one she liked and pulled it from the group. "This might do."

Mrs. Simmons couldn't stand it any longer. "Are you needing a dress made? For a special occasion?"

"Oh, yes. A most special occasion." She pushed it aside and continued to browse.

"Well, what's it for? I might be able to help you find what you're looking for if I knew why you needed it."

"Oh, didn't I say? I'm getting married next month. Jess is making my bridal gown."

The woman's eyes bugged out. Her tongue darted out and moistened her thick lips. It reminded Nora of a large frog. She knew she was being awful, but she couldn't help it. She let the woman flap in the wind a minute longer.

"Who is he? Who're you going to marry so fast? You've hardly been in town at all."

A low voice from behind answered, "She's marrying me."

CHAPTER 22

Jack strolled across the store, boots clicking along the hard floor. Seymour Simmons thrust out a hand and pumped his before slapping him hard on the back.

"I declare, Jack, you stole the prettiest girl out from everyone. Congratulations!"

His eyes met Nora's. "I think we're a good match." He crossed to her and placed an arm about her. "Your daddy's looking for you."

Nora turned to Mrs. Simmons. "I'll let Jess know what I liked. If she finds something she's pleased with—"

"I guarantee she'll find something to her liking. We carry the best fabrics between here and Denver." The woman grudgingly added, "Tell her to get herself over here. She'll be able to find what you need."

Mrs. Simmons squinted up at him. "High time you married, Sheriff. Can't expect these miners to settle down when the town's lawman acts footloose and fancy-free."

Jack ignored her comment and smiled at Nora. Without taking his eyes off her, he said, "Just had to wait until the right lady came along, ma'am. Now that she has, I'm putty in her hands."

They said goodbye to the storeowner and his wife and walked out into the afternoon sunshine.

"Putty in your hands," she murmured. "Didn't know how well you could tell a whopper."

If only she knew how much she affected him.

"Had to pull that old gossip's leg, that's all. You were doing a fine job of teasing her yourself."

Nora laughed. "How long were you standing there?"

"Long enough to hear you reeling her in like a fish on a line."

He tucked her hand through the crook of his arm as they stepped out into the street.

"Let's go to my office."

"I thought Papa needed me."

"Not as much as I do." He tugged gently on her elbow. Jack watched her eyes widen at his remark, followed quickly by a trace of a smile.

"I finished writing two articles for the *Silver Bluff Gazette*. Ben's typesetting them now."

"The Appletons?"

She nodded. "It's our page one story."

"They're well thought of in the area." He paused. "Seth agreed to sell to Kessler a few minutes ago."

"I bet Mr. Kessler didn't act a bit surprised." She stopped. "What are you not telling me?"

He raised an eyebrow. "Why would you ask that?"

"You mean besides the fact you told me to stay away from them? Your eyes go hard, Jack, when the name Kessler is mentioned."

He tightened his jaw. He hadn't wanted her to pick up on anything. He knew it would only give her curiosity an itch which needed scratching.

"Nothing specific." He gave her a reassuring squeeze. "I guess I don't like Kessler having any interest in your newspaper operation." He opened the door to the jail and ushered her inside.

"It's only twenty percent. His investment is more

speculation. If we grow, he'll eventually gain a steady profit. If we go bust, he hasn't lost much."

"But you'd lose everything you have if it's not a success."

"That about sums it up," she said in a light manner, though he saw the strain on her face.

"Then we'll buy him out."

She rolled her eyes. "Weren't you listening? Papa and I can't do that. Every dime we have is tied up. After a year—maybe two—if the paper starts to make money, we might be able to think about it but—"

"I meant *I* would buy him out." He stared at her. "That's the *we* part."

Nora looked at him skeptically. "You have that kind of money?"

"I have a small nest egg I've tucked away through the years. I was a bounty hunter before I worked in the silver mine. Made darned good money since both were dangerous jobs. Haven't had a need to spend much of it."

"You were a bounty hunter? Why, they're the meanest, most despicable, most feared men on earth!"

"Am I despicable?"

She softened, unshed tears glistening in her eyes. "No. Am I despicable because I cry at the drop of a hat?"

"No," he said slowly, a fire building in the pit of his belly. He glanced down at his shirtfront. "But you do seem to get an awful lot of my shirts wet."

"I'm sorry," she whispered. But she didn't look sorry at all. What she did look was damned delicious, with her eyes bright from tears and her mouth trembling slightly.

He moved to kiss her. Unfortunately, he was interrupted.

Seth Appleton opened the door. They sprang apart

quickly. The homesteader took in the situation and smiled.

"I hear congratulations are due. Mrs. Simmons told me all about it when I went to finish up loading the wagon."

Jack whistled low. "Is there anyone she hasn't told by now?" He pulled his watch from his vest and glanced at the time. "I'd wager she's been in possession of that bit of knowledge a good quarter-hour now."

Appleton chuckled. "Mrs. Seabury and Mrs. Malone were both in the store when I was. She told the three of us. Don't know if anyone else heard it beforehand."

He grinned wryly at Nora. "Our engagement may outscoop the *Silver Bluff Gazette*. Are you sorry you told her?"

She gave his hand a squeeze. "No, I knew what I was doing. I'm proud to be marrying you, Jack Duncan."

His insides turn to mush.

৩৬৩

THE FIRST EDITION OF THE *SILVER BLUFF GAZETTE* came out two days later. Nora and Albert had argued about what day of the week to publish. Ben had solved the problem.

"Why don't we bring it out on Saturdays? Most farmers outside town stock up then. The miners only work until three that day. They might buy a copy before they go get drunk that night. People'll want to have it read, I reckon, before they come to church on Sunday, so they can talk about what they read *after* church."

Nora hugged Ben. "You, my friend, are a genius."

He grinned. "If'n I get any smarter at this newspaper business, I just might have to up and go to New York and seek my fortune there." He scratched his chin. "Or mebbe San Francisco. I hear it's a pretty place."

Jess swatted him with a cup towel. "You ain't going nowhere until I get this wedding dress made and even then, you best be sticking around."

Ben winked at his wife. "You think?"

She turned demure. "I hope so."

He walked slowly toward her. "I'd say you ain't getting rid of me, woman." Ben swept his wife into his arms and carried her out of the room, her mock protests weak.

"I hope you and Jack will love each other the way they do." Albert looked at Nora fondly. "Your looks already tell me you do."

She blushed. She'd thought she had loved Paul with all her heart, but marriage to her boyhood sweetheart turned out to be a nightmare relationship with a virtual stranger.

Now, she would be marrying for a second time. Did she really know Jack? Did any woman ever really know the man she married?

He'd been fairly quiet about his past. The part about being a bounty hunter surprised her. From everything she'd read about them, they were men who were ruthless and dangerous, even more so than the men they hunted down.

Of course, her first impressions of Jack were of a man mixed with danger and ill manners. Had he changed? Or did she view him with different eyes?

The thought of the physical side of marriage had her in knots. She'd found the two times she'd engaged in the marital act messy, short, and painful. She'd assumed Paul had been satisfied by his grunts and collapse upon the bed. The encounters left her empty.

Jack's kisses had the opposite effect. If his kisses were any indication, she might actually come to tolerate being in his bed. She wondered if he could kiss her while he was having relations with her. That would make things more agreeable. She could put the rest from her mind and concentrate on his sweet kisses. Thinking about the kind of man he was, Nora knew he had to be better at things than Paul. That comforted her.

Albert helped push these thoughts from her mind. "I'm heading over again to see how we're selling."

He had only been gone a few minutes when Marguerite arrived, ready for a little gossip.

They sat down to tea. Marguerite picked up her cup but then placed it back down. "I'm too excited to drink and talk."

"Talk first and then drink."

"Oh, Nora, you don't seem excited at all."

"I may be if you tell me how the reaction is. I haven't gone out today on purpose. I don't think people would be honest with me, anyway. I'm too closely involved for them to give me their true opinion."

Marguerite beamed. "Then I'm happy to report that the *Silver Bluff Gazette* is the talk of the town. I heard all morning people have been picking up copies at the general store. Two of my girls went over first thing and let me tell you, honey, they are not the kind that jump right out of bed."

"Did they like it?"

"Of course! Everyone has hungered for news—any news—so when they see quality writing and loads of information, they can't help but be impressed."

"Papa went over to Mr. Simmons' place around noon. He said it was bustling. He went back a few minutes ago."

"I heard most everyone from the outlying areas came in at first light to stock up." She grinned. "And get their newspaper."

Albert burst through the door at that moment. He

couldn't have been gone longer than ten minutes, which accounted for his flushed face.

"Papa, you're wheezing like a horse that's run the race of his life," Nora scolded. "Did you run all the way from the store?"

They settled him in a chair. Marguerite put a cushion behind his back while Nora fetched him a glass of water. He drank it greedily and laid his head back against the top of the chair.

Finally, he opened his eyes. She caught their gleam.

"We're a success. Every subscriber has picked up his first edition at the general store. Five minutes ago, Mr. Simmons sold the last copy printed."

Tears of joy sprang to her eyes. "Every copy? Why, we printed thirty extra!"

"We can't assume every issue will sell as well, but we are off to a magnificent start."

He took Marguerite's hands in his and kissed them soundly. "I think I'll be able to support you, my dear. Oh, am I glad we left Monroe behind. Nora and I have found both professional and personal satisfaction here in Colorado Territory."

"And in so little time. I wish you would have come years ago, Albert," mused Marguerite.

He shook his head. "The time wasn't right, my sweet." He closed his eyes again.

"Are you tired, Albert? Would you like to rest a bit before dinner? Nora said Jack's coming. You know you'll want to trade stories with him."

"Maybe I will lie down for a bit."

Marguerite helped him to his feet and down the hall to his bedroom. Nora figured she would stay with him while he fell asleep.

A knock at the door startled her. She answered it and was surprised to find Chin there.

"Please come in, Chin."

She saw the grave expression on his face and knew something was amiss. "What's wrong?"

"I heard Mr. Kessler talk with Mr. Ken. They're mad about what you wrote. He said you made them look bad. Mr. Kessler says he'll try to shut you down. Mr. Ken said you need to learn your lesson."

Chin looked at her. "I'm scared for you, Miss Nora. They're very bad men. I'm afraid they'll hurt you like they hurt the other girl."

CHAPTER 23

A chill coursed through Nora.

"What girl?"

Chin looked frightened. "I can't talk about her. Mr. Kessler said she did bad things." He paused, his eyes reflecting sorrow. "I'm scared, Miss Nora. I believed him when he said she was bad and had to be punished. Now . . . I'm not so sure."

She led Chin to a chair. "Please sit. Tell me what happened." She resisted the urge to whip out a pencil and jot down every word he uttered.

The servant took a deep breath. "It was two, maybe three days after they came to live in Mr. Stevenson's house. Mr. Stevenson was a very good man. He told me to take care of my new boss and do whatever he said.

"Mr. Kessler came with the other Mr. Kessler. First thing Mr. Ken asked about was women in town. He said, '*Long time since I had woman. Need to fix that.*' I told him about the saloon in town."

"Did he visit the saloon?"

"Yes. He came home late. Made lots of noise. Tien slept through it, but Sung Moon and I heard him. He was very drunk. Mr. Ken gets mean when he drinks."

"Tell me about this girl." Nora deliberately kept her

tone soft and reassuring. She could tell Chin was having a difficult time getting out his story.

"Next day, he sent me in the buggy with a note. I went upstairs and saw Miss Marguerite. She read it and laughed and told me to wait. I waited outside." He shook his head. "Those ladies didn't have clothes on. Sung Moon would not want me there.

"I waited for an answer. Miss Marguerite brought a piece of paper and a girl with her. She told me to take the answer and girl with me. Miss Marguerite told me the girl would spend the night. She said to tell Sung Moon to make her a good dinner because she was gonna entertain Mr. Ken."

Chin begin fidgeting in his chair, much as Robby would if called upon in school when he didn't know the answer.

"Go on, Chin."

"That girl rode back with me. She was in a tight dress. Her bosom almost spilled out." He blushed. "She was nice, though. Talked to me the whole way. Said she was new here. Moved from New Orleans. Gonna make lots of money and go home rich. When we got back, she went upstairs. Mr. Ken was waiting. He wanted wine. I brought it. Later, he wanted food and I brought that, too." Chin winced. "I saw the girl. Her eye was swelled up and she had a red mark on cheek.

"I asked if she was okay. Mr. Ken said she tripped and fell."

"So she stayed that night?"

"Yes. Two more after that. He gave a note for me to take to town. He said don't worry Miss Marguerite and tell her about the girl tripping. He didn't want her mad at the clumsy girl. I didn't tell that. Miss Marguerite said it was okay for girl to stay. She's new and didn't have many customers."

"Then what happened?"

"Both Mr. Kesslers left for the mine. Mr. Kessler

said to leave the girl alone since she felt bad and needed to sleep. But Sung Moon heard her crying. She went to comfort her." Chin shuddered. "The girl was hurt. She said Mr. Ken hurt her. Sung Moon tried to help but we were so afraid."

"Did the Kesslers find out you saw her in that condition?"

Chin frowned. "I don't know. I heard Mr. Kessler tell her to write a note to Miss Marguerite and say she doesn't like the West. That she was going home. She wrote the note. I took it to town. Sung Moon went, too. Mr. Kessler wanted her to get pickled pig feet from Mr. Simmons. When we came back, Mr. Kessler said the girl left with Mr. Ken in the buggy. He said she was a bad girl. Not good for the town. Mr. Ken took her to Denver so she could go home."

Chin looked at Nora and took her hand. "Mr. Ken came home the next day. He told me to forget about the girl. She was very bad. Then he left for two weeks. No one ever mentioned her after that."

Sweat beaded on the Chinaman's forehead. "I found her suitcase in the closet one day. I pushed it far into the back. I didn't tell anyone, not even Sung Moon. I put it out of mind. I didn't think about until now."

He squeezed Nora's hand. "You're good to us, Miss Nora. Good to Tien. I don't want them to make you leave like this girl."

She controlled the raging emotions within her. She didn't want Chin upset any more than he was. "Thank you for sharing it with me, Chin. I will be very careful. I won't visit either Mr. Kessler. If I see them in town, I'll make sure I stay next to Jack."

"Mr. Jack Sheriff will protect you. He'll be a good husband." He stood. "I must go now. I want to find a different job and not work for Mr. Kessler."

. . .

Nora accompanied him to the door. "Be careful, Chin. Don't talk to either Kessler about this."

She watched him leave. He turned once. She waved, a smile pasted onto her face. She finally shut the door and leaned against it, her energy sapped.

What kind of men could behave in such a fashion? Beating women. Burning a family's livelihood. Killing a cherished pet? She shuddered, frightened that they'd come to a town where such evil existed.

Marguerite entered the room. "Your father's fast asleep. Why don't we—" She stopped short. "What's happened? You're as white as a starched sheet."

Nora walked unsteadily across the room and collapsed into a chair. "Chin came while you were with Papa." She related everything he'd said.

"I do remember that. The girl was named Sally Lovelace. Pretty little thing. Young, too. Had only been here a few days when Ken came for his first visit and saw her." Marguerite brought her hands to her face. "I thought it a bit unusual to send her out to Kessler's place, especially when he wanted her to stay a few days. But I had no reason not to trust him."

"You received the note from her as Chin said?"

She thought a moment. "Yes. She'd been here such a short time and had kept to herself. Girls come and go quickly at the saloon. I never thought to question her decision. I sent the few things she had out to Kessler's place and promptly forgot her."

She exhaled loudly. "I feel awful, Nora. I could've helped Sally."

"Don't blame yourself. You couldn't have known."

Marguerite's eyes widened. "Jack would never have stood for this. He would—"

"We aren't going to tell him."

Marguerite's face showed her outrage. "How can we keep this from him?"

"He's already upset enough about Seth. He's been

working on that day and night, trying to find some proof of the Kesslers' involvement. It's too late to help Sally. Don't burden him with this."

"I see what you mean." Marguerite hesitated. "I won't mention it to him for now. We may eventually need to."

"I agree. We will. When the time is right."

❧

THE LAST STRAINS OF *BRINGING IN THE SHEAVES* faded. Nora set her hymnal in the pew beside her.

"Mama," whispered Robby. "Can Tien and I go fishing? Ben said he'd take us."

She glanced over at Ben. He nodded.

"All right but you need to come home and eat dinner first. You can go afterwards."

"But Mama, the—"

"I said eat first. Fish later."

He rolled his eyes. "Okay." He gave Tien a thumbs-up and his friend burst into a toothy grin.

Nora stepped into the aisle. Jack took her elbow and guided her out the front doors. The day was cool and crisp. It smelled of sweet grass and the rain from the night before.

They greeted the Seaburys. The reverend flashed her a smile.

"I do believe you have a success on your hands, Mrs. Cantrelle."

"Thank you. I'm pleased at how the layout looked."

Mrs. Seabury interjected, "The *Silver Bluff Gazette*'s first issue is wonderful. The articles were so informative. I look forward to each edition."

Nora took her hand. "I must thank you for parting with your recipe for scones."

"Scones?" Dr. Malone and his wife stepped up next to them. "The minute I saw that cooking column, I told

Mrs. Malone you were a genius. The women alone will buy up every copy."

"And clamor to be the featured recipe, I'll daresay," added Mrs. Malone. "Don't you worry, Anne. I don't care how many people will try to imitate your scones. No one can make them like you."

Mrs. Seabury blushed. "Thank you, Iris. I do put a lot of love into each batch."

Jack spoke up. "I'm glad Nora has the recipe now, ma'am. I'd hate to run off the morning after we're married just so I could sample a few of your delicious scones."

She playfully punched him in the arm. "I may send you off, sir, just to have some peace of mind."

"The wedding's next Saturday, right, Jack?" the reverend asked.

Nora's mouth fell open.

Reverend Seabury looked confused at her reaction. "That is what you wanted, Sheriff?"

Nora shook her head. "Jack, if you keep moving up the date, I'll find out we were married a month ago."

He slid an arm around her waist. "You can't blame me for being too eager, darlin'."

"Do you really want to be a married man in just six days?" she asked.

"I could cotton to the idea."

She decided to throw caution to the wind. "Why not?"

Those gathered around them voiced their approval.

"Did you have a time in mind, Mr. Jack?"

Nora turned and saw Jess, hands on her hip, foot tapping impatiently, as she awaited his reply. Jess finally caught his eye.

Jack had the decency to look sheepish. "Whatever's good for you, Jess. As acting mother of the bride, it's really your show."

"Then let's make it for five while there's still good

light. We can come back for a buffet supper and then dance until midnight." Her eyes sparkled. "You are gonna save a dance for me, Mr. Jack?"

Ben moaned. "Mr. Jack, you watch out now. This here lady's middle name is Twinkletoes. She'll dance all night long if we let her."

Jack laughed. "Then I better dance with her early because I'm afraid she'll wear me out."

The crowd around them laughed heartily. After a bit of small talk, they begin to break up and head their separate ways. A few called out congratulations to Nora on both the newspaper's first issue and her upcoming vows.

Jack led her over to his cart and handed her up.

"You never bring this to church. Why today?"

"I thought you'd come back to my place for a little while. Got something to show you."

"Wait a minute. Let me tell—"

"She already knows. Just sit back and relax."

Nora did. Jack's arm went around her shoulder. She snuggled close to him, basking in his warmth. The trees they passed were starting to change their leaves from green to various autumn shades. She'd never seen such a wide variety of color.

"Colorado's beautiful," she proclaimed.

"Not half as pretty as you." He stole a quick kiss and then turned his eyes back to the road.

They arrived at his place a few minutes later. He shooed her into the house while he unhitched the horse. Nora stepped in and stopped. Something large sat in the middle of the floor. It was wrapped awkwardly in brown paper and had a huge yellow ribbon tied around it.

She backed up a few steps and then turned to find Jack standing inside the door, watching her.

"Go ahead. Open it."

"What is it?"

"It's your wedding present," he said softly.

She blinked several times, hoping the moistness in her eyes would flee. She walked slowly to the center of the floor and knelt next to the wrapping.

"I really couldn't get it wrapped like a real gift should be. It was too big."

"Don't apologize." She smiled up at him. "I love it."

"You haven't even seen it yet," he said, slightly exasperated.

"But it's from you, so I know I'll love it." She gazed at the shape.

"Go ahead. Open it."

"Don't rush me. Let me savor the moment."

It touched Nora that he'd been thinking about this. That he'd wrapped it himself. That he was eager for her to see what it was.

Finally, she untied the ribbon and set it aside. Like a child at Christmas, she tore into the wrapping with a loud shriek, ripping it away and tossing it over her shoulder.

She stared at it in wonder, no words coming.

Jack finally spoke. "It's a hope chest."

"Yes," she said softly, her gaze fixed upon the chest.

"It's pine. I know you've said you like pine."

"I adore pine." She gazed at it lovingly.

"Do you like it?"

She heard the hesitancy in his voice. That caused her to spring to her feet and fall into his arms.

"I love it. I love that you made it. I love you."

She kissed him, the first time she'd ever initiated a kiss between them. She poured into it all the love that had been growing inside of her. A love that she really hadn't known existed until this moment.

He finally broke the kiss, his breathing coming in short spurts.

"You really like it?"

"Yes." She kissed him once more, a soft touch that barely grazed his lips. "I like it a lot."

"I give this hope chest to you in good faith, Nora. I pray you'll store your most special items in it and maybe even a good dose of hope that we'll be rocking out on that porch when we're eighty-five. Maybe ninety."

"I'll be eighty-five. You're the one that'll already be ninety."

He cupped her chin. "I hope we'll die in each other's arms in our sleep, at least fifty years from now, with good times in our memories and no secrets between us."

He drew her close, resting his chin atop her head.

No secrets.

And here she already hid one from him.

"Jack . . . there's something we need to talk about."

He pulled away from her and looked her in the eyes.

"It's about the Kesslers."

CHAPTER 24

"**Y**ou are the prettiest bride I've ever seen," Jess declared.

Nora stared at the image reflected in the oval mirror. She barely recognized herself. Jess had piled Nora's hair high atop her head, making her seem even taller. Her eyes were bright and her cheeks flushed as if she'd raced Robby to the newspaper office and back.

It was the dress, though, that made her seem truly beautiful. In the short time they'd had, Jess crafted a vision of loveliness. A soft shade of sky blue, it had a rounded neck and long sleeves trimmed in lace. A tight bodice flared out into a very full skirt, thanks to several stiff petticoats underneath. It made her a vision of elegance.

She tried to calm the butterflies that raced through her stomach, wondering if fairy tales really did come true.

She'd told Jack she loved him, and she'd meant it. It surprised her to attach such a powerful word to all the jumble of feelings raging within her, but the minute she uttered the words, they had seemed right.

Nora didn't worry that he hadn't responded accordingly. Jess told her long ago that many men were too stoic to admit romantic feelings aloud. Jack Duncan struck her as that kind of man.

Hopefully, those feelings were buried deep inside him. She banked on this. After the way her first marriage turned out, she couldn't take a chance. Jack had her trust. She hoped, one day, she would have his love.

"Mama! You look like a queen!"

She caught Robby's expression in the mirror. His open-mouthed amazement spread into a wide grin.

"I feel like a queen. You look pretty handsome yourself."

He tugged at his shirt collar. "Ben helped me. Grampy was too tired. He said he had to rest."

Nora looked at Jess, her smile bright, hiding her concern with Robby present. "I think I'll go check on Papa. Why don't you finish getting ready, Jess?"

She walked down the hall and tapped lightly on her father's door.

"Papa? May I come in?" She waited for a reply. "Papa?"

Her heart slammed against her chest at the lack of response. Panic thickened her throat. An unspoken prayer crowded into her mind. She pushed it aside as she turned the doorknob and pushed the door open.

Albert was slumped on the floor, his face turned away from her. She ran to his side and dropped to her knees while she turned him over. He was an alarming shade of white.

"Papa!"

Nora tried to rouse him unsuccessfully.

"Ben! Get Dr. Malone! Now!"

She cradled his head in her lap, whispering words of comfort that went unheard.

THE CHURCH WAS FILLING UP. JACK TRIED TO swallow the nerves that suddenly rumbled through him. He'd heard murmurs about cold feet before a wedding. Was this what people meant?

None of Nora's family was present yet. He'd hoped at least Ben and Jess would be here by now. He figured Nora and Albert would leave the house and walk over just before the ceremony began. That was in less than ten minutes.

He stepped out the door. A hard slap on his back startled him. "How you holding up, boy?" Dr. Malone asked.

Jack grinned. "I've been better," he admitted.

The physician was going to stand up with him. Jack wasn't close to anyone in town and wondered who he should ask. Albert would have been his first choice if he wasn't escorting Nora down the aisle. He'd thought about Robby, but Nora said he was too young. Robby had a tendency to giggle at solemn occasions, and she didn't want to ruin the ceremony. She trusted Jess to keep him in line in the pew.

Reverend Seabury would have been his next choice, but that wouldn't be possible since he would perform the ceremony. Finally, he'd asked Doc Malone. The man's presence already had a calming effect on him.

"Got myself worked up mighty fine before I got hitched," said Malone. "I was shaking so bad my daddy didn't think I'd be able to stand during the vows."

Jack looked at him in surprise. Cyrus Malone was the most unflappable man he knew. It did him a world of good to hear that he, too, had been nervous on his wedding day.

"Daddy sent my brother back around the corner to our house to fetch a bottle of brandy. My daddy was a doctor, too. He used it for medicinal purposes." Malone chuckled. "He said nerves qualified for a good-sized medicinal dose."

"Did it help?"

The physician laughed. "Well, at least I was able to stand up. Between Daddy on one side and Iris on the other, I made it through." He grinned sheepishly. "Still don't remember much of it, though."

Jack kicked a rock in front of him. "I don't think I'll need any brandy. I want to remember my wedding day."

He took a deep breath to calm his jitters. He'd been through years of fierce battle. Brought in dangerous outlaws. Crawled in the bowels of unsteady earth seeking silver.

None of that compared to getting married and becoming an instant father.

He wondered how Nora was holding up.

Cyrus Malone caught his eye. "Let's go inside, son. It's almost time to start. You want to be at the front when Nora comes floating down that aisle. There's not a prettier sight than when a man catches sight of his bride."

The men reentered the church, walking down the aisle alongside the windows. Several people spoke as they passed. The best Jack could do was nod. He tried to swallow but his mouth was drier than a desert.

"Doc! Doc!"

He recognized Ben's voice as it echoed through the silence in the church. He and Malone both reacted quickly, darting up the aisle to meet Ben as he approached at a run.

"Come quick. It's Mr. Albert. He's in a bad way."

"Get my bag, Jack. It's next to Iris." Malone hurried from the church.

Jack grabbed the bag that Mrs. Malone held up and quickly followed. As he stepped out into the fading light, he saw the Pendletons alight from their buggy, Mrs. Pendleton complaining about their tardiness.

He needed to get Dr. Malone there fast. He motioned the other two men into their cart.

"Emergency, folks."

He caught the reins up and signaled the horses. They took off at a fast trot down the street.

A thousand thoughts ran through his mind, none coherent.

They arrived at the Le Fall homestead and scrambled from the cart. Jack leaped over the picket fence that surrounded the new home, Ben and Doctor Malone close behind. Jess motioned them down the hall and ushered them into Albert's room.

Nora sat on the bed next to her father. Her gaze met Jack's. He saw the haunted fear in her eyes. Though her voice quavered, she described to the physician exactly how she'd found Albert.

"We placed him on the bed and covered him with blankets to prevent shock. I can't waken him, though."

"You did just fine, Nora," the doctor comforted. "I need everyone to leave so I can examine my patient."

"I want to stay," she said firmly.

"Of course, dear. Everyone else out."

Jack reluctantly left the room, his jaw clenched. Albert looked dead to him. He wondered if Nora was fooling herself and only thought him to be alive.

His heart went out to her. She had already suffered so much and now on what should be one of the happiest days of her life, tragedy had struck.

He paced the parlor, nervous energy bursting from him. Jess sat stiffly in a chair, dry-eyed. Ben stood behind her, his large hands on her shoulders, occasionally giving her a reassuring squeeze. Marguerite had arrived with Mrs. Malone and the Seaburys and sat huddled in the corner.

Jack suddenly wondered where Robby was. He stepped outside to search for him and saw a small, booted foot peeking out from under the porch. He bent down.

"Robby."

A sniffle echoed under the porch.

"Come here, son."

Robby scooted out from his hiding place on all fours and stood shakily, his eyes swollen with tears.

Instinctively, Jack held out his arms. The little boy ran to him and buried his face in Jack's shoulder, his body shaking with silent sobs.

He returned to the porch and sat in the swing, Robby's arms locked around his neck. The motion was a tonic to them both and slowly the boy relaxed his grasp. Jack didn't know how long they sat this way before he realized darkness had fallen. He glanced down and saw that Robby was asleep. He rose carefully with the boy in his arms and walked toward the door.

The screen opened. Dr. Malone stood in the doorway.

"I'll take the boy. Go to Nora, son."

Jack handed the sleeping bundle over. He steeled himself for whatever lay ahead.

CHAPTER 25

Nora stood by Albert's bed. Instant relief washed over Jack when he saw the covers pulled to the old man's chin and not tucked over his head.

"How is he?"

She wrapped her arms about her. "It was a stroke. Dr. Malone isn't sure yet how much damage has been done. Papa could face partial paralysis. He could be dead in the next hour."

Jack moved to her, wanting to comfort her, but she threw an arm out.

"Please. Don't touch me."

Her words hit him as hard as a slap.

"Why?"

She gave him a bitter smile. "Because even now, with Papa hovering between life and death, all I *can* think about is you touching me. I wish you could sweep me up in arms and kiss me until I'm breathless. Make me forget all this."

She shook her head. "I feel lower than a snake for wanting you so much that I hurt." She rubbed her eyes. "I'm sorry. I wanted this day to go so well."

"So did I." His voice was barely a whisper. "There's nothing wrong with needing someone, Nora. It was like that in the war. So many bad things happening all around you. Sickness and death so close, you breathed it in with every gasp for air."

As he spoke, Jack took the few steps necessary to close the gap between them. He pulled her close, his chin resting atop her head, glad that he could simply hold her.

She trembled in his arms. He held her lovingly, with no words, trying to transfer his strength into her. He wanted to tell her it was good to want to feel alive, to shout it from the hilltop, but that wasn't what she needed to hear now.

Jack looked at their image reflected in the mirror. Nora looked so lovely in the dress Jess had made. He hoped she would still wear it on their wedding day. A selfish thought poked him in the ribs. He wanted Albert to live—because he couldn't live without this woman for an entire year of mourning.

Now, he felt like the snake. He wasn't a praying man, but he said a quick, heartfelt prayer for his friend's survival and for Nora's peace of mind.

"Nora."

A hoarse whisper called from the bed. They sprang apart. She dropped to her knees next to the bed.

"Papa?"

"I can't . . . I can't . . . Nora, I can't move."

❦

"THE PARALYSIS COULD BE TEMPORARY. THEN AGAIN, it could be permanent."

Nora released a deep sigh. "You're telling us you don't know."

Dr. Malone nodded sadly. "I'm afraid you're right on that point." He closed his medical bag and met her eyes. "These things can take time. Even the best doctors back East couldn't tell you more than I have already."

She saw the defeated look in the physician's eyes and knew her harsh tone had put it there. Nora laid a hand on his sleeve. "I'm not doubting your skill, Dr. Malone."

"That's a normal reaction, dear." He shifted his bag from one hand to the other. "The best thing to do is let Albert get some rest tonight." The doctor looked at the small circle gathered around him. "That goes for all of you. Does anyone need a sleeping draught?"

Marguerite spoke up. "That won't be necessary, Doctor. I'm sure we'll all want to sit a spell with Albert during the night."

"I'll walk you to the door," Nora offered.

She stepped onto the porch with him and drew the door closed behind her.

"Would you like a private word, Mrs. Cantrelle?"

She nodded. "I realize Silver Bluff's a small town and we all seem to know each other's business. I have a favor to ask."

"Go on."

"The *Silver Bluff Gazette* is our livelihood. We've wagered everything we had to move West. If it fails . . ." Her voice faded. She swallowed the lump gathered in her throat. "We simply have to make a success of this venture."

"How can I help?"

Nora saw nothing but kindness in the physician's eyes. It gave her the courage to continue.

"I'd like to keep the paralysis quiet. For now."

Dr. Malone quickly caught on. "Shall we say Albert's not up to visitors? That he tires easily?"

"That's exactly what I had in mind. If this continues, I could let everyone know he's feeling better and is working at home. Doctor's orders." She gave the physician a half-smile.

"You never know. The scene you paint could well come to pass."

"I'm a realist. I've had to be. My mother died when I was young, and for all Papa's good qualities, his head is often in the clouds. The war, too, taught me to prepare myself for the worst."

Dr. Malone placed a hand on her shoulder. "Can you run the *Silver Bluff Gazette* alone?"

Determination filled her. "I've written a majority of the stories for quite a while. Papa would write an editorial from time to time. Often, we'd talk over story ideas, but I was always the one to get the articles on paper."

"And Ben?"

Nora smiled. "Ben writes the headlines that attract attention and typesets all the work. Lately, he's been learning how to create advertisements and handbills." She shrugged. "I guess we'll both take on a little bit more responsibility."

"May I pass along a small piece of advice?"

"Of course."

"Let Marguerite and Jess do most of the nursing."

"But—"

"They need something to do. You'll be far too busy to sit at Albert's bedside fourteen hours a day and run a newspaper. I'm not saying abandon your father. Just let the others—"

"I know what you're saying." She pulled a handkerchief from her pocket and wiped her eyes. "Thank you. For everything." She put her arms around him and hugged him fiercely.

"Papa will get better. I know he will."

He had to. The thought of seeing him waste away was too much for her to bear.

"Miss Nora, I done told you what Mr. Kessler said. We got to be patient."

Nora continued determinedly down the street in the early morning light, chin thrust up, ready to take on William Kessler and the world. Ben matched his strides to hers.

"Nothing good'll come from this, Miss Nora. Mark my words."

She stopped in her tracks. "I won't be kept waiting any longer, Ben. Kessler's already put you off about discussing this paper delay. We can't sit on it any longer."

She continued in long strides until they reached the edge of town and beyond. Ben tread silently beside her. When they reached Kessler's place, Nora halted in front of the gate.

"I'd like you to wait here."

Ben started to speak then shook his head slowly. "I've known you since you were a baby. You were stubborn then and way more now." He crossed his arms and leaned against the fence. "Go on, now. I'll wait for you here."

"Thank you, Ben."

She opened the gate's latch and hurried up the walkway before her courage failed her. Chin answered her knock and solemnly shook hands with her.

"Welcome, Miss Nora. You've come to see Mr. Kessler?"

"Yes, Chin."

He showed her in and seated her on a carved oak bench in the main hallway. She studied the patterned swirls in the carpet until he returned and escorted her upstairs to a spacious office.

"Come in, Mrs. Cantrelle." William Kessler was seated behind his desk puffing on a cigar, shirtsleeves rolled up as he pored over a map spread across his desk.

To Nora, this was the first slap in the face. No gentleman back home would have dared received a lady without his coat on. Even though the West was much more casual than the South, she knew the good manners that had been drilled into William Kessler were now sorely lacking.

On purpose.

"Good day, Mr. Kessler. I'm here to inquire about the paper delays that have occurred this last month. Ben told me you'd put him off about—"

"I'm not used to doing business with lackeys," Kessler said bluntly.

"Ben is no lackey, sir. He is a valued employee and family friend who deserved a valid answer."

He blew a perfect ring of smoke in her direction. "I don't believe we'll have any more problems now. Our new foreman took a bit longer than I expected to learn the ropes, is all. That and the fact that we were behind in our delivery schedule. You shouldn't experience any more lags."

"When will the paper be delivered?"

"Tomorrow." Kessler extinguished his cigar. "How is Albert doing? It's been over a month since he's been at the office."

"Papa is doing as well as can be expected. Dr. Malone says he's coming along nicely."

"You've been late coming out with the last two papers. I wonder if I shouldn't bring someone in to run it for you until Albert gets back on his feet." He smiled daggers at her. "As a partial investor, I would hate to see the *Silver Bluff Gazette* go under."

Nora held her temper in check. It wouldn't do any good to lose it. "Things are under control. *If* our paper supply is delivered on time. I'd hate to think spotty deliveries were an attempt to sabotage the *Silver Bluff Gazette*."

"And risk my investment? You obviously know nothing about business, Mrs. Cantrelle."

"Then maybe you could explain things to me sometime." She glanced at the opened map on his desk. "Perhaps how to buy real estate, for instance?"

"Retract those little claws, Nora."

She turned and saw Ken Kessler in the doorway. Despite her uneasy feelings about him, he was a welcomed sight compared to his older brother.

"Good day, Ken. I was just leaving. I have a newspaper to put out." She glanced at William Kessler before turning back to his brother. "I'm relieved that Mr. Kessler has assured me I won't have any more problems doing that—now that his problems at the paper mill have been resolved."

"Then I'll see you out."

Ken took her elbow and moved her through the doorway and down the stairs. He paused in the front hall as they reached the door.

"Guess I won't be getting that home-cooked meal you promised me." He gave her a wry smile.

Maybe Chin had been wrong, and Ken wasn't as bad as she'd thought.

And maybe she could find out a few things from him.

"I don't have time for cooking these days, but I wouldn't be opposed to a buggy ride. It would be a welcomed break from all my work."

He tilted his head and studied her a moment. "I guess you'd need to check with the sheriff to see if he'd allow you to go for a drive with me."

She bristled inwardly but thought she could use this to her advantage. Let Ken Kessler think she was affected by his taunt.

"I'm my own woman. I don't need permission from Jack to go for a ride."

"Tomorrow afternoon? Surely, you can take an hour from piecing together your stories."

"What time?"

"How about two o'clock?"

"Three would be better."

"I'll call on you at three." Ken took her hand and lifted it to his mouth. He brushed a quick kiss upon her knuckles and released it before she could protest.

Nora stepped aside as he opened the door. "Until tomorrow."

She nodded and went down the stairs. Ben was still waiting by the picket fence.

"He said the paper deliveries would be on time from now on. We'll receive our expected shipment tomorrow."

"Hmmm."

"He wanted to bring someone in to run the *Silver Bluff Gazette* until Papa got back on his feet."

"Hmmm."

Nora stopped. "Do you want to know what I told him?"

Ben pulled his hat lower onto his brow and shrugged. "Don't need to know. I got a pretty good idea."

She stewed over her encounter with their minor investor the entire way back to town.

"I'm going to go home and feed Papa and then check on Robby and Tien's lessons. I should be back to the office in no more than an hour."

"Don't forget to eat something," Ben advised

"I'll bring us both something back and we'll eat together. All right?"

She waved as he set off in one direction and she in the other. As she passed in front of the bank, she heard her named called out.

"Mrs. Cantrelle? Mrs. Cantrelle? That is you?"

A woman in her mid-forties approached. She was tiny but wore a formidable look on her face. Nora dreaded their encounter, remembering how Jack had warned her to keep her distance from this woman.

"Hello," she said in a friendly but guarded tone.

"You must be Mrs. Witherspoon. I've heard you've been out of town for some time."

The banker's wife gave her an appraising look. "Finally, we meet. I had a terrible head cold and then missed you before I went to visit my sister. Been gone a good spell now."

"It's nice to have you back in Silver Bluff. Have you been able to catch up on things in the *Silver Bluff Gazette?*"

Millicent Witherspoon pursed her lips. "That's exactly what I want to take up with you, missy."

Nora frowned. "You may address me as Mrs. Cantrelle or Nora."

The older woman ignored her remark. "Let me tell you, missy, that I have gripes aplenty about your so-called newspaper. Mr. Witherspoon tells me you've been late in getting out your editions two times in a row. We are not paying for lackadaisical efforts."

She pushed her glasses back onto the bridge of her nose. "And I can't believe I've been back for two whole days without you coming to see me. Any newspaper worth its salt would want to let its readers know about my trip."

"And the fact you are now home and ready to receive callers?"

Mrs. Witherspoon stamped her foot. "Of course." She shook her finger at Nora. "You haven't even asked for my recipe for black currant jelly. Everyone in Silver Bluff knows I make the best jelly in Colorado Territory. How do you answer that?"

Before Nora could reply, Mrs. Witherspoon added, "You can't. That's all there is to it. What kind of business are you running? I felt the need to speak to Mr. Kessler about things."

Nora's eyes narrowed. "Why would you do that?"

"He's the most important man in this town, so mannerly and gracious. Mr. Kessler assured me that although a woman was in charge for the present, he knew you'd come to your senses in time."

"Oh, he did?"

"Yes, missy. Mr. Kessler and I know that a woman should be in the home, caring for her man and having babies."

Anger simmered through Nora and she refused to hold her tongue any longer. This exchange would not end with Millicent Witherspoon having the last word.

"While the *Silver Bluff Gazette* is interested in all the citizens of this town, it recognizes the fact that no one person is more important than another, Mrs. Witherspoon. Certainly we will report on your visit with your sister—if space allows. Furthermore, I will not permit you to stand in judgment of the efforts my family has made in getting this newspaper off the ground. Yes, there have been delays in our supply chain but those will be cleared up."

The older woman's jaw dropped. Not a sound came from her. Nora doubted anyone had ever called out Mrs. Witherspoon for her bullying.

"Furthermore, I couldn't care less for the opinion of Mr. Kessler. I plan to run this newspaper even after I marry Sheriff Duncan. I will continue to run it while I carry and birth his children. And I will do a damned fine job of it."

Nora took a few steps and turned back to the spiteful woman. "And I cannot abide black currant jelly. Good day, Mrs. Witherspoon."

As she strolled away, Nora had to stifle the laughter that threatened to bubble up.

❦

JACK STARED IDLY OUT THE WINDOW, TIRED OF THE paperwork in front of him. He caught sight of Millicent

Witherspoon pointing her finger in Nora's face and grinned.

His day had just become considerably more interesting. He watched Nora begin to say something, only to be cut off immediately. He didn't want to have to arrest his fiancée for manslaughter. He was afraid it would come to that by the look on Nora's face. He stood, ready to step out when he heard the rumble of the noon stage.

The two women moved back as the horses roared by and came to a halt near them. A lone man in a dark suit stepped from the carriage, straightening his collar. The driver removed a trunk from atop and handed it down to the stranger. His stance seemed familiar.

No passengers waited to board, so the driver took up the reins again and urged the horses forward. More than likely he would water the horses at the trough behind Seymour's before continuing on to Wyoming.

The visitor paused and tipped his hat to the women. Jack immediately recognized him as Thomas Morrison, Kessler's mystery guest from before. He exchanged a few words with the pair.

It bothered him that he recognized Morrison from somewhere, but he couldn't place him.

If he did, he might have a better idea what the Kesslers were up to.

CHAPTER 26

Jack ambled into the general store, his boots clicking along the wooden boards.

"Morning, Jack."

Seymour Simmons handed him a blueberry muffin sitting on the counter. He wolfed it down. Mrs. Simmons wasn't much of a cook, but he hadn't had a bite this morning. When he'd gone to gather eggs, he'd found two dead hens, with a third cowering in the corner. He figured a fox had broken into the hen house. Cleaning up the blood and feathers reminded him of what a mess the war had been. It also killed his appetite.

Seymour chuckled. "You must be hungry the way you're gobbling down that muffin." He sighed as if bored, but Jack caught a restlessness in the storeowner.

"Spill the beans, Seymour. I can tell you've got something to say."

The man nodded sagely. "Got some news, all right."

Jack studied him carefully. Seymour's eyes gleamed with hidden knowledge that was seconds from eruption.

"I done gone and sold the general store," he blurted out. "Made a dilly of a deal."

He felt the wind knocked out of him and barked out, "Who'd you sell to?"

Seymour grinned like a jackal. "That's the beauty of the deal. I sold out to Mr. Kessler."

"What?"

"He's made me a few offers in the last weeks. My Jane's been pressing me to take him up." Seymour wiped at imaginary crumbs on the countertop as he spoke. "Made a tidy profit and I will continue to run the store at a handsome salary. It's the best of both worlds. Security for the future and still a good living in the here and now."

"Gotta run, Seymour." Jack tipped his hat and strode out quickly. He'd be damned if he'd congratulate Seymore and his deal with the Devil.

He crossed the street and returned to the jail, slamming the door when he reached it. He walked a few steps and kicked the trash can across the room, swearing loudly.

The fact that Kessler now owned all of the land around town and much to the north and south of it was old news. He'd thought things through a thousand times.

Water rights? No. He hadn't invested in cattle or shown any interest in it.

Mining? The silver mine was producing steadily. Kessler made no move to open any new shafts on the land he'd acquired.

The railroad. That was the only thing left. What he'd just found out from Seymour Simmons confirmed his suspicions.

Jack fought the sour twisting in his stomach. He crossed to the window and looked down the street at the store. He couldn't blame Simmons. He was set for his old age with the sweet deal.

Only last night, Jack discovered Silver Bluff's hotel was now in Kessler's possession. The news didn't surprise him. Zebulon Hall and his wife had always liked Denver better anyway, with its conveniences and quality of society. They'd spent most of the past year there.

By slowly taking over the town, Kessler would earn a pretty penny if it became a major stop on the railroad. Jack was certain that railroad would also come across all the land bought up by Kessler in the last few months.

What else did the bastard have up his sleeve?

At that moment, William Kessler himself walked into the jail with another man. Immediately, Jack looked over the stranger accompanying Kessler. He was just under six feet, wiry in build, with green eyes that glittered. His smile was false as he removed his hat, uncovering a bald pate speckled with freckles.

"Jack, I'd like you to meet Spank McHardy."

He nodded warily. He offered his hand only to size up the other man's shake. It was firm but the sweating palm betrayed the McHardy's nervousness.

"Silver Bluff's grown so much in the months I've been here." Kessler smiled broadly. "I thought it was high time to get you some help. Spank here's your new deputy. You'll teach him the ropes, of course."

"So he can take over my job?" His words hung in the air. He finally added, "My contract's up in a month. Are you implying that it won't be renewed?"

Kessler cleared his throat. "I can and will deny that, Sheriff. Spank's here to ease some of your burdens. No offense should be taken."

Light footsteps sounded on the boards outside the door. Nora swung open the door. She didn't seem surprised to see William Kessler there.

Nora announced, "The *Silver Bluff Gazette's* been vandalized."

Spank whistled low. "You must be the lady writer. Miz Cantrelle. Mr. Kessler's told me about you."

She ignored the stranger. "Equipment was damaged.

I'm uncertain how long the delay will be before we can begin production again."

Her voice was strong, but Jack knew the inner struggle her words brought. He longed to comfort her, but he knew Nora would want to stand strong in front of Kessler.

His gut screamed that William Kessler was responsible for what had happened at the newspaper office, as sure as he'd been that Kessler had torched Seth Appleton's place. This might bankrupt the Le Falls.

"I can check things out for you, ma'am," said Spank affably. "Let's just—"

"No," Jack interrupted. An eerie stillness bathed the room. No one moved. He met McHardy's eyes. "I'll take care of Mrs. Cantrelle."

He took Nora's elbow and led her outside into an overcast day. He could smell rain in the air. It would be here within the next few minutes.

She held herself stiffly as he guided her along. "Aren't you going to ask me about my new deputy?"

Her eyes widened in alarm. "Your what?"

"Kessler had just introduced me to my new right-hand man when you walked in." He shrugged. "Looks like I'll be out of a job soon."

She gripped his arm tightly. "He can't do that, Jack."

"He can and will, darlin'. I had a contract with Stevenson. Kessler can cut me loose if he chooses. It's up in less than two weeks. Looks like I'll be training my successor in Kesslerville."

She looked at him quizzically. "What are you saying?"

"Well, they might as well rename the town after our beloved Mr. Kessler. Seems he's bought out the hotel and the general store."

Nora laughed bitterly. "I can't even write about it now, much less prove he sabotaged my presses."

"What all's wrong?"

She shrugged. "I'm not sure. The minute we saw the damage, I hightailed it over to your office. Ben's assessing the damage."

They reached the newspaper office and went inside. Ben was trying to lift one of the toppled presses.

"Let me give you a hand," Jack suggested.

Between the two of them, they righted the press and surveyed the damage.

"Not as bad as I thought," Ben said. He walked from one end of the press to the other, studying it carefully. "Not like it's been smashed. A few parts will need to be replaced."

"Would they have those parts in Denver?" Nora asked.

Jack looked at the last vestige of hope on Nora's face and saw a brief smile when Ben told her he thought so. Then despair shadowed her eyes again.

"Even if they do, we have no money. We've pawned the few jewels Mother brought into the marriage. We sold off all the fine furniture back in Monroe, piece by piece. We don't have any room in this house to take in boarders as we did before."

The bleakness on her face aged her by a decade. Ben enveloped her in his huge arms.

"We'll get by, Miss Nora. We won't let this get us down. We've gotta be strong for Mr. Albert." The gentle giant stroked Nora's hair as if she were a child again. Jack had an image of a young Nora with skinned knees, coming to Ben for comfort.

"You're damned right we'll get by." He slapped Ben on the back. "Let's go see Seymour. He can help me wire my bank in Denver."

CHAPTER 27

"**Y**ou can't do that," Nora declared.

Jack gave Nora a look that would freeze boiling water. "I can. And I will." He gazed at her steadily, daring her to contradict him. Being Nora, she did.

"Jack, you can't protect me from all the world's evils. This is something Ben and I will work out." She looked pleadingly at her friend. "Won't we, Ben?"

"We have to do what's best for Mr. Albert," Ben said without hesitation. "He doesn't need this borrowed trouble. If'n we take Mr. Jack up on his offer, we can get back on our feet and have him paid back in no time."

Nora looked as if she needed more convincing.

"Weren't you the one who told me you wanted to do more than put out a newspaper?" he asked. "You said with the town growing, there'd be handbills to circulate for new businesses. Signs in stores to be printed. Brochures and maps and plenty of—"

"I see where you're going but I hate to take charity."

"Weren't you listening in church last Sunday, woman? Even I couldn't gather wool when the good reverend spoke. He said the three greatest things were faith, hope, and charity. I'm offering you all three."

He wanted to take care of her. Damn, if he hadn't

picked a woman with an independent streak a mile and a half wide.

"At least if we were married—"

"We *are* married, darlin'. At least in my heart of hearts. We committed that day to be together. Albert's getting sick hasn't changed a thing. I don't care if it takes another month of Sundays before I say the official vows and slip that ring on your finger. You've already got my heart."

"Oh, Jack."

She wrapped her arms about his waist, resting her head against his chest. He held her a moment, savoring the rush of warmth that flowed through him. Then he gave her a brief squeeze and lifted her chin with his finger.

"I can wire my bank in Denver. Most of my funds are there. More private that way."

She smiled. "I can't imagine why you wouldn't want Mr. Witherspoon reporting on your financial affairs to his missus."

"That battle-ax spews everything she knows to weeds in a field. That's exactly why the bulk of my money's safe in Denver."

He turned to Ben. "Can you leave immediately?"

"I'll need to see about getting a horse and cart."

"You're welcomed to my wagon. It's strong and roomy because of the furniture I transport. I'll need my horse, but Seymour can rent you his two. We can go arrange that now."

Jack caught Nora's hand and held it a moment. "This will work out. Just have a little faith."

"With a generous dash of hope and charity?"

He grinned.

ALEXA ASTON

"Everything's all but finalized. Come the spring, the railroad will run through here clean up into Wyoming." Thomas Morrison packed the tobacco tightly into his pipe. "You bought all the land we spoke about?"

William Kessler nodded. "Yes. We used a little pressure a few times but I'm the proud owner of this town and anything else that comes up in it or around it for miles and miles. Cost most of what I had, but thanks to you, Tom, I'll regain every penny a thousand-fold."

Morrison gestured, pipe in hand. "As long as you can produce reliable deeds, William. I'm serious about that. The U.S. Congress doesn't fool around. I have strict instructions on the documentation needed, once the decision's been made and we approach the owners of the land needed. I'll need to see originals for all sales and maintain copies of all deeds for the government's records."

He chuckled. "We became masters of paperwork during the war, Tom, didn't we?"

Morrison nodded. "As quartermaster, I had a code book to go by. My accounting background helped."

"Your ingenious way with things other than numbers helped, as well." He clapped Morrison on the back. "I never could have managed to slip a fortune through the lines without your help. I haven't forgotten that."

Morrison blew smoke into a perfect ring. "Neither have I, William. My time's come now, though."

"I told you to be patient. You were. I'll have the gold transferred into your San Francisco account by week's end. My lawyer's coming through to make sure every 'i' has been dotted."

"I get the rest after the announcement is made?"

"Of course." He crossed to his picture window and looked out possessively at Silver Bluff. "Spank's already in Silver Bluff learning the ropes, courtesy of Sheriff Duncan."

"How do you plan to get rid of Duncan? Seems like he won't take to all the gambling halls and businesses you intend to start. If he plans to marry that lush little piece, she's the kind that'll want schools and civic pride."

"Stevenson had him on contract. It's close to being up. I won't renew it."

"Probably a good thing."

"Why?"

"You don't know?" Morrison smiled sarcastically and took another puff. "He once served under your command."

"What?" Kessler felt the blood rush to his head, causing him to go lightheaded for a minute.

"He wasn't there long. Transferred out to front-line duty. Probably had all those foolish notions of being a hero for the Union. He's lucky to be alive. It was early in the war when he shipped out."

He shook his head. "He's never said a word."

"He plays his cards close to the vest," Morrison noted.

Ken Kessler threw open the door and interrupted their conversation. "Have you seen my diamond stickpin? I could've sworn I left it—"

His brother touched his own lapel self-consciously. "And why would you need it? Where are you going?"

Ken smiled as he spied it. He walked to William and deftly lifted it, placing it on his own suit coat in a quick motion.

"Still slick as spit, Ken."

"Thank you, Tommy Boy."

"You didn't answer me," Kessler said gruffly, although he had a pretty good idea that it involved a woman. "Where are you going?"

Ken grinned impishly. "On my way to see Nora Cantrelle."

He threw his hands in the air as Morrison cackled. "What does her fiancé have to say about that?"

"She's not married yet."

Kessler placed a hand on his brother's shoulder. "You're playing with fire. Jack Duncan's no sucker."

Ken patted his pomaded hair, his lady-killer smile already in place. "Later, boys."

꧁꧂

NORA RUSHED IN AND RAN SMACK INTO JESS, telling her, "Someone broke into the office and ruined some of the parts to the printing press. Ben's going to Denver to get the replacements we'll need."

Jess' eyes narrowed. "With what?"

She shrugged. "I sold Robby to a childless couple passing through."

"Miss Nora, you are bad to the bone."

She twirled around. "I'm just so happy, Jess. I thought everything was too far gone. The darkest hour is only sixty minutes, though. I think we're due a little sunshine in the Le Fall household."

"Is Mr. Jack helping out?"

She turned quickly. "How did you know?"

"He's a decent man."

"He's wiring his bank in Denver. Ben'll be able to get what he needs and use Jack's wagon to bring the parts back. Hopefully, we can be up and running again in a week. Less if things go well. Papa need never know."

"You don't think he'll miss Ben?"

Nora shook her head. "You know he has his good and bad days. We'll manage." She sighed. "I'll go look in on him and then I'll be going out for a while."

Jess frowned. "Where are you going?"

"If I tell you, I don't want any lectures."

Jess mumbled to herself.

"I'm going for a drive with Mr. Ken Kessler."

"What?"

"You heard me. I think I can pump him for information about what his brother's up to. He's bought up the town and everything around it. I'm going to get to the bottom of this whether you approve or not."

Nora went down the hall and quietly entered her father's room. A window was open, admitting a cool breeze. She covered him with a patchwork quilt and then slipped an item from his dresser drawer before she went to her room to freshen up.

Her hands trembled as she brought the brush to her hair. What she was doing was dangerous. Chin's words echoed in her head. That girl, Sally, met with foul play at Ken Kessler's hands. She would be in a vulnerable position. Yet she didn't know any other way to find out what William Kessler's plans were.

She dashed off a note, telling where they would be. She hoped it was strictly a precaution. She didn't expect Ken to become violent. If he did, she was prepared. She picked up the revolver she'd taken from Albert's bureau and checked to see that it was loaded. She slipped it into her reticule and returned to tidying her hair.

Ken Kessler called exactly at three.

"My, you're prompt."

"I thought someone used to meeting deadlines could appreciate that." He gave her a winning smile and took her elbow to guide her along the path.

"Anywhere particular place you'd like to go?" He lifted her into the buggy and walked around, climbing in and taking up the reins.

"Let's take the west road out of town and see a little of nature."

He gave her a sideways glance. "Don't want your neighbors to see us out and about?"

She bit her tongue and smiled sweetly. Gossiping women were the least of her concerns. In Monroe, this little outing would have caused an uproar. Out West, things were much more informal. What she was concerned about was avoiding Jack for the moment. He would blow higher than a whale if he knew what she was up to.

Ken turned the horse and headed back in the opposite direction. They rode in silence for a few minutes. She was conscious of his thigh pressed against hers. She began to wonder if this had been such a good idea after all.

He took the reins in one hand and leaned back, draping his other arm along the back of the seat. Nora thanked her stars that the nuns had drilled excellent posture into her. She did not want her back to brush against him under any circumstances.

"Will you tell our sheriff about this little sojourn?"

"Jack doesn't run my life," she snapped. "Unlike your brother, who runs yours." She hoped to provoke him into revealing something of importance.

Ken stopped the horse. "I am sorely offended. I thought you realized I assist my brother. William can't do a thing without me."

"So he's the brains and you're the muscle?"

He sneered. "I know as much and maybe more than he does."

"Then why has he bought up all the land in and around town, pushing people out right and left? Has he found another mother lode of silver? Will he open another mine?"

Ken frowned. "You think you know it all. For your information, the railroad is coming through soon. That's why Tommy Morrison's been in town. He's with the Congressional commission sent to investigate the best route to lay track. It's going to make William a mover and shaker in these parts. He's going to be governor when Colorado becomes a state. I'll be with him every step of the way."

He looked at her intently. "You could, too. With me."

"You're crazy. I'd never leave Jack."

Ken grabbed her tightly by her upper arms. "You're a flirt and a tease, Nora Cantrelle." He pulled her to him, forcing a hard kiss.

Revulsion filled her. If she hadn't realized it before, in that moment she knew Jack Duncan was the only man for her. She jerked away and spit on her attacker.

Stars flared immediately. Nora hit the ground hard, landing awkwardly on her hip. It took her a moment to realize that Ken had slapped her so hard she'd fallen from the buggy.

"You cock-teasing whore! You're like all the others," he roared.

He tossed aside the reins and jumped to the ground, his face angry with menace. Nora reached inside her reticule and removed the pistol. She pointed it up at her attacker.

Ken froze. She saw the indecision in his eyes.

"I will use it," she promised as she cocked the gun.

He swallowed hard, his eyes narrowing as he studied her.

"You're done in this town, Nora Cantrelle. I'll make sure you never print a single page of that damned newspaper ever again."

"You can't stop me," she told him, willing the hand that held the gun to remain steady and not betray how frightened she truly was.

"You think I can't? How wrong you are, pretty lady. Your idiot father is on his last legs. Everyone in town knows he'll be dead soon—and then where will you be? You think that little ragtag family of yours can protect you?" He snorted. "Two old former slaves and a young boy wet behind the ears won't offer you much protection."

He snapped his fingers. "I could wipe them all out,

just like that, including that whore who hangs around your father and the damned sheriff who's sweet on you." Ken shook his head. "I'm the brains behind everything, Nora. The puppet master pulling my brother's strings. And you have just made the biggest mistake in your life when you decided to cross Ken Kessler."

He cursed at her, kicking at the gravel before he mounted the cart. Her heart hammering wildly in her chest, Nora watched him drive off in a blind rage.

CHAPTER 28

Nora walked stiffly along the bumpy road. Every step hurt, but she forced one foot in front of the other, willing the pain in her hip to fly away.

She was lucky and knew it. A wave of thankfulness washed over her. She was alive. It was more than she could say for poor Sally. Her gut told her the girl was long dead.

At least she'd forced Ken's outburst no more than a mile from home. It made for less ground to cover. Nora was grateful they were the first house on this side of town. She didn't want to explain her frazzled appearance to anyone. She'd taken enough risks as it was, going for a drive with Ken Kessler.

She squinted and saw home. Home. A simple word for such a sweet place. Nora wondered how long it would remain home to her. She longed to marry Jack and begin her new life with him, but she had to be practical. Until Papa was back on his feet, she needed to stick close by. If his days were numbered, she didn't mind sacrificing a little personal happiness for the extra time with her father.

Jess came into sight, bent over a washtub behind the

259

house. If Nora were lucky, she could slip inside unnoticed. She wasn't in any mood for *"I told you so"*—though she realized she deserved it.

She quietly opened the gate and went up the front walkway. Robby and Tien must be off with Ody. Thank goodness the dog wouldn't announce her presence to Jess with his yip.

Going into her bedroom, she stripped off her torn dress. Bruises splayed along her arms. She poured water into the basin and bathed her face. It was sore from the slap and still red. At least the slap had been open-handed and shouldn't leave a mark. She hoped no swelling would appear. She didn't want to concoct a story about it.

Nora rubbed her right hip. What hurt more than the sore hip was her wounded pride. She brightened, though, remembering the information she'd gleaned about the railroad and William Kessler's alleged run for governor. That would be an interesting race—if it happened. She couldn't wait to tell Jack what she'd discovered. If they could prove Kessler had advance knowledge of the railroad or influenced the choice of route in any way, charges of impropriety could be brought. She wondered if anything could be done about the pressure he used to purchase land, and whether or not those families might be entitled to regain their property.

She changed clothes and heard the clock chime in the parlor. Time to feed her father some broth and fresh bread. He still had trouble chewing because of the partial paralysis along his right side. She teased him about his crooked smile but her attempts at humor fell flat. He was despondent and she couldn't blame him. She wondered if he would ever recover physically. His illness was very different from Paul's.

Nora went to the kitchen door and opened it. "I'm back, Jess. I'll feed Papa now for you."

She ducked back into the kitchen, guilt weighing heavily on her. Jess taught her to be a lady. Her actions today were far removed from that notion.

She decided to look in and see if Papa might be awake before spooning out the broth Jess had burning low on the back of the stove. She walked to his room and quietly pushed open the door.

Nora studied her father from the doorway as he slept. He was no longer the giant she worshipped in her youth, full of vim and vigor. He was just a man and a frail one, at that. It took her by surprise how much he reminded her of her mother on her sickbed—the pale, pasty skin. Even the slack mouth Genevieve had worn.

She brought a handkerchief from her pocket and walked closer to wipe the drool from the corner of his mouth. He looked so weak. A half-formed prayer touched her lips before she stopped herself. She better watch what she prayed for. God had already answered her prayers twice. She didn't want His interference anymore.

Papa slowly opened his eyes, blinking several times before focusing on her.

"Is Marguerite here?"

"No, Papa, she's with the Seaburys this afternoon. Would you like me to send for her?"

He nodded, his breathing labored. "Fetch the reverend, too."

Nora brushed a quick kiss upon his brow and left the room. She followed the voices she heard. Robby and Tien had returned and were playing in the yard, throwing a stick to Ody and having him return it.

She walked out onto the porch. "Robby. Come here, please."

He tossed the stick out again for Ody and trotted over. "Hey, Mama. We've taught Ody how to fetch."

"That's a good trick to know." She smoothed his

hair. "I need you to go see Reverend Seabury and ask him to come visit right away. Marguerite, too."

"She's there making scones. Tien and I stopped and ate some." He made a face. "Hers weren't very good but we ate 'em anyway. Maybe she'll get better."

"Maybe she will."

Robby motioned to Tien. The boys opened the gate, ushering Ody through.

She had a quick thought. "Robby," she called. "On the way back, see if Jack's around. I'd like him to come over, too. If you can't find him, leave word with Mr. Simmons."

Robby's eyes lit up. He exchanged a grin with Tien. "Maybe he'll give us a peppermint candy." The boys took off running, Ody barking behind them.

Nora went back inside to wait at her father's bedside.

❦

HALF AN HOUR LATER, REVEREND SEABURY AND Marguerite had arrived. Robby told Nora that Jack was out with his new deputy, but he told Mr. Simmons to pass along the message.

They all gathered in her father's small bedroom. Nora had lit the lamps, bathing the room in a golden glow. Albert held out his good hand. Marguerite went to him, taking it in hers as she sat along the bedside.

"Will you marry me now, my love?" His voice was weak. "I can't offer you much but my good name."

"I never asked for more than that, Albert."

"Reverend?"

"I'm here, Albert." Seabury stepped closer and laid a hand on Albert's shoulder. "I'll begin whenever you're ready."

Her father took a slow breath. "Go ahead. I'm not going anywhere just yet."

The minister started the wedding ceremony. Nora was sorry Ben wasn't there to share in it. She reached for Jess' hand and held on tightly.

Jack slipped into the room halfway through the vows. He'd gotten Robby's message and hightailed it over. He had not asked Spank McHardy to come along.

Once the last "*I do*" was uttered, Reverend Seabury pronounced them man and wife. Marguerite knelt and kissed her new husband gently.

"I think we might need to let Albert rest a bit," she told the assembled group.

Jack turned to move into the parlor and then heard his name. He faced Albert.

"I need . . . to see Jack," the old man said.

Everyone filed past him. He touched Nora's cheek as she went by and then when the way was clear, he moved across the room to the narrow bed.

"Take care of . . . both my girls now."

One look told him that Albert knew he wouldn't live through the night.

"I will," he promised. "I'll be having a touch of whiskey with you as soon as the doc says we can."

Albert closed his eyes. Jack stood there a few minutes, not wanting to leave his friend alone.

"I want Nora."

"I'll get her." He walked down the hallway and caught Nora's eye. She came to him.

"He wants to see you."

They both returned to the sickroom. She knelt beside her father. "I'm here, Papa." She stroked his hand.

Albert had trouble getting his words out, but his meaning was clear. "Make a go . . . if you can . . . of the paper. If not . . . other things. You'll always have Ben and Jess. Give . . . pocket watch to . . . Robby. When he's older."

"Papa, you can give it to him."

Jack heard the raw emotion in her voice. He placed his hand on her shoulder and squeezed it.

"Take care of Marguerite. No life for her at saloon . . . maybe not even here at all. She knows I put . . . paper in your name. Watch out . . . for her. Trust . . . in Jack."

He fell silent. Jack didn't know how long they stood there before Albert asked for his new wife.

Nora squared her shoulders and fetched Marguerite. She fed everyone some cold chicken, but no one ate much. Finally, Reverend Seabury said he would head home.

"If you need me at any time, Mrs. Cantrelle, send for me."

"Thank you for your kindness."

Jack offered to walk the minister home. "I need to check on a few things around town," he told Nora quietly.

"Go ahead. Get some rest, Jack. I have a feeling I'll need your strength tomorrow."

He gave her a brief kiss. She went back to check on her father.

Marguerite said, "If you don't mind, I'd like to sit up with him tonight. Alone."

Nora gave her a hug. "Of course." She brushed a kiss on her father's brow. "Sweet dreams, Papa."

She tried to sleep but images from the past crowded into her mind. She dozed off and on and awoke exhausted. She waited until she heard a cock crow in the distance before she arose and slipped into her dressing gown. Robby slept peacefully next to her, the very image of Paul. It took her by surprise, but then it had a thousand times since his birth. She'd known Paul her entire life and so she knew what he looked like at every stage of his life. She only hoped that Jack's steady influence would contribute to the boy's already sweet temperament. She wanted her boy to be nothing like his father.

She pulled the covers up and brushed a quick kiss on Robby's brow. Tiptoeing down the hall, she entered her father's room without a knock. Marguerite turned, tears staining her cheeks. When Nora saw those tears, she knew her father was dead.

CHAPTER 29

J ess opened her door quietly. Nora was dressing in the faint light.

"I heard you up, Miss Nora," she whispered. "How is Mr. Albert?"

She walked closer and helped Nora pull up the gown. Nora heard her gasp and braced for what she knew would come.

"Will you please fasten the back, Jess?"

Jess roughly pulled the material closer together and began buttoning it, muttering under her breath. She knew that was a bad sign. Jess finished the job and took her hand.

"Miss Nora, I know you saw me looking at those bruises. They are ugly things in the half-light. I can imagine 'em in broad daylight."

Nora was in no mood to offer Jess answers. "Papa's dead."

"Oh, sweet Jesus," Jess whispered. "Baby. Come here."

She gave herself up to the smaller woman's embrace, comforted by the warmth of the only mother she'd ever really known. Finally, she pulled away, brushing away tears.

"I'm going to Reverend Seabury's. He's always up early."

"Would you like some coffee before you go, child?" Jess smoothed her callused hand across Nora's brow.

"No. I'd rather not wait. Go ahead and put a pot on to brew. Take some to Marguerite." She kissed Jess' cheek. "I won't be long."

❧

JACK FOUND HIMSELF AT REVEREND SEABURY'S DOORSTEP NOT LONG AFTER DAYBREAK. HE WASN'T A RELIGIOUS MAN. HE'D LEARNED LONG AGO TO LIVE BY HIS OWN CODE OF ETHICS. YET HE FOUND COMFORT IN THE REVEREND'S PRESENCE AND THE MUSIC IN HIS CHURCH EACH SUNDAY.

"Have another scone, Sheriff." Mrs. Seabury heaped first one, then another onto his plate.

"That's already four, ma'am."

"Who's counting?" She poured him a second cup of coffee as a knock sounded at the door.

The minister rose. "I'll get it, my dear." He went to the door. "Why, Mrs. Cantrelle, why are you out and about so early?"

"Papa's passed on. Would you help me plan his services?"

Jack swallowed the unchewed scone in his mouth and washed it down with a swig of coffee. Her rose and met Nora as she entered the room. Her eyes were swollen and red, a stark contrast to her face, which was drained of color. He wrapped his arms around her, wanting to comfort her. He felt her sharp intake of breath and pulled away.

"What's wrong?" he asked sharply.

"Nothing." Her voice was barely a whisper. "I fell from the back porch yesterday. I had too much on my mind and wasn't paying attention." She rubbed her hip. "Hurts like the dickens."

He noticed the slight swelling on one side of her face. "Did you hit your face, too?" He stroked a thumb gently across her cheek and she winced.

"I . . . don't remember. Maybe," she said vaguely.

Jack thought her evasive but now wasn't the time to dwell on this. "How's Marguerite holding up?"

"She has a calm about her. She expected it."

Reverend Seabury asked, "Would you like the service performed tomorrow? That would give you time to notify everyone. Albert was popular in Silver Bluff. I'm sure there'll be a good turnout."

"Tomorrow is Saturday. That would give more people a chance to pay their respects," Jack noted.

"I only wish Ben were here."

"He won't be back for several days, Nora. It'll take him a couple of days there and back, plus whatever time it takes to get the money and find the necessary parts."

"Let's go ahead then." She gave Reverend Seabury the names of a few hymns Albert loved and filled in some facts about his background for the clergyman.

"I'll get to the eulogy right away," the minister promised. "May I drop by later in the day?"

"Of course." She shook his hand.

"Let me walk you back," Jack said. He took her arm and led her out into the street.

As they walked slowly as dawn broke, she promised, "I will repay you, Jack. Somehow, no matter how long it takes. I just hope the paper will sell now."

"The work's always been quality, Nora."

"But most of the bylines were Papa's. I wonder how the town will accept me coming out from behind his name and taking full credit for what I've been doing all along."

"It won't matter. People know you. Your writing will speak for itself." He gave her a soft, reassuring kiss. "We'll make a go of this. We're in this together."

They reached the Le Fall homestead. "Do you want me to come in?"

She shook her head. "No. I need to work on Papa's obituary. Will you drop by later?"

"You know I will."

❦

IT WAS WHAT THEY CALLED INDIAN SUMMER IN THE South. A fall day that lost its crispness and cool breeze, only to be replaced by a lone day of warmth and bright sunshine. Papa would have liked being laid to rest on such a day.

Nora busied herself scraping plates, handing them to Jess to be stacked and washed. The funeral had been over several hours ago. Most of the town returned home with them, bringing a variety of covered dishes. She feared the table would collapse with all the laden goods.

"It's hard to believe he's gone," she said sadly to Jess.

Jess smiled. "Mr. Albert was a good man. I'll never forget how he gave us our freedom after Miz Genevieve passed on." She shook her head. "Not many men would be that brave. Mr. Albert, though, he did it because it was right."

Nora hugged Jess. "I'm glad I have you and Ben. I don't know what I'd do without you." She hesitated a moment. "You will be staying on, even with Papa gone?"

Jess pulled her close and embraced her fiercely. "We're family, Miss Nora. You know that. And family sticks together, through thick and thin."

She sighed her relief and went back to the dishes. She chatted happily with Jess until strong arms wrapped around her unexpectedly. She gasped.

"Still hurting, darlin'?" Jack asked. He rubbed her arms gently. "Maybe you should let Doc Malone check you out."

"I'll be fine," she told him. "Excuse me a moment. I need to check on our guests."

Jess mumbled under her breath and began dunking dishes into the pan of water, scrubbing with more than elbow grease, her rag flinging water everywhere.

"What's wrong, Jess? What did that plate ever do to you?" Jack teased.

"Nothing. She's just a stubborn, hard-headed child with no more sense..." The rest of her sentence trailed off as Jess attacked the plate again.

"Don't be so hard on her. Anyone could fall. She's had a lot on her mind."

"Is that what she told you?" Jess snorted. "Then explain those bruises up and down her arms."

"What do you mean?" Jack's belly suddenly felt as if he'd swallowed lead.

"I saw 'em on her. A man put 'em there." Jess looked at him accusingly.

He was bewildered. "Jess, I swear, it wasn't me."

"It better not be."

"Then who?"

The servant started to speak and thought better of it. She closed her half-opened mouth and picked up her dishrag.

Jack studied her a moment. "You know. Or have a good idea."

She avoided his eyes and kept on with her task.

Jack went looking for Nora.

He sauntered through the house, still crowded with the people who'd attended Albert's services and burial. A few had started to leave. He opened the porch door and walked out, scanning the yard, and spotted Nora talking with Mrs. Malone and Sung Moon.

Nora saw Jack heading their way, his eyes flashing

fire and brimstone. She excused herself and met him, wondering what he was so worked up over.

Through gritted teeth he said, "We need to talk."

"I think that most people will be—"

"Now." He took her arm and escorted her around the house. No one was there. Jack took her wrist and pushed up her sleeve. It was rimmed in elastic and slid easily up her arm.

Nora immediately pushed the material down and Jack away from her. He took a firmer hold of her wrist and forced the sleeve up again as high as it would go. Her pale skin was mottled with blue and purple bruises, evenly spaced on her arm. He took the other arm and did the same. It, too, was a match.

"Who did this?"

She heard the effort in his voice as he tried to control his emotions. "It was just a misunderstanding."

"With whom?"

At that moment, Jack looked like the man Nora first saw when she arrived in Silver Bluff. He seemed more dangerous than any criminal. She didn't dare lie to him. She could only hope to soften the blow.

"Ken. Ken Kessler."

Jack swore softly. "Why?"

Her words rushed out in a torrent. "I needed answers. We needed answers, Jack. About William Kessler and what he's doing to this town. He's too wily. I thought Ken seemed easier to reach. He—"

"You flirted your way to the answers." He grabbed her roughly and instantly regretted it. A flash of fear sprang to her eyes and he knew Ken Kessler had touched her in the same way. He released her and took a step back.

"Explain what happened."

"I went for a buggy ride with him. I found out Thomas Morrison is with the Congressional railroad commission. Kessler's not after silver. He's received advance word on where the railroad will be built. That's why he's bought what he did and ran off others when they refused to sell.

"I meant to tell you, but Papa asked for Marguerite when I got home. All of a sudden, he married and died in a matter of hours. Everything was a whirlwind." She looked at the ground. "I would have told you."

Jack's gut tightened. "And the rest?"

Nora looked up at him, tears threatening to spill. "He got a little fresh. Tried to kiss me. I handled it, though. I'm fine, Jack. Really."

"I'll kill him."

He turned, ready to find Ken Kessler. Ready to kill him. Nora tugged on his arm, clinging to him.

"Jack, no, please. No."

He had the strength of ten men at that moment. Nora had no chance of stopping him. He strode to the front of the house. Both Kesslers were coming down the porch stairs. Ken reached the bottom, smiling.

He never knew what hit him.

CHAPTER 30

All Jack saw was a haze of red. Nora had been hurt.

And he hadn't known it.

He had to protect her. He'd promised Albert he would. *By God, she was his.* What hurt her, hurt him. He would give his life for this woman.

His arms and legs strained against something. He came out of his fog and realized someone was restraining him. He saw Ken Kessler lying crumpled on the ground, bleeding. Both his nose and mouth gushed blood. Jack caught a glint in the man's eye, which was starting to swell.

"Find out something, Sheriff?" Ken taunted. He pulled a handkerchief from his pocket and dabbed his mouth. "I'd say you have your job cut out for you keeping a woman like Nora Cantrelle satisfied." He whistled low. "But she sure tastes mighty sweet."

Jack had to be held again. "I'll kill you! I swear I will. Don't touch her again. Don't even look at her."

Ken laughed and dropped his head back onto the grass. Jack looked at the crowd gathered around him. Every eye he met looked away.

He shook off the hands that held him and moved away into the house. If he hadn't known it before, it was a certainty now. His career as sheriff—maybe even his life in Silver Bluff—was officially over.

"DIDN'T I TELL YOU NOT TO MESS WITH THAT spitfire? She's pure trouble and her beau, too." William Kessler pulled a cigar from his pocket and then tossed it aside. "You probably got nothing out of her for all your efforts. Women like that may flirt a good game, but their legs are locked at the knees."

His brother rubbed his jaw. "At least that cowboy didn't break it." Ken reached up and tenderly stroked his nose. "Can't say the same for this." He picked up a hand mirror lying on the nightstand next to him. "I think my new nose will give me character." Ken laughed harshly. "After all, I guess I shouldn't be prettier than my women."

Kessler exploded. "I've told you before to keep your private life quiet. I don't want to clean up after any more of your messes. It was easier during the war. It's much more difficult now. Especially in a small town."

Ken groaned. "Not the girl again. Sarah? Sally? It only happened here once and that's because my temper got the best of me." He touched his temple and winced. "I didn't touch that trollop of a Southern belle."

"Well, you did something to rile up Jack Duncan. I've got enough on my hands easing him out and Spank in. I don't need this kind of spectacle played out in front of the whole damned town. The deal with Morrison is almost complete. I transfer the gold to his California account the day after tomorrow, soon as Bill Tompkins looks everything over.

"Lie low until then."

Ken grinned lazily. "I guess I could fill up on Sung Moon's cooking." He slapped his belly.

JACK RAISED HIS HEAD FROM THE DESK. IT WAS STILL early. He'd come in when it was barely light, nursing a whopper of a hangover and sore knuckles.

It had been foolish to brawl like a kid in a school-yard fight. Especially with the likes of Ken Kessler. He was mad at himself for such immature behavior—and hopping mad at Nora.

It was his job to seek out wrongdoing and bring justice to the town. Why was she trying to do a man's job? Why'd he become involved with her? She was nothing like the women he was normally attracted to. He liked them quiet and submissive, totally dependent on him.

Yet Felicity had been all those things. Had he ever really loved her? Maybe she'd done him a favor when she'd married his brother. It had given Jack the opportunity to move West and discover more about himself. *It had led him to Nora.*

Despite the fact that she was driving him crazy, he couldn't imagine life without her. Quiet? No. Submissive? Never. Independent? As a hellcat. But she brought a rich texture to his life. He wouldn't trade her for all the silver in Stevenson's mine.

Turn her over his knee? There was an idea.

He worried how he would provide for her and Robby, since he was certain he'd be out of a job soon. Should he grovel to Kessler and go back to the mine? Or could he somehow help Nora and Ben? He didn't know the first thing about running a newspaper.

Jack opened his bottom drawer. He sighed and removed the half-empty bottle of whiskey reserved for his afternoon talks with Albert. The man had become a good friend and father figure to him over the last few months. The empty space in his heart throbbed painfully.

Returning the liquor to its place, he lifted his ever-present chunk of wood instead. He slipped out his pocketknife and began turning the wood over and over. Soon, he was lost in its feel. The smoothness of the wood. Even his pounding headache receded.

The door swung open, crashing loudly against the wall, startling him from his reverie. William Kessler strode in. Before Jack could react, Kessler threw a solid punch, smashing him in the face.

Jack fell backward in his chair, hitting the ground hard with his head. He came up quickly from the floor, his head reeling with blinding pain. Others stood before him, restraining Kessler. He blinked, his blurred vision slowly clearing.

Something was incredibly wrong. Kessler wasn't the kind to throw his own punches. Instead, he served as a puppet master, pulling the strings of others that did his dirty work.

"What in hell is going on?" he demanded.

Chin Lee came forward. Jack immediately picked up on the Chinaman's nervousness. He hesitated and looked around behind him. He saw Seymour Simmons nod, encouraging him to speak.

"Say your piece, Chin."

"I have bad news, Mr. Jack Sheriff. Very bad news." Chin swallowed hard. "I found Mr. Ken dead behind the stables a few minutes ago."

His stomach sank and hit rock-bottom.

Ken Kessler dead?

William Kessler glared at him as he rubbed his knuckles. "My brother's dead and you're the only one with a motive. The whole town heard you yesterday. You had it in for him. They all heard you can't keep your woman satisfied."

Jack lunged for him. Chin stepped between the two men.

"No, Mr. Jack Sheriff."

He took a cleansing breath and met Kessler's eyes.

"I may not have liked your brother, but I walk the right side of the law. I don't murder men."

"I guess you forgot about the war, Private Kessler."

Startled, he stared at the mine owner.

"Yes, Sheriff, you were under my command. For all I know, this beef may go back to our war days. The incident with your . . . fiancée . . . could simply have been the icing on the cake."

Spank McHardy arrived and looked immediately to Kessler. Jack spoke up quickly.

"I'm the law in this town. It might be Kesslerville now, but it's still my town."

"Not anymore." Kessler reached over and ripped off the silver star pinned to Jack's vest. "Arrest him."

Spank McHardy already had his gun in hand. Jack hesitated a moment before unbuckling his gun holster. He slammed it on the desktop and turned to walk the short distance to a cell. He pulled the iron bars closed behind him on the way. The clang of the metal catching in the lock sent shivers deep into his soul.

❧

NORA SIPPED HER COFFEE, MISSING HER FATHER'S company at this time of day. They had planned things carefully over a cup of brew on a daily basis. If they weren't discussing stories to write, then there were always other things to mention—the good pie eaten the day before. Robby's progress in spelling. The fishing to be done.

Perhaps Ben would like to join her in this ritual. They had so many details to work out now. She hoped Silver Bluff would accept them as a team. The Southern widow and the freedman. She laughed at the reception they would have received in Monroe.

"I hope you're safe, Ben," she said aloud, "and

finding all we need." She figured it would be at least two days before he returned.

A loud pounding sounded at the door. Nora knew no good news came at this time of the morning. She hurried to the door and opened it to find Chin Lee standing there. He began instantly rattling away in what Nora could only guess was Chinese.

"Come in, Chin. Calm down. It's okay." She did her best to quieten him, but Marguerite, Jess, and Robby all appeared in their nightclothes. Marguerite had stayed in Albert's room after yesterday's funeral. She told Nora she was unsure of her plans. Nora had been only too happy to have her nearby.

Chin finally wound down. Jess thrust a cup of coffee into his hands, and he drank from it greedily. That seemed to do the trick. He grew silent, but his hands shook as he held the mug. Finally, he drained its contents and handed it back.

"Why are you so upset, Chin?" she asked.

"Mr. Jack Sheriff was arrested for murder."

Nora gasped, as did the other two women. Robby gripped her hand.

"I went to milk the cow. She bellowed as if she were in pain. The horses were skittish. I went to get them feed." He shuddered. "I found Mr. Ken there in a pool of blood. His head was all bashed in. It was hard to know it was even him."

Nora willed herself not to fall apart. "And Jack was arrested? By whom? There's no proof. No witnesses. This is outrageous!"

She got little else from Chin, who kept expressing his sorrow for bringing her such bad news.

"Thank you, Chin. I know you took a chance coming here."

"Mr. Jack Sheriff is good to me. To us. I know he wouldn't do that."

Nora saw the servant to the door and quickly

dressed to go directly to the jail. Marguerite tapped on her door.

"Shall I go with you?" she offered.

"No. I want to see him alone."

"Would you like me to visit Kessler? I don't know if would do any good, but I'll try."

She bit her lip. "I can't tell you what to do." She slipped on her boots and quickly laced them. "I have to go."

As she walked to Jack's office, she passed Mrs. Witherspoon, who snubbed her. It would almost have been comical if the situation wasn't so serious. She entered the jail. Spank McHardy was there, feet propped on Jack's desk. He waved his hand around the room as if it were his kingdom.

"Here to see Jack?" He chuckled. "Who's stopping you?"

"I prefer to speak to him alone."

McHardy shrugged and slipped the toothpick from his mouth. "Suits me." He sauntered out the door, fingering the star pinned onto his vest.

She approached the bars. She wished the deputy would have let her inside the cell. She needed to touch Jack.

He sat on a bunk, eyes glued to the floor. Nora tried to look at him as a jury might. He was large, powerful, and sullen at the moment. He looked as if he could have killed a man, especially if pushed. She was guilty of putting Jack behind these bars. Even if he'd done nothing, her thoughtless actions caused enough suspicion to place him inside this cell.

He hadn't acknowledged her yet. He had to know she was here.

"Jack?"

Without looking at her, he said, "Leave, Nora. Don't come back."

CHAPTER 31

Jack didn't want Nora to see him like this. He took pride in wearing the badge. He'd now been stripped of it—and his pride, too.

He couldn't protect her from a cell. He'd done nothing wrong, but William Kessler would railroad him all the same.

His only choice was to escape. He had no way to prove his innocence. He'd left Nora's last night and gone home. He stayed there the rest of the night, sitting in the dark for a good portion of it, drinking shots of whiskey until he finished the bottle.

He awoke before first light, assuming he'd passed out once the bottle was empty. He lay slumped against his sofa. His limbs were stiff and sore.

Escape would be his only means to stay alive. But escape meant no future with Nora. No home. No kids. No job. He'd always be on the run. A new alias in every town. Living a vagrant's life.

But at least he'd be alive.

Jack looked at the shock on Nora's face. Well, maybe half-alive. He couldn't imagine a life without this woman. She meant everything to him. Yet he couldn't ask her to give up her identity, her stability. She had a son to raise. A job she loved. Family who loved her.

Kessler wouldn't stay in Silver Bluff forever. He had bigger fish to fry. He would leave Nora alone. She could grow here. With the prospect of statehood growing, floods of people would rush in. Somewhere, there would be a man for her, a good one, and she'd forget all about Jack Duncan.

"You're crazy to think I'd leave!"

Nora interrupted his thoughts. Her green eyes burned hot in her pale face. Her mouth trembled in fear or fury.

He was afraid to find out which.

"Do you think I'm so shallow that I'd run at the first sign of trouble? Or was that all talk, us being married in your heart? Marriage is for better or worse, Jack Duncan, and believe me—I've known worse."

"All I—"

"The war was bad enough. People I'd known my whole life, marching off for a lost cause. They might have believed in it, but I never did. I was raised to accept others for who they are.

"I married a man so changed by the war that he returned a total stranger. I stuck by him and those vows we made. He came home a cripple. Not because he was missing an arm and leg, but in his mind. I did everything to get him out of that bed, but his mind had turned lame.

"I stayed. Fed him his meals. Bathed him. Read to him. Fussed over him. All the while, he complained. He wanted a life that would never exist again. I got no love. Only heartache. I cared for him and raised the son he never glanced at. I wrote most of the stories we published under my father's byline. Those articles wouldn't have been accepted by others in Monroe society. They'd turned their backs on me long ago. I had a liberal daddy who'd freed his own slaves back in '51. That made all of us suspect.

"I married out of my class and was shunned by polite society. I didn't cry to Paul about it because he had too much on his mind. I kept things going. Sold off everything not nailed down. Even took in strangers to board with nary a complaint.

"And I survived." She looked directly in his eyes. "I know what *for worse* is, Jack. I've been to hell and back, so don't expect me to fold the tent and head for greener pastures at the first sign of trouble."

Her cheeks were flushed. Her eyes blazed with anger. She stood right next to the bars. Jack reached through and grabbed her shoulders and pulled her close for a searing kiss. It branded her as his. Or maybe it was the other way around.

Time stood still. He wished he could gather her up in his arms. He ached at her touch. He finally pulled away.

"Okay."

She narrowed her eyes. "Okay what?"

"Okay. You can stay."

He bent and brushed his lips against hers once more. He stroked her cheek with a callused thumb, then captured her hand and brought it through the bars. He pressed a fervent kiss into her palm and took her hand in both of his.

Nora pulled her hand back as if scalded. "I can't think when you do that!" She shivered. "We've got to figure out how to free you."

Jack smiled at her. "Business before pleasure?" Her mouth pursed as a schoolmarm before a naughty boy.

"Silver Bluff doesn't have a judge, so there's no bail to post," he informed her. "The circuit judge comes through once a month. He rarely has to stop."

"When is he due next?"

"About a week from Tuesday. Today's Sunday so that's ten days or so."

He watched her eyes dance with a quick light. She had thought of something.

"I'll be back," she promised. "It won't be until this afternoon. Reverend Seabury will have services to conduct this morning and I'll need his help." She began to back away from his cell. He could almost see the wheels turning in her head.

She blew him a kiss. "Don't go anywhere." She smiled at him. "And don't give Spank any reason to rough you up."

Jack nodded as she left.

❧

WILLIAM KESSLER RUBBED HIS EYES. THEY WERE DRY and red. He'd never been close to anyone except his brother. Ken looked to him in any given situation, sure that his older brother would take care of him. Their parents hadn't. Bob and Martha Kessler undoubtedly were the coldest people on the planet. They'd stressed hard work and long prayers over any sign of affection. The two Kessler boys depended upon each other from the beginning.

And now Ken was dead.

"Damn Jack Duncan!" Kessler slammed his fist on the desk, scattering the papers in front of him.

"Am I interrupting?"

He looked up to see Thomas Morrison. Thank God, he still had a few people he could trust. His old quartermaster had helped him amass a small fortune during the war. It seemed like Providence when Morrison contacted him after Morrison landed the position on the railroad commission. With his inside information on where the railroad would be built, they both would become wealthy men.

Then it was on to politics. He wanted Morrison to stay in Silver Bluff and run his establishments. They would bring in good money, but he didn't want to be closely associated with them. He planned on returning to Denver and making it his base of operations. Morrison was hesitant, though. Probably visions of all that gold that would soon be in his bank account made him leery to settle down in Silver Bluff. Still, the town was on the edge of booming. It would be a good place to be, with lots of action.

"I wanted to see if—"

A rap at the study door caused Morrison to pause.

"Come in," boomed Kessler.

Chin Lee poked his head through a narrow opening. "Guests, Mr. Kessler, sir."

He wasn't expecting anyone. Ken wouldn't be buried until tomorrow afternoon. He was in no mood for visitors.

"Send them away, Chin."

The servant shook his head. "They say they have important business with you, Mr. Kessler, sir."

He grew impatient. "Who the hell's here?"

The Chinaman's eyes grew large. "Lots of people. Reverend Seabury, Dr. Malone, Mr. Simmons, Mr. Nelson, Mr. Spivens, and Mrs. Cantrelle."

His best guess said this was about Jack Duncan being locked up. Might as well get it over with.

"Show 'em in, Chin."

"Shall I leave?" asked Morrison.

"No. Stay."

Moments later, the group filed in. Damn, Nora Cantrelle looked good enough to eat. For a minute, he understood his brother's obsession with the sassy Southerner.

Dr. Malone addressed him first. "Mr. Kessler, we've come to speak on behalf of Sheriff Duncan. There doesn't seem to be any sense in holding him in that tiny jail cell until the circuit judge comes through. I know if he gave his word, he'd stay out at his place."

"His word?" Kessler's blood ran hot. "*He killed my brother*. You trust him at his word?"

"You have to admit, Mr. Kessler, there's no proof that links Sheriff Duncan to your brother's murder."

"Just his threat in front of the entire town, which he carried through hours later." His heart pounded wildly.

Sam Spivens spoke up. "I've known Jack Duncan since he worked in the mine, Mr. Kessler. You won't find a better man. He may have shot his mouth off because he was upset, but I guarantee he had nothing to do with your brother's murder."

The others assembled murmured their agreement, all except for Seymour Simmons. At least he knew which side his bread was buttered on, unlike Spivens, his own foreman.

"Of course, he'll run. He's got no job. No family ties. He was a former bounty hunter. I think he'd shake the dust of this town so fast our heads would spin."

"Not if he was married," added Reverend Seabury.

Kessler looked quickly at Nora. "You're willing to marry a man that might hang in two weeks?"

"I have enough faith in Jack and the legal system to know that won't come to pass."

"Let's be reasonable, Mr. Kessler," said Dr. Malone.

He knew they were right. He also wanted the town folk to remember he'd been fair in such a painful situation.

"If I can place an armed guard outside his house, he can go." He looked to his foreman. "Pull six men from the mine. Parker, Cross, Heckton, Miller, Oldham, and Brucker. Three shifts, two men a shift. No days off. Time-and-a-half pay. If Duncan leaves town, you'll be held responsible."

"Agreed. I'll find the men and speak to them."

The group filed out from his office silently. Kessler reflected on this new situation. It could make things much easier. He knew no court of law would convict Duncan with such flimsy evidence. If he were stopped in an escape attempt, however, that was another thing.

Too much might be made if Jack were killed trying to break out of jail. Suspicion would be placed on Spank —and indirectly, on him. Set-ups of this kind were common in a rough land.

But what if Jack were caught by his own, those who toiled in the mine? Would an innocent man run away from his new bride? From his responsibilities to her and her son and from his day in court, where he could clear his name? He didn't think any sympathy would lie with the town's ex-sheriff in that situation.

Visions of Duncan with a bullet through his head seemed mighty sweet. He knew exactly which man to approach in order to make that happen.

CHAPTER 32

Jack nodded politely, wondering what was going on. Mrs. Malone, Mrs. Seabury, and Jess came calling on him shortly after noon. He'd even seen Robby outside through the window, playing on the porch with Tien Lee.

The ladies brought him dinner, for which he was grateful. He'd forgotten the last time he'd eaten. Usually with a prisoner, Mrs. Simmons provided the meals, and he dreaded what she might send over. He'd twice eaten food she'd cooked and realized why Seymour was so skinny.

Mrs. Seabury was telling stories of her childhood in England. While moderately interesting to the women, it had put Spank McHardy to sleep within the first ten minutes. Each story went on longer than the one before. Jack knew something was in the works, and it sure wasn't this little tea party.

The door swung open. "They're here!" Robby cried out, causing Spank to fall from his chair. The ladies tittered as the deputy picked himself up and dusted off his pants.

A large group filed into the office, but he only had eyes for Nora. She wore the dress Jess had made her for their wedding. Her hair was swept up high with tiny daisies worked through it somehow. Those green eyes gleamed with some hidden knowledge.

She'd never been more beautiful.

He rose from his cot and came to the bars. He grasped them until his knuckles turned white. All those assembled gathered around in a semi-circle. Dr. Malone was speaking quietly to Spank. The deputy wore a surprised look.

What the hell was going on?

McHardy strode to the wall and took the ring of keys from their hook. The ladies stepped aside as the cell door was unlocked.

"Come on out," Spank ordered.

Jack moved slowly as if in a dream. Everyone grinned at him like he was a cat just let out of a bag.

Except he didn't know what the secret was.

"Join hands," Reverend Seabury instructed. He opened his Bible as Nora took Jack's hand.

"What the—"

"Hush," she whispered. "Just listen."

"Dearly beloved, we are gathered today in this . . . place . . . to celebrate the union of Jack Duncan and Nora Cantrelle."

"What?" He looked at the crowd and back to Nora. "You've got to be crazy, darlin'. You're already a widow once. If we go through with this, it'll be twice before you can blink."

"Jack." Nora looked at him steadily. "I have enough confidence to believe this will all work out. Do you have any objections to marrying me?"

His heart nearly burst with the love he had for her. "No," he said softly.

"Then I suggest we let the good reverend continue." She turned back to the minister and nodded.

Jack heard the words flow, but they didn't have much meaning. They all ran together like a swift stream rushing along. He tried his best to follow, but Reverend

Seabury's voice ran as smooth as dripping honey. He lost track of the time.

"Jack?" Nora prompted.

"Come again?"

The minister spoke the words and he repeated them, gazing at Nora with wonder. She did the same, holding tightly to his hand.

"We need a ring," Reverend Seabury said.

"Use mine." Mrs. Malone slipped her wedding band from her finger and handed it to her husband. He, in turn, gave it to Jack.

"It's worked well for us all these years," the doctor quipped.

"Nora's is at my house," he told Mrs. Malone. "I'll be sure yours is returned to you shortly."

Iris Malone smiled sweetly at him. "All in good time, Sheriff."

He placed the ring on Nora's finger and echoed the minister's words.

"You may now kiss the bride," Seabury proclaimed.

Jack hesitated a moment, still in shock from the suddenness of the affair. Nora reached up, took his face in her hands, and pulled his lips down to hers.

The minute they touched, he felt a longing pour through him. He pulled her close and kissed her, gently at first and then with more passion. He continued kissing her until he became aware of laughter all around. He pulled away reluctantly and looked around guiltily.

"Glad you could come up for air, son," Dr. Malone joked.

Everyone laughed, and then hugs and kisses were being exchanged. Arms wrapped around his leg. He looked down to see Robby clinging to him. He lifted the boy high.

"You married Mama."

"Yes, I did. And you, too."

The boy's eyes grew round. "You did?"

"I sure did," he assured him. "We're all a family now, Robby boy. We've made a commitment to each other."

"Are we gonna live at your house now?"

Jess slipped the boy from his arms. "Yes. But not tonight, young man. Your mama and Mr. Jack need a little privacy."

"Mrs. Duncan?"

Jack saw Nora turn, a smile on her face at being addressed with her new title.

"Cart's waiting," said Dr. Malone. "You'd best get going."

She turned to him. "Ready?"

He looked out over the room. "Thank you," he said humbly. "It means so much for each of you to be here. I'm only sorry Albert and Ben weren't with us." He turned to Nora. "And if certain matters are settled, we'll do this again, proper-like, in the church."

He placed his arm around her waist. "Shall we go?"

The group saw them out and called words of good cheer as Jack took up the reins. It was his own cart and horse. He didn't know who'd managed that trick, but it gave him comfort. He raised a hand and waved goodbye as they took off, then placed his arm around Nora's shoulder.

"This was your best idea on how to get me out of jail?" he teased.

She shrugged. "Seems like you've traded one prison for another. Except this one's the permanent kind." She held up her hand to inspect her ring. "It was kind of Mrs. Malone to loan us her ring."

He took her hand and brought her fingers to his lips. "You can have your own the minute we get home."

She snuggled closer to him. "All right."

They rode for a minute in silence before he asked, "You went to Kessler?"

"Yes. All the men who attended the wedding came

with me. They spoke of how your word was good enough to keep you in Silver Bluff, if Kessler had you released." She wrinkled her nose. "He seemed to think you'd run faster than a dog in heat since you had no ties to the town."

He grinned. "So, we tied the knot to keep me here?"

"I know you would've stayed regardless. Still, I was feeling a bit selfish. If this was the only way to have you all to myself, so be it."

Jack marveled at his new wife. She had courage and strength of mind to bear up to incredible adversity. It gave him hope that maybe they would weather this storm.

He pulled into the yard and tugged gently on the reins. He jumped from the cart and reached for her, drawing her down the length of him. When her feet touched the ground, he still held her about her waist.

"Did I tell you how much I love you, Mrs. Duncan?"

Nora stared at him a long moment. Her mouth trembled. "You've never said that before."

"I've felt it for a long time, sweetheart. It just takes a bullheaded Yankee a while to admit to it. Especially when it involves a sweet Southern flower." He pressed his mouth softly against hers for a lingering kiss.

"Let me get the horse unhitched and taken care of. Why don't you wait for me on the porch?"

"I'll be there."

He led the horse into the barn as Nora went around to the front of the house. Butterflies had exploded inside her stomach, and now they fluttered so that she was next to breathless. She knew what would come next. She was scared but she knew it wouldn't be like her time with Paul. Jack's kisses had proven that.

Still, she was at a loss as exactly how things would pass. It happened so fast the first time with Paul and it hurt so much. Jack was larger than Paul in every way. She hoped she would be brave and not cry as before.

She'd cried with Paul that second time, too, but that was after the act was done. He'd rolled to one side and she had done the same, wishing for a closeness that never came. He'd left the next day, and Robby had been the result.

Nora wondered what it would be like to have Jack's child. She couldn't imagine loving anyone more than she did Robby, but she knew each baby brought its own sweetness into this world. Just from watching him with Robby, she knew Jack would make a fine father.

If only he were around to raise the baby.

Almost against her will, she found herself praying.

Please, God. Oh, please, God. Keep Jack safe. Don't let him go to his death for a crime he didn't commit. Don't punish him for my careless stupidity. Please love him and take care of him. Take care of us, God.

Her thoughts frightened her. The only two heartfelt prayers of her life had resulted in two deaths

Don't kill Jack, God. I'll die in his place but don't let him die.

She collapsed into the chair on the porch, her head in her hands. She refused to cry. Cry on your wedding day and you'll have something to cry about every day, the old saying went. She bit her lip to still its trembling.

Warm hands lifted her face. Jack knelt next to her. "It's all right, honey. I won't hurt you." He stroked her cheek.

"It's not that. I'm so worried about—"

He placed a finger against her lips. "No talk about any of that. Not now." He kissed her forehead. "Let's go inside."

Nora stood and was suddenly swept off her feet. She clung to Jack's neck. "What are you doing? Put me down, silly."

He grinned lazily at her. "It's the custom, Mrs. Duncan, for a husband to carry his bride across the threshold." He walked a few steps and pulled back the screen door, then turned the knob and opened the door. He stepped inside and reversed the process. The house was quiet and dark inside. No shades had been opened.

"Prepare for me to worship your body, Mrs. Duncan."

She felt the blush rush up her neck.

door, then turned the knob and crossed the floor. She stopped near the dresser and . . . the room was . . . quiet in total darkness. Its shades had been drawn.

. . . apparent . . . for . . . possibly . . . or . . . looking. Was Dianne . . . ?

. . . might get . . . mother . . . up the stairs . . .

CHAPTER 33

J ack slowly brushed his lips across Nora's. They were soft, warm, and giving. Lazily, he traced their outline with his tongue, first clockwise and then in reverse. He sensed her stillness, as if she had stopped breathing.

He eased her feet to the floor and encircled her in his arms. Her green eyes shone bright with excitement and what he guessed was a little fear. He would lay those fears to rest.

He took her hand, which fit perfectly in his. "Come here."

Jack led her across the room to his desk. Opening a drawer, he pulled out a wad of cotton stuffing and placed it on the flat surface of the smooth pine. He slipped Iris Malone's wedding ring off Nora's finger and placed it on the desktop before he unwrapped the cotton. Nora's gold wedding band shone brightly.

Jack lifted the ring and held it between them. "I give you this ring in good faith, my love. May it see us through good times and bad—and may its circle of love hold us together forevermore."

Lifting her trembling hand, he slipped the ring onto her third finger. He bent and kissed the ring itself.

"I'll kiss this ring every morning as a sign of my love

for you. I promise you that every time I do, I'll tell you that I love you."

He threaded his fingers through hers. "The words have been hard in coming, Nora, but I know that's the kind of thing a wife likes to hear. I'll do my best to let you hear it from cock's crow until the cows come home."

A lump formed in his throat. He paused, reining in the flood of emotions rippling through him. "I will honor you, protect you, and love you until the day I die."

Jack kissed her then, a long, searing kiss. His hands pushed into her hair, spilling pins and daisies to the floor. He couldn't seem to get enough of her mouth. The kisses they'd shared before didn't compare to the sweetness of this moment.

He swept her into his arms again and carried her to his bedroom. Their bedroom. He placed her on the bed and stepped back. Nora reached for him.

"Just a minute, honey. It's too dark in here. I need to see your beauty shine."

He lit a candle next to the bed and another one atop the dresser. A soft, golden glow bathed the room.

As he turned, he thought an angel from heaven had come down to rest upon his bed. Waves of golden hair fanned out across the pillow. He slipped off his boots and came back to the bed.

Nora watched Jack approach, her heart pumping wildly. His dark hair spilled across his forehead. She reached up to brush it back. He caught her wrist and turned it to his mouth. Tiny shivers raced along her spine as his tongue played with her throbbing pulse. Sensations new to her made her eager for his touch.

She stretched her arms to his shirtfront and pushed a button through its hole. The look of surprise that crossed his face pleased her. Boldly, she repeated the action until they were all undone, at least those above his waist. His shirt was tucked into his pants.

Nora slid a hand inside the shirt, running it along Jack's muscled chest. His quick intake of breath gave her pause.

"No, go ahead, honey," he reassured her. "You're doing just fine."

She pulled his shirttail from his pants and unfastened the remaining buttons. Jack loomed above her now, and she ran her hands along him. His chest was matted in soft brown hair that trailed down to his flat belly and below his waistband. As her fingers danced along his chest, exploring the ridges and planes, his eyes closed. A smile a sunning cat would wear appeared on his face.

He threw off the shirt and slipped onto the bed next to her. Nora turned on her side to face him, all the while stroking him as if he were a cat. She raked her fingers through his thick, brown hair. It felt like silk against her fingertips. His eyes closed and the smile returned.

With abandon, Nora pressed a kiss against that beautiful chest. It amazed her how hard his muscles were. He cupped her nape, his thumb rotating in a lazy circle that had her pulse pounding wildly.

"Mrs. Duncan?"

She thrilled at hearing her new name on his lips. "Yes, Mr. Duncan?"

"You have marvelous hands." He caught them in his and kissed each finger tenderly. "But I'm the one that wants to pleasure you."

He pulled them to a sitting position and then up onto their feet. "I want to love every inch of you. I can't do that while you're dressed."

Jack spun her around and wrapped his arms about her waist, drawing her to him. He nuzzled her nape, pressing hot kisses along it, his stubble slightly rough, causing tingling sensations.

"We don't want to hurt Jess' masterpiece, so we'll take it nice and slow."

He proceeded to undo every button that ran along the back of her wedding gown. With each one came a kiss in its place, thirty in all. When all were undone, he slid the dress from her shoulders to her waist.

"Step out of it, hon. I'll lay it across the chair so it won't wrinkle."

She eased the gown down her hips and to the floor. He collected it and placed it neatly over the chair back and turned to her.

"I don't know much about petticoats. Maybe you could help me figure out what to do."

Nora helped him with the ties. He was a fast learner. He eased down her stockings and removed them and her shoes. Soon she stood in nothing but her shift.

"My God," he whispered.

She raised a hand self-consciously, but he caught it.

"Don't cover a thing, darlin'. You are perfection." She heard the wonder in his voice and shivered.

He lowered his head to her breast and pressed a hot kiss upon it. Without warning, he captured it in his mouth, through the thin material. Nora gasped, her knees going weak. He suckled it as Robby had as a babe, but the sensations flowing through her weren't in the least bit motherly.

Jack moved to her other breast and Nora needed more of him. "Jack?"

He lifted his head. "What, sweetheart?"

She sensed her blush rising to her roots, but she gamely said, "Could you do that without my shift in the way?"

His hands slid up to her neck. "I'll do whatever you want, my love. Remember that. If I go too fast or too

297

slow, just tell me. I want to please you. I want you to remember this night forever."

She nodded, afraid to trust her voice. He kissed her then. One kiss slid into another, until she wasn't sure if it was one or a thousand. His hands went from her waist to her breasts, where his thumbs rotated methodically around her nipples. Over and over they ran, until she thought she would scream.

"Touch me again with your mouth," she managed to gasp.

Jack slid his fingers under the straps of her shift and brought them along her arms until the shift fell to her waist. He trailed hot kisses from her neck down to her breast. This time, she reveled in the rough feel of his stubble along her skin.

Then his tongue touched her nipple, and it was like lightning had struck. Nora gasped and clung to his shoulders, her nails digging in deeply as she tried to steady herself. He massaged it with his mouth and tongue, pulling, tweaking, lightly biting first one, then the other. A dizziness swept over her as waves of pleasure rippled through her.

He steered her to the bed. She fell across it, her breath coming in jagged spurts. He took the hem of her shift and suddenly she was freed from it as he tossed it onto the floor. Cool air from the room enveloped her. She shivered.

Jack's body came close to her, radiating a heat that warmed her instantly. It also intensified the ache that had begun in her womanly parts. The dull throb between her legs which had sped up began pounding rapidly, an instant beat that demanded attention. Nora wanted him suddenly, wanted him there, knew she couldn't live if he didn't fill her.

"Jack." She barely recognized her voice. It was filled with raw need.

"I know, baby. I know. Be patient."

He ran a callused hand across her stomach, back and forth. The throbbing magnified. She swallowed hard and bunched the coverlet under them in her fists. His hands smoothed along the curves of her hips and onto her thighs. She tightened them reflexively.

"Easy, sweetheart," he murmured into her ear, his warm breath causing a flutter to run through her body, anticipation building within her.

Jack ran his hand along her nestle of curls and cupped her gently. A warm rush seemed to come from her.

He smiled. "You're already ready for me," he said, easing a finger inside her slowly. Instinctively, she tightened around it, her hips rising.

"Oh, Jack . . . oh . . ."

"That feels good?"

"Yes, oh—"

She sucked in a sharp breath as he repeated the motion, moaning softly as he stroked her. Her head whipped from one side to the other, her hips rising each time. He kept his hand in place and ran his tongue from her belly up to her mouth. His pupils were large and dark as the candlelight danced shadows across his face.

Nora took that handsome face in her hands and pulled him close to her. He kissed her hard, possessively, his tongue thrusting in time with his fingers. She growled in the back of her throat, a trill that seemed to delight him as he made a similar noise in response.

She felt her juices spill from her as she cried aloud. "Oh, Jack. Oh, Jack!"

Jack quickly unfastened his buttons and sank into Nora. She was tight, so tight. Hotter than he'd ever known. All his love for her spread through him like wildfire as he thrust into her, again and again. Her gasps became music to his ears.

Then it was over and he was kissing her, her eyelids, her brow, her cheeks, her mouth, nipping the tender lobes of her ears. He flipped to his back, taking her with him, holding her close, never wanting to let her go. She was all woman, all his, and he'd fight through the fires of hell for her.

He brought her head down to his chest and stroked her silky hair. Her breath came in quick spurts. He loved the feel of her breasts on his chest, of her weight atop him, the smell of lavender wafting around them. He loved the slick sweat of their bodies against one another, the curve of her buttocks under his hand.

He loved her. Every inch of her.

How had he ever lived without her?

He held her tightly to him, wondering at his luck at finding her. Would that luck hold? He didn't know how he'd get out of this mess with Kessler, but he would. He couldn't have his life end now. Not when it was just beginning, for that's what these precious moments held. A new life. One with Nora by his side. He would be the best man he could be because she brought it out in him.

"I love you," he said, his voice raw with emotion.

"I never knew..." she began, hers full of wonder.

"I know." His hands pushed through her hair, massaging her scalp.

"Mmm. That feels . . . so good." She sounded sleepy. He thought about all she'd been through and knew she had to be tired. He turned to his side and wrapped her in his arms. She snuggled close. Soon, her breathing evened out.

It took all his control not to wake her and do it again.

Jack rested his chin on the top of her hair. "We'll get out of this, Nora," he promised in a whisper. "Somehow, we'll find the answer. And live the lives we were meant to live. Together. Forever."

NORA WOKE ENVELOPED IN WARMTH. HER LIMBS were heavy. She felt almost as if she had been drugged. She grinned—because she'd drunk from the cup of love, the most potent drug of all. Jack's touch had been nothing like Paul's. She had reveled in it, ached for it, wanted it again and again.

Her new husband had awakened her once in the night, his mouth on hers, his hands working their magic. Their lovemaking had been sweet and slow. She wished she could stay in his bed—their bed—forever.

But she worried about what lay ahead. The thought of a noose around his neck brought a winter's chill to her heart. She had to prove he wasn't involved in Ken's death. To do so, she must find the real killer before the circuit judge arrived and convened court.

Nora became aware of Jack stirring. His arms, already surrounding her waist as they spooned together, pulled her even closer against him. He softly bit her earlobe and a frisson of pleasure danced through her. She pushed back against him in a lazy stretch.

"Good morning, Mrs. Duncan." One arm moved from her and caught her left hand. His fingers entwined with hers as his lips met the ring on her hand.

"I love you," he said, making good on his promise of the night before.

"I love you," she echoed.

He released her hand and wrapped both arms around her again, locking his hands together at her belly. Nora knew utter peace in that moment, wrapped protectively in the cocoon of her husband's arms.

"Are you tired?" he asked.

"A little but it's a good kind of tired." She glanced over her shoulder and smiled shyly at him.

Jack smiled back, his hand massaging her belly and moving lower. Nora's breath hitched in surprise at his intimate touch. He parted her folds and stroked her slowly at first, gradually increasing his motion, his fingers conjuring a love spell. Soon, she moved against him, caught up in the rhythm he'd created. She shuddered violently, her body shaking as waves of pleasure rippled through her.

She sighed in utter content.

"Oh, no, darlin', we're not finished just yet," he teased. He turned onto his back and lifted her above him. She could have sworn she was flying. Jack eased her onto his rigid shaft. It went deeply inside her. Her eyes opened wide.

"What are we doing?" she asked shakily.

"Whatever you want to do, sweetheart. You're the boss."

She rested her hands on his shoulders. His chest glistened in the early morning light. Slowly, she began to move, tentatively at first, then more freely as he caught her rhythm. This really was flying, like riding the fastest horse against the wind. Nora had never experienced such freedom and pleasure as they both climaxed together.

She fell across him, winded, kneading her hands against him like a kitten.

"Jack, you're going to wear me out," she proclaimed.

He grinned. "I'd like to die trying."

Suddenly, his stomach rumbled noisily. Hers responded in kind. They both began to laugh.

"We never ate last night," he said.

"I guess we forgot."

He lifted her from him, and an instant loss ran through her.

"I'll go draw some water for coffee. You stay here."

He kissed the tip of her nose before he rose and slipped on his pants. Nora marveled at the figure he cut. And he was hers. All hers. She smiled broadly.

"Happy?"

She nodded. "Very." She blew him a kiss.

He left the room. She snuggled back into the pillows and began to drift into sleep.

Suddenly, Jack's angry voice carried through the partly opened window.

"Why in God's name are you on my porch, pointing a gun in my face?"

Nora bolted upright and reached for her clothes.

CHAPTER 34

J ack watched Jamie Parker lower his shotgun. He threw open the screen door and grabbed the man by his shirtfront.

"Drop your hands, Jack."

He turned to find Fess Cross coming around the side of the house, aiming a gun his way. "We've got our orders, Jack. Turn him loose."

He released Parker and stepped back.

"What's going on, Fess?"

"Kessler agreed you could be under house arrest as long as he could place a couple of men on you, twenty-four hours a day, until the judge rides through."

"One in front and one in back?" he asked.

Parker nodded. "We know you wouldn't go anywhere, Jack. You ain't one to run, much less kill somebody, even if it's a sorry mess like Ken Kessler."

"Watch your mouth," Cross warned. "We're getting good money from Mr. Kessler." He looked apologetically at Jack. "We won't be in your way, Sheriff. Just stay inside and we'll stay outside."

"Can I draw water from the well for my coffee? Feed my hens or horse?"

Both men shook their heads. "Sorry. Kessler's orders. We're to shoot if you set foot off this here porch."

"Damn." He marched back into the house and slammed the door hard enough for the windows to rattle.

Nora met him, hair askew, trying to button up the back of her dress. Her glance told him she'd known about this arrangement all along.

"Thanks for informing me I'm a prisoner in my own home. I can't even fetch a pail of water."

"It was the only way." She looked at him imploringly. "Would you rather be sitting on that hard, narrow bunk with only Spank for company?"

He glared at her. They stared at each other a good minute until a knock sounded at the door.

"See who it is, will you? I better not stir from this chair or they might shoot me."

She answered the door. Parker handed her a bucket of water. "For coffee, ma'am. I think the sheriff could use a little. I'll tend the chickens and his horse."

"Thank you."

Nora went into the kitchen and began making breakfast. Jack stewed until she called him in. They ate in awkward silence. He found he'd lost his appetite.

"Are you finished?"

He looked up to see Nora standing next to him, her mouth set. Her face wore that pinched look of a woman trying not to cry. He pushed his plate away and stood. She took it and his empty coffee mug to the sink. Jack watched the slump of her shoulders. He couldn't let this go on.

He went to her and wrapped his arms around her. She stiffened at his touch.

"I'm sorry, hon. I'm not upset with you. It's just this whole mess I'm in. I feel so helpless."

She turned to face him. "It's me you should be mad at. I'm the one who put you in such a pickle. If I hadn't gone looking for trouble, you wouldn't have said the things you did to Ken and you wouldn't be stuck here like a caged tiger."

She pulled away from him. "I've got to go."

He caught her hand. "Will you be back?"

"Do you want me back?"

"Of course." He gave her a quick kiss, hoping to reassure her.

"I'll bring a few clothes later on. We can get the bulk of my and Robby's things after this is settled."

He felt the unspoken words hang in the air.

If he didn't hang for murder.

"Nora, I need to let you know about my money. The deed to this land. Where things are."

She broke the contact between them, a stubborn look on her beautiful face. "I don't want to hear about it. I don't need to know. You'll be fine." Then the tears began to fall.

He brought her close as the sobs started and comforted her. "Shh, it's okay. It'll be fine, love." He lifted her chin and wiped away her tears. "Let me button the rest of your dress. I'd hate for you to make a spectacle of yourself in public," he teased lightly.

She returned to the bedroom when he'd finished and brushed her hair and splashed water on her face. Before she left, she asked him, "Do I look the least bit presentable?"

Jack smiled at her and nodded. He kissed her goodbye and saw her out the door. When she was gone, he went to his desk and sat. Pulling out a fresh sheet of paper from a cubbyhole, he wrote *Last Will and Testament of Jack Duncan.*

"ARE YOU CERTAIN YOU'VE UNDERSTOOD EVERYTHING I've said? I can't afford any mistakes," Kessler explained.

The man nodded.

"Make sure you're the one posted at the front door. In fact, I'll send Spank along to check on things. When the trouble breaks out, Spank may even shoot, but it will be after you've fired. He'll back up your story, whatever it is. Work it out with him."

Kessler took a sip from the tumbler of water. "Make sure Nora Cantrelle isn't there."

"Why?" The man chewed thoughtfully on his toothpick. "I thought we could do it at night, like he's slipping out under cover of dark."

"No. The little tramp'll be with him then. She's too smart. Too suspicious for it to come down when she's around." Kessler thought a moment. "Let's make it for late tomorrow afternoon. It'll seem like he's had time to think about it. I'll send her a note saying I need to see her."

The man laughed harshly. "Why would she want to talk to the likes of you?"

"I'll say it's regarding my plans for the town, something to draw her out. Her nose for news will do her in." Kessler drained the glass. "I'll arrange for you to pull your duty this afternoon to set up the routine. We'll move tomorrow. When do you go on?"

"Two. Two until ten tonight."

"After this is over, you can accompany me to Denver. I'll be wanting a personal bodyguard. Interested?"

The man flicked his toothpick into the wastebasket. "Sure thing, Mr. Kessler."

They shook hands.

◈

AS THE CLOCK CHIMED FOUR, NORA STOPPED AND locked up the newspaper office. She wanted to get home and see Robby for a few minutes before she returned to Jack's place. It was hard to think of it as being home.

"Nora."

She turned and saw Marguerite and Chin Lee approaching. The Chinaman rubbed his hands together nervously.

Marguerite smiled brightly and quietly said, "Nora, unlock the door and let's go in. We need to talk. Don't ask any questions." She smiled again and called a greeting to a passing miner.

Nora played along. "Please, come in."

She slipped the key into the lock and opened the door for them to enter. As she closed the door, Marguerite reached over and turned the lock into place.

"We don't have much time. Chin has taken great risks to come here. Listen to what he has to say."

She took in Chin's agitation. "I must warn you and Mr. Jack Sheriff. I heard Mr. Kessler tell a man to shoot Mr. Jack Sheriff in the head. He said to pretend Mr. Jack Sheriff tried to escape town. The man is supposed to do this tomorrow."

"Which man?"

Chin shrugged. "I didn't see what he looked like, Miss Nora. I only listened at the door. Mr. Kessler wants Mr. Jack dead. Mr. Kessler told the man he will send you a note to get you to come away. Then the man will kill him. The new deputy is supposed to help."

"So he'd have someone to back up his story." Her blood turned to ice. "Thank you, Chin. I appreciate all you've done for us. Go back to Kessler's now. Stay out of his way, for God's sake."

The Chinaman nodded and slipped out the door. Nora turned to Marguerite. "Who do we turn to? Spank is the law and he's in cahoots with Kessler. Who would even believe me if I said Kessler had arranged to have Jack killed?"

She slammed her fist on the desk. "He doesn't even have a gun. They took his at the jail." She thought about Albert's, still in his bureau, since she'd returned it there after her outing with Ken. She would be sure to get it.

"We've got to protect him somehow." Marguerite took a handkerchief from her pocket and wiped her brow.

"The safest place for him is jail," reasoned Nora. "There's no way out of that cell, so they couldn't pretend he was escaping." She paused. "I've got to talk him into going back for now." She looked at Marguerite. "But how?"

CHAPTER 35

J ack was happy to see Nora. She returned just after sundown, toting a pie from Jess and a picture Robby had drawn for him.

"I've missed you. I never knew how lonesome I could be without you around."

She smiled. "I had a long day, too. Why don't we cook supper and talk over it?"

"Are you hungry for other things?" Her blush simply deepened his need for her. "Come here, Nora."

She walked to him almost reluctantly, her eyes downcast. It gave him time to think. "Are you sore, honey? Is that what's ailing you?"

"No," she whispered.

"Then what's wrong?"

"Nothing. Let's not talk."

It must be this Kessler thing hanging over them. It was the only thing he could think of. Well, he knew a few ways to take their minds off that. He took her hand and led her into the bedroom. Candles were already lit. He'd turned back the bed and fluffed the pillows. A bottle of wine stood on the table with two glasses.

She took in the scene. "I can see you've been busy."

"I plan on being a lot busier."

He made love to her once, slowly, almost as if in a

dream. After they'd shared a glass of wine, entangled together, his passion built again. This time, he took her hard, fast, as if there was no tomorrow. She clung to him, calling his name over and over as he soared to a new height, bringing her with him.

Spent, he drew her close and dozed. When he awoke, he reached for her but the bed was empty. She sat in a chair, watching, dressed again.

He smiled at her. "Guess you're ready to eat?"

"Yes. Why don't you throw some clothes on?"

She left the room, an odd expression on her face. He couldn't place what was bothering her. He slipped into his shirt and pants and hurried into the other room. Nora stood at the window, looking out. He could see the shadow of his latest guard dog standing on the porch.

Nora hoped that Kessler only got to one man. If it was true that Jack was destined to be murdered sometime tomorrow afternoon, then she had to play the odds and believe that the two men on duty outside weren't dirty.

"Whatever happens, Jack, will you go along with what I do or say?"

She saw his confused expression. "What are you talking about?"

"Never mind." She sighed and steeled herself for what was about to unfold. She picked up a glass vase on a table.

Raising her voice to a shout, she said, "I can't believe you would walk out on me now, Jack Duncan. For all I know, I could be carrying your child. Your baby, Jack! He'd never get to see his daddy or understand why he ran away at the first sign of trouble."

Nora hurled the vase through the air. It crashed into the front door. She heard footsteps hit the porch.

"Why are you doing this, Jack? I thought marriage meant something to you. I thought you'd be different from my first husband, but you're just as sorry as he was. No, don't touch me."

She hated the look on his face, one of surprise and disbelief. Jim Oldham came hurdling through the door, his rifle drawn.

"Stay back, Sheriff. Charley! Get in here now!"

Charley Miller flew through the back door, his gun leveled at Jack, as well.

"Damnation! Will you tell me what's going on?" He glared at her as if she'd lost her mind.

"Back away, Mrs. Duncan. Don't go to him."

Nora began to cry softly. "Oh, Jack, they'll have to take you back to that jail cell now." She wiped her sleeve against her eyes. "Why did you ever try to leave?" She let her jaw go slack. "Unless . . . you really did kill Ken Kessler? Oh, God." Her sobs started and, this time, they were real. The look in his eyes at her seeming betrayal caused them to be genuine.

"What game are you playing, Nora?"

"Sheriff, I'm afraid you'll have to come with us," Oldham said.

"The hell I will! I'm not going anywhere until I find out what's going on."

As Jack stared at her, Oldham took a step toward him and hit the back of his head with the butt of the gun. Jack took a wild swing going down but didn't connect with anything.

As Miller took out a pair of cuffs, Oldham apologized to her. "I'm sorry you had to see that, ma'am. We'll take him back into town and lock him up again. I'm sure you can visit him there."

Nora saw how reluctant they were. She nodded tearfully and fled to the bedroom. She hated herself in that moment and knew Jack must, too.

JACK AWOKE WITH A KILLER HANGOVER. HE LICKED his lips but tasted no liquor. Odd. Anytime he'd ever drunk this much, his mouth was as dry as a desert. And then he got a taste of Nora. That was the last thing he'd drunk of.

He sat up, his head exploding. He brought up his hands and felt the knot on the back of his head.

It all came back to him.

Nora had betrayed him. For some reason, she'd accused him out of the blue of trying to flee Silver Bluff. She'd caused such a ruckus that the two jackasses Kessler assigned rushed in and popped him before he got any kind of explanation from her.

What had gotten into her? She'd acted odd, even said something about going along with her. Then she'd shattered a vase and accused him of being as no-good as her first husband. Why hadn't she told him what she was about to do?

He knew her too well. She was up to something and he didn't like her playing with fire. He couldn't keep her safe locked up as tight as a drum. Why had she wanted him back in this cell?

Jack looked out and saw Miller sitting at the desk. He guessed the man had stuck to him like glue since Spank was probably still home cutting Zs. Earning that time-and-a-half Kessler was so eager to pay. He heard steps outside and hoped it was Nora.

It was the next best thing.

Ben entered the room talking ninety to nothing. "I hurried back as fast as I could, Mr. Jack. The trip went well. Our presses will be rolling tomorrow." Then his voice died down as he saw Jack sitting on a bunk behind bars.

"What's going on?" Ben looked at Miller.

"You'll have to ask him." Miller walked across the room and pocketed the key ring hanging on the wall and then stepped outside.

"This ain't funny, Mr. Jack."

"Do you see me laughing, Ben?" He shook his head. "Pull up a chair." He briefly told Ben about Albert's death and his threat to Ken Kessler after the funeral, and how Kessler had been found dead the next morning.

"Nora got me out of jail by marrying me. She talked Kessler into the idea that I wouldn't run if I had family ties."

Ben frowned. "Then why are you in jail now?"

"Heck if I know. Kessler kept two men on my property at all times. They had orders to shoot me if I let a big toe creep off my porch. Then last night, Nora goes berserk and accuses me of trying to sneak out of town and leave her behind. They dragged me back here."

"Miss Nora must've had a reason to do what she did."

"I think she's lost her reason, to tell you the truth." Jack stood and paced the few steps he could manage. "I'm afraid I'll go stir crazy in this cramped place. Circuit judge won't be here for another week."

Ben flashed a smile. "Nope. He's back in the last town, Mr. Jack. I heard about it when I took the horses back to Mr. Simmons now. He said the judge came early to the next town over. They caught two Sioux who were horse thieves. Their trial was yesterday, and the judge'll give his verdict this morning. He should be along by early afternoon, I suspect."

The door flew open, and William Kessler interrupted their conversation. "What are you doing back in jail?"

Jack noticed how upset Kessler seemed and decided to push him. "What's it to you, Kessler? I'd think you'd want me here. Judge is on his way. He'll be here later today. Can you wait a few more hours for justice, or would you rather go and hang me now?"

Kessler flushed brick red. "You're not worth the

rope." He tripped over the trash can on his way out and kicked it across the room in anger.

No sooner had Kessler left than Thomas Morrison appeared in the doorway. "I came to tell Spank good-bye, but I see he's not here. I was going to catch the noon stage today since my business is finished. When is your circuit judge riding through, Sheriff Duncan?"

"Funny you should ask. He'll be here later today."

Morrison nodded. "Sir," he addressed Ben. "Would you do me the favor of telling Mrs. Duncan I need to see her at once?"

"Yes, sir. I'm heading over to the house now. I'd wanted Mr. Jack to help me unload some equipment, but he's a little busy right now."

"Tell you what. Ask Mrs. Duncan to meet me at your newspaper office in one hour. I'll help you unload your goods and then I'll have a little chat with her."

He tipped his hat to them both. "Good day, Sheriff."

Jack and Ben stared at each other. "What was that all about?"

CHAPTER 36

Nora was sitting with Jess, fiddling with a piece of toast.

"Miss Nora, you've played with that enough. Put some jam on it and eat it."

She tossed it onto the plate. "I'm not hungry."

"What are you moping about? Why are you even home? I thought you'd be with Mr. Jack."

Nora pushed away the plate. "Jack's back in jail."

"Oh, Lordy be. What on earth happened?" Jess studied her carefully. "He didn't try to run, did he? Not Mr. Jack. I won't believe it."

She heard the sound of a wagon passing by. It stopped in front of their house.

"Ben?" She looked at Jess and they both jumped up and hurried to the door. Sure enough, Ben was coming up the walk.

"Good morning to you both." He picked up Jess and twirled her around before giving her a solid smooch. Then he turned to Nora. "Miss Nora, something powerful's coming down." He walked into the house and stopped suddenly.

She caught the glint of tears in his eyes as he said to her, "I was sorry to hear about Mr. Albert. He was a good, good man."

"You were a good friend to him, Ben." Nora took his giant hand in hers. "It's just you and me running the paper now. Did things go well in Denver?"

He brightened. "Yes'm, they did. I got what I needed and even stopped in town at the jail to get Mr. Jack to help me unload things." Ben looked at her reproachfully. "He was in jail."

"I know."

"He told me all that went on. I ain't sure why you got him put back in there but there's more."

Her stomach flipped over once. "What?"

"That Mr. Morrison came in while we were talking. He said he'd help me unload the wagon if you meet him over to the office. He wants to see you now. Seemed to be really important."

Nora was puzzled. "What could he want?"

Ben shrugged. "Don't know. Just think we'd best get over there."

They rode in the wagon, Ben telling her where he'd gotten the parts and for how much.

"Got a deal on a couple of pieces. We'll be saving Mr. Jack some money." He smiled in satisfaction.

She placed a hand on his arm. "I know I could never get things up and running again without you, Ben. I hope you know how much you and Jess mean to me."

He chuckled. "Well, we are family. And family sticks together."

"Agreed."

They pulled up at the office and found their visitor already waiting. Nora jumped down from the wagon.

"Mr. Morrison."

"Mrs. Duncan." He inclined his head to her. "I'm here to help your man with a little moving and then it's imperative that we speak. I have some valuable information for you."

She tamped down her mounting curiosity. "We do

appreciate your help. I'll make some coffee while you unload things."

Within fifteen minutes, the men had all the equipment parts in the shop.

"I'll get right to things, Miss Nora. I think by this time tomorrow, we'll be printing anything you've written."

"Thank you, Ben." She handed him a cup of coffee and another to Morrison. He took a swig of it.

"Hits the spot, ma'am."

"Are you ready to talk?" Nora offered Morrison a seat and sat in the chair opposite her.

"What I have to say is not pretty, Mrs. Duncan. I would ask that you curb your reporter's inquisitiveness and not interrupt my tale."

Her curiosity grew but she agreed. She took up her pencil and opened the tablet before her, ready to jot down any pertinent facts he offered.

"I grew up in a town southeast of Boston. Good people. We may have lacked in material things, but there was always ample love. It was there I first met the Kesslers."

Nora bit her tongue to keep her questions at bay.

"I fell between the two—older than Ken but a bit younger than William. It was a middling-sized town, and though we knew of each other, we didn't run in the same crowd, mostly due to our ages and class.

"When the war broke out, I was eager to fight, but I'd had trouble with my back. I'd been out of work for some time. Then I learned of a quartermaster job that was open for the regiment training nearby. It would require no active duty, merely ordering supplies and pushing around papers. The pay was decent." He paused. "William Kessler was in charge of the unit."

Nora took a deep breath. She'd always wondered about the Kesslers' backgrounds, especially after Jack alluded to knowing things about them. She wondered if Jack knew Morrison, as well.

"Little did I know that while I was making things run smoothly for William Kessler, his brother headed over to court my girl. If I'd had wind of it, I would've nipped it in the bud. Ken Kessler always had a reputation as a ladies' man."

Morrison took another sip. "Maude was dazzled that a Kessler paid notice to her. Her family had come down in the world. Money invested in ventures that had failed. She was impressed by Ken's good looks and fine manners. In the meantime, our regiment got transferred down South. Didn't actually see much fighting. Kessler still had too many connections for that. We went first to Virginia, then later Tennessee. And that's where I made my mistakes."

Nora saw Morrison's hand tremble. "What mistakes?"

"I was greedy. Wanted to change my sweetheart's mind. Give her and my family things they'd never had, things I'd never been able to give them." Morrison sighed. "Somehow, William Kessler knew it. He was always one who could sniff out a man's weakness and use it against him."

He paused and sipped on his coffee thoughtfully. "I began making out false requisitions. Doctoring others. I helped Kessler ship confiscated Southern goods up north as his personal baggage. He gave me a small percentage of the profits for my work. Even though I took all the risks, he gained all the wealth."

"No one suspected?"

Morrison shook his head. "After two years, Kessler got transferred to the War Department, courtesy of an old friend. He took Ken with him. I stayed on as QM, but shipped out to a different unit, to a colonel who'd passed through a few months earlier and had taken a liking to me. Colonel Green was from an influential family and had served in Congress before the war."

He slammed his fist down on the table. "Let me tell you, I walked the straight and narrow for the colonel and have ever since. After the war, he returned to Congress and took me with him. I served on his staff two years and then his ties got me placed on the railroad commission."

She sat up expectantly. Finally, things were falling into place.

"I went home. My two brothers died in war. One at Chancellorsville and one at Shiloh. It was a hard blow, but I still had hope that Maude would come around and marry me. I hadn't received any letters from her in a long time, but I believed in my heart that we belonged together."

Morrison teared up. His voice began to shake. "Ken Kessler did more than his share of sweet-talk with my girl. After we shipped down South, Maude found out she was expecting a child."

"By Ken?"

He nodded. "Ken Kessler was the only one that had been coming around. Maude died in childbirth. Her mama gave the baby away. Said he had eyes like Ken. She couldn't stand to look at him."

Nora's head reeled. She thought of the young woman who'd been used by Ken Kessler and the heartbreak Mr. Morrison had suffered.

He took a cleansing breath. "I decided I would kill Ken Kessler in revenge for taking my sweetheart from me. Thought I'd take big brother William for a ride, too. It's taken a while but it's finally all in motion."

Nora asked, "The railroad coming through? Kessler buying everything up and running people off?"

"Exactly."

"And Ken's dead." She jumped to her feet. "How could you kill him and let Jack take the blame? He might hang for it!" She raised her hand to strike him, but he caught her wrist.

"Wait a minute. I'm not through. I didn't kill Ken Kessler—and neither did your husband."

She jerked her wrist from him. "Then talk fast, Mr. Morrison and tell me everything you know. The circuit judge arrives soon. I won't let Jack die." She sat back in the chair, arms crossed, watching him with wary eyes.

"I reeled William Kessler in like a fish on a long line. He only thinks the railroad will come this way from Denver and up into Wyoming. It won't."

Morrison grinned, his tiny teeth resembling those of a shark. "I advised him where and when to buy. After all, he trusted me. He spent a good part of his fortune made during the war on the surrounding properties for miles in both directions. Then he provided me two separate payments in gold to my account in San Francisco. That pretty much will wipe him out."

"And Ken?"

"I'd had plans to kill him. I wanted him to suffer as my Maude had. I wanted to try and place the blame at William's doorstep, but it didn't work out that way."

"What really happened?"

"Before I could act, I overheard Ken and Spank McHardy arguing. It was the same night of your daddy's funeral."

"Can I talk to you, Ken?"

"Not now, Spank. I'm going out."

"Uh, I don't think Mr. Kessler would approve."

"Since when have I needed William's approval?" Ken *laughed, and then he stared at Spank. "I get it. You're supposed to keep me here."*

"Well, Mr. Kessler did mention he wanted you to stay out of trouble, especially with Sheriff Duncan mad at you."

"Nice try, Spank, but I need a woman. When I get that urge, nothing can stop me."

"At least talk to me a minute, Ken. I want you to help me ask for a bigger cut in the action."

Ken laughed. "You're a lackey, Spank. As Silver Bluff's sheriff, William will expect you to turn a blind eye to anything rotten that goes on in this town. He'll compensate you nicely for it, but Morrison will get the big piece for running everything— the saloons, brothels, the gambling halls. That'll be his job."

"What if I want more? If I wore diamond pins and fancy clothes, the ladies'd want me like they do you."

Ken roared. "Spank, listen up. You're bald, short, and ugly. I can't imagine three worse things in a man."

"You're a crude, selfish, pretty boy."

"That's the best you can do?"

"Ken walked out the kitchen door toward the stables. I watched Spank step out and follow him inside. He was in there a long time and then came out, looking around, guilt written all over his face. He went to the trough and dipped his hands in and then wiped them on his trousers.

"I went out to the stables and found the body. It wasn't quite what I'd planned but it suited my purposes. No one was around. William had gone into town to meet with the local banker. Kessler had given the servants a night off. I was the only one around to see what happened."

"How could you not speak up? I think of everything Jack has suffered—"

"Oh, come on, Mrs. Duncan. He's spent a couple of nights in jail and at least one with his new wife. Don't tell me he didn't enjoy that."

Heat filled her cheeks. "I still don't see—"

"I wouldn't have let Duncan hang. I'm not that cruel. It took any heat off me, in case William Kessler got an inkling what I was truly up to. Now that I have confirmation of the money in my account, I can speak my piece and enjoy the shock on Kessler's face. It will be sweet indeed."

"You're a hard man, Mr. Morrison."

A shadow crossed his face. "War makes you hard. That and any dealings with the Kesslers."

Morrison rose. "I just wanted to share my story with you first. I'm sure you'll have plenty to write about now. People like to read about the downfall of the high and mighty."

"Why have you told me all of this?"

Morrison slipped on his hat. "I admire your spirit, Mrs. Duncan. I think you've had a hard row to hoe, and it's about time the sun shone on you."

He sighed. "You also favor my Maude quite a bit. Maybe I'm getting sentimental as I age, but somehow, I fancy her looking down on me, pleased that I told you."

Morrison paused. "I'll make my way over to wait for the judge. Promise me you'll keep this under your hat for now."

A bitter taste stung Nora's mouth, but she nodded her agreement. She had no desire to give William Kessler any kind of warning. She'd have to avoid seeing Jack, though. One look at her face and he'd know she had something to hide.

CHAPTER 37

Jack held the razor to his face, willing his hands to stop trembling. He squeezed his eyes closed and swallowed. He didn't want to appear before Judge Moss covered in nicks. He took a deep breath and let it out slowly.

His hands now steady, he touched the blade to skin and slid it downward in a smooth stroke. His eyes never left his image as he shaved away the growth of beard. He was grateful Ben had brought him a mirror. It made the job easier. It also let him see just how bad he looked.

He hadn't gotten much sleep the night before, first stewing over Nora's strange behavior that had landed him back in jail. Then he'd lain awake trying to figure out what she was up to. Exhausted, he'd slept lightly, waking time and time again, reaching for her. They'd only slept together that one night, and yet his hands searched for her before his eyes ever opened.

She was definitely under his skin.

He finished his shave and dipped his hands into the basin of water, again courtesy of Ben, who'd also gone to Jack's place and returned with fresh clothes. He slipped into them now. The feel of the crisp cotton shirt against his skin gave him renewed hope. At least

Judge Moss wouldn't be greeted by an accused murderer sporting rumpled, dirty clothes and rough stubble.

He stole a glance at Spank, feet up on the desk, hat pulled low over his eyes. The man slept more than he was awake. Jack wished he could throttle Spank for the sheer pleasure.

Seymour Simmons slipped a head inside the doorway. He coughed loudly to announce his presence. Spank didn't move.

"You might want to shake his foot," Jack suggested.

Seymour did just that. Spank jumped to his feet, hand slapping against his side for his gun.

"It's just me, Spank," warned Seymour. "I came to tell you things'll be starting in about ten minutes."

The new sheriff grunted. "Church ready?"

Church?

"Filling up nicely." The storeowner gave Jack an apologetic glance. "Whole lot of folks have turned out for the proceedings."

He realized that the Methodist church would offer the most substantial venue for what he assumed would be a large audience seeking an afternoon's free entertainment.

"Well, let's get rolling, Jack." Spank inserted the key into the lock and stepped aside so he could pass.

He strode halfway across the room in only a few steps. It felt terrific to stretch his legs again.

"Uh, Sheriff. I mean . . . Jack . . . we need to slip these cuffs on you." Spank shifted his weight from one foot to the next. "Orders, you know."

He looked Spank in the eyes. "Kessler's orders, you mean."

Spank fastened the handcuffs around Jack's wrists and locked them behind his back before he took Jack's arm. "Let's get going."

Seymour rushed to open the door. They stepped out into a cool, crisp day. Jack took a deep breath of the sweet mountain air. If he had it to do over again, he'd want to take Nora on a picnic on a day just like today.

They walked down the center of the street. A few passersby scurried in front of them, probably hoping to get the last remaining seats. He wondered how long it would take for Judge Moss to hand down a verdict. If it was as speedy as he suspected, he might be swinging from a tree in a couple of hours.

His stomach turned sour. He hoped they'd give him some time alone with Nora. Just a few minutes. He didn't know if he'd have much to say, but he wanted to hold her close once more. Run his fingers through that silky hair. Steal one last kiss. He also needed to tell her about his will.

They mounted the steps of the church and entered. It had the familiar smell he'd come to love. Echoes of *Bringing in the Sheaves* tugged at the corner of his mind.

His eyes swept over the room. He recognized the Malones and Seaburys. Chin Lee and his family. The Nelsons. Even Sam Spivens, the mine's foreman. He nodded to an entire row of miners themselves, men who'd obviously given up a half-day of work to show him support. He hoped Kessler would stop at taking the money out of their paychecks and not fire them outright for their absence.

Then he caught sight of Nora. She was turned slightly in the pew, one hand on its back, holding on tightly. She flashed him a weak smile. He fought to keep the tears at bay. If anyone had told him a couple of months ago that a simple glance at a woman—and a Southern woman at that—would cause such strong emotions in him, he would have laughed at their pathetic attempt at a joke.

Instead, he found himself wanting to live. The feeling was stronger than any he'd ever experienced. And he wanted that time spent with this woman, loving her. Her strength of character was as beautiful to him as her angelic face. Somehow, he had to make Judge Moss see he was innocent.

Spank led him to a table set to the side. It surprised him when Spank released him from the cuffs. Before he could say thanks, Judge Moss entered through the side door. He walked straight to the pulpit and addressed the crowd.

"Keep your seats, folks. I don't stand much on formality."

Jack studied Moss in a new light, that of prisoner to judge. The magistrate had a shock of white hair that was thick and unruly. He was dressed in a sober black suit that had seen better days and was as thin as a reed. He couldn't help but wonder if Moss came straight here after a meeting with Kessler. Kessler owned the town—but did he own this man?

He glanced around and saw the mine owner sitting in the third row, watching him through narrowed eyes. Hatred as thick as honey flowed from him. Jack stared back. He wouldn't be the first to look away.

"I met in chambers earlier with a Mr. Thomas Morrison, so I don't think this proceeding will take long."

The room began to buzz. People turned left and right to catch a glimpse of the stranger in their town. Jack spotted Morrison in the back row.

Morrison gave Jack a tight smile before he rose and walked to the front of the church. He paused, waiting on instructions from Moss.

The judge snapped his fingers. "Get this man a chair."

Quickly, a folding chair was produced. Moss signaled for Morrison to be seated.

"Do you swear to tell the truth, the whole truth and nothing but the truth, so help you God?" Moss roared.

"I do." Morrison sat up expectantly.

"Mr. Morrison, would you please relate the events of

last Saturday night to those present, as you did to me in private not an hour ago?"

As Morrison spoke, Jack was spellbound by his narrative. Although he listened to the man's words, it was Kessler he focused on.

Until Morrison began to explain Spank's involvement. Then he turned his attention to Silver Bluff's newest lawman. His bald pate shone with sweat, and his cheek twitched visibly.

"When I went into the barn after Mr. McHardy left, I discovered Mr. Kessler. He was missing the diamond stickpin from his lapel. He was also dead."

"You're a liar!" Spank rose from his chair, fear visible on his face. "I never touched Ken. The Kesslers have been good to me, just like they have been to you. Why, you're a rich man now, Tommy, thanks to them Kesslers."

Judge Moss spoke up. "If we were to search your person or premises, we wouldn't find this said stickpin, Mr. McHardy?"

Spank's terror got the best of him. Jack had seen men spooked in the war, panic turning their minds to flight. He recognized that look on Spank as the man bolted from his seat. Instinct took over as Jack jumped from his chair and tackled the deputy, grateful that the cuffs had been removed earlier. He found them inside Spank's pocket, pulling them out. As he slapped the restraints on, Ken Kessler's stickpin rolled across the floor.

When Spank caught sight of it lying there for all to see, he blubbered like a child stung by a bee. He looked to his boss for support. "Do something, Mr. Kessler. I'm being railroaded."

Judge Moss interrupted. "Proof enough for me." He climbed down from the pulpit and scooped up the flashy piece of jewelry. He brought the object close to Spank's face.

"Did you do it, son? Did you kill Ken Kessler or not? Remember, you're in God's House."

Words failed Spank but he nodded.

"Lock him up, Sheriff. Execution'll take place in the morning."

Jack realized the judge was speaking to him. A stir of pride rippled inside. "Yes, Your Honor."

Jack lifted Spank to his feet and caught sight of Nora. He grinned at her like a lovestruck schoolboy as he walked his prisoner down the aisle. They left the church and headed for the jail. This day would be forever ingrained in Jack's mind. It was perfect. The slight chill in the air. The sunshine streaming down. The fresh smell of fall in the air.

Until a shot rang out.

CHAPTER 38

Nora pushed past people left and right, trying to keep Jack in sight. A steady drone of gossip filled the church. Everyone seemed to have an opinion on the Kessler murder. It was least of her concerns.

She slid past Chin and gave him a quick wave. She had so much to be grateful for concerning him. If Chin hadn't come to her, Jack might have been shot and killed before Morrison stepped forward with his testimony.

The wind had picked up since she'd arrived at the church and whipped her skirts as she went through the front doors. She fought to keep them down as she hurried to catch up to her husband. She knew they would have a more private reunion later on, but she needed to touch him for a moment, to make it all seem real.

He wasn't making it any easier for her. His long strides put him a good twenty yards in front of her. She lifted her skirts and pushed ahead.

Then a shot rang out, its crack carrying over the wind. Jack staggered and fell to his knees. Time froze. Nora quickly scanned the nearby rooftops and caught a whirl of black cloth. It immediately disappeared. In that moment, her heart told her Kessler was behind it. She ran to her husband.

"Jack!"

She dropped to her knees next to him. Bright red stained his white shirtfront. He wore a stunned expression as he reached for his shoulder.

"Who..."

Without thought, Nora reached over and grabbed the gun still in Spank's holster. She leaped to her feet and ran into the alleyway between the general store and the new law office Harve Nelson had begun last week. Whoever shot Jack had been on top of Seymour's store.

Barreling down the narrow passageway, she heard a horse snort.

Please, God, let me be in time.

As she emerged from the alley, a figure mounted a sorrel horse. Nora raised the pistol and fired off a shot. Having never discharged a weapon before, she was unprepared for the recoil. From her hand up along her arm and into her shoulder, a painful vibration rattled enough so that she dropped the gun into the dirt.

Voices then surrounded her. People were everywhere. Two of the miners she'd seen at the church pulled the man from his horse. He was shouting obscenities, cradling one hand in the other, his fingers bloody.

"Hot damn! She shot the gun right out of his hand."

Nora walked shakily back to where she needed to be. She had to find Jack.

Let him live, God. Let Jack be safe.

She turned the corner and ran into Reverend Seabury.

"Come with me, Nora. They've taken Jack to Dr. Malone's."

He took her trembling arm and led her there. She was grateful. Her mind was in such a jumble she barely remembered her own name, much less where the physician's office was located.

The minister opened the door and ushered her in past the gathering crowd.

"God bless, Doc, will you hurry?"

She broke out into a huge grin. That was her Jack, all right. Nora ran the few remaining steps from the small waiting room into the doctor's examining room.

Her husband of less than a week was stripped to the waist, sitting on a tall table. A dark spot graced his shoulder, his chest bloody. She assumed that was the entry point of the bullet.

"Gotta have clean hands, Jack. One of my medical school friends swears by it. Says it keeps infection from setting in." Dr. Malone finished drying them and turned, spying her.

"Glad you could make it, young lady. My patient is giving me what-for."

The pain all but left Jack's face as he saw her. He held out a hand and she took it, smothering it in kisses.

"If you'll help him hold still, Nora, I need to dig out this bullet. It's pretty shallow and won't take me but a minute. Lie down, son."

Jack eased back onto the table. She continued to hold his hand, her eyes never leaving his. He grimaced, clenching his teeth, and then he relaxed.

The doctor held up a long set of tweezers with an object between them. "Got it all in one try." He grinned. "You're a lucky man, Sheriff Duncan."

Her husband smiled at Nora warmly. "I know, Doc."

ॐ

NORA DOODLED ON THE PAGE IN FRONT OF HER, THE presses noisily cranking out tomorrow's edition of the *Silver Bluff Gazette*. A tap on her shoulder startled her. She turned to find Chin beaming.

"Finished my handbills, Miss Nora."

He handed the stack to her for approval. She glanced at it thoroughly. Although she'd proofed it before Chin ran them, she had learned in the month he'd worked for her part-time that he needed this careful inspection in order to be satisfied with his own performance.

"Perfect, Chin," she hollered to make herself heard. "Why don't you head on home? I'm sure Sung Moon could use your help for tonight's dinner party."

Chin took the sheaf of papers. "I'll take them to the law office and then go home. See you later, Miss Nora."

She smiled as she watched him leave. Chin had learned rapidly under Ben's tutelage. She was glad to have the extra hand, even if it was only for a few hours a week. Silver Bluff had grown rapidly in the last six months.

Besides the law office, a livery and feed store had gone in, as well as a dentist. A teacher had been hired for the completed schoolhouse, which freed Nora from preparing lessons for Robby and Tien.

She looked at the watch pinned to her dress. She'd better leave now in order to have time to bathe and dress before heading over to Marguerite's. Robby would go home with Ben and stay overnight.

"Ben," she called out. "I'm leaving."

He nodded while he continued his explanation to Robby. She smiled seeing the two of them together. So many of the things she'd learned had come from Ben. Nora hoped that he would be around for many more years. Between the two of them, they would make a newspaperman of Robby, a third generation to carry on the business.

Nora wrapped her shawl around her. April in Silver Bluff was nippy compared to the warmer climes of Monroe, but she wouldn't trade her life here for any other. Everything had worked out so well. Mike

Heckton was jailed for attempted murder, squealing like a stuck pig that it had been William Kessler who instructed him to kill Jack.

Before Kessler had been tried and found guilty, he declared bankruptcy. The mine had been foreclosed on, only to be purchased by Marguerite, who'd surprised them all with her large nest egg. She told Nora she'd always had a head for business, much of it learned at the elbow of Burke Stevenson, the mine's original owner.

Now Stevenson was back in town. His son had recovered from the mine accident and although he'd lost both legs, Bran was running a bank branch for his new father-in-law. Stevenson, lonely for the wide-open spaces of Colorado, had returned and promptly asked for Marguerite's hand in marriage.

Marguerite had shared with Nora how she'd always been fond of Burke. "Nothing like Albert, you understand," she'd declared. "Your papa brought sunshine into my life, even if it was only for a short while. Still," she confided, "I always got along well with Burke. I imagine we'll grow old together as Silver Bluff grows up."

Nora left her office and walked along the street, dodging mud puddles from the previous evening's rain.

"Good afternoon, Nora."

She turned and waved at Seth Appleton. "Good to see you, Seth. Are you settling in?"

He crossed to her. "Yes, indeed. It was mighty nice of Jack to find where we'd gone and send word for us to come back."

She smiled. "He is a good man. Just like your Annie has."

Seth blushed. "Oh, go on." He pushed his hat low on his brow. "Well, tell him I said hello. And that we'll be having you to dinner soon, once we get things settled."

"We'll look forward to that."

Nora continued down the street until she reached the jail. She met Casey Lowell coming out.

"Good day to you, Mrs. Duncan."

"How is Gertrude doing these days?"

Casey frowned. "Most ornery beast on the planet, that mule. Sheriff just told me I might be able to get rid of her. Said Seth Appleton's back in town and might need a mule for spring planting."

"I just saw him not two minutes ago down the street."

Casey tipped his hat to her. "Then I best be going, ma'am." He limped off, favoring his right leg.

She opened the door. Jack was sitting at his desk, running his hands through his hair, paperwork spread out in front of him. Without looking up he said, "Casey, I told you—"

"Casey's running down Seth right about now."

Her husband's head shot up. A smile spread across his handsome face. "Come here, you."

Nora went to him and he pulled her onto his lap.

"Jack, I'm getting too heavy—"

"No, you're not." He wrapped one arm around her waist and placed a hand on her rounded belly, rubbing it gently. Suddenly, his eyes grew wide. "Did you feel that? Wait. There it goes again!"

She grinned. "I felt it for the first time this morning. You were already gone." She loved the look of amazement mixed with love on his face.

He kissed her belly, then her hand, and finally her lips. Nora sighed in contentment.

"Happy?"

"Very."

"I'm sheriff again. Robby's thriving. The *Silver Bluff Gazette's* prospering. And we've got a sweet bundle to look forward to by summer's end." He touched a hand to her cheek. "I love this life we've created together, Nora Duncan. I love you."

Jack took her mouth in a long kiss, one full of passion and promise.

Maybe the dinner party could wait.

ABOUT THE AUTHOR

A native Texan and former history teacher, award-winning and internationally bestselling author Alexa Aston lives with her husband in a Dallas suburb, where she eats her fair share of dark chocolate and plots out stories while she walks every morning. She enjoys travel, sports, and binge-watching—and never misses an episode of *Survivor*.

Alexa brings her characters to life in steamy historicals, contemporary romances, and romantic suspense novels that resonate with passion, intensity, and heart.

Keep up with Alexa
Visit her website
Newsletter Sign-Up

More ways to connect with Alexa

www.ingramcontent.com/pod-product-compliance
Lightning Source LLC
Chambersburg PA
CBHW01448100726
47899CB00010BB/3201

* 9 7 8 1 6 4 8 3 9 1 1 1 8 *